THE TIES THAT BIND

a novel by

TOM BREW

Printed by HNE Printing, Greenfield, Indiana

Library of Congress Control Number: 11766484891

ISBN 978-0-9858021-1-0

For more information on the author,
visit tombrewsports.com or
e-mail at tombrewsports at gmail.com

For the three of you,
and the next two of you,
and the others to come.

For my mom, my brothers
and all the friends and family
who have stood by me.

And lastly, for the
compulsive gambler
who still suffers.

1

He had his favorite couch, the family room television set and, of course, the trusty remote. He had a first-in-weeks Mountain Dew poured over ice and some chilled carrots to munch on, and on a hot Thursday afternoon in mid-August this was all Danny Bridges needed.

It was good to be home.

In the past five weeks, Danny had spent four of them at basketball camps and AAU tournaments around the Midwest, sandwiched around recruiting visits to Central Michigan and Bowling Green. It was non-stop basketball in the middle of the summer, and Danny was loving it. As Danny was about to start his senior year at Crossroads High School in Schererville, Indiana, he was suddenly very much in demand with college basketball coaches.

Suddenly being the operative word.

In the crazy mixed-up world of college basketball recruiting, Danny hadn't been much more than a blip on the radar the past few years. You'd never find him on any Top Five lists, or even Top Twenty for that matter. Oh, he was always a good player, all the way back to the fourth grade, when he slipped on a basketball uniform for the first time with his best friends at St. Mark's School in Schererville. Danny's mother Mary, who never missed a game, still keeps a picture of that first game on her dresser mirror. Little Danny, the smallest kid on the floor, made his first three shots, made four more later and a couple of free throws and his team won 41-15. They never lost a game all year. Mom kept score every game, and all her scorecards were still stashed away in a file.

Danny could always play – and he played always. He was a natural athlete; quick, great hand-eye coordination, and smart. Not only did he always know where he was supposed to be, but he also knew where everyone else was supposed to be, teammates and opponents alike. The game didn't matter; he played them all. Basketball, baseball, football, even hockey in the winter on the frozen ponds behind the Brent farm or the Shell station. He was always a student of the game and wise beyond his years.

But he also was very short. He was a Thanksgiving baby and an active young child. He probably should have waited another year to go to kindergarten, but his mom sent him anyway when he was still several months shy of his fifth birthday. Danny's two best friends in the neighborhood, Nick Vincent and Kenny Dockery, were both almost a full year older and they were going, so it seemed like a good fit. Plus she had son No. 2 at home – a 10-month-old named Michael – and a third child on the way, her doctor had told her a few weeks earlier, which was shocking news. Having Danny at school all day would be a nice break for her, and she knew Danny was ready anyway. He always did everything early, puzzles, books, even newspapers at a young age, sports sections only of course. With his best friends going, she knew it was right, and Danny was all for it.

As they all grew older, Danny and his pals were inseparable in Scher-erville, a suburb in the very northwest corner of Indiana where U.S. 41 and U.S. 30 – the original "Crossroads of America" – intersected. They weren't far at all from downtown Chicago and just down the road from the steel mills and oil refineries that lined the Lake Michigan shoreline along northwest Indiana. It was more where the suburbs met the farms when Mary and Carl Bridges had first moved there, but it was all suburbs now, a fast-growing community with lots of big families moving in on a regular basis. The kids would play ball all day, then dash home in time for dinner. Danny was good, and so were his friends. They'd take on anyone their age, or even a few years older, and pound them. They were competitive, but friends first and they always had fun.

Danny was the smallest of the bunch, but it never deterred him. He had to handle a few jokes and some ribbing, which was fine. He would prove himself on the court, a joy to watch even as a youngster with a basketball on his fingertips. And he had such a strong arm that he was a natural at baseball. He could throw hard and he loved the nuances of the game, always making suggestions to his grown-up coaches even as a Little Leaguer. Even though his mother hated the idea of him playing football, she knew not allowing it would never fly, not with all of Danny's friends playing. And when one of his first youth football coaches, a former college football quarterback himself, showed him how to grip and throw a football, the coach knew almost immediately that he had something special in Danny. He was little, but he could throw.

He was a scrawny 5-foot-6 when he arrived at Crossroads High, and barely 120 pounds, but he played quarterback on the freshman football team, started every game all winter with the basketball team and was 4-0 as a pitcher in the spring with the baseball team. He worked hard and always played well, even against bigger classmates. He was confident without being arrogant, and had a burning desire to always get better.

The summer before his sophomore year he had a growing spurt, which made everyone happy except for his mother, who always looked for sales and had bought his school pants months in advance. By the time school started, Danny was pushing 6-feet and had been back to the mall twice with his mom exchang-ing clothes. His meticulous mother, of course, always kept the receipts. That was a good thing.

When his junior year started he was about 6-1, and most everyone in Danny's family figured that would be it. No one in the family was very tall. Danny's father, who wasn't around much past Danny's eighth birthday, was only 5-foot-9 and his mom was just 5-4. Danny's maternal grandfather was 6-1, tall for a man born before the turn of the century, but that was about it. Danny was a point guard, very quick, a great ball-handler, a great passer and, as a child of Indiana hoops, a great shooter. On a team with only one senior and no height, Crossroads went 16-6 his junior year and everyone expected big things the next year. He and his best buddy Nick were great athletes who won a ton of games together. Danny was the better basketball player, but he was also a good high school quarterback on the football team. Nick was a football stud and a solid, workhorse basketball player. They were inseperable, on and off the court.

Because Danny could shoot the ball and handle it so well, several mid-major colleges were showing some interest in him as a junior, but not much. Danny knew that a scholarship of some kind – athletic or academic – was the only way he could get to college without a ton of loans, considering the family finances and all. So he paid attention to his own game and where he thought he measured up to other kids, either during the season or during the summer at AAU tournaments or camps. He first thought he'd be a small-school kid, maybe Division III schools like Wabash or DePauw, but he played very well as a junior, especially against good competition. He showed he could shoot, but his passing skills and – more importantly – his leadership skills really stood out.

But what Danny didn't expect – and neither did anyone else – was another growth spurt. It started near the end of his junior season. He could tell something was going on, because his legs hurt all the time just like they did when he grew almost five inches in six months a few years earlier. It was happening again and when he went to his first camp that summer, they measured him in shorts and socks at 6-foot-5.

Coaches from the country's best programs started to take notice, especially that first week of camp. Playing against kids with much bigger recruiting reputations, he was scoring well every day and playing sound, selfless basketball, something that rarely happens at most all-star camps. Practically overnight, as one camp rolled into another, Danny was becoming the talk of the summer tour. At the second camp, a Nike thing, he scored 30 points in the championship game, making 7 of 8 three-pointers with nine assists and no turnovers. He won camp MVP.

He wasn't a mid-major recruit anymore. He had become a stud high school basketball player, which means something special in a basketball-crazed state like Indiana that idolizes its stars.

The Michigan State coach said hello on his way out, and so did the new guy at Georgetown. People were noticing. People noticed too when he got to Bloomington, Indiana for his last camp of the summer. This was meant to be low-key, a relaxing way to end the summer, something he'd done every year since he was 9 years old. The Indiana basketball camp was always a highlight for him, but this time it was different. This time, all those little fresh-faced kids were looking up to him.

So were the coaches, who had known Danny for years and now were drooling over his sudden progress during the past few months. This time, Indiana's legendary coach, Henry Garrison, looked at Danny as more than just a camper dropping down his two hundred dollars for a week of fun and a t-shirt. No, Danny was more than that now. Danny took part in all the scrimmages with the best players at the camp and did drills with many of the current Indiana players who were working as volunteer counselors. It all led to a ten-minute conversation on the morning of the last day between the legendary coach and all-grown-up Danny, who idolized the man, a gentle Southerner who had found a home in Indiana long ago and became a legend.

"So, you want to come to Indiana?" the coach asked at the end of the conversation. "Is that something you'd want to do?"

The question totally floored Danny.

He loved IU, loved the coach and loved all the tradition of a basketball school that had won seven national championships, five under Garrison during his 28-year tenure. Every player who had spent four years under Garrison at Indiana had been to at least one Final Four. Danny knew his stock had been rising with the college coaches all summer, but had it risen this much?

Indiana?

Really?

"Coach, I was born in Indiana and I was raised in Indiana. I've loved Indiana basketball my whole life. I've probably won 5,000 IU games in my driveway making a last-second shot. And if you think I can play here and you want me here, then just ask and I'll be here.

"I think I did just ask." the coach said with a smile.

"Well then, yes, of course. It would be a dream come true. I'll have to talk to my mom but, yes, I'd love to come here."

"What about your father?"

"They've been divorced for almost 10 years and I really don't have a relationship with him. I haven't even talked to him in a long time. It's really just my mom."

"OK, that's fine. What about your grades? They good?"

"Yes, 3.8. Screwed up a few science courses along the way, but that's it. SAT's are already done, and I did well. The NCAA Clearinghouse already has all of my paperwork"

"Well, go home and think about it, and I'll have one of my assistant coaches call your coach. Maybe we could do your official visit before school starts for you."

"Sure," Danny said. "This is my last camp. I've got a few weeks off now, other than work. I'm sure either weekend would be fine."

"Let's do it this weekend then. Let's shoot for that."

The coach and the kid shook hands and Danny headed off, a huge smile on his face.

"Hey Bridges!" the coach shouted from across the floor. "You know if you come here you're going to have to learn how to play some defense, don't you?"

"Yes sir, coach. Yes, I do."

"Good. It's very good that you know that."

* * * * *   * * * * *   * * * * *

So those were Danny's thoughts three hours later as he flopped down on his couch in Schererville. He was tired from a grueling month and glad to be home after the three-hour ride from Bloomington, but his mind was racing now. Could this really be true? Could Coach Garrison really want him? Could he really be a Hoosier?

It was all happening so fast. Just a few months earlier he thought he'd be a Mid-American Conference kid, or maybe a big step up to Butler because he really liked the coach there. But he wasn't even sure how much they liked him.

And now? Indiana?

A dream come true.

Danny flipped on the TV and the Cubs were on WGN, playing a late Friday afternoon game at Wrigley Field in Chicago. Danny watched, but not intently. He was a Cubs fan, but now his mind was all about Indiana, all about the championship banners, the candy-cane warm-ups, the greatness of Assembly Hall and the hysteria that grips every corner of the state in those years when the Hoosiers were good, which was all the time lately. Thousands and thousands of kids grow up in all corners of this basketball-crazy state hoping someday that Coach Garrison would ask them to play at Indiana.

And for Danny, that day was today.

Danny was obviously excited, but fear gripped him too. Sure, he was a good player and, yes, even he was surprised at how well his summer had gone against some great competition. But the one question that continued to run through his head was this: "Am I really good enough to play basketball at Indiana?"

In about the third inning, Danny's cell phone rang. It was Will Jackson, his high school coach at Crossroads. Jackson was 40 years old and a former great small-college basketball player himself. He won a state championship coaching at Anderson High School with all-everything Michael Trickett, and then arrived at Crossroads the same year Danny did. He loved to win, pushed his kids hard and ran the program in a first-class fashion. "Welcome to Crossroads University!" he would always say with a smile when greeting visitors to the school. He always thought Crossroads should be a dominant program, and he was hired to make that happen. In three years there, everyone loved having him as the head coach, and everyone in town hoped this hard-working guy would take them to the promised land. The thought was this group could be Crossroads' best in years.

Will Jackson was a worker, always pushing kids to get every last drop out of them. But he also had a great sense of humor and he thought now might be a good time to have a little fun with his standout point guard. He had already gotten a call from Tony Carter, an assistant to Garrison at IU, so he knew about the offer. He and Carter became close during Indiana's successful recruiting of Trickett a few years earlier, so they had a nice conversation. He also knew IU wanted to get the visit scheduled quickly and get the deal done. It was all just verbal this time of year – Danny couldn't sign a letter of intent until November – but they still wanted the commitment and they wanted to be done with this recruiting class.

"So how was Bloomington?" Jackson asked. "You didn't embarrass us down there, did you?"

"It was fun. I didn't want to leave. In fact, it was so good …"

"What, did you win the egg-toss contest again like when you were 10?" he said, interrupting on purpose.

"Can I call you a smart-ass without having to run a million gassers tomorrow? Can I? No, Coach Garrison offered me a scholarship"

"Yeah, I already heard. Coach Carter called me a few minutes ago. They want you to take your visit this weekend, get them all your academic papers and make a commitment. They want you to do it fast because they only have one scholarship left. You're the fourth and that's it. If it's not you, they'd probably want to sign Kenny Monroe from Bloomington High School, and that's kind of awkward right now because the kid is practically Coach Garrison's neighbor, for Christ's sake. They don't want Kenny to miss out on something else if they can't take him at IU."

"Well, my mom gets home from work at 5. I'll talk to her and I'll call you back tonight. I was supposed to work Saturday morning, but I can take care of that."

"One other thing," Jackson said. "Mike Carey, the reporter from the Lake County Star-Press, called and wanted to talk to you about your summer. I told him you were still gone and wouldn't be available to talk for another week or two. I told him that because Coach Carter doesn't want you talking to anybody about IU until you've decided for sure and it's all done. You know how Coach Garrison is. He hates all that media stuff. So no papers, no web sites, no chat rooms, no nothing, OK? That'll just upset Coach Garrison."

"No problem. I won't be talking to anybody. I'll call you after my mom gets home."

"Danny, I know you might be thinking you're not good enough to play there, but let me tell you this: You're not! But get one more year of my excellent tutelage and you'll be ready. We've got several things to work on and I'll need your undivided attention from here forward. That's what IU wants, too. You know what I mean, right?"

"Yeah, I know what you mean. You know I work hard and I'll continue to work even harder. That's never been an issue with me."

"Jeez, Danny, sometimes you're not as smart as I think you are. I'm not talking about your work ethic, I'm talking about football. No football this fall, OK? We need you to get better, and IU wants you to get better and stronger. They don't want you getting hurt playing football. It's their last scholarship and they aren't taking any chances. It's part of the deal, OK? It's the only way they'll agree to give that last scholarship to you."

"Damn, Coach, I wish you were kidding but I know you're not. I've had a million thoughts running through my head today and not playing football ever even crossed my mind. That sucks."

"I know it does, but times change, Danny. Basketball's your future now and your dream is coming true. You can go to Indiana. Look, you've taken some hits on the football field and you've been very lucky you haven't ever been hurt bad. But why risk it? We have an excellent chance to have a special winter and football's just football. I mean, you're a good quarterback and all, but you can easily be replaced. You need to make this commitment to IU and make the most of it. Plus, Coach Garrison isn't going to budge on this. He wants you, but he only wants you in one piece. He's a tough son of a gun."

"Yeah, but telling him that I'm going to play football anyway would probably be a lot easier than telling Nick I'm not going to play. He's a tough son of a bitch too, and he's my best friend. He's going to be pissed. We've always played football together."

"He'll understand. He'll be happy for you, Danny. Hell, we all are. It's

Indiana."

"I know," Danny said. "I'm very happy too, I really am. I'm just not look-ing forward to talking to Nick about this."

They hung up after a few minutes. "Great," Danny thought. "Time to go disappoint a friend."

His best friend.

2

Danny and Nick Vincent were the best of friends since they were three years old. While basketball had turned out to be Danny's best sport, Nick was a football stud. They had played everything together all these years and with one year left at Crossroads, they figured their senior seasons would be one last stroll together before heading their separate ways.

Nick always had Danny's back. He was bigger, stronger and tougher than anyone his age or even close. He wasn't a bully in any way, just someone you wouldn't want to mess with. And messing with Danny meant messing with Nick. Everyone in and around Schererville knew it, even the older kids.

When they played youth football together, Danny was this little quarterback who could throw the ball well, but his main job was to simply hand the ball to Nick. He was a beast on offense as a running back, but mostly Nick loved playing defense. He was a middle linebacker, strong as a bull and fast. He loved destroying people and thoroughly enjoyed the viciousness of football. Getting out his frustrations by burying an opponent was nothing but pure pleasure to him.

And while Danny was a late arrival to the big-time recruiting game in basketball, Nick had been a five-star football recruit since his sophomore year. He actually played six games with the varsity as a freshman, something almost unheard of in football at a big school like Crossroads, but then started every game at middle linebacker as a sophomore, leading the county in tackles and earning All-State honors. He had a great junior year, making over 200 tackles in 12 games on defense, and rushing for just over 1,000 yards on offense on only 150 carries. He was the state's Defensive Player of the Year. He was a bit over 6-foot-3, and was 235 pounds of rock-solid muscle. Every major college in America wanted him.

Something else that was almost unheard of was that Nick was the No. 1 prospect at middle linebacker on every big national recruiting service. That never happens. Biases always set in somewhere on these lists, but in Nick's case there was no question he was something special. He ran a 4.55 in the 40-yard dash, was a perfect physical specimen and was technically perfect as a tackler. He could pick and choose where he wanted to go. He was a big-timer, no question, a player who would head off to some college campus for three years, maybe four, then be a certain first-round draft pick in the National Football League. He was that good.

Nick wasn't the type of person to get all worked up over being in the recruiting spotlight. He was quiet by nature with strangers, and opened up to only a few people, if at all. If something was bothering him, he'd talk to Danny or his older brother Tony, and that was about it. He hated it when the newspapers ran big stories about him. He didn't like talking to the reporters and he didn't like that they made such a big deal about him. It was a team game, and he didn't like being portrayed as an individual.

Coaches and recruiters called him all the time in the periods they could. Recruiting-service hacks always bugged him too. It wasn't uncommon for 40 or 50 college coaches to be in the stands on a football Friday night. Nick didn't like it much at all, really. He had a plan for his recruiting, just to avoid all the hype. He was going to spend the summer narrowing his list to five schools, he was going to take his official visits as soon as he could and he was going to make a decision early to get it over with.

That was the plan; whether or not it would work was another matter. Nick just wanted to be left alone to play. He loved playing football and enjoyed basketball all winter in his role as a brutal power forward. Even though he was always playing against guys much taller, he was a superb rebounder and a great defender. He also set the meanest, nastiest picks you could imagine. He'd make sure Danny and the others would get open, and for a shooter like Danny, Nick's presence on the court brought new meaning to having a best friend at his side.

But now this Indiana thing had come up for Danny. It was something that was going to put their relationship to the test, and that's something that neither had much experience with. They had been friends for more than a dozen years now and they knew each other very well. Big arguments could probably be counted on one hand, and they usually revolved around a girl, a bad hand of poker or Danny wanting to get home by curfew and Nick, who would always have the final say, not really caring all that much what time any of the guys got home. No, this was a relationship of kids growing up mostly on the same page. They liked all the same stuff, liked going to all the same restaurants, liked being with each other. With the exception of Nick's temper and Danny's more laid-back demeanor, they were basically the same kids.

But since they were in the fourth grade, the two of them had never played a school game without the other during football and basketball seasons. Danny played a lot of AAU basketball without Nick, but at school they were always together. Now, Nick was getting ready to start his senior year of football and Danny wasn't going to be there.

And that wasn't good.

Danny figured Nick would get home from work about 6, so he thought he'd wait to see his mom at 5 when she got home, share the good news about the

IU offer with her, then go to Nick's later that night to tell him. Telling Mom would be great; telling Nick was going to stink. But he had a plan.

Right about the time the Cubs were going to their bullpen in the seventh inning, Danny heard his mother pulling up the driveway. She stopped about half-way up – she never parked on the basketball court portion of the driveway when Danny was home – and got out as her son popped out the side door to greet her.

They shared a hug, and it was a nice moment, one of many they've had through the years. Danny was lucky; he had a good mom, which made up for his father not being around much when he was a kid and not at all, for the most part, for the past 10 years or so. Danny also was lucky his mother loved sports as much as he did. She never missed a game and juggled schedules to make sure Danny got to every practice or camp. Danny always appreciated it.

Good kid had a good mom.

"I'm so glad you're home. I've missed you so much," Mary said. "It seems like you've been gone all summer. Now I'm going to keep you at home for a few weeks."

"Well, Mom, we've actually got one more trip to make. We have to go to Bloomington again this weekend and you need to come with me."

"Bloomington again? Why?"

Danny couldn't help but smile, but at the same time he started to feel tears well up in the corners of his eyes. The moment was starting to overcome him.

"Coach Garrison wants me to come play at IU, Mom. He wants me to play at Indiana University. He offered me a scholarship this morning. Can you believe it?"

Mary grabbed Danny and hugged him as tight as she ever had. She was so happy for him because she knew this was a dream come true for her boy. It was for her, too. She also loved Indiana basketball. She never missed a game on TV and if she couldn't watch a game live, she'd record it and make sure she didn't hear the score until she got home. Now, she'd get to watch her boy at Indiana.

"Danny, that's just so great. So what do we have to do?"

"Coach wants me to take an official visit this weekend, make sure I'm 100 percent on it and get everything in order. We can go down Saturday morning and come back Sunday afternoon, so you won't miss any work. I'm 100 percent sure, but it would be good to take the visit and find out everything I need to know about the academics and all that. They only have the one scholarship left that's not com-mitted to someone, and they want me to make up my mind."

"Your mind's made up, right?"

"Of course."

"Then let's go celebrate. Your brother has a sleep-over and your sister doesn't get back from her trip until Sunday, so it's just you and me. Do you have plans?"

"No, Mom. Not now. I have to go see Nick later, but I have time for dinner. Let's go get some pizza. I've been craving Angelo's for a month."

* * * * *   * * * * *   * * * * *

Danny ate too much at Angelo's, but he loved every bite of it. He dropped his mom off at the house, parked the car then decided to walk down to Nick's house, which was just down the street then left around the circle. He'd made the walk a thousand times, but never once was he so nervous. As happy as he was about the whole Indiana thing, he was still concerned about telling Nick.

It seemed odd. You'd think the first reaction would be good, but Danny also understood how much playing together meant to Nick. He knew Nick was going to be disappointed. The question was: How much?

When Danny strolled around the corner, Nick was out in the driveway cleaning his truck. They met with a handshake that quickly turned into a hug, both of them smiling. They hadn't seen each other in three weeks, which was a long time for them. Danny was busy playing basketball and Nick was busy working 60 hours a week for his brother Tony. He was a bricklayer who had his own successful business and Nick was his bitch all summer. Tony worked him to death as a laborer, but Nick loved every minute of it. It beat working out in a gym and he loved making fifteen dollars an hour all summer. Nick had never lifted a weight in his life, and didn't have to. His brother made sure of that.

"What's up, man? It's good to see you," Nick said. "I was wondering if you were home. I pulled in your driveway on my way home from work and knocked, but no one answered."

"Yeah, I went to dinner with my mom. We had something to celebrate."

"Really?"

"Yeah, Nick, really. Indiana offered me a scholarship today, and I'm going to take it. How's that for news?"

"Jesus, Danny, that's incredible. Good for you, man. Your nice little summer paid off, didn't it? He must have surprised the hell out of you."

"He did. I mean, Coach Garrison came over this morning, near the end of one of our shooting drills. I just figured he was being nice. But he asked me to come talk to him and we just walked through the corridors at Assembly Hall. We talked for about five minutes, and then we were right by the door to the locker room. He opened the door and walked me in then he asked me if I wanted to play there. Man, just looking around was so cool. I told him yes and that was that. I grabbed my stuff and walked away and then he gave me some grief about learning how to play defense."

The two best friends walked into the house and grabbed a soda to drink.

"There is one thing, though, Nick. And you're not going to be happy about it."

"What's that?"

"Well, they don't want me to play football this fall. It's their last scholarship and they don't want me to get hurt. I figured you'd be pissed and I hated to have to tell you. I hate letting you down."

"Well, you prick. You frigging prick," Nick said as he stormed out of the kitchen, heading toward the screen door out to the back porch. Danny trailed behind, saying nothing. This had to soak in, and he knew it.

Out on the porch, with a warm summer's night breeze blowing through the trees, Nick turned to Danny and stared him in the eyes.

"If we're not going to play football together, then you better do this for me. We better win a damn state championship in basketball and when we do, you have to tell everyone you couldn't have done it without me."

Nick started laughing, and Danny followed along. What a relief. He was thrilled that Nick could make light of the moment. He was pleased that it was out there now, and nothing was being thrown in anger, especially himself.

"You know, about a month ago at work I was telling my brother about a dream I had, that you got hurt real bad in a football game."

"That's a bad dream."

"Not really. In the dream I had to run it like 50 times, so it was no big deal."

"So you're not pissed? I figured you would be."

"Man, I understand. Look, you're not that great anyway …"

They just looked at each other and smiled.

The best buds, they were good.

TOM BREW

3

$\mathbf{A}$s expected, the trip to Bloomington went well. One of the Indiana assistant coaches played the role of tour guide most of Saturday. He showed Danny and his mom around Assembly Hall, then, when one of the coaches' wives took Mary to lunch, they showed Danny one of the dorms and the Athletic Learning Center, a new building that had just been built near the football stadium. They had lunch downtown at the Trojan Horse, then went back to Assembly Hall to wrap things up. Danny and Mary met with an academic counselor and a tutor for about an hour, then it was agreed to meet later for dinner.

Coach Garrison – a soft-spoken but stern disciplinarian who played and coached at Vanderbilt with great success before coming to Indiana three decades earlier – was out of town on a speaking engagement for the Fellowship of Christian Athletes, so the plan was for Danny, Mary, the assistant coaches and Garrison to meet for breakfast late on Sunday morning. They started breakfast without him at the Tudor Room, but when he did arrive, it was with a quick apology. His flight had been late.

"It's a pleasure to meet you," Mary said with a big smile, introducing herself to the coach she had marveled at watching as a fan for nearly 30 years. "It's so nice to finally meet you."

"Pleasure's all mine, Mrs. Bridges. You have a great son here, the kind of kid we like to have in our program. If he works hard and does everything he's told – and I mean everything – he'll do just fine here. I understand you had a chance to talk to the academics people yesterday and they really do a good job with our kids. The business school is the best in the country and they stay on top of things. They communicate with us very well. Academically, I can't imagine Danny will have any problems."

"I'm sure he'll do just fine, Mr. Garrison," Mary said. "I've stressed it to him for years and I know it's important to you, too. So, between the two of us, he'll know he's being watched. But he's always been a good student, so I'm not worried."

"I'm not either. And from a basketball standpoint, he'll have a lot of work to do. I understand you follow our program pretty close, so you know we've got a lot of great kids here right now and we've been fortunate enough to have another nice recruiting class. But if I didn't think Danny could play here – and play well here – I wouldn't have asked him to come. He'll fit in well, he'll have a nice career and he will get a great education, on and off the floor.

"So we're set then, Dan. You in?"

"Absolutely, Coach," Danny said. "I know I can't sign until November, but you have my word and you have my commitment. I'm here, and I'll let every other coach know right away. There's a newspaper guy in my hometown that's been wanting to talk to me for a while. He's been good to me, so I can tell him now, right?"

"Sure, we want you and you want us. As far as I'm concerned, we're done. Now, about this football thing. Coach Carter told me you've talked to your coach about this, and you're good with it.

"Well," Danny said, but he was cut off instantly by Coach Garrison.

"Listen, Dan, we all reach a point in life where we have to make some decisions. Your time is now for that. Look, you've grown, but you haven't filled out. You need to get stronger and you need to keep working on your basketball skills. You have a chance to be a special college basketball player, but it takes effort. I can guarantee you that you will never know what hit you when you get here, we'll work you so hard. Embrace it, Danny. Know that you're doing the right thing."

"Oh, I do, Coach. It's just that I feel like I'm letting my friends down. But they understand too. They know how much this means to me. We've got a chance to have a pretty special basketball season together, so that's what we'll do. It'll be OK."

With that, everyone said their goodbyes and the Danny and Mary headed back north to Schererville. It was around noon and their work in Bloomington was done. It all went well and Danny was relieved to have it behind him. He really didn't mind the recruiting, other than not really knowing what the final result was going to be. Things kept changing so quickly, he never had a good comfort level for where he might end up. Now this, so fast, and it was done.

It was a good thing.

On the ride home, Danny spent most of the time on his cell phone while his mother drove up Highway 37 and then Interstate 65. He called Coach Jackson and filled him in on the quick weekend. He called Nick, and they made plans for Sunday night with the rest of the guys. It was the last night of the St. Mark's church festival, and that was always a can't-miss local event. Everyone in town went, hung out with their friends, ate plenty of food, and danced all night to the band. Nick was glad Danny was on his way home, and they promised to hook up by 6.

About a half-hour from home, Danny's phone rang and he didn't recognize the number. He said hello, with some hesitation.

"Danny, this is Coach Carpenter at Purdue. How are you today?" Kevin

Carpenter was the new head coach at Purdue, IU's arch-rival, and he was just start-ing his second year there. They had never met, though Danny did remember seeing him at the Nike camp a few weeks earlier in the summer, the night he went off for 30 points.

"Danny, we've never really had a chance to get to know each other and I wanted to call you today to see if there's a chance we could come up to your school and talk with you a little bit about what we're trying to accomplish here at Purdue."

Danny paused for a moment, gave a little smile to his mother, and contin-ued on.

"Coach, with all due respect, I think you should know I committed to In-diana this morning. No offense, but it's always been a dream of mine to play there and for all the times I pretended I was making the winning shot for Indiana in my driveway, it was usually Purdue I was beating when I made it. I'm real happy with my decision, but I do appreciate you calling. Everybody tells me great things about you."

"Well, Danny, congratulations then. I feel bad we didn't get to you sooner. We kind of screwed up on our recruiting of you, and I feel bad about that. Please don't make me regret that too badly in the future, OK? You're a great kid, from everything that I hear, and I truly do wish you the best. Good luck."

"Thank you, Coach. I'm sure I'll see you down the road."

Danny looked at his mom and laughed.

"Purdue," he said. "Told them no."

"Of course you did," his mom said, laughing herself. "And if you hadn't, I would have. Your sweet mother would have never let you go to Purdue. That would have been way too hard for me to watch, you playing for them. I'm glad you're going where you're going. That's going to be fun."

"It is, Mom. I can't wait."

* * * * *   * * * * *   * * * * *

Parking was always a disaster at St. Mark's Fest, especially on the last night, so Danny, Nick and Kenny Dockery just walked the half-mile from Nick's house. There were easily a couple thousand people there on a warm late-summer night, and they all were enjoying the food, the rides, the bingo and the music. Behind the short white picket fence, the adults enjoyed the beer garden and the gambling, and there were plenty of both.

The weekend-long festival was the church's big fundraiser of the year, and it was a cash cow. Three nights it ran, and every year the locals set their calendar around it in late August. It was the last fun weekend of the summer before school started. Friday night was the fish fry, Saturday the chicken and corn roast and Sunday the big steak fry. The church would get all the food donated, then charge $10 a head to feed everyone. They'd feed 800 or so people every night, so do the math. That alone would rake in at least $25,000. They also made their money off the rides, a huge auction of donated goods, the quarter bingo games and the car raffles. But they made most of their money off the beer garden and the gambling tables. The pastor usually turned a blind eye to the contradiction of it all, because it was for a good cause. The tables and the beer brought in the people, and the money just flowed in. The church would rake in at least $150,000 a year, sometimes more, especially when the weather was good. It paid for the majority of school tuitions, which the parents loved. It wasn't that way at most Catholic schools.

Every year, it got bigger and bigger. Now there were dozens of blackjack tables, over-and-under tables and roulette wheels. People won money, but the house raked it in. For every $5 blackjack hand played, the player had to throw in a buck for the church. It was a quarter to the church at the dollar tables. It added up quickly. They added poker tournaments a few years ago once the poker craze had kicked in, with big percentages going to the church, making even more money.

Danny, Nick and the gang, of course, were too young to venture behind the white fence into the promised land. No one under 21 could get into the beer garden, and that should have been the rule in the outdoor casino too, but since it was a church function, they let anyone 18 and over play the games. The boys longed for the day – and it was getting close – but for now they hovered around the periphery. The usual routine since they were little kids rarely changed. You always went to the festival, you just found different things to do.

Any gambling was still out, so it was food and drink, and listening to the music – and decent little local soft-rock cover band. Flirting with the girls usually came into play, but not this year. Danny and Nick both had girlfriends now, and this had been going on for about five months for Danny, and a little longer for Nick. The girls would be here soon, after a birthday party.

Candice Wren was the perfect first girlfriend for Danny. She was an athlete herself, an excellent golfer, and an outstanding student who had moved to Indiana from New Jersey prior to her freshman year at Crossroads. She studied hard, worked hard at her golf game and had very nice but strict and successful parents who pushed her hard to succeed. Her father was a powerful executive at a steel company and her mother a successful real estate agent, both New Jersey natives who passed along their love of Bruce Springsteen to their daughter. She wanted to be a doctor, a pediatrician, and was very focused on her goals. She had just received an early acceptance letter from Northwestern, the prestigious university just north of Chicago in Evanston, and was eager for the next phase of her life to begin. Without question, she was something special.

Candice and Danny were a lot alike. Both were goal-oriented and were never much for the dating scene until now. For Danny, basketball was No. 1 and academics were a close 1-A. Candice's priorities were similar, just reversed slightly. School always came first for the straight-A student, then family, golf, friends and church.

Boys were way down on the list, at least until Danny came along.

Neither really had much time to date, but last spring they sort of found each other. They had always been friendly with each other at school, but their closest groups of friends didn't really hang out together. That changed one Saturday night at a pizza party right after the end of the basketball season. They chatted each other up for about an hour and found they both enjoyed it. A few days later they had lunch, then went to a movie a few weekends later. It was nothing serious, but they enjoyed each other's company. With prom about six weeks down the road, they mutually agreed to go with each other, without either of them having to awkwardly ask the other. They had a fun night, looked great together in the pictures and had been together ever since. They didn't see a lot of each other, only when they could, but that was fine with both of them. They had a lot of fun together and Candice was even turning Danny into a Springsteen fan as well.

Now, Abby Parsons, she was a different story. She'd had a crush on Nick Vincent since the first day of their freshmen year. She was boy crazy, a little wild, and always had to have a boy on her arm. That boy now was Nick. She'd spend every minute with Nick if she could, and they had plenty of alone time together since both of them usually had empty houses. She was a cheerleader, a very average student, but loaded with personality and plenty of good looks. She was all Nick could handle, and Nick could handle a lot. An active sex life made Nick happy. Abby too.

When the girls finally arrived, Abby ran across the lot and jumped into Nick's arms, giving him a huge kiss with a loud hello, Candice just rolled her eyes, gave Danny a little hug and a quick kiss, then whispered something about Abby being a little too wound up. "She's just driving me nuts," Candice said. "I'll be ready for a little quiet time with you. She just never shuts up"

Candice and Danny had only seen each other maybe three times in the past six weeks, between his basketball stuff and her summer golf schedule. After Danny's scholarship offer, they'd only had one night together where they were in town, and Candice's family had something going on. They spent an hour or two together, but that was it.

"I know you love the fest and all, Danny, but I'd just love it if we could go somewhere else and maybe just have a nice quiet dinner or something. I miss you, and we've got so much to talk about. You think you could pull yourself away from all this?"

"Yeah, I think so. Nick's been itching to play poker anyway and I think he's up to something. He won't care if I bail. Let's maybe spend about a half hour here, then we'll go, OK? My mom is over there playing bingo with my aunt. Why don't we say hello to them real quick. She's been asking about you."

Danny gestured to Nick that they were leaving for a while. "Where you going?" he said.

"Say hello to my mom, then we might go get something to eat. I haven't seen much of Candice lately. Plus, this is kind of lame. I don't really feel like hanging out around here tonight."

"Well, I am. Got my hundred bucks right here and I'm going to play the big final poker tournament. My brother's collecting the entry fees and he doesn't give a shit about me being a few months shy of 18. Nobody's going to say anything. I'm going to kick all their asses."

"Good luck, man. Show those old codgers something."

Thirty minutes turned into an hour before Danny and Candice could get in all their hellos – and all their goodbyes – and make their getaway. As they were walking across the field to Candice's car, they walked along the sacred white fence and Danny shot a glance at Nick, totally in his element, mixing it up with the adults at Texas Hold 'Em. The field of 90 poker players was down to about 50, and Nick had a nice stack of chips in front of him. Nick saw them, then flashed nine fingers at Danny, along with a big smile. He had already turned his 1,500 chips into 9,000 and Nick, the young poker wizard, was well on his way.

Danny and Candice had a nice leisurely meal at Chili's, chatted for a couple of hours, made out a little in the car, and then Candice dropped Danny off at home.

Walking into the house, Danny's phone beeped.

He had a text message from Nick.

'Finished fourth. Went all-in with king-high flush, prick had the ace. Oh well. $495! I'll take it. C U tomorrow."

4

As the gambling and drinking finally died down late on a Sunday night, Ben Richardson was glad to see a parking spot open right in front of his house. Ben ran The St. Jude Serenity Center, a treatment facility and transitional living center in Schererville for people dealing with gambling addictions, and it was right next door to the church at St. Mark's. The big two-story house used to be the church convent, where there was room for a dozen or so nuns to live. Ben owned the house now, and his beds were often filled with sick compulsive gamblers, some sicker than others.

Ben was 50 years old and had grown up in Schererville. He had been through his own share of gambling problems, but hadn't made a bet now for almost 15 years and had devoted his life to helping others with gambling problems. He had worked at a treatment facility in Florida for a few years, and then decided to come home to Indiana and start something here, because he knew the need was there, especially after a half-dozen glitzy casinos opened along Lake Michigan a decade earlier. He had his own life in order and had some good fortune a few years earlier. That's when he talked the church into selling him the convent, which had been empty for a few years and in desperate need of repair. It seemed like the perfect place for a treatment facility, and he'd been running The Serenity Center out of it now for about five years and it was going well. His work was very rewarding, and he was enjoying the slow-paced life again in Schererville. He still snickered at his St. Jude reference in the name of the place: the patron saint of lost causes and all. He treated a lot of very sick people – both in group therapy and individual sessions – and he loved every minute of it.

It was good to be back at home, living a rewarding life.

It was also good to be away from Schererville on this weekend. He currently had three clients at the house, enrolled in various stages of a 28-day in-house program, and three other houseguests, guys who had been receiving treatment and were now tackling the world on their own again. Ben offered transitional living services for these addicts, so they could work their way back into a normal lifestyle while still being surrounded by people who were trying to tackle this insidious disease as well. They went to a lot of Gamblers Anonymous meetings, had a lot of great conversations about recovery with Ben over meals and helped out around the house. As long as they were staying clean and working on their recoveries, Ben liked having them around. Some stayed for a month, some for six. That was Ben's limit. They all helped each other out, living their recoveries one day at a time. For the guys in the midst of hard-core rehab, it was nice to have the other guys around as shining examples that their recoveries could work, as long as they worked at it.

With all the gambling going on with the festival, Ben didn't want anyone to be surrounded by temptation, so everyone left Saturday morning for Milwaukee and went to a Gamblers Anonymous mini-conference for two days. Ben spoke at a few sessions and for the others it was good be surrounded by hundreds of other recovering gamblers and learning more about how best to go forward in their lives. They got back early enough for everyone to get a good night's rest. They would be busy on Monday.

One of the deals Ben worked out with the church when he bought the convent was that he would help the church maintain its grounds. Ben had a landscaping background, so cutting grass and trimming and edging was right up his alley. The guys in the house in their transitional living phase would help out too, a way to keep them busy and feel positive about doing something good. They plowed snow in the winter and kept all the grass cut around the church, the school, the cemetery, the sports fields and all the parking lots the rest of the year. During the summer, a few of the local kids also helped out for a decent wage, and Ben, with the blessing of the pastor, did the hiring. It was the good kids in the parish who got the jobs, and Danny was one of those kids. He'd worked at the church for two years in a row whenever they needed them, and Ben was great about working around his sports schedule. It was just a handful of hours every week, but it was spending cash all the same.

The Monday after the festival meant there was lots of cleaning up to do. The parish volunteers had put away all of the big stuff late Sunday night, and Ben and a few of his guys got the grounds back to normal. Danny helped out too for about four hours. He had a nice chat with Ben while they were working, and Ben was thrilled to hear all about his experiences at Indiana. Ben was an IU graduate, and a big fan. He was a big fan of Danny's too. What a nice fit, he thought. Ben was a marginal player back in the day in high school at Crossroads, but he was at least part of the school's first very good team about 30 years earlier, a team that had a great regular season but lost in the first round at sectionals. He loved basketball and still played often to stay in shape. He was thrilled to know someone who was going to be a part of the Indiana University basketball program.

Danny left about 2 p.m. to go to the high school. He wanted to work out while the football guys weren't around. Practice started on Monday, an early workout at sunrise, then a second workout for the football guys about 6. He still felt a little awkward about the whole thing, and didn't mind giving it some time. So he figured he'd work out at about 3, then Coach Jackson had lined up an interview with the reporter from the local paper. He was coming by the school about 4:30 to talk to Danny about the Indiana decision. Danny figured he could get all that done before all the football guys got back to school.

After his workout, Mike Carey from the Star-Press was waiting with Coach Jackson in the basketball office. He had already interviewed the coach, and now was waiting to wrap things up with Danny before heading back to his office.

"Hello, Danny," Carey said, rising out of a chair to shake hands when Danny walked in. "Congratulations on the IU thing. You know, as reporters we try to remain impartial, but that still is an Indiana University diploma hanging on my wall. So I'm glad you're going there, and even more glad that now I have another reason to get to Bloomington every once in a while. I still love it down there, even though it's been five years since I graduated. It's a great place to go to college. You'll have a blast."

Danny thanked him for the kind words and then sat down for a 20-minute chat with the reporter, and it all seemed to go well. Danny talked about how it was always his dream to play at Indiana and how he was glad that his summer had gone well enough for him to get the chance. He talked about the things he wanted to work on and only for a few minutes did they even talk football.

As near as Danny could remember, Carey only asked him the one question: Are you going to miss playing football?

Danny remembers his answer vividly, because it was the same thing he had told Coach Garrison the week before in Bloomington. He felt like he was letting down his friends by not playing, but that he also had to look ahead to his future and do what was right for that. He had a lot of work to do physically and he had high hopes for his senior season at Crossroads in basketball.

End of interview, a shake of the hands, and they went their separate ways. Danny thought it had all gone well enough. He jumped into his mother's car and drove to Candice's house for dinner with her and her parents.

* * * * *   * * * * *   * * * * *

Danny was usually an early riser. He liked to get in about a two-mile run in the morning, especially in the summer when the days were long and the weather was good. But on this Tuesday morning, his first move was to stroll down to the end of the driveway for the morning paper. He was curious to see what Mike Carey had written about him.

He peeled away the first two sections of the paper to get to the sports section, and there he was, down near the bottom of the front page, right corner. It was a small mug shot, and all there was underneath it was:

Bridges commits to IU, Page 6
Crossroads High QB to focus on basketball

Danny was puzzled. Page 6? No front-page story, after granting him an interview first before telling any other newspaper or recruiting website? And why is he calling me a quarterback in a basketball story?

Then Danny saw why, on second glance. It wasn't pretty. He took a closer look at the bold front-page headline, under a "Sports Special" banner:

"Era of 2-sport stars dying?"

It was a big headline, with a subhead underneath it talking about pressure from college coaches to pick one sport.

Danny didn't like where this was going, but he read on:

By Mike Carey
Star-Press Sports Writer
SCHERERVILLE – Crossroads High School football coach Mitch Elliott and offensive coordinator Jack Bowen, close friends for more than 20 years, have been looking forward to the day when Bowen's son, sophomore standout quarterback Ryan Bowen, took the reins of the Marauders' offense.

They just didn't expect that day to be Monday.

Bowen lined up under center with the first team when Crossroads began two-a-day practices Monday. The 6-foot-4 sophomore has unlimited potential, but his future is now after the sudden announcement that Danny Bridges, the Marauders' starter the past two years and projected starter this year, would quit the football team to concentrate on basketball. Bridges committed to Indiana University basketball coach Henry Garrison last weekend and will play basketball next year at IU.

The scholarship offer came with this caveat: That Bridges not play football this season at Crossroads.

Is there something wrong with high school sports when college coaches start dictating what talented high school seniors should be doing with their final year of school?

Of course, there is.

"Shit." Danny said, shaking his head, wondering where this was going. Then came the whammy.

Garrison, through an Indiana University spokesman, refused to comment for this story.

"Great. Just great." Danny said to no one in particular. "I'm a year away from setting foot in Bloomington and I've probably already got Coach Garrison pissed off at me."

Carey's story didn't get any better. A few paragraphs later, he used Danny's quote – "I feel like I'm letting my friends down by not playing football" – but didn't use the second half of the only quote Danny gave him about football a day earlier, the part where his coaches and teammates understood, and that everyone was on board with his decision, that this was best in regards to Danny getting stronger and having a great final high school basketball season.

Near the end of the story was a quote from Elliott, who had been Crossroads' coach for 15 years. He had talked about his meeting earlier in the week with Danny, after he had returned from Bloomington. Danny had met with him and Coach Jackson, and Coach Bowen was there too. Danny thought that meeting had gone well, and he even considered Coach Bowen a friend. They'd spent countless hours together a year earlier, watching film and going over game plans. Young Ryan, a freshman at the time, was always there, too, learning as much as he could from Danny and his father. Danny enjoyed the mentor role, because he knew Ryan was going to be great someday. Coach Bowen had been Danny's coach in youth football and he'd known Ryan since he was about 8.

Elliott's comments were scathing, and caught Danny off-guard.

"I know this is a basketball state and all," Elliott said in the story, "but it's wrong when someone like Danny, who's a very good high school quarterback and would certainly help us win some games, isn't allowed to play football. We have a pretty good football team too, and it's wrong for these big-time college coaches to tell a kid what to do.

"It ticks me off. It really does."

The story, of course, failed to mention that Elliott had played college football at Purdue, works their camps every summer and has, like most Purdue fans, a deep dislike for Indiana University, especially its basketball program. It was an easy cheap shot for him to make.

The story ended with a quote from new Ridge Central football coach Bo Tyler, who had coached against Bowen last year as the junior-varsity coach at Ridge Central and had several sons who were two-sport athletes. Ridge Central had owned Crossroads in football for several years, ever since the two high schools – Munster and Highland – merged into one 3,800-student super-school about five years earlier to better compete with all the huge super-schools around the state. The two coaching staffs didn't like each other much. But Tyler, who had a son who was a senior on Ridge Central's basketball team and knew Danny's basketball prospects well, also could be impartial with his assessments.

31

"I've seen Ryan Bowen first-hand, and he's a great quarterback who will probably play Division I football someday," Tyler was quoted. "I've also seen a lot of Danny Bridges in the past couple of years, and he's a much better basketball player than he is a football player. If they go 6-4 instead of 7-3, what does it matter if Danny doesn't play football? It's not like they're going to win anything big in football anyway."

Danny, at last, had reason to smile. As upset as he was about the article, at least he knew all his Crossroads High School pals were going to be more upset with Coach Tyler's comments. Tyler thought what most people did, that Crossroads was good but not great in football. He was just speaking the facts; and Danny knew he was probably right. They were what they were. They weren't going to win any state titles in football, but basketball was different.

Stay the course, he thought. He knew he made the right decision, and he knew it hadn't been an easy choice to make.

He was a basketball player now, and that was OK. That's what he needed to remember.

5

Danny was supposed to work at St. Mark's on Tuesday morning, but when it began raining about 45 minutes after he started cutting grass back by the school soccer field, he brought the mower back into the garage and Ben invited him in to dry off and have a late breakfast.

The Star-Press sports section was lying on the dining room table.

"Nice story, Danny. You're a big-timer now," Ben said.

"You think that's nice? I felt like he threw me under the bus. He came out to school yesterday to talk to me and we probably talked for 15 minutes or so and he asked me one question – one question! – about football. Then there's this whole big story about me not playing football. He made Coach Garrison look like an idiot. It kinds of makes me mad, to be honest with you."

Ben had been interviewed for hundreds of stories in his day – some good and some bad – so he knew what Danny was going through. He had something of a love/hate relationship with the media.

"Danny, one thing you have to learn about newspapers is that they're always going to write what they think they need to write, not what you wish they would write. You can't ever let it bother you, especially when you know you're doing the right thing. If they misquote you, then you can be mad. Or if they take a cheap shot at you, then get mad. But when they write something different from what you expect, just take it with a grain of salt. They make one of those newspapers every day. No one will remember tomorrow what they read today."

Ben has had his name in the papers many times, and not always for all the right reasons. As a younger man, he was arrested three times, once right after college for lipping off to a cop in a bad mood after a traffic stop, once later in life – after the gambling had kicked – for shoplifting and another time for writing several bad checks. He spent a few nights in jail, but was lucky enough to have good lawyers. Especially when his gambling was in full force, Ben lived life on the edge. He got caught twice and should have been punished even worse than he was. He got away with much more.

The best thing that ever happened to Ben was asking for help when his life hit rock-bottom. He was running a four-star restaurant/bar with complete autonomy on the north side of Chicago and had total control over his time and other people's money. He was winning more than he was losing gambling, but he was betting a couple thousand dollars a day by then, was totally consumed with gambling and was totally ignoring his job. People were starting to notice. He'd take money from work – a popular spot just down the street from Wrigley Field – gamble with it, then pay it back down the road. If he was short, he would borrow the money from sleazy loan sharks on the streets, then pay them back as fast as he could He was robbing Peter to pay Paul, and he was on the verge of everything blowing up in his face. When he got arrested on the bad check charges, his mother came and bailed him out of jail. When they got in her car, she asked Ben where he wanted her to take him, because she was dropping him off and turning her back on him.

She was done with all his crap, and was telling him so.

For her, this was the end of the road. She had had enough.

"Either come with me to get help, or say goodbye forever. It's your call," his mother had said that day.

Since Ben had no money, debts out the ass and nowhere to go to escape this mess, there was only one answer at that moment, whether he believed it or not.

"I need help, Mom. Please, help me."

Not really sure what he was wishing for, Ben walked into an ambush when he entered his mother's house. His only brother was there, as was the the owner of his restaurant and two gambling treatment professionals who had done hundreds of interventions with addicts on the edge, or over it. His brother told him they were done bailing him out as a family and that he had to get help immediately, or they would call the police about the money Ben had stolen from his own mother a few months back to pay off a loan shark. His boss said his job would be waiting for him in a month if he went to get help, and if not he'd call the police about all the cash he let flow from the night club registers to his bookies and the horse tracks and casinos on a nightly basis.

When the two treatment guys started talking, Ben was already a beaten man. He knew he'd been bitten hard by the gambling bug and needed to get out from under it. He just didn't know how.

These two men did.

"Have you had enough?" the one said. "That's the only question I have for you, and it's really that simple. If your answer is yes, then we don't have any more questions for you, we'll have answers. We can help you from this moment forward.

"But if your answer is no, that you haven't had enough yet, then we don't have any other questions for you either. We'll just let you go back to doing what you're doing now, and we'll hear about you getting arrested, or we'll hear about your funeral. Or both. It's as simple as that.

"So, again, I'll ask you this question: Have you had enough?"

Broken and beaten, Ben was smart enough to understand that he really did need some help. The two men explained that they wanted Ben to come to Florida for three weeks with them, and they would help him. They weren't asking, his mother said. They were telling.

He had no choice, so Ben agreed to go.

The two men drove Ben to his apartment in Chicago, where he packed some clothes quickly into a suitcase, and grabbed a few personal items. Within two hours, they were on an airplane to Tampa, and a few hours later, well past midnight, Ben was in a hospital, locked in his own room, staring across the table at two men he had never met before this night, but who were about to become his two best friends.

They were going to save his life, and they did.

Ben went through an intense three weeks of treatment, clearing his head of bad thoughts and his body of bad behavior. He was fortunate that it all made sense to him. After just a few hours of conversation, he thoroughly understood that he was a compulsive gambler, was being totally controlled by the disease, and needed to do something about it. It was embarrassing to be hospitalized, but he got the point. He was a mess, and they were going to help fix him. He had to be broken down first, then put back together. This was the first step. He spent hours each day in one-on-one therapy, spent several more hours in his room reading, and spent each night out of the hospital with several recovering addicts, going to Gamblers Anonymous meetings. It was reassuring to know he wasn't the only one with this problem, and he was grateful to know there was a way to get his life back in order. As much as gambling had been consuming his life a few weeks earlier, now recovery was all that was on his mind.

He moved into a treatment facility after the hospital, went to 76 meetings in 90 days, and started to feel like he could breathe again. He had flown to Chicago briefly, spent a bit of time with his mother and brother, but left to come back to Florida a few days later. He told the restaurant owner that he needed some more time to get well and needed a change of scenery. He thanked him for getting him help, but told his boss he didn't feel comfortable coming right back into that same bad work environment he had just left. The owner understood Ben needed to make changes in his life, and he wished Ben well. Ben got a job in Florida at a landscaping company, went to meetings almost every night and worked on getting better. Days turned into weeks, weeks into months, months into years. In his third year of recovery, he become a certified gambling treatment counselor, started working part-time at the treatment center he had stayed at in Florida and learned as much about the disease and the recovery as he could.

When all the casinos started opening on the lakefront in northwest Indiana, Ben thought it would be the perfect time to move back north. There was very little organized help for compulsive gamblers in Indiana, and he thought he could help. Year after year, he did more and more. And now he was 50, comfortable as he could be in his role, and enjoying life. He was a wise man, on lots of topics, and didn't mind sharing his stories. Danny loved their conversations, which were almost never about gambling, just sports, family and life. With no father around, Danny tended to rely on Ben a lot for fatherly advice, and both seemed to thoroughly enjoy that kind of a relationship.

"You know, Danny, one thing I learned a long time ago is to worry only about the mountains, not the mole hills," Ben said as they finished off the last of the eggs and sausage. "I wouldn't worry about what he wrote at all. Look around you. Your coaches understand, your friends understand, your family understands. You are a great basketball player and you're surrounded by a lot of other great players this year. We only get a handful of chances to do something special in our lives, and you've got a chance to do something special right now. So just do it, and make the most of it.

"Give your all to making your basketball season memorable. Make sure you make the special moments in your life unforgettable. Just grow from this experience with the writer. It will happen again, trust me, Just learn from it. Learn from everything you go through. That's what makes us stronger as people."

"You always make a lot of sense, Mr. Richardson. Thank you for the advice," Danny said. "I appreciate it. I really do."

The rain still hadn't stopped, so Ben handed Danny $60 and sent him on his way. School started the following Monday, so they agreed that Danny would work one day after school and Saturday mornings. "Eight or 10 hours a week won't get in the way until basketball season starts will it?" Ben asked. "We'll be done cutting grass every week by mid-October anyway."

"Maybe let's keep it to six, if that's OK. I really need the money, but I also need to be working out too."

"Whatever you need," Ben said as they shook hands. As they walked out the back door, Ben walked over to his car and called Danny over. "Here, Danny, take this. It's an Outback Steakhouse gift certificate for fifty dollars that someone gave me. Take that girlfriend of yours out for a nice dinner before school starts, OK?"

"That's really nice. Thank you so much," Danny said. "I will, and she'll love it. We both love that place. Thanks."

6

Danny had the luxury of being able to pop right out of bed when his alarm went off, so Monday's first day of school started just like all of them for him. Up at 6, he took a quick run of 2-plus miles that took about 15 minutes, grabbed a shower and then some breakfast before Nick pulled into his driveway a few minutes before 7. That was their routine, which rarely changed. There was one exception. On the days when Danny's mother already had made homemade bread, Nick would be forewarned – usually by Danny's mother – and he'd get there about 15 minutes early. They'd slice and toast up an entire loaf of bread, each dunking about a half-dozen slices or more of the best buttered toast you've ever eaten into a mug of steaming hot chocolate. It was a rare treat when Mary made bread, because it took her so long and time wasn't a luxury she had very often. So when she did, Nick was sure to be there to enjoy the feast.

But on this first day, Danny settled for a few poached eggs on English muffins and a large glass of juice. When Nick pulled up, he grabbed his backpack and gym bag, tossed a bottle of Gatorade in the pouch and headed out the door.

Another year. The last one.

"Here we go again, my friend," Nick said as Danny hopped into his truck. "The last year. Should be fun."

"Yeah, it's going to be great, man. We'll have a blast. How were two-a-days?"

"Three weeks of hell, which you completely avoided. We didn't have a single practice rained out, which kind of sucked, but at least we got a lot done. Bowen's been good at quarterback. I'll say this about him. I used to think he was a little smart-ass, but he's been busting his tail. He's learning the offense and he's staying after practice, throwing with the receivers and really working on the playbook. I think he's going to be all right. We're still going to throw it a lot, even with you not there. We put in a lot of one-back-set stuff, which I like, but we're probably going to throw out of it more than we run, depending on the situation."

"I've thought of you guys often, believe me," Danny said. "That's why I've tried to get my workouts done when you guys weren't there. I don't want to be a distraction. I'm sure it'll all settle down now that school starts. And a game Friday already. You think you'll be ready?"

"Yeah, it's just Southlake, so it shouldn't be a real battle anyway. They're the perfect first opponent for the kid to get his feet wet, plus it's at home, which will help him a lot. He'll be more comfortable there. You know how it goes, though. It'll be nice just to hit someone else for a change. Can't really beat the crap out of my own teammates, you know. I'm ready to blow up some other people."

Danny gulped down the last of his Gatorade as they pulled into the parking lot, and grabbed his things. "You decide on your five visits yet? I know you wanted to have that done by the time school started."

"Yeah, I think so. Sure on four of them. Michigan and Ohio State for sure, and Notre Dame, definitely. I have to visit there, but I don't really think they're a serious candidate. All those years of rooting against them is still hard to shake, even if they are good again after all these years."

"I can relate, and you know I've got you covered there. Still hate them. Ever since the first day they marched us over to church in grade school on a Friday morning and made us pray for a Notre Dame victory, I couldn't stand that. Still haven't ever gotten over it."

"Me neither, but I have to at least visit and keep them on my list. My brother, stinking Irish fan that he is, he would never forgive me and neither would half the people in this town. So I'll go visit, at least. And Florida State's the fourth. I wanted to at least keep one warm-weather school on the list and I like them a lot better than Florida or Miami. USC's just too far. I really want to stay close enough that my brother can drive somewhere on game days. The fifth one, I'm not sure yet. Not sure I really need a fifth, but we'll see."

* * * *   * * * *   * * * *

As they walked across the parking lot toward the school's front door, Candice came over to meet them, dressed in a cute pair of jeans and a sleeveless red button-down top that Danny had bought her on his last trip to Indiana. She looked gorgeous.

"Dude, you got lucky there," Nick said as he walked away. "She gets cuter and cuter every day."

"I know," Danny said. "She's great."

The two embraced and gave each other a quick kiss. They had just left each other 12 hours earlier. Danny thought it would be a great idea to take Candice and her parents to Outback with his gift card, and they had a great time at dinner the night before. Danny's mother came too, and it was the first time all five of them had sat down for a meal together. Danny and Candice enjoyed it, and the parents all seemed to enjoy each other's company as well. Danny had planned on paying, with Mom's help for the difference, but Andy Wren refused and was adamant about paying the bill. He took Danny's gift card but gave him fifty dollars in cash in return. "I know you'll spend it on her anyway. It's no different from me giving it to her," he said. It was a nice way to end the summer, and now here they were, starting their senior year.

"Good news," Candice said. "Saw Crissy Brown this morning when we were getting our locker combinations and I switched with her. Now we're locker neighbors. I'm not down with all the W's now."

"That's great. So now every time I forget something, you can rescue me. And maybe I'll see you a few more times during the day."

They only had one class together, but the same lunch, so they mapped out their day ... and their nights. They'd be busy this semester, but both thought the same way. Schedule their time together and make it happen. And that's what they did. Danny wanted to work out every day after school Candice,wanted to practice since her golf season was starting in a week. She was one of those rare golfers who loved to practice as much as she loved to play.

"So Tuesday night, come over for dinner and hang out. Study with me. And Friday, you're all mine, okay? Come to school with Nick, but I'll give you a ride after school. I have everything planned. We'll eat an early dinner at my house first and then go to the football game together. You promised we'd do that, right? Be together for the game? You said that might make it easier for you."

"Of course we're together for the game. I think that'd be great, and the day with you too. That's perfect. And I'll just go out with Nick and the guys after the game for a little while. Sounds like the perfect plan."

Danny actually loved being back at school. He looked forward to getting into the school routine again, and getting on with what was certainly going to be a fun year. He had a relatively easy schedule, one that didn't include any more science classes, and his first-period history class was with Coach Jackson, which was perfect in case some before-school shootarounds ran long. His only class with Candice was his last one, Honors English IV, with Mrs. Wesson.

Mrs. Wesson was one of Danny's all-time favorite teachers. She was a tiny woman, barely 5-feet tall and not an ounce over 100 pounds. She was in her early sixties and had been teaching at Crossroads for nearly 30 years. She taught all honors courses and Danny had her twice before. She wasn't a sports fan, but she appreciated hard-working kids with good manners, and Danny certainly qualified there. She enjoyed reading Danny's papers, and challenged him often because he was such an insightful writer. And if she needed a student to do a chore for her during class, she'd often ask Danny to help her out.

Mrs. Wesson was glad to see Danny in her class, and Candice too. The two were walking down the hallway hand-in-hand toward Mrs. Wesson's door when their teacher was coming toward them from the other direction. She gave them both a nice smile as they reached the door together.

"I have to admit," Mrs. Wesson said, "I think it's very nice to see the two of you together, all hand-holdy and everything. You make a very cute couple."

"Thank you, Mrs. Wesson," Candice said with a nice smile. "But seriously now, hand-holdy? Is that even a word? And coming from you, the keeper of fine and proper English?"

They all laughed.

"You get my point, Miss Wren. You get my point." And then she whispered into Candice's ear: "He's such a good boy. I'm glad you're with him."

"So am I," Candice said, still smiling. "He makes me very, very happy."

* * * *　　* * * *　　* * * *

Danny walked into the Wren house about 7 on Tuesday night, and Mr. Wren said hello over a platter of chicken breasts that were on their way to the grill. Late dinners at the Wren house weren't uncommon, since both of Candice's parents had hectic and successful careers and Candice was often off doing her thing at the golf course until close to dark. Danny was starving after a long day of school and a hard two-hour workout, so a nice meal was sounding very good to him. It was a beautifully warm late summer evening, so Candice and Danny sat outside on the porch and drank sweet tea while Mr. Wren cooked away. They were nice and comfortable all stretched out on two lounge chairs.

After all the chicken and corn was gone, they studied together for a little while, then curled up on one lounge chair together, under a cloudless, star-filled sky, alone at last while Candice's parents left to run a few errands.

"This is nice," Candice said, squeezing Danny's arm. "Very nice."

"Yes it is," Danny said with a smile.

"It's nice to be alone with you. And it'll be nice to relax together on Friday before the game."

"Every day with you is nice, Candice. I'm loving every minute of it."

The two curled up even closer together, happy as can be.

* * * *　　* * * *　　* * * *

The first football Friday of the fall had arrived and everyone at Crossroads High was excited. The Star-Press had done their extensive high school football special section that morning, and Nick was on the cover, in a caricature along with three other local players, one from Ridge Central and two from Merrillville, who would all be serious Division I recruits that fall.

Mike Carey's long story was very nice, and Nick even liked it because it wasn't all about him. It had a reference high in the story about him being a Mr. Football candidate, the award given to the state's top player every year. Even the team preview focused more on the new young quarterback, Ryan Bowen, and his three speedy young receivers, with just a one-paragraph mention about Danny not playing, which was nice.

Life was moving on for everyone. That was good.

All the writers made their picks, and they had Crossroads as low as 6-4 and as high as 8-2 in their predictions, some as high as second in the conference behind Broadway High School, the big school up the road in Merrillville that was loaded and ranked No. 2 in the state. Others picked Crossroads third or fourth, which was about right. They had some players, but aside from Nick they were young and small, and had lots of question marks.

For Danny, it was a surreal morning. It was game day, but not for him. He was just going to be a fan this night, instead of the starting quarterback. And he was, surprisingly, just fine with that.

Nick, as expected, was juiced up on the ride to school. He'd be wound into a frenzy by kickoff at 7:30, and his excitement level would build through the day.

"I've gotten into my routine of practicing without you, but I have to admit it's going to be a little strange without you out there tonight," Nick said. "But I'm sure it's going to be even more strange for you, just sitting up there watching. I'm surprised you're even coming."

"Really? Why would you think that? I'm not going to miss any of your games, man. There's one weekend where I have to go to Bloomington, but that's it. Actually, Nick, I'm really looking forward to my day. Candice's mom left this morning for a trip, so Candice is going to make me dinner at her house, then we'll come to the game. And I'll go out with you guys afterward for a while. It won't be so bad. I'll just try not to be too critical from the stands."

The day passed quickly. Danny found Candice after the pep rally at the end of the school day and the two headed off to her car, hand in hand.

"This is nice, leaving school with you in the middle of the day," Candice said. "We never get to do this."

Never was an apt description, because they hadn't ever left school together. Both were usually in workout mode after school, so the break was nice for both of them on Friday. They made a quick stop at the grocery store, and were to Candice's house by 4.

"My mom went to Florida this morning for the weekend and Dad is in Chicago all day on business, then he's got a dinner up there and won't be back

41

until 10," Candice said. "So we've got the house to ourselves, with my dad's only orders not to burn the house down while I make you dinner. Help me with that, OK?"

"I think you're perfectly capable of making tacos without burning the house down, but I'll keep an eye on you," Danny said. "Both eyes, the whole time. From head to toe, with a pause or two in between."

They traded smiles, and hugged for a while.

The Wrens, as you would expect from a successful, hard-working couple, had a beautiful home in St. John, about five miles or so south of the high school. It was a little over 4,000 square feet, four bedrooms, four baths, a huge den for mom and dad to work out of and a gorgeous pool and spa out back. Candice's room was upstairs, and she had a room to sleep in and another to study in, both attached to the same bathroom. The kitchen was huge, right off the family room, and Candice flipped on the television with the remote while they laid all the groceries on the counter.

"Come here, you," Candice said as she pulled Danny toward her by the hand. She gave him a long, passionate kiss, then a cute smile with a nice hug.

They made their tacos together, laughing and smiling the entire time. Then they curled up on the couch together to relax and watch a movie. It was a nice moment for the two of them. In just a few minutes, Candice fell asleep on Danny's shoulder. He laid there, admiring the moment, feeling Candice's heartbeat on his arm as they cuddled up together. This was new to him, but so, so great. He couldn't have been happier.

Candice slept for about a half-hour and woke up with an adorable smile on her face as she looked up to Danny. She just grinned, without saying a word. She didn't need to, because they were both thinking the same thing. How wonderful. They kissed for a while, then Candice hopped off to change clothes for the game. Danny stayed on the couch, mindlessly watching the movie. Life was good.

Candice popped down the stairs and grabbed her car keys. They took off for the game, happy as could be.

"I guess when you fall asleep in my arms you really are my girlfriend now," Danny joked as they jumped into the car to go to the game.

"Yep, you're stuck with me," she said.

* * * * *   * * * * *   * * * * *

Danny and Candice got to school about 20 minutes before kickoff, and as they were walking through the gate hand-in-hand, one of the reporters from the Star-Press was there, along with a photographer who was clicking away as the two walked into the stadium.

The reporter introduced himself to Danny, and Danny shook his hand. But that was the end of the pleasantries.

'Why are you taking our picture?" Danny said.

"I'm covering the game tonight and Mike Carey wanted me to do a sidebar on you not playing, and what it's like to be watching the game," he said. "He wanted me to make sure we got some pictures."

"Well, where is he? I want to talk to him. And did he even talk to my coach about this, like he's supposed to? This is the first I'm hearing of this."

"He's not here. He's in Merrillville doing the Broadway game."

"Well, I'll be honest. I don't like this," Danny said. "Those are my friends out there playing, and they've been busting their butt for a month in the hot sun getting ready to play a game. I'm just a high school senior going to a football game with my girlfriend. That's not a story. If you write a story about me tonight, you can tell Mike Carey that I will never speak to him again. I don't think he'd want that."

"Can I just ask you a couple of questions?" the reporter said.

"No!" Danny said. He was getting angry now, and Candice squeezed his hand a little tighter. "You call Mr. Carey and tell him what I said. It's not fair to my friends out there. Write about them. I do not want you writing a story about me."

"OK, I'll call him. I'm sorry, Danny," the reporter said. "I didn't expect it to be a problem."

Danny and Candice quickly walked away. It took a lot to get Danny upset, but this certainly did. He was angry, and this was the first time Candice had seen this side of him. "Don't let him bother you," Candice said. "Like you said, you're just a kid watching a football game with his girlfriend. So go take your girlfriend over there and buy her a Diet Coke, then let's go sit down."

Danny knew she was right. "Thanks," he said. "You're definitely saying all the right things today, aren't you?"

Candice smiled. "That's what perfect girlfriends are for, right?"

"I certainly can't dispute that. You really are the perfect girlfriend."

They grabbed a couple of drinks from the concession stand and as they headed to their seats, Danny spotted Coach Jackson. He walked over and – calmly this time – told him about being accosted at the gate by the reporter and photographer.

"I made it pretty clear to him that I thought it was unfair to be writing about me tonight when it's those guys that are playing," Danny said. His basketball coach agreed.

"I have Mike's cell phone number. I'll call him and make sure he understands," Coach Jackson said. "I'll find you before you leave and let you know that I got a hold of him."

As the game started, Candice and Danny sat near the back row with the other students, mostly Candice's friends. Candice, of course, was doing a lot of whispering as the game started, and there were a lot of smiles back and forth since most of her friends didn't get to see her and Danny together all that often. Danny watched the game, keeping an eye on Nick and young Ryan Bowen, who was wearing Danny's old No. 12 jersey, which was a bit of a surprise Danny wasn't expecting. Crossroads – bigger, faster and stronger at every position against their lesser opponent – had no trouble beating Southlake. Ryan played well, Nick was dominating on defense, and the Indians won 37-7. Nick had 13 tackles and even though he only ran the ball five times on offense, he did score a touchdown. The game came and went, and Danny was fine. He enjoyed just being there, with Candice at his side.

Candice made plans with a few of her girlfriends to get some pizza after the game, so Danny said his goodbyes at the gate.

"I hope you had a good Friday." Candice said as they kissed goodbye.

"It was the best. Loved every minute of it. Call me when you get home, OK? I won't be late. Just going to Nick's with the guys for a little while."

As Danny strolled toward the locker room, he ran into Coach Jackson, who was on the phone. Turned out it was Mike Carey, the reporter from the Star-Press, on the other end. All was good.

"Hey, Danny, Mike apologizes. They had some extra space and the story idea was a last-minute thing, and he's sorry he didn't call first. They're just writing about the game, and a sidebar on Ryan. He said there's a nice picture of you and your girlfriend standing in the bleachers clapping, but that they would run it small. The picture of Ryan will be the big one. I figured that'd be OK."

"Yeah, I guess. I just didn't want to take anything away from those guys. They're the ones working hard."

"Not to worry. He wants to stay on your good side. In a few months, you're his golden boy."

Danny chose to wait outside the locker room, not wanting to intrude on the players' territory. One of the first players out was Ryan Bowen, who noticed Danny immediately and came over to say hello. Danny congratulated him on his first win as a starter and slapped him on the back. Nick popped out a few minutes later, and the two of them took off toward Nick's house. "A good win," he said. "Got to hit some people, got a win and no one got hurt. It's all good. Now let's go get a beer. I'm thirsty."

They ordered a pizza on the ride and another carload of guys showed up at

Nick's house right behind them. The cooler of beer was ready, ice cold, and Nick threw down a couple quickly. Danny passed and hung out for a while, but then headed for home early.

As Danny walked home, Candice called a few minutes before midnight.

"So your Friday is almost over, and I had to call one last time. I hope you enjoyed your Friday with me. I tried to make it a perfect day for you."

"Perfect doesn't even do it justice, Candice. It was a great, great day. Now get some sleep. I love you."

They hung up, and smiled their smiles. Ah, young love.

TOM BREW

7

Since **Danny hadn't worked** all week, he had plenty of grass to cut at St. Mark's on Saturday, but that was fine with him. It was a beautiful September day, sunny, high 70s, low humidity. It was a good day to do some mindless riding on the tractor, especially with the memories of his fun Friday with Candice still fresh on his mind.

That morning after his run, Danny grabbed the newspaper out of the driveway to be sure that Mike Carey had been true to his word. Sure enough, he was. The game story was out on the front page, with a nice picture of Nick making a tackle. The sidebar of Ryan was inside, with a big picture of Ryan talking to Coach Elliott and his dad Jack Bowen, the offensive coordinator, on the sidelines. Inset into the story was a small picture of Danny and Candice, clapping in the stands after a touchdown. They looked great together, as they always did in pictures. It was just a small black-and-white picture in the paper, but on the newspaper's web site, the photo was there in color, so Danny downloaded it and saved it to a disk. He went to the photo store, made a couple of quick 8-by-10 enlargements, added the date to the bottom then bought a nice frame. He bought a cute little card for Candice, wrapped up the framed picture and ran it over to Candice's house.

Danny couldn't stay long, but Candice opened the present quickly and saw the picture all framed and looking great. Danny had added the quote that was above the picture in the paper too – "I'm just a high school senior going to a football game with my girlfriend." At the bottom, Danny had added the date with one other line – "I love my Fridays!!" – and Candice laughed.

She hung the picture on her wall immediately. Then they left, Danny off to work and Candice off to the golf course to play 18 holes with her father and then work on her short game.

Nick stopped by about 2 with sandwiches and sodas and Danny talked more about his wonderfully peaceful Friday afternoon with Candice. A couple hours later, Ben Richardson emerged from the St. Jude Center with a cold drink in hand. Danny was about finished, so the drink was a pleasant sight.

"Danny, do you have your mom's car here with you today?" Ben asked and Danny nodded. "Can you work for another hour and help me? I've got a lot of people coming to the house tonight, and I need some things at the store. Would you mind going to get them for me, and I'll pay you for another hour?

47

Danny said yes, and ran off to get a dozen 2-liter bottles of soda, chips and dip and some cups. When he came back, Ben paid him and then gave him an extra $20 for helping. A $70 day beats a $50 day any time, Danny thought.

Ben was getting ready for lots of visitors because his usual Saturday night Gamblers Anonymous meeting was a big deal tonight. It was Ben's 15-year anniversary of refraining from gambling, and a big celebration was planned. Ben figured about 70 people would show up, but more than 100 crowded into the big first-floor living room for the meeting. They were there out of respect for Ben, who was so involved in reaching out to help the compulsive gambler through northwest Indiana and the Chicago area. Those in recovery, whether they had been in for a just a few weeks or the veterans who had been in for decades, all loved listening to Ben share his stories.

This night was no different.

Ben admitted he was overwhelmed with the turnout and was grateful to have so many close friends in the program. His voice cracked when he started to speak, but he gathered himself and began his therapy, all from the heart.

"You know, when we were reading from the Gamblers Anonymous book earlier in our meeting, I got kind of stuck on that subject of dealing with this disease, and the consequences of prison, insanity or death. There's a price we pay for being sick compulsive gamblers, and I'm no different. Fifteen years of clean time means nothing tomorrow if I don't attack today the same way I did the last 5,400-something days. I know what's out there for me if I don't live my life right. I've done the prison thing because of my gambling. I've done the insanity thing, for sure. I was totally insane when I was gambling. And death? When you sit all alone on a picnic table in the middle of the night, with a loaded gun in your hand, wondering how your life got so out of control, that's damn scary. I did that. Sat there for hours, just thinking. And praying. You guys who've been around me all these years know that I never bang on that religion drum, but it's the spirituality that matters. I kept praying that night for God to give me some kind of answer. Somehow, I got off that table, walked to my car and came home. But I still wouldn't stop gambling. Walked away from that gun and picnic table and still made bets the next week. Thank God I got arrested a few weeks later and my family stepped in and got me some help. I've been here ever since, 15 years later. But it could have all ended that night.

"That's what this disease does to you. I could have pulled the trigger just as easily that night, believe me. I was hurting that much. So death? Yes. I've had to deal with it. Thought about it, didn't do it, and still gambled the next week. How sick is that? The whole insanity thing we've all experienced. We are clearly out of our minds when we're gambling and I don't think any of us could ever dispute that. And prison? Man, I spent four days in jail because of my bad check charges, and before that I used to always think that jail might not be a bad place to hide for awhile. But after those four days, I never wanted to go back. The things I saw. Man, it was horrible. And the food? Worse than you can ever imagine.

"Prison, insanity or death, those are our options if we don't live our lives right. You guys have heard me say over and over how I get through my day every day. I wake up every morning and tell myself that I'm not going to make a bet today and that I'm going to work on being a better person. I ask for God's help with those two goals, and I ask this program and the people in it to help me every day. Those two things go hand in hand. I can go a day without making a bet, but if I ever stop working on being a better person, then I am going to be primed for a slip. I can't stay away from gambling unless I'm working on being a better me. I have to be strong, so I can fight off those urges. I still get them, 15 years later. And I'll get those same urges for 15 years more, I'm sure. That's why I have to be strong. And if I want to be a better person, there's no way I can gamble, period. If I ever went back out there, I would self-destruct very quickly. I know how quickly I got sick 15 years ago. It wasn't years of dangerous living, it was just a few months, but it took me right to the edge.

"So that's why I'm here tonight, to get my help with not making a bet today and working on being a better person. You guys and girls help me with that. And I'm getting through the day clean again, with your help, so thank you for being here with me. This is a celebration for me, but it's really more a celebration of this program. I guess I am proof that it works, if you work it. So I'm going to keep on working, and I look forward to every one of you helping me. Thanks. Thanks so much for being here. Now let's go live life the right way every day. Let's eliminate the insanity. Let's not ever think about putting ourselves behind those bars, or putting ourselves back on that picnic table, with gun in hand. Let's live life, and love every day that God gives us."

Everyone clapped as Ben finished, many dabbing tears away from their eyes. Ben's powerful words always hit home with this group. He seemed like such a good, solid person now, but every time he told that story of the picnic bench – and the gun, the loaded gun – it hit home with those people who've been there too. Every time Ben spoke at a meeting, everyone in the room was always glad they were there to hear it.

As the meeting ended and people broke into smaller groups while eating, one of the newer members who didn't know Ben well asked him about his treatment center, and how that all got started.

Ben never minded telling the story, because it always hit home with compulsive gamblers, especially the newer members trying to find their way.

"About eight years ago, not long after I started working up here as a treatment professional, I met a young man named Aaron Maxwell who was severely addicted to gambling, probably as bad as I've ever seen, and drugs and alcohol too," Ben said. "He had tried to stop many times, but he always relapsed. He was an only child and his father, who was very wealthy, had bailed him out many times. When they finally came to me for help, he was a mess. He was suicidal, but he also had people out there who wanted to kill him. He had borrowed something like $40,000 from some loan sharks in the Albert Calabria crime family over on the south side of Chicago, and when he couldn't pay them back like they wanted, they were ready to kill him. Once we got him hospitalized and settled down, his father put him in the treatment center where I was working and we started trying to work on some pressure relief for him. A friend of someone in the program who used to be a cop knew someone in the Calabria family. He arranged a meeting with me and this kid's father, and we made a deal with them. We told them he'd pay them back a thousand dollars a month and that we were working with him to never gamble again. They said they'd do it, but then about two months later the kid got caught playing in a high-stakes poker game downtown. He lost a bunch of money there too, and when they found out about it, someone took him out to a bad part of town and beat the living daylights out of him, just to send him a message. He kept on gambling and hiding from his father and a few months after that, they found him dead in a dumpster in a very bad part of town in Chicago. The Calabria people denied knowing anything about how he died, and no one had any proof, but we kind of knew. They just don't put up with any crap.

"It was a horrible thing to go through, because his father was the sweetest man, really did all he could to help his son, but the kid just never figured out how to stop gambling, no matter how much people tried to help him. The father and I kept in touch occasionally, and a few years after that he got colon cancer and only had a few months to live. He asked me to come see him one today, to tell me he sick, and we talked for a long time. I had told him before about my goals to start a full-blown treatment center for compulsive gamblers one day and he offered to help. He also knew about my gambling history, so he had his lawyer set up a trust that allowed me to buy this home from the church after his death. The trust provides for a set amount of money each month to keep it running and help the occasional gambler who really needed help but couldn't afford to pay for it. I have no control financially over the money or the house, which is good. And for every success story that's come out of this facility in the past five years, I thank that dear man for the opportunity. He knew I tried everything I could with his son, and he was grateful enough to want the next person – someone else's son – who came along who might get the right help. I share that story with a lot of my clients here, because I want them to know that sometimes even perfect strangers are rooting for them to succeed in their recoveries, and to succeed in their lives.

"That's why I'm grateful, every day. We've been able to help a lot of people here, thanks to the generosity of that man."

* * * * *   * * * * *   * * * * *

Many people believe in the whole Six Degrees of Separation thing, and more often than not it can be true.

So when mob boss Albert Calabria knows a former cop who knows Ben the treatment center director who knows Danny the basketball player who knows Nick the football player – that's five – and Nick lives with his older brother Tony, that's an interesting paradox.

Because Albert Calabria knows Tony Vincent, the 29-year-old brother of Crossroads High School football star Nick Vincent.

And knows him well.

Tony Vincent has been a sports bettor for quite a while, and for years he placed his bets with Joey Risone, a Calabria family low-life who ran his bookmaking operation out of the back room of a bar in Chicago Heights, a grimy industrial town about 20 miles west of Schererville and 20 miles south of Chicago. Tony won more than he lost, but not by much, and he never minded throwing back a few beers with Joey on Thursdays, which was settle-up day each week. It was a good day to drink a bit for a bricklayer, especially after a long hot summer day. And when Albert needed a deck poured at his mansion, Joey arranged for Tony's company to get the work, at a very good price, of course.

Tony brought Joey a few new gambling clients now and then and never once was late paying Joey if he had a losing week. Even the weeks he broke even, he'd still go over for a few beers, just because it was a Thursday tradition. Joey was gruff, a high-school dropout but loaded with streets smarts. He knew how to be a bookie, and how to maximize his profits. He followed the games close, followed his bettors even closer, and was a cash cow for the family, because he had several high-rollers who lost much more than they won. Joey liked Tony, mostly because Tony was fun to hang around with and because Tony didn't disrespect Joey. To some extent, they became friends, too, even though Tony was a hard-working bricklayer by day. The gambling was just fun for him, $50 here or a $100 there, maybe $200 tops. It was nothing big.

But it could be, and Tony knew it.

When Joey was drinking too much, he also talked too much. Tony knew all about his business. He had four or five guys taking bets for him all across the city and the south suburbs, and everything got pooled through Joey every night. They had more than 150 clients in Illinois. They all paid when they lost, or they suffered the consequences, physically or otherwise.

What you have to know about bookmakers is this: They don't care which team wins the game in most cases. Their goal is to get action bet evenly on both sides of a game, then collect the 10 percent fee the loser pays. If you bet $100 on a team and you lose, you owe $110. Bet $1,000 and lose, you owe $1,100. It's called vigorish, or the vig. That's how bookmakers make their money.

Joey talked so much that Tony knew what kind of money he was making. Joey once told the story of an NFL playoff game a few years back where they had bets of more than $50,000 almost exactly the same on both teams. They didn't give a hoot who won. They were making $5,000 that day no matter what. Same thing happened two weeks later on the Super Bowl. They made another $20,000 just like that, with bets divided equally and not a single play to sweat over.

What a great gig. And Tony wanted in.

About two years ago, after several beers with Joey, Tony put a bug in his ear. What if, Tony said, he started rounding up new clients in Indiana, ones that wouldn't conflict with Joey's client base. They could be partners on the new stuff, and they'd both make some more money. More in the pool meant more vigorish.

Nothing was said for several weeks, but then one Thursday Joey pulled Tony in the back room of the bar one hot summer day. Some of his ugly mope friends were in there too.

"How many clients you think you can round up before football season? New ones or ones we steal for other books over there."

"Maybe 15 or 20 for starters," Tony said. "Maybe double that by the time the season starts. I run into guys who want to gamble all the time."

"OK then, here's the deal. You can do your own thing in Indiana only, you can take the bets and call me every night with them. You pay me $300 a week for that through football and basketball season, plus 20 percent of your profits each week. You don't have profits one week, too bad. You still pay the $300. You always pay the $300. And you always pay your fair share of the profits, or there will be trouble, got it? This isn't personal, it's business. You want in, you pay. Deal?"

"Deal!" he said. Now, he was a bookmaker on the side too, and he had to answer to Joey, a member of the Calabria crime family. Business was brisk from the beginning. Tony probably made $40,000 during football season and another $20,000 during basketball season. He paid his tribute weekly, and his profits, and when it was all said and done, Joey got about half of Tony's $60,000. Mob boss Albert Calabria was happy with Joey, who was happy to tell his boss about his new cash stream in Indiana, and his new boy over there, Tony Vincent, bricklayer by day, bookmaker by night.

Albert Calabria was happy. Joey Risone was happy. Tony Vincent was happy. Everyone was happy.

Like most bookies, Tony had more clients who lost money than those who won. All in code, of course, Tony kept track of his clients and their bets on the computer during that first year of taking action. He had about 30 guys who bet across northwest Indiana, and only eight actually made money on the year.

Only one guy won more than 65 percent of his bets, and that was someone who only bet in small amounts anyway, mostly $20 or $25 a game. He was just a kid, he always paid on time if he lost that week, and he always knew where to find him, so Tony didn't even worry about it. Not one minute.

Why should he?

It was his little brother, Nick Vincent.

TOM BREW

8

Mary Bridges didn't have many rules for her oldest son Danny, and she didn't really need to. He was that good of a kid. He had been the man of the house for almost 10 years now since Mary had divorced Carl, and even though he still wasn't 17, he was expected to do more than the average teenager. Most importantly, he was expected to be a role model for his younger brother Michael and his sister Kathy, who were four and five years younger than he was. He kept the yard looking good, the snow plowed in the winter and helped his two siblings with homework and school projects whenever possible.

Mary's only real rule was that Danny always be home on Sunday morning, so the four of them could go to church together at St. Mark's. As busy as they all were, Mary thought it was important that they have some time together as a family, and Sunday mornings seemed like the perfect time to plan on that without too many interruptions. Danny didn't mind one bit. He always made sure he did all he could for his mother, who certainly would have preferred not to be a single mother. But Carl Bridges was a jerk, plain and simple, and her decision to divorce him was one that everyone agreed with. He was an alcoholic with a work ethic problem – he didn't have one – and they were better off without him. Even as busy as Danny's days were with school, working out and spending time with Candice and his friends, it was nice to spend the morning with his family. It was fun, too, when Candice would meet them at church, and then occasionally go out for breakfast or come over to the house for one of Mary's fine meals. Mary enjoyed having Candice around almost as much as Danny did.

Almost.

Sunday afternoons in the fall usually meant watching football, oftentimes with Nick. They each were Chicago Bears fans, Nick off-the-charts rabid, Danny not so much. Still, it was fun watching the games together, usually at Nick's house.

So when Danny's cell phone rang after church, he was glad to see it was Nick. He wasn't seeing Candice until dinnertime, so his day was free.

"Hey genius, get over here for some football and some fun," Nick said. "And bring your laptop and your wireless card. We have a little experiment to try today."

Danny laughed a little laugh, only because he knew Nick was up to something, but he wasn't sure what. Nick's history said it was going to be fun anyway.

"Not a problem. Give me 15 minutes," Danny said. "Just got back from church and I need to do a few quick things here and then I'll be over."

"Kickoff's in 20, so hurry up," Nick said. "Can you stay for the whole game?"

"Sure," Danny said. "I've got nothing going on all afternoon. Game's at noon, be over by three, and I'm not picking up Candice until 6. So we're good."

"OK then, but hurry up. And don't forget your laptop."

Danny walked over to Nick's house, laptop bag tossed over his shoulder, and he settled into the living room a few minutes before kickoff. Nick's older brother Tony came out from behind the locked door of his office just as the game started, his ears still humming from the barrage of phone calls from his gambling clients just prior to all the early games starting. He grabbed the remote for the TV, flipped on the Bears-Lions game, set the picture-in-picture to another game and flopped down in the recliner with a bunch of papers in one hand and his laptop in the other.

About 10 minutes into the game, the Lions struck first, scoring a touchdown on a trick play. Nick and Danny groaned. Tony looked up from his papers and laptop and smiled.

"Actually, that's not a bad thing. The Lions keeping it close today would be a good thing. You guys can have your Bears victory, but keep it under 12 if you would."

Danny didn't pay much attention to the comment, but he knew what Tony meant. After adding up all the numbers, Tony surmised that the Lions keeping it under the 12-point spread wouldn't be a bad day's work.

Nick concurred. He was actually betting against the Bears. "A nice little 17-10 win will be just fine. That's too many points for a team like the Bears with a suck-ass offense."

Danny rolled his eyes. "How much?"

"Just twenty-five dollars. Got to be a good boy now that the slave driver I call my big brother isn't giving me any work now that school started. Just the Bears and another twenty-five on the Packers to destroy the 49ers. We're going to get it all back in about hour anyway. That's why we needed you to bring your laptop and your wireless card."

"OK, so what's your big plan? Why do you need me?" Danny asked.

"Well, Tony and I thought we'd try something and since you're almost – and I said almost – as good a poker player as I am, we thought you could help. We're going to play a little online poker and make a few bucks."

"I'm not playing poker for money online, Nick. First off, I don't have much money, and second, I'm not going to spend it playing cards. A ten-dollar game with the guys every once in a while is one thing, but that's just for fun. I'm not doing that."

"Hey, it's not your money, it's ours. We just need a third hand, a third set of eyes, a third IP address and a third opinion."

"Clearly, you've thought this out, so tell me what your grand plan is, Nick."

Tony laid down his papers, and put his laptop on the large coffee table. He looked up at the TV, flipped the channel over for a minute to check the other scores, and then laid out the plan for Danny. This was Tony's show.

"Here's what we're going to do. We have the three of us, and three computers. Nick and I will log on to our Poker Kings accounts, and we've set up one for you too, and we put two-hundred dollars on it. We'll all enter the same forty-dollar nine-player sit-and-go tournament and it's our damn goal to finish 1-2-3. We figure if we all know what each other has, that's a third of the cards being dealt that we already know. We can work together, stay in hands when we need to, bail out of them when we have to. We thought we'd try it and see how much it helps having the insider knowledge on the other two hands.

"And it doesn't cost me anything?"

"Nope. It's our money and our accounts. But what we'll do is split anything we win four ways, the three of us and the snack fund. We'll all just work together."

"Sounds like a nice experiment," Danny said. "Let's get those snacks then, and get to it."

"Alright!" Nick said. He was ready to go.

So the three of them logged on, and entered their passwords. Danny had to laugh at what Nick did for him. "Your sign-on is WrensBoy and your password is Candice. And you only use this when you're with us."

"Sure, I'm very curious about this anyway. I'm just a third opinion."

When they got to the site, they picked a forty-dollar game down the board, where no one had yet entered. It cost each of them forty-four dollars (the vig, of course), which was already in their accounts. Nick logged on first, and they figured they'd wait until two more players joined before Tony entered, so they could be staggered around the table. When that happened, Tony signed on, and then Danny took the seventh spot. A few minutes later, the game began.

All three smiled.

When the table popped up, they learned their first lesson. The order they entered the tournament had nothing to do with seat assignment. Tony was in the first chair, not Nick. Danny was across the table, and Nick in the immediate seat to his left.

"Actually, that might be good," Nick said. "We'll have to see. And next time we know just to all log in at the same time."

The first hand got dealt and they immediately realized that some insider knowledge is a good thing. Tony was dealt a pair of kings, Danny had nothing but Nick had a pair of aces. Nick would have certainly pushed hard with his aces, and Tony would have been in real trouble in the small blind when the action got around to him.

"Killer kings," Tony said. "Anyone but you and I'd be picking my nose after one hand."

They had all started with 1,500 chips and one of the other players bet 200. "Good. Let him," Nick said. "See, this is perfect. Now we can double-team him."

Danny folded with nothing, of course, and Nick set the trap. "I'll just call him, then you call too, Tony."

They did, and everyone else folded. Nick and Tony were in with one other player, and they both roared when the flop came King, Jack, 4.

"See, I love this already!" Tony said. "This guy isn't going to know what hit him."

The guy checked, and they looked at each other. "Nick, bet a 100, and just call, Tony, so he thinks you just might be limping along," Danny said. Nick and Tony looked at each other, nodded their head and did so. The other player also called.

They really laughed when the turn came, a beautiful ace of spades. And they laughed even harder when the other guy went all-in. He had two pair, aces and jacks.

"Perfect example of teamwork. We would have killed each other otherwise," Tony said.

Nick went ahead and called the all-in, and Tony bowed out gracefully. The river came, nothing, and Nick raked in the pot. He suddenly had 3,445 chips. Normally, he would have won that hand on his own anyway, but Tony clearly would have been sitting on the sidelines after one go-round. The plan worked.

They played a dozen more hands, and knowing what each other had certainly helped. One hand, Tony would have usually chased a flush, but he could already see three other diamonds, so he didn't. Nick was dealt a pair of sixes one hand, but Tony had the third six and Danny had the fourth in a bad hand. They all got out. The extra knowledge prevented losing hands as much as it helped winning hands.

Good cards also helped, and before long they were down to five players, the three of them and two others. Nick kept getting the best cards and he conservatively kept betting and winning against the others. They were quickly learning that the conservative approach was best, even though it was totally out of character for the Vincent boys. Tony knocked one guy out who was chasing a straight draw, and his odds weren't good since he'd seen the two cards the guy needed; Danny and Nick each had a 10.

Danny wasn't getting any cards, so he didn't have a chance to play many hands. But his cards were so bad that he didn't have to bet and lose at all either. Nick had more chips than the rest of the table combined, and decided to call when the fourth player went all-in with a pair of nines. Nick had the ace and king of diamonds, hit a king along the way and the fourth player was out.

In forty minutes, their first experiment turned out great. Three players cash, and they were the last three standing. They all laughed.

"Now what do we do?" Danny said.

"Well, you need to finish third since we might be using our accounts without you sometime, so just bet almost all of your chips and then fold when Nick goes all in. Then just bet the little bit you have left all-in on the next hand and hopefully you'll lose. Let's see, that $132 total to play and we just won $400. That's $268 in less than an hour."

Danny went all-in and lost to Nick, then Tony did the same and it was over.

Tony stood up, pulled some cash out of his pocket and gave Danny a fifty-dollar bill and a few tens. "Here's your money. Thanks for the help," Tony said. "Now, let's watch some football."

Nick was glad to have won at poker because he had guessed wrong on the Bears, who were thumping the Lions by halftime. So were the Packers, so it was a break-even football day for him. They all ate lunch together and laughed, and Tony smiled away. He was having a very good day with his little gambling ventures, despite the Bears' rout.

"Almost break even," his big brother said. "You owe me two-fifty for the vig. Pay up, little brother."

After the Bears game, Tony had one other idea.

"Let's try this. I'm going to go into my office and log back in to Poker Kings, plus my instant messenger account. You guys do the same thing out here, but when the game starts we don't talk, just instant message each other with which cards we get dealt, then we'll talk things through only on the IM. It'll be a good test if we decide to do this someday when we all can't be here."

So they played one game that way, and it was all working fine until Nick, who was short-stacked, went all-in with a straight and got beat by a flush he didn't see coming. He was out and Danny and Tony were still around, with three others. Tony wasn't getting any cards and couldn't play much, but it did help once when

Danny had a pair of eights, and Tony had the third one. He was going to call a big bet from another anonymous player, but thought better of it and folded.

It was a good thing. He would have lost.

Tony hung on for dear life while Danny kept wiping players out. They got down to three players, and Tony finished third. Heads-up with some stranger, Danny never got any cards and ran through his stack slowly. He finally went all-in with an ace and an eight, but didn't hit and lost.

Still …

Even with just a second and third, they made money. Tony handed Danny another nine dollars and their experiment was done. It works. Even the instant messaging went fine. They tried it twice and won money both times. Danny walked away with almost eighty dollars.

"I'm glad you're here, Danny," Nick said. "We tried this just the two of us and lost four games in a row. The third player makes a big difference. We needed you and your computer."

"You could just buy another computer and another wireless card and do it yourself," Danny said.

"What would be the fun in that?" Nick said. "So now you get a free dinner tonight with Candice. Enjoy."

Danny got ready to head for home. He packed up his laptop and grabbed his money off the table.

"Need a ride to school again in the morning?" Nick asked, smiling. He knew the answer. Danny rode with him almost every day. "Because if you do, I need to get gas tonight and could use some cash. Twenty dollars ought to do it."

Danny smiled, and looked at his stack. "I guess I can't say anything, can I?" Danny said. "You want the fifty-dollar bill, or the rest of it?"

"That twenty will do it. Thanks, man. See ya."

Tony yelled goodbye from the other room, but he didn't sound too happy. The afternoon games must not have been going his way. Danny didn't care. He was about to see his girlfriend, and he had dinner money in his pocket and enough left over to buy a few groceries for his mother on the way home.

Every day is an adventure with Nick, he thought.

Every day.

9

As it did most years, fall was coming and going quickly in northwest Indiana. As the calendar rolled through October, the weather was changing dramatically. More often than not, it was 50s and rainy, sunshine giving way to one gloomy gray day after another.

Danny didn't care. Other than his morning runs, he wasn't outside much anyway.

His two months of workouts had been paying off. He was much stronger now, having gained about 10 pounds of all muscle and could taste basketball season being right around the corner. Four weeks of the football season had passed and Danny still had no regrets about not playing. That decision, troubling at the time, had turned out for the best. The Crossroads football team was 3-1, three easy wins against teams it was supposed to beat, and just the one loss to No. 2 Broadway in the third week. Even if Danny had been playing, they weren't going to beat them anyway. Broadway was that good, the talent discrepancy too much, especially early in the season. But they were winning enough, and everyone on the team was having fun. The papers weren't even mentioning Danny not playing any more.

For Danny, football games now were more about hanging out with Candice and worrying about his basketball-playing buddies not getting hurt. So far, so good. There were three guys who played both sports, including one other basketball starter, and in a selfish sort of way, Danny was already thinking about basketball season.

Nick was all about football for now, of course. He had finally lined up his five visits, and the first was coming this weekend to Michigan. He had narrowed down his short list to Michigan, Ohio State, Notre Dame, Florida State and Wisconsin, and official visits were planned for all five schools. He had Michigan and Notre Dame in back-to-back weekends, Ohio State and Wisconsin a few weeks after that, then Florida State at the end, the weekend after Thanksgiving when the Seminoles were playing arch-rival Florida.

Mike Carey from the paper was at a practice earlier in the week, but Nick told his coaches that he didn't want to talk to him about the recruiting situation. He never really liked talking to reporters at all, especially for stories like this, because the spotlight was solely on him. He had always been uncomfortable with that.

"Not yet," Nick told his coaches. "I don't even know anything solid myself and I'm not going to have people guessing. Just tell him I'd rather wait three or four weeks."

Nick wasn't saying much, but that didn't stop the recruiting web sites from guessing away. One of the pro-Notre Dame web sites actually ran a picture of Nick and his older brother Tony after a Crossroads football game, one where Tony was wearing a Notre Dame football jacket. Nick laughed when he saw it. He was laughing at all of it, really, especially since his short list had been finalized and all the conjecture had started.

"All those sites are amazing, some of the stuff they write." Nick told Danny on the way to school one morning. "One of them said Michigan was the favorite, because that's where I was taking my first visit. Crazy. One of them said Florida State wasn't seriously on my list, that I was just looking for a place to visit once it got cold. That's nuts. If I had to guess now, I'd say it's probably Michigan No. 1, then Florida State No. 2. Or visa versa; I really like Florida State. Notre Dame doesn't really count, not yet at least, and Ohio State and Wisconsin I want to look at, but they're not knocking my socks off just yet. Well, maybe Ohio State a little. There's still so much to know. I'm really excited about Michigan. I'm curious to see how that's going to go. I want to make sure I make the right choice."

Danny was glad his recruiting stuff was over and wouldn't have to worry about it during his season. That's the one plus basketball kids have over their football counterparts. More and more now, the basketball recruiting was done in the summer and by the early signing date in November, it was done. There were no distractions during the season.

Nick had a ton of distractions.

The phone calls, text messages and letters from dozens of colleges were getting old. Even after narrowing his list, several colleges still called. Nick wasn't one to want to just chat, so he ignored them as much as he could.

He also wasn't real happy with his high school coach, Mitch Elliott. Nick had been dominating on defense, and was living up to all his billing. He was playing at an All-American level, no question about it. But Nick still liked running the ball and he wasn't being involved much in the offense. He only had 22 carries in the first four games, and only played in about a quarter of the offense's snaps.

Throw in the fact that his crazy girlfriend Abby was driving him nuts and most of his time at home was spent alone with Tony gone so much, and Nick had a lot going on without much support from anyone else. For someone who tended to get annoyed easily, this was an easy time for Nick to be ornery. He was.

Danny usually could sense Nick's moods pretty well, but he had a lot of his own distractions now and he wasn't spending nearly as much time around Nick with football out of the equation. He was missing a lot of the signals he would have normally noticed right away in his best friend.

So on the Monday night before his first recruiting visit, Danny was surprised by a phone call from Nick. He wanted him to come over, and he wanted to talk. Danny found that to be odd.

Come over to watch a game, yes. Come over watch a movie or cook out some food, yes. Order a pizza, sure.

But just talk? It sounded like an odd request.

Danny rushed right over.

When he got there, the house was dark except for the television in the family room. Nick had the disk the coaches gave him of Aberdeen High School's offense, his opponent from about 30 miles east that was coming up Friday night. Nick had it in his laptop and had run a cable to the TV to break down the film. Otherwise, all the lights were out.

"Hey man, what's going on? You OK?" Danny asked as he walked in the room.

Nick was quiet for a moment. "Do you ever have a hard time sleeping? I can't seem to sleep hardly at all anymore. I'm up all night, millions of things running through my head, and it's driving me nuts. I've just got a lot of things frustrating me right now and it's hard to shake this "feel-like-crap" sort of feeling. A couple of nights ago, I was up until like three in the morning. Happens all the time now. Tried reading, didn't help. Wound up playing cards online for like three hours before I finally fell asleep. It sucks, man."

"Well, you know me, Nick. I don't sleep long every night, but I sleep like a log," Danny said. "That's never been a problem for me, at least not in the past few years. What's bugging you the most? Maybe you just need to work on things one topic at a time. Is it the recruiting?"

"That's part of it, a big part really, but everything just sort of spins off of that. I'm kind of sick of dating Abby and I need to end that. I definitely don't want a girlfriend when I go away to college and I'd probably be better off if I broke up with her now instead of later in the year. I'm not real happy with football right now either. It's going well and we've been playing good, but I'd like to do more on offense and the coaches barely include me in anything. Coach Elliott will talk with me all day long about defense, but him and Coach Bowen aren't even using me on offense. Hell, last Friday I only ran the ball three times. I think Coach Elliott is still pissed I wouldn't visit Purdue, because of his ties to the coaches there. But hell, if I'm not going to go to Notre Dame, I damn sure ain't going to Purdue. And I don't know, it's just weird around here. Tony's hardly ever around here anymore, so I'm just here by myself a lot. It gives me too much time to think, and that's not always a good thing for me. There's just so many things that are going to be changing in the next year and I guess I'm kind of feeling the pressure. I feel like I really need to make the right choice with college. It's kind of freaking me out a little."

Nick got quiet for a second, and leaned up on the edge of the couch. He leaned forward toward Danny, not more than a few feet from his face.

"You know what the hardest part is right now? I just keep thinking at night, when it's getting so late and I'm getting so pissed off, that I just wish my mom could walk through my bedroom door and tell me good night. Times like that, I really miss her. I even miss my dad yelling at me to turn down my music and go to sleep. I know it's been a few years now, but there are times when I still really miss them. Right now, they're on my mind all the time."

Nick's mother died of breast cancer when he was eight and his father passed away not even a year later, from a heart attack at age 49, which was way too young. A lot of people said he really died from a broken heart. Nick's parents were high school sweethearts and had been together for 30 years. Nick's mom was only 48 when she died. They had Tony, and then 10 years later Nick came along, a huge surprise, when both of his parents were in their 40s. Nick's dad just wasn't the same after watching his bride die a slow and very painful death. Less than 10 months later, he was dead too.

Here was Nick, just 9 years old, suddenly without both parents. They left the house to the two kids and from there his older brother basically raised him. There was talk about him living with an aunt for a while, but Tony would have nothing of it. Neither would Nick. They were brothers, and they'd be just fine, thank you very much. And for eight years it had been just fine.

But that didn't mean Nick still didn't miss his parents.

"That's natural you're going to miss them, Nick. I could never imagine getting through a day without my mom. Even my dad, for all his problems and how little we talk, at least I know he's still there, somewhere. It just seems like you've got a lot on your plate now. I'm no great purveyor of wisdom, but it seems like maybe you just need to solve some of these issues one at a time. Get the Abby thing behind you. I know she'll cry and cry for a while, but then she'll get on with her life just fine. You can talk with the coaches anytime. They'll listen to you. And the recruiting thing? The fun's just starting now. Just enjoy your visits and take your time making a decision. You can't sign until February anyway. It's four months away. Don't worry about making a mistake, because you've got five great schools on your list anyway. Whichever one you choose, you'll be happy. Just enjoy it."

Nick knew Danny was right, right about everything. And in reality, Nick knew all of that too. It was just good to hear it from someone else.

"And by the way, my mom's making bread tonight, so come by early tomorrow morning and we'll have some toast and hot chocolate."

"Ah, I feel better already!" Nick said. "Thanks Dan, I really appreciate you coming over. Not to get sappy or anything, but I really appreciate your friendship. Thanks for helping me through this. I knew I could count on you."

"Always, man. Always, and forever. Any time you need me, just say so. That's what best friends are for. And I'll keep this between us."

"Thanks," Nick said. "I appreciate you keeping it quiet."

* * * * *   * * * * *   * * * * *

There are good things and bad things about having a compulsive personality trait, and for Nick the good part kicked in right away. He got right to confronting all his issues and fixing all his problems. By lunchtime Tuesday, he had his brief conversation with Abby, and it was over. She cried and cried, of course, loud enough for everyone in the hallway to hear her, but Nick comforted her enough by telling her he'd promise they'd be friends forever. That probably wasn't going to happen, but it worked at the time. And since Nick had study hall the last period of the day, he told Coach Elliott he wanted to meet with him. They agreed to huddle as soon as school ended, so Coach Bowen, who didn't teach at the school, could be there too.

"I bet I know what this is about," Coach Elliott said. "You want the ball, don't you?"

"Well, yeah," Nick said. "And at the very least, I'd like to know why I'm got getting it. You guys are barely giving me a chance and I'd like to know why."

"Well, there's two big factors, Nick. First of all, when we looked at the schedule, we figured the first half of the season was more than likely going to play out as scripted. We should beat Aberdeen Friday to be 4-1 and that's what we figured was going to happen. We needed to get Ryan comfortable at quarterback and if we're going to beat Broadway, our best chance of that is in November in the playoffs, not in September. So we haven't wanted to play all our cards and, yes, that's affected you. But secondly, and most importantly, we didn't want to wear you out early either. You've played every down that matters on defense and you're playing great. You're the best high school linebacker I've ever seen, Nick, and that should be good enough for you. Everyone notices how great you've been playing. You want more and we understand that, but we'd also like to save you for the time that it matters most, and that starts next week when we play those pricks at Ridge Central."

"Look, I feel fine after every game. Running the ball 10 or 15 more times isn't going to wear me out. I'm in great shape, I'm healthy. Just give me a chance."

"We will. Starting next week. I'm sure you've noticed that whenever we're in a one-back set, we've been throwing out of it 90 percent of the time. We want that on film. We want defenses spread out. And when we get to Ridge Central, we plan on running you out of that set a lot, especially on passing downs, so you get some good matchups. They won't be ready for it. Look, Nick, we'd like to think we know what we're doing here. We've got Ridge, Porter Central and White Hawk back to back, all tough games but all winnable games, games that can make our season. You'll be a big part of it. So just keep doing what you're doing, and understand what we're doing. But be prepared this Friday. If we get a lead early, you may not run it at all. We want to keep that element of surprise for Ridge Central. You know how much we hate those pricks. We want to beat their ass, especially on their own field."

Nick left Coach Elliott's office feeling much better. As he headed to the locker room, Danny was coming the other way.

"Abby, check. Coach Elliott, check," Nick said. "Even the weekend at Michigan is set. That's a load off. Thanks for pushing me to get this stuff done."

They went their separate ways, and Danny couldn't help but smile.

His friend, his best friend, was back.

10

On Thursday, Coach Will Jackson called Danny out of lunch and asked him to come to his office.

"Two things, one immediate," Coach Jackson said when Danny arrived. "Ben Richardson called me a few minutes ago and wanted me to get a message to you. He has two tickets to the Cubs' playoff game tonight all of a sudden and wanted to know if you'd like to go up to Chicago with him."

"You're kidding?" Danny said. "I'd love to go, but I can't. Candice has her golf regionals today and I really need to go watch her. I can't miss that. Let me call him, though, and thank him anyway."

Danny picked up the phone, and Ben answered on the first ring. He thanked Ben for the offer, but told him about his plans. "Yeah, I want to be the good boyfriend first," Danny said.

"That's more important," Ben said. "Plus, the Cubs are down 0-2 in this series already. You may not be missing much."

They chatted for a few more minutes, and then Danny pulled the phone away from his mouth. "You want to go?" he whispered to his coach. Jackson nodded. "Hey, Mr. Richardson, Coach Jackson would love to go if you'd like."

"Sure, put him on. It would be fun to catch up with him."

Coach Jackson and Ben talked for a few minutes to set up plans, and then said their goodbyes. They were occasional golf buddies in the summertime, but hadn't seen each other for a few months. This would be fun for both of them.

"OK, secondly," the coach said. "The basketball schedule. It's changed a little. I got a call yesterday from a group in Indianapolis. They are playing two doubleheaders at The Fieldhouse in downtown Indy the Saturday after Thanksgiving, and they've invited us to play. I accepted, of course. It's a last-minute thing. They're trying to use the building more, to cover their budget deficits. We'll play the late game in the night session, at 8:30. And we're playing Anderson, which should be a lot of fun for you guys, but a little weird for me. I called the coach over at Aberdeen and he agreed to move our opener up from that Saturday night to the Tuesday night before Thanksgiving.

"The Tuesday night? That's my birthday. That'll be fun."

"So will Indy. We'll get the nice bus and go down early and watch all the games. All eight teams figure to be ranked in the Top 20 or close, they said, so it's nice to get the invite. Of course it helped too that you committed with Indiana. That kind of put us on their radar. And, in a perfect world, it's great preparation for March. It would be nice to reach the Final Four and already have had some experience in playing there. That's a lofty goal, of course ..."

"Yeah, but it's a goal we have. We all do," Danny said. "Anything short of not making it to the Final Four in Indianapolis will be a disappointment. And Anderson will be a good test. They're going to be tough, right?"

"Well, they're very young, but they have a lot of speed. They're not real big either, but they always have a ton of talent. Their seniors would have been eighth graders when I left, so I know a few of them pretty well, but not many. Their two best players are both sophomores, but I don't know much about them."

Bring it on, Danny thought. He was looking forward to the exposure, especially in a beautiful 18,000-seat arena that was home to the NBA's Indiana Pacers and the high school state finals.

He was also looking forward to his afternoon. High school girls golf isn't exactly a spectator sport, but Danny had gone to a few of Candice's matches earlier in the fall and was glad he did. Now it was regionals, a big deal, and he wanted to be there. Candice wanted him there, too. There was a chance it might be her last competitive sporting event, although she was hoping not. Her goals for her last golf season were simple. During the season, she wanted to shoot a round under par (and did), wanted to win an invitational (and did), wanted to win regionals and wanted to finish in the Top 10 at the state meet, which would give her an All-State medal and her picture up in the gym on Crossroads High School Wall of Honor. She was ready, and was glad Danny was there, along with her parents and a few other friends. The meet, which featured about 100 girls from the northern quarter of the state, was on her home course at the country club, so she felt good about that too.

Danny got a kick out of watching her play. She was talented, as Danny had seen up close a few times, playing together in the summer. Danny was a marginal golfer at best, and played maybe five times a year, just for fun. Breaking 90 was his usual goal, but after his last growth spurt his golf swing was a mess. The first time they played, Candice shot 74 and Danny 92, a stroke-a-hole difference. Candice loved every minute of it, and enjoyed ribbing Danny about her whitewash.

Candice played really well at regionals. She made two birdies on the front nine, had one bad hole on the back, but strung together a bunch of pars before making a birdie on the 17th hole and another on the 18th hole, making a long 30-foot putt. Danny watched every shot with her parents and marveled at how cool and composed Candice stayed all day, never getting flustered or frustrated, even after that bad double-bogey. She shot a 1-under-par 71 in one of the first groups out, so she had to sit and wait for all the other scores to be posted.

No one else came close. When the tournament finished about an hour later, Candice had won by three shots. She was regional champion, and earned the right to compete in the state meet near Indianapolis a week later. Another goal accomplished.

"Let's go celebrate," Candice's father said after his daughter received her huge first-place trophy. "You pick the restaurant, my dear."

As they walked to the car with Candice's clubs, Andy Wren put his arm around Danny and talked softly into his ear. "Can you imagine the catch she's going to be, a gorgeous doctor with a golf game like that?" he said with a smile. "You better hang on to her."

"I certainly plan to, Mr. Wren," Danny said. "You know I think she's wonderful, and I can't believe I'm saying that to her father."

"I hope you do, Danny. We like you too."

Candice, ever the perfect girlfriend – and the perfect daughter – knew that Danny and her dad probably wanted to pay attention to the Cubs' playoff game, so she picked Angelo's, the pizza place with the sports bar that everyone loved. It was a good choice, unanimously approved by all. Only slightly embarrassed, Mr. Wren made Candice bring in her trophy, and they put it right in the middle of the table for all to see. Candice picked the table, a big one back by the big screen, her favorite table in the place.

It was the table where her and Danny had first sat and talked last spring. It was a great first conversation, and had led to the first date, and so on and so on.

She hadn't forgotten.

And never would.

Mr. Angelo, who had owned the restaurant for 30 years and was quite the golfer himself, came over to the table and congratulated Candice. He went back into the office to get his camera, and gathered the group up for a photo. Candice smiled, with trophy in hand, boyfriend on one side, parents on the other. It was a nice day for Candice, and Danny was glad to be a part of it. He enjoyed his secondary role of supportive boyfriend. It was a nice feeling. Candice was smiling all night, so proud of herself and also so thrilled to be enjoying her big day with Danny. More than once, she hugged him during dinner, simply thrilled that the two of them were together.

"Hopefully we'll take some more pictures this winter, Danny," Mr. Angelo said. "We'll put them up on the wall side-by-side."

That would be great, Danny thought. That would be just great.

* * * * *   * * * * *   * * * * *

Nick **had quite** the good weekend himself. After the easy win against Aberdeen in Valparaiso, as expected, he and his brother Tony left straight from the game and stayed in a hotel about an hour away in southwest Michigan, at the Two Paws Casino. They grabbed some food to go on the way and Nick showered after they checked in. They'd sleep there and drive the three hours to Ann Arbor early in the morning.

With the time change, it was close to midnight by the time Nick got out of the shower. He had sprained his ankle a bit during the game. Nothing major, but he figured some ice might not be a bad idea. Tony was already down in the casino.

Nick was amazed at the thoroughness of the Michigan recruiters. When he told them of his travel plans earlier in the week, the recruiting coordinator John Jefferson – who was also Michigan's linebackers coach, which Nick liked – called ahead to make sure the Vincents were well taken care of at Two Paws. The school couldn't pay for the room or anything like that because of NCAA rules, but they made sure the hotel manager gave them the best discount he could give any pre-ferred client in his hotel. They got a $300 suite for fifty bucks.

After the ice, it was about 12:30 and Nick couldn't sleep, so he threw on some clothes and went down to check on Tony. Tony was playing poker and had a big stack of chips in front of him, which Nick admired.

"Having fun?" Nick said, startling his brother a bit.

"Yeah, I love this place. I'm up $400 already in about an hour."

"Well, don't forget the 6 a.m. wake-up call. We need to be on the road by 6:30."

"No problem, little brother. You're driving, though. I'll be sleeping."

Come morning, Tony was true to his word. Going on about three hours' sleep, he was awake enough to get in the car, but that was about it. Nick drove the three hours into Ann Arbor and Tony never moved. He followed directions closely and parked in a lot near the athletic center. They checked in, and there were about 20 recruits there for the day.

Nick and the other recruits watched the game together, and then were es-corted into the locker room for halftime. Michigan was up 24-3 at halftime against a bad Illinois team, so it was a fairly quiet locker room. No coaches screaming, just a lot of small groups gathered together, going over specifics by position. After the game he got to meet the coaches, had a nice dinner as a group, then got the students-only tour of the campus – and the nightlife – from some of the current players.

Nick was the plum of this recruiting group, along with a running back from Detroit and a quarterback from western Pennsylvania. He got about 15 minutes alone with head coach Larry Traine and John Jefferson, the linebackers coach and their lead recruiter. They made their best pitch and did their best to make Nick feel comfortable, right up to having a blue Michigan jersey on a hanger, with the name and the number (Vincent, 44) that Nick admired.

"Nick, I know this is your first visit, but here's what we'd want you to remember about the University of Michigan when you leave here," Coach Traine said. "We think this is the perfect place for you. We've seen all your games on film, and Coach Jefferson here has seen you in person several times. You know we have a senior middle linebacker right now, and we both are firmly convinced that you can play here right away. We haven't had too many freshmen start at middle linebacker, but we'd certainly give you every opportunity to make that happen. We really want you here. You are our first choice, our most important recruit. You will love it here and we will certainly get you ready for the next level. You'll be on national TV every week and you'll have millions of fans watching your every move. There's nothing better than the Michigan football tradition. And we're close enough to home that your brother and your friends can come up for games as often as they'd like."

Nick really couldn't argue. He had plenty of fun with the players that night as well, and drove home firmly convinced that his original pecking order didn't need to change. Michigan was tops on the list, and it would take some serious swaying for that to change. He saw all the right things; they said all the right things. It was a perfect weekend.

Danny was right, Nick thought. Just enjoy the experience.

So far, it wasn't so bad.

* * * * *   * * * * *   * * * * *

At school Monday, Coach Elliott made a point of seeking out Nick early in the morning. He wanted an update on the Michigan trip, but more importantly he had game plan in hand, and wanted to get Nick involved early.

And he also wanted Nick to get devious with him.

Nick gladly obliged.

The coach's plan was this: Today would be a good day for Mike Carey from the Star-Press to come out and finally do his big Nick Vincent recruiting story. Nick had just returned from Michigan and Crossroads was 4-1 heading into its showdown with 5-0 Ridge Central, their biggest and most-hated rival, so the timing was perfect for some media attention. Coach Elliott was true to his word the previous weekend in the Aberdeen game, only playing Nick on offense for about six plays, giving him just one carry. Coach Elliott wanted Nick to talk about his recruiting stuff, but also talk about focusing on defense this year and how not playing offense had been the plan all along and he was glad to be able to focus on leading the defensive unit.

And that's exactly what happened. The reporter came out, Nick's answers led to all the right follow-up questions and the story in the next day's paper was all about Nick the middle linebacker, and how much he enjoyed Michigan, but how he was also looking forward to going to Notre Dame this weekend (a lie) and making his three other recruiting trips (true).

The Crossroads coaches loved the article, and so did Nick. He also loved what was going on in practice. They had about five running plays for Nick that they hadn't used all year, and they worked on them hard every day. They were going to shock Ridge Central with a new look, and they were hoping their little scheme in the newspaper would help throw off the Ridge Central coaches as they prepared their defensive game plans.

When Friday night rolled around, the atmosphere at the sparkling new Wicker Stadium was incredible. The stadium held about 10,000 people and it was almost full. The local cable TV channel was there too, doing the game live. Ridge got the ball first, went three-and-out and punted. Nick made two tackles, including a big sack on third down.

Crossroads went on offense, the field spread with its four wide receivers and Nick alone in the backfield with young quarterback Ryan Bowen. As hoped, Ridge answered with a slew of defensive backs spread all across the field, too. On first down, they ran a draw play, Nick broke a tackle and gained 12 yards. First down. He ran two quick-hitters for four and five yards, and then on third-and-1, Bowen faked a handoff to him and hit a receiver on a quick slant route for six yards and a first down.

Nick kept running hard, getting positive yardage every time. Coach Bowen was calling a great game. When the teams got to the line of scrimmage, he'd scan the defense and yell out an audible to Ryan when necessary. If the defense bunched up, then they'd throw outside. If they stayed spread out, Nick ran up the middle or off-tackle. Finally, 16 plays into the drive and nearly nine minutes later, Nick scored from two yards out to make it 7-0.

On defense, they held Ridge to another three-and-out, Nick forcing a fumble on third down that Ridge maintained. After the punt, the offense again was efficient as could be. Fourteen plays and 82 yards later, Nick scored again, this time on a six-yard run off tackle. There were only three minutes left in the half, and so far Crossroads had run 30 plays to Ridge's six. It was 14-0, and their perfectly scripted game plan had worked like a charm. Nick had 13 carries for 108 yards already and Ryan Bowen was a perfect 8-for-8 passing. You could see the frustration mounting on the Ridge Central sidelines.

The dominance continued throughout the game, though not to the same extreme. Ridge finally scored early in the fourth quarter, but by then it was already 24-7. Continuing to grind things out, Crossroads ran out the clock and danced off the field with an impressive 31-7 victory. Nick finished the game with 17 tackles on defense and 229 yards rushing on 25 carries, none of which went for negative yardage.

It was a game for the ages, one of the greatest individual performances anyone at Crossroads had ever seen. It was vintage Nick Vincent.

He kicked their ass, almost single-handedly. He had his moment, his memory, his high school scrapbook game that would be talked about for years.

After the game, Nick could barely contain himself. The Crossroads students had rushed the field afterward, and as Mike Carey from the Star-Press searched out Nick for an interview, he was surrounded by a bunch of students, including a grinning Danny Bridges, just some high school kid watching a game with his girlfriend.

"Right here in this story, here's Coach Tyler of Ridge Central quoted as saying that we weren't going to win anything big in football," Nick screamed to the reporter, a grin stretching from ear to ear.

The quote was from the story about Danny quitting football prior to the season starting.

"Well, you can tell Coach Tyler for me that we think coming onto their field and destroying them – destroying them! – *is* something big. It's really big. We've been waiting for this game for two months and it was worth every minute of the wait. What do you think of us now?"

About 15 yards away, a few students were congratulating Ryan Bowen. Nick called him over. "Ryan, you talk to this reporter now. I'm done. But one last quote, Mr. Carey. Our coaching staff deserves a lot of credit for this game plan and Ryan deserves a lot of credit for executing it perfectly. It was a total team effort, so make sure that's how you write it."

Nick marched off, helmet in hand raised over his head. On his way to the locker room, he got hugs from everyone, including his brother Tony. When he found Coach Elliott, they embraced, pleased over a job well done.

"Now that was fun," Nick said. "I can't wait to watch the replay on TV. It couldn't have gone any better. Now let's do it again next week."

Nick found a moment to be alone with Danny. "It's amazing how much fun that was. I hate those pricks and we flat-out kicked their ass. They didn't stop us all night."

"Yeah," Danny said, slapping his friend's shoulders. "I think you're going to sleep well tonight."

"Like a baby!"

11

It **must have been** the bad karma from the planned Notre Dame visit. Nick Vincent was figuring he was going to have a bad weekend, he just didn't expect it to start on Friday night. In the middle of their season-defining three-game stretch, the Indians screwed up at Porter Central, a very good Class 3A school with a great football tradition. They were evenly matched but, to be honest, Crossroads was probably a little better. But every break kept going Porter's way in the third quarter and they upset Crossroads, 21-13.

Ryan Bowen had a tough night. He fumbled in the second quarter when he got blindsided on a pass play, leading to a Porter Central touchdown. In the third quarter he had a pass tipped and it was intercepted and returned for a touchdown. It was too much to overcome, and Crossroads fell to 5-2 on the season. Nick wasn't happy. He played well on defense, but never got much of a chance on offense. It was a hard-fought game between two good teams and they just came up short. It happens.

So when Nick made the hour-and-change drive east to Notre Dame the next morning for his official visit, he was a bit on the irascible side. He really didn't want to be there, and the sting from losing the night before wasn't helping his mood either. Even though his brother was a huge Notre Dame fan, Nick never fell under the spell of the Fighting Irish mystique, even though they were undefeated this year and ranked in the top five for the first time in years. The Friday morning prayers for a Notre Dame victory in grade school always got under his skin and Notre Dame hadn't been a serious national title contender for going on two decades, until this year. You had to be an old-timer, more or less, to remember that Notre Dame was supposed to be the go-to destination for big-time recruits. Even for the current Catholic kids from northern Indiana, the thrill just wasn't there. If anything, the fact that Notre Dame was off to such a hot start this year bothered Nick even more. He hated all the fair-weather fans who came out of the woodwork whenever Notre Dame got it going. He disliked them that much.

Even before he got there, Nick couldn't wait to go home.

He did all the same things he had done the week before at Michigan, getting the tours, meeting the coaches, seeing all the history. Nothing mattered. He was in a bad mood, bordering on sullen. He hadn't felt this low since the night he talked to Danny about being so depressed. He answered questions when asked, but

75

didn't say much and didn't talk a lot with many of the other recruits. The coaches talked to him about how important a recruit he was to them and how they needed him to help continue to restore the legacy.

In one ear and out the other.

Right after dinner, Nick left South Bend as fast as he could and drove straight home. In his mind, Notre Dame was clearly out. He also decided on the way home that Wisconsin was out, only because he couldn't see himself getting excited about a trip there either. He had nothing against the coaches or the school, but they were his fifth choice at the time he added them to his list anyway, and that was that. They were still at the bottom of the list. He was looking forward to seeing Ohio State in early November and he was definitely looking forward to the Florida State visit, but Michigan was still No. 1 in his mind and it just seemed like a good time to start narrowing things down. It was a hectic couple of weeks. He was tired and in a bad state of mind. He got home about 10 and went right to bed.

Lights out, dark house, dark mood.

* * * * *   * * * * *   * * * * *

In direct contrast to Nick's somber mood was the beaming smile on Danny's face. He was having a great weekend. He had been invited to Blooming-ton for the weekend along with Coach Jackson as Indiana's basketball team started its preseason practice. His coach was kind enough to leave very early on Friday and stop in Indianapolis to watch Candice's second and final round in the state golf tournament. She hadn't played all that well the first day, shooting 77, but bounced back on Friday with a 72, finishing sixth in the state and earning a coveted spot on the All-State team. Danny was proud of her, and Candice was proud of herself and glad Danny was there.

They said their goodbyes Friday afternoon and Danny headed off to Bloomington with Coach Jackson. The other three recruits in his class were there as well. They met as a group Saturday morning, and had a meal with the entire Indiana basketball team and coaches. Danny was loving every minute of it, as was Coach Jackson, who had a chance to catch up with Michael Trickett, who had played for him in Anderson when the two won a state championship together the year before Coach Jackson came to Crossroads. Michael was Danny's host for the weekend, and the three of them had a great time. Michael provided a wealth of information for Danny, and promised to take him under his wing in the fall.

Michael had met Danny for the first time during the summer, at the camp where Danny got the scholarship offer. Even Michael noticed that Danny had got-ten bigger during his three months of workouts. "I thought you were a stick this summer, but it looks like you've bulked up," he said. "You'll need it here, man. The Big Ten is so physical." That was saying a lot coming from Trickett, who was built a lot like Nick, only taller. He was 6-8, about 255 pounds and very solid, a tough-to-stop post player when he could stay healthy. Michael was an NBA prospect coming out of Anderson, but he had battled injuries most of the early part of his career, first a knee, then a shoulder. He missed his entire sophomore season and was redshirted, so he was glad to have two years left at Indiana. He was hoping to make the most of it, and still make professional basketball a career. Everyone went to the Indiana-Minnesota football game at noon, then went back to Assembly Hall to prepare for the first Indiana basketball practice of the year, an open-to-the-public hoops festival that was simply meant to be an hour of fun. It was. Coach Garrison and his staff put them through a few fast-paced drills, introduced everyone to the crowd of 15,000 and then oversaw a loose 20-minute scrimmage at the end, along with three-point shooting and slam-dunk contests.

This was all a year away for Danny, and it was a bit overwhelming. Indiana was a Top 10 team this year and had only two seniors. They were going to be great next year too when Danny arrived, and he was thrilled to be a part of it. He saw plenty of talent on the floor and was looking forward to being there in Bloomington

But first …

Michael Trickett did a great job of grounding Danny at dinner. It was just the two players, plus Coach Jackson and IU assistant coach Tony Carter, who had recruited Trickett and knew Coach Jackson well. Michael's talk was all about making the most of his senior year at Crossroads, and accomplishing his ultimate goal, winning that state title.

"Danny, there was no greater feeling than standing at center court in Indianapolis, getting handed that state championship trophy. Coach Jackson tells me your team this year reminds him a lot of our team that won it all, a team with lots of weapons and a lot of selfless players who gave their all every day. I hope so. We had a special group and those memories will stay with me forever. We put all that time in and we think everything will just continue to get better. That hasn't happened for me here, with all the injuries, but I'm still having a blast. You will love it here at Indiana. I'm enjoying playing basketball here, but I'm also so grateful for what happened that last year at Anderson, and I want you to make sure you make the most of your senior year too. Stay focused on your season, and if you have any questions about things here at Indiana, just call me any time. I'm looking forward to you being here."

Coach Jackson had nothing but great things to say about Michael Trickett to Danny on the ride home. Coach had known Michael since he was a 10-year-old, a talented youngster from the projects in Anderson, a true rust-belt city that had been hit hard when its once-proud automotive industry basically disappeared. He was raised by his grandmother and had watched two older brothers fall into the drug-selling trap and get shipped off to jail. Basketball had become his diversion, and Coach Jackson had become something of a surrogate father to him. He grew up relying on Coach Jackson, and to be able to celebrate a state championship together meant a lot to both of them. Coach Jackson would have never left Anderson for Central Lakes if Trickett had still been around.

"You'll have no better friend to rely on than Michael when you get to Bloomington," Coach Jackson told Danny. "He's a good kid, a hard worker and very coachable, so he'll be able to help you with what you need to know. He thought he was well prepared when he got here, and you'll be too. Of course, he got to bring a championship ring here with him. You going to do that, too?"

"That's the plan, Coach. I'm looking forward to practice starting Monday and hopefully will get all our football guys to us without any injuries. So far, so good and they've only got a few weeks left, more than likely. For Nick's sake I hope they can get past Broadway in the sectionals, but I just don't see that happening."

Coach Jackson looked over to Danny and smiled. "A loss wouldn't be the worst thing. I wouldn't mind three weeks of practice with everyone, instead of one or two. But that stays between you and me, of course."

"I know, Coach. I'm just glad they've had a good year and Ryan's played well without me around. That was my concern in the summer, but it's turned out for the best. They've done well, Nick's had a great season and I'm in the best shape of my life. I'm finally up over 200 pounds for the first time, so I'm ready to go."

"Yeah, they have to be happy with how it's gone. And that game Nick played at Ridge Central, man that was something. It was one of the most incredible performances I've ever seen in a high school football game. He may not win Mr. Football, but he's definitely the best football player in the state. He's the best high school football player I've ever seen, and I've been watching football for a long time."

"Yeah, it's hard for a defensive guy to win Mr. Football. Almost never happens, especially with some quarterbacks and running backs having big years on the best teams. But you know how Nick is. I don't think he cares either way. But you never know. He has such a great reputation on all those recruiting websites and coaches see those, too, so he might get enough votes."

"How do you think his mind-set is going to be for basketball? Will all the recruiting stuff distract him?"

"I don't think so," Danny said. "He'll have all his trips taken before we start playing, except for that last trip to Florida State the week after Thanksgiving. He'll miss a couple of practices, I'm sure, but just that one game. I think he'll have his mind made up before signing day, which is Feb. 4, I think. He won't be distracted. And you know how he is. When he laces up those shoes, he'll be all business out there. For years, we've talked about our chances to do something special, and he really wants it too. Nick is very modest, and he never likes talking a lot about himself, especially in interviews with the newspapers. But he also knows how much people take history seriously around here, and he wants his legacy to be something special. With his football career being what it's been, and what he's done in basketball so far, if we have a big year and get to Indy, he might very well go down as the best athlete ever in the history of Crossroads High School. That'll mean something to him."

"I'm definitely glad he's on our side," Coach Jackson said.

"Me too," Danny said. "I've felt that way since I was about three feet tall."

* * * * *   * * * * *   * * * * *

Nick still wasn't feeling good Sunday morning when he woke up, so he called Danny early in the morning, hoping to catch him before church. Mrs. Bridges answered the phone when she called. They chatted for a few minutes; Mrs. Bridges liked Nick and held a special spot in her heart for him, with all he had been through with losing his parents. She could even sense on the phone that Nick wasn't very cheerful, and she always knew how to solve that problem.

"Nick, breakfast will be ready in about 15 minutes. Pancakes, sausage and orange juice. Please come join us," she said as she handed the phone to Danny. "Tell him he *has* to come for breakfast," Mary said.

Danny said hello and they each had a lot on their mind. They had busy weekends and Danny could sense the tone in Nick's voice that he wasn't happy. So he pressed him on coming over for breakfast and finally Nick acquiesced. Church was still more than an hour away, so they could eat and have plenty of time to talk.

Danny took the proactive approach when Nick got there and dove right in to telling Nick how great his weekend was in Bloomington. He figured the good stuff might cheer Nick up a bit, and it seemed to. Nick was genuinely enthused about Danny playing basketball at Indiana and his joy over Danny's fun weekend was genuine. After they plowed through Mary's pancakes, they went into Danny's room to talk.

"Hey, I wanted to ask you. Did you meet Ronnie Moats this weekend at Notre Dame, the linebacker from Chicago?"

79

"Yeah, I did," Nick said. "We talked for a little while at the game. Why?"

"Well, I noticed on the MyRivals.com site this morning that he committed to Notre Dame last night. He must have had a good visit."

"He must like it a hell of a lot better than me," Nick said. "I couldn't wait to get out of there."

Danny's computer was already on, so he flipped to the story on the website IrishIllustrated.com site, a very-pro Notre Dame site, the one that had run a picture of Nick and his brother earlier in the fall. The story gushed on and on about Moats, who was an all-city linebacker at one of the famous Catholic high schools in Chicago.

"Here, Nick, check this out. I'm sure you'll be thrilled with this line." Danny said. He read it verbatim: "Coaches can't comment on recruits, of course," the reporter wrote, "but people have told me Moats was the most important linebacker on their recruiting list."

Nick laughed.

"That's not what they told me yesterday. Bastards. Well, to be honest, I don't give a shit anyway. I'm not going there, was never going to go there and I can't wait to cross those bastards off my list. To hell with them."

The two pals talked some more about the visit, and about how Nick didn't feel like being there all day Saturday anyway. He was sure it had something to do with losing Friday's game, but mostly it was just the whole Notre Dame thing. They were never really a serious contender for his services in his mind anyway, so he knew he was just wasting his time there.

Nick explained the Wisconsin decision, which wasn't difficult. He just didn't feel like they could ever get past the other three schools on his list and he didn't want to waste their time, or his. They were a team on the rise, with a quality coaching staff that he genuinely liked, but it just didn't seem like the right fit.

"Well, that's good you'll at least let them know early. That's being fair," Danny said. "You talk to Coach Elliott about this at all?"

"Just out of courtesy. He doesn't really care where I go. I'll probably call him today just to let him know that Notre Dame's out. That'll make him happy. He's a Purdue guy through and through and he would have hated if I had gone to Notre Dame."

Danny mentioned his conversation with Coach Jackson about the Mr. Football voting and Danny, of course, was right on about Nick's thinking. "I'm not going to win that, even though I probably should. You know what's funny is that Deshawn Milton at Broadway or Steve Mahoney, the quarterback down at Meridian Hills in Indy, are probably the favorites to win it and we're all going to Ohio State together on the same weekend. That'll be fun. They've been putting up big numbers, so it'll be hard for a linebacker to win. It might have been different if I had played more on offense, but that was really OK with me. We picked our spots there, and it paid off."

The Bears were off on Sunday, their one bye week of the season, and a few minutes later Danny's phone rang. It was Coach Jackson. "Hey, Mike Carey wants to talk to you today for a short little story on our Bloomington trip. Slow news day, I guess. Can he call you?"

Danny smiled and slapped Nick on the shoulder. "Sure, but I have a better story for him. Give me his number and I'll call him now," Danny said.

Nick look puzzled.

Before Danny called the reporter, he looked at Nick and smiled again. "They don't need to be writing about me going to some practice. Why don't you tell him about narrowing your list and take your shots at Notre Dame? It'll be fun and he'll eat that up. He'd probably love to have a juicy little story today."

"Sure, why not?" Nick said. "Might as well have a little fun. Be nice to remind those Notre Dame coaches that they're missing out on their No. 1 linebacker."

Danny called Mike Carey's cell phone and said hello. "Mr. Carey, you have a vote for Mr. Football, right?"

"Yes, I do. So does our columnist here. Why?"

"Have you decided on who you're going to vote for yet? You think Nick has a chance?"

Carey, of course, had no idea Nick was standing right next to Danny. "The vote takes place right after the state finals and I'd probably be leaning toward Deshawn Milton, because I like voting for a local kid whenever I can. Especially if they make a long run in the playoffs, he'd probably get my vote. Nick's a great player. I'd probably vote him No. 2, even though he's the best player I've ever seen. The position players always get the edge in those things.

"Well, they shouldn't. Nick's that defensive player that comes along once every 20 years who should win it, don't you think?" Danny was being very persuasive. "You need to take up his cause."

"If it was between him and someone from downstate, I probably would. But it wouldn't be fair to Deshawn to ignore him. They're undefeated and he's got like 1,500 yards already in eight games. But you know I think the world of Nick. I'd have no problem voting for him if it comes to that."

"I hope you do," Danny said. "So you need a good story today? I've got one for you. Nick just narrowed his list to three schools. That's a good story on a quiet day like today, right?"

"Sure, it's really good."

"Well, Nick will give it to you today and not say anything to anyone else. So it's all yours. Just remember we're doing this favor for you. Maybe you can do a favor for us sometime."

"I get your point, Danny," the reporter said. "I get your point."

Danny handed the phone to Nick, who told the reporter he only had five minutes, because he had to go to church. They smiled at each other over that one. But he gave him the list, told him he was down to Michigan, Ohio State and Florida State in no particular order, said the obligatory nice things about the Wisconsin decision then went on and on about how he could just never see himself at Notre Dame. He gave the reporter the anecdote about having to pray for Notre Dame victories as a kid and gave him another good anecdote about how he planned on smiling at church today with the memory of it all. It was a short, quick interview, but perfect for Nick to vent and perfect for the reporter who needed a good Monday story.

He had one. Trashing Notre Dame was always good copy and any Notre Dame football story always generated a lot of hits on the newspaper's website, good or bad.

Nick hung up and Danny glanced at his watch. "It is time for church. You coming with me? You should. Candice is coming, too. You could congratulate her for the All-State thing."

"I'm not going to church," Nick said. "Look what time it is." Danny knew it was a few minutes before 11. Church wouldn't be over until a little past noon. "Got a few things to do before kickoff at noon."

Danny shook his head and laughed at his friend.

"I'm a bird-watcher today," Nick said as he headed out the door. "Need the Eagles and Falcons early, and the Cardinals late. I need a good Sunday."

"You've already had a good Sunday," Danny said.

"Yes I have," Nick said as he scooted out the door, hugging Mrs. Bridges goodbye as he grabbed a few more sausage links for the walk home. "It's been a fun morning."

Nick walked home realizing he had never even had a chance to say anything to Danny about being so depressed the night before. Maybe he didn't need to. He felt fine again now, and that was all that mattered.

Some good days, some bad days. They were going to come and go.

He was happy now, and that was all that mattered. Plus, there was football to watch in an hour, and money to win.

Hopefully.

12

On **the night** Ben Richardson and Coach Will Jackson went to watch the Cubs get swept out of the playoffs at Wrigley Field, they had a beer and a sandwich at a bar across the street from Wrigley before the game. While they were there, they ran into Mark DiPolitto, a former detective for the Chicago Police Department who now worked in the organized crime division with the FBI. Ben had met Mark several years ago when Aaron Maxwell, one of his treatment center clients who had fallen off the wagon, was murdered on the south side of Chicago. DiPolitto was the detective in charge, so they talked off and on about a case that never got solved.

DiPolitto had his ideas, but he couldn't prove anything and it went no-where. It was just another case of an out-of-control addict getting killed. Sad to say, it happened all the time. But for Ben Richardson, it hurt deeply, because this was a gambling addict that he couldn't help, which is never good, and he was a kid who had come from a good family. It was a sad ending.

Mark and Ben had occasional conversations because Mark had referred a friend with a gambling problem to Ben and they occasionally collaborated on some speaking engagements for Ben, as well. They didn't talk often, but they were certainly friends and it was nice to run into each other on this cold October night.

Mark grabbed a beer at the bar and sat down with Ben and Will. They all were paying attention to their watches, because first pitch was less than an hour away. So they talked, but it was short and sweet.

"How's the new thing going at the FBI? It working out for you?" Ben asked.

"Well, it's certainly different, but I'm enjoying it," he said. "It's more big-picture stuff now than that day-to-day street-pounding that I had been doing with the police department. I've got many more people working under me, but many more bosses above me too. And, of course, I'm still basically dealing with all those organized crime lowlifes, so that hasn't changed. But we've done some good things, which has been rewarding, and we're working on some even bigger things now, which has been exciting, too."

"Ever talk to your old Chicago detective buddies?"

"Sure, all the time. There's still a lot of information-sharing."

After a bit of baseball conversation, the talk veered back to the case of

Aaron Maxwell.

"So nothing ever came of that investigation?" Ben asked.

"No, try as we might. Look, we have a pretty good idea that Joey Risone's crew had something to do with it, but we have absolutely no proof. We've never heard a word from anyone and we have zero clues. Not a stitch of evidence. If I had to guess, I'd say I'm probably 50 or 60 percent sure that he was involved with one or two of his guys, but I'm also 40 or 50 percent certain that something else might have happened too. Look, that kid was back doing cocaine all the time and he could have very easily been in that bad part of town buying drugs. It could have been a drug deal gone bad, or it just could have been some gang punks who just didn't like seeing a white boy in their part of town. We'll always keep our ears open, of course, but we may never know what really happened. We'll never forget him, but frankly, with his father gone now too, there's no one left in his family to report anything too anyway."

"Well, I'll never forget him," Ben said. "That really hurt, just not being able to get through to that kid. And his father was such a kind, generous man. All he wanted to do was help his son, and all the money in the world really wound up not mattering. It was a great lesson for me for what I do, that no matter how hard I try, I can't always get through to everyone."

"But you try," Mark said, "and that's the important thing. The work you do is very important. I wish there were more people like you."

They all said their goodbyes and headed over to Wrigley. In a matter of hours, the Cubs were beaten again and the Chicago baseball season was over. On the ride home, Will couldn't help but harken back to Ben's conversation with Mark DiPolitto before the game.

"You know, all these years I've known you and known what you do there at your treatment center, I never really put it together that sometimes you're dealing with life-or-death situations," Coach Jackson said. "That must really get stressful for you, day in and day out."

"Well, no matter what we do, there are stresses in every job," Ben said. "I'm sure you have your share of stressful days too. Years of experience have helped me a lot, and my own experiences have helped too. I know now that I can't reach everyone. Hell, the success rate is pretty darn low, if you really need to know. But to me, for every one person who gets it and winds up having a better life, that makes it all worthwhile to me. It's very gratifying. You can't win them all, but the ones you do win, you feel really good about. It really is all about just getting better a day at a time. I'll take the wins any way I can get them."

"Spoken like a true Cubs fan, Ben," Wilson said.

"Yep, wait till next year once again. Another baseball season in the books."

"And another basketball season right around the corner," Coach Jackson said. "I can't wait. It's going to be fun."

* * * * *   * * * * *   * * * * *

Before a basketball season could arrive, there was the matter of getting through the rest of this high school football season and keeping all his basketball guys healthy. Thankfully for Coach Jackson, that happened. Nick and the boys won their last three regular season games to finish 8-2. The final home game, an easy win against a bad South Hammond team, turned out to be a nice night. They retired Nick's number 44 at halftime and the ceremony was beautiful. Lots of people said lots of nice things, and Nick truly appreciated the gesture. So did Danny, who watched every minute from the stands with Candice.

The playoffs started with a quick rematch against South Hammond, this time on the road, but the results were the same, another easy victory in the pouring rain. The sectional pairings, made by a blind draw, meant Crossroads got undefeated Broadway in the second round, this time at home. And this time, again, in the pouring rain.

Even though Broadway's Deshawn Milton was only 68 yards short of 2,000 yards rushing on the year, he was used as more of a decoy in this game as a way to keep middle linebacker Nick Vincent occupied. Broadway just had too much speed on the outside and in the sloppy conditions, they took advantage of knowing where they were going against the struggling Crossroads defensive backs. They scored with regularity and their great defense kept Crossroads at bay, winning handily 27-10. Nick played well, but Broadway showed how much of a team game football really was, attacking away from Nick whenever possible. Broadway was just better overall.

When it was all over, Nick and Deshawn Milton congratulated each other at midfield. Milton ran the ball only nine times for 41 yards, and the decoy plan had worked.

"I hope you took that as a sign of respect," Milton said. "We knew we didn't want to bang heads with you all night."

"Hey, you guys are just better than we are. I hope you win all the rest of them," Nick said. "Next week you can get your 2,000."

They clasped hands one more time and said they'd spend more time together on Saturday, since they were both making their visits to Ohio State that weekend. Nick went off and showered, then met Danny, Candice and the gang at Angelo's for pizza. It was too cold and it was raining too hard to hang out outside, so pizza sounded good.

Danny was curious what kind of mood Nick was going to be in, and he was pleasantly surprised that Nick came in nice and fresh and laughing with everyone.

"I've got no complaints," Nick said of his football season. "We won a lot of games and just got beat by a better team. I had a lot of fun and I'm walking away healthy. To be honest, I'm kind of glad it's over. Two straight weeks of practicing and playing in the rain hasn't really been a lot of fun."

Together again now, Danny thought. Just like old times.

* * * * *   * * * * *   * * * * *

On that first Monday after the football season, Nick and the rest of the football guys joined up with the others for the first full-squad basketball practice. It was a good time for Coach Will Jackson to get everyone's mind on the task at hand – which was to make the most out of every practice and get better as a team.

It was all basketball now.

Nick was ready. His weekend recruiting trip to Ohio State went well. He liked it a lot, liked the coaches and players he spent time with and certainly kept Ohio State on the list with Michigan and Florida State. He was amazed at how much attention was paid to him, and how much time coaches and players alike spent bad-mouthing Michigan. They hated each other, and it was obvious. Knowing Nick had already visited Michigan and was seriously considering them, they used that as their hook to push Nick their way. Nick didn't mind one bit. He loved everything about that rivalry, and kept an open mind all weekend. If he had to put them in order – and he was glad that he didn't – it was probably still Michigan, then Ohio State, then Florida State, but that was certainly subject to change. He was still very much looking forward to his Florida State visit at the end of the month. The idea of sunhine sounded great after weeks of cold, rainy days.

Some basketball issues came and went quickly as well. The November signing period started and Danny signed his letter-of-intent to Indiana at a quick ceremony at the school. Mike Carey from the Star-Press was there with a photographer and wrote a nice story about Danny signing. The story also included Tyrone Wells of Gary Northside signing with Northwestern; they were the only two Division I basketball recruits in the county.

Carey also wrote a short story about the first state basketball poll that had been released. Gary Northside was ranked sixth in the state, Crossroads was 13th and North Hammond was 18th. Coach Jackson thought they might be higher, but the fact that they weren't wasn't a big deal to him. It gave him extra fodder for his first sit-down with the team.

They gathered in the locker room around their coach, the first of many meetings over the next four months. Coach Jackson made sure to set the proper tone.

"I know you guys have thought about winning a state championship for quite a while now and I'll be totally honest with you. I've thought about it, too. We can sit here and talk about that, but you know what? There are all sorts of teams sitting in their locker rooms this week having the exact same conversation. Hell, we're ranked 13th in the state right now, so I know at least 12 teams think they're better than us and more capable of winning a state championship than we are. There are probably 12 more behind us who are thinking the same thing too.

"Now, do I think we're capable of winning a state championship? Sure I do. Do I think we're good enough today to win one? I don't think we are. We have to make the most of every practice and get better every day. I like everything about this team. We have stars, we have depth, we have balance and we're capable of playing a lot of different ways. Those are all good things. But if we're going to have success this season, we have to be good every day. It takes nine wins in the tournament to win a state title, and that means playing nine good games. Seven out of eight, or three out of four, isn't good enough. It just takes one loss to ruin the dream. So we need to push it and work on things. Let's get better every day and see where it leads us. We have a great opportunity, so let's make the most out of it."

They headed out to the court, Danny and Nick walking out side-by-side. "Thirteen, my ass," Nick said. "That's a huge mistake. Someone will have to pay for that."

Danny couldn't help but laugh at his friend … and smile.

It was nice to see Nick so focused already.

* * * * *   * * * * *   * * * * *

Two weeks of practices went well and the season was ready to begin. All the football guys had gotten the kinks out and the practices had been high-paced and competitive. Crossroads had its two stars, Danny and Nick, and about six others who were all going to be key contributors at one time or another during the season. The fight for playing time was on, but everyone, down to the last man, knew this was a team-first thing. Only Kenny Dockery, who was still fighting an ankle injury from the end of the football season, missed any practice time, and that wasn't necessarily a bad thing.

This first week of the season was going to be interesting. The home opener on the Tuesday night before Thanksgiving against Aberdeen was going to be fun. It was the first game against an inferior opponent, on Danny's birthday no less, and it was also the night that the fall sports athletes who made All-State would get honored at halftime and their portraits put upon the Wall of Fame.

There were only two this year – Nick and Candice. Danny would be a happy spectator for that one.

The Crossroads fieldhouse held about 4,000 for basketball on a normal night and it was full for the opener. The students, who were very much looking forward to this season, had their own section and they came prepared, all wearing jeans, white hard hats and their white STATE CHAMPIONSHIP: UNDER CONSTRUCTION T-shirts. They marched into the fieldhouse in unison about ten minutes before tipoff and immediately started making lots of noise. In the last two minutes before tipoff, they all sang together.

"Happy birthday to you … Happy birthday, dear Danny …"

Danny couldn't help but laugh. He gave the student section a little bow on his way to the bench, appreciative of the gesture.

The game went very well. They were precise on offense and got good shots all night long. They had a 10-point lead by the end of the first quarter, a 16-point lead at halftime and a 25-point lead to start the final quarter. Danny played just two minutes in the fourth before Coach Jacksons emptied the bench. Crossroads won 81-55, with Danny's 27 points leading the way.

Nick added 14 points and 14 rebounds and Coach Jackson, quite frankly, was happy with how everyone played. There were no signs of first-night jitters, just a veteran team focused and on a mission. Even the young guys played well. It was just one of 20 regular season games, but it was a nice one to have out of the way. They were 1-0, and everyone was happy. You can't win them all if you don't win the first one.

* * * * *   * * * * *   * * * * *

Getting to 2-0 was going to be a daunting task, because they had to do it without Nick Vincent, who was off in Tallahassee, Florida for the weekend taking his official visit to Florida State. After three weeks of rainy, dreary weather in Indiana, Nick was duly impressed when his plane landed Friday afternoon and it was a sunny, 80-degree day. He got the tour of the campus on Friday, an early dinner at one of the local hot-spots where a serious happy hour was going on for the fired-up student body and then he was taken to a huge pep rally and bonfire that night.

One thought kept running through Nick's head all day long:

"I have never seen so many beautiful women in one place in my life!"

The warm weather certainly helped. One gorgeous Seminoles girl after another – in short shorts or gorgeous sundresses – kept turning Nick's head. It was a great campus, a great student body and a great football program. He loved everything about his visit, especially the intensity inside the stadium on that Saturday afternoon, when Florida State spanked their arch-rivals Florida with a three-touchdown rally in the fourth quarter. Nick loved everything about his visit and as he flew home late Saturday night, he knew he now had some serious thinking to do. He could see himself at all three schools still on his list. In his mind, for now, it was a toss-up between Florida State, Michigan and Ohio State. His Florida State visit was that good.

As Nick flew home, Danny and the rest of his Crossroads teammates took the court at The Fieldhouse in Indianapolis against Anderson, Coach Jackson's old school. Without Nick, he decided to go small and put both point guards – Kenny Dockery and sophomore Javier Hernandez – in the starting lineup. He knew it was going to be a loose, free-wheeling game and going smaller and quicker wasn't a bad thing. As the last of four showcase games, he wanted to make sure his team made a good impression around the state.

Coach Jackson sure wished Nick would have been there. But he understood that this weekend was Nick's only chance to get to Tallahassee, so he didn't make a big deal of it. He spent an inordinate amount of time watching film of Anderson's first game and had the team ready with several plays he wanted to run against them early.

Danny was the focus in all of them. On their first possession, Danny got free with a little back-screen and scored on an easy lay-up. Then he hit two straight three-pointers and got free on a little curl through the lane.

Four shots, 10 points. A quick 10-2 lead. For the thousands of fans in the stands who didn't know much about Indiana recruit Danny Bridges, they were getting an eyeful. Anderson's coach called a quick timeout. They just weren't a very good defensive team this early in the season and Crossroads' precise and disciplined patterns were giving them fits. By halftime it was 44-20 and Crossroads wound up cruising to a 85-60 victory. Danny finished with 34 points and that was without playing even a minute in the fourth quarter.

Impressive.

Everyone in Indiana knew who Danny Bridges was now.

About halfway home on the bus ride, Danny's cell phone rang. It was Nick, who had just landed at Midway Airport in Chicago.

"Hey, man," Nick said. "How'd we do?"

"Who is this?" Danny deadpanned.

"Smart ass," Nick said.

"Well, just as I predicted, we didn't miss you one bit. Completely pounded them. Won by 25 and had a big lead the whole game. Everyone played great."

"How many did you get?"

"I had 34. An easy 34 too. They tried to play man against us early and we screened them to death. And when they went to a zone, we hit about six three-pointers in a row. They never had an answer for us and everybody really played well. It was good to win without you, just so you know we really don't need you."

"Oh, OK," Nick said.

"How was Florida State?" Danny asked.

"Great. Fell in love about a thousand times. The girls there, they're just incredible."

"And the football?"

"The girls, Danny. They're just incredible."

The two best friends talked for another 20 minutes, laughing and joking and jabbing each other as the miles and barren cornfields ambled by.

Smiles abounded.

13

The cool, rainy dreariness of November finally rolled into the bone-chilling month of December, but it certainly stayed plenty warm inside the Crossroads High School fieldhouse on most nights. The basketball season was progressing nicely with three more easy wins. They were 5-0 heading up to North Hammond for an early-season showdown between two of Northwest Indiana's best teams. North Hammond was 5-0 as well, and both were ranked in the Top 10 in the state now, North Hammond fifth and Crossroads tenth.

Danny was playing great basketball, averaging nearly 27 points per game, and so was Nick. They had won all five games by double digits and hadn't really had a high-pressure game yet. That changed against North Hammond, whose quick wing players kept attacking the basket and scoring at a rapid rate. They jumped ahead early and never let up. Kenny Dockery, whose ankle still wasn't 100 per-cent, was starting at guard with Danny but was having all sorts of trouble guarding quicker players. Danny got his points, but they couldn't ever slow down North Hammond long enough to get a lead. They got within three points on a few occa-sions in the fourth quarter, but eventually lost 78-71.

Any dreams of a perfect season had vanished. That was a never really a goal anyway, not with their difficult schedule, but it was still never easy to deal with a loss.

Unless you're a great coach like Will Jackson.

Losses, especially early in the season, did serve a purpose. For one, it got his players' attention, knocking them down a peg or two. It gave him the chance to remind them that maybe they weren't as good as they thought they were and that they had to continue to work even harder in practice. Secondly, it gave a coach like Jackson a great window to his team, to see its flaws and what needed to be cor-rected before the state tournament rolled around.

And, at least for now, he didn't like what he was seeing.

This issue with Kenny Dockery at guard could be a problem, he thought. Everywhere else, things were good. Danny, of course, was the best player on the floor every night. Nick was a solid contributor at power forward on both ends of the floor and Bobby Nickerson, the skinny 6-9 junior center, was doing just fine in the middle. Rick Tiller, the 6-4 junior forward, was a nice compliment to Danny on the wing, a good shooter and slasher who didn't handle the ball particularly well but could certainly score.

For Coach Jackson, this was a situation that needed gentle handling. Kenny Dockery had grown up with Nick and Danny. They'd been playing together since the third grade, but as Nick and Danny grew into talented college-level athletes, Kenny was just a slow, plodding 6-footer who could shoot it but not do much else. For years and years, he could defer the ballhandling responsibilities to Danny, but now as Danny had grown, Coach Jackson really wanted him to be more of a constant scoring threat on the wing than the primary ballhandler at the point. Kenny was struggling in a new role, not only in the games but in practice as well. Javier Hernandez, the speedy 5-10 sophomore who had transferred in from Chicago during the summer, gave him fits in scrimmages because he had such quick hands and was a pesky defender.

In a perfect world, Coach Jackson would start Hernandez, but there were other things to consider. If he benched Kenny, would he lose him for good? He certainly didn't want that, because he did like Kenny's experience and calmness on the floor. And it was a long season. He would hate to increase Javier's role and then have it blow up in his face. With so much at stake, it was a delicate balancing act.

But he also had a window to experiment. Their next three games before Christmas were all at home and all against inferior opponents. If he had to mix things up, this was a nice 10-day window to try things.

So he called a meeting of his three seniors, and laid out the plan. He was a little sneaky, filling in Danny ahead of time so he could be prepared to be supportive of Kenny in the meeting. It was that important. They all met in Coach Jackson's office about 15 minutes before practice was scheduled to start.

"Guys, we're six games in now, almost a third of the way, and I've had a chance to see what we're dealing with here," Jackson said. "Look, we're 5-1 so there's certainly nothing to panic about, but I do think we have a few issues and I think I have the cure. One issue we've had is our ability to handle the basketball in pressure situations and our ability to guard quick people on the other end. Also, there's been times where we're just not getting good perimeter shots other than from you, Danny. I think some of that's coming from our rotation and who's been playing with whom. I need to do a better job of that, and I want to make some changes."

Danny knew what was coming and he was curious to see how his friend Kenny would react.

"Kenny, I'm going to go ahead and start Javier at the point and I want you to be the first guy off the bench. Here's why," he said, not pausing at all so Kenny couldn't jump in. "Javier's got great ballhandling skills and he can help us pressure

92

people better on defense. He's not a good shooter, but if he's out on the floor with Danny, Nick and Rick, then we don't really need him to score and maybe he can play more relaxed and not be so nervous. I want him to get comfortable and I want you to come off the bench for him. But I also want you to come in first for Bobby a lot of times, so we can go small and go with more shooters. I want to do that this Friday, because White Hawk isn't big. I want to practice that this week, with you and Javier on the floor at the same time too and Danny at a wing with Rick sliding down to the four and Nick to the five. That way Kenny, your primary job is to shoot, just like the old days. This might help you."

It was all well played by Coach Jackson. And it worked. Kenny understood his limitations and his place in the pecking order.

"Hey coach, to me it's all about winning. I am what I am as a player. Whatever it takes to win every night, that's what is most important to me. I'll do whatever you need me to do."

It was what everyone wanted to hear.

Practices went well with Javier in the starting lineup. So did the games. They won easily all three times, including the first game against White Hawk, their rivals to the east in Crown Point. Javier got more comfortable every day and Kenny played well in a back-up role. The first game, as planned, he came in for Bobby Nickerson and they went small. He hit his first two jumpers and scored a bunch more in garbage time when all the starters, except Javier, were on the bench. All three wins were by at least 15 points, so they went into the Christmas break 8-1 and feeling good again. The last game before the break, against an undisciplined Gary Washington team, Danny went nuts. He scored 18 points in the first quarter, had 32 by halftime and early in the fourth quarter, he hit a three-pointer to hit 50, breaking the school record by a point. It was a special night. Danny made 18 of 25 shots, including 8-of-9 from three-point range, and they broke 100 for the first time in school history. Javier Hernandez, the speedy young sophomore, also tied a school record with 19 assists. He proved, too, that he belonged.

Coach Jackson had defused a potential problem and turned it into a plus. It was behind-the-scenes coaching at its best.

* * * * *   * * * * *   * * * * *

Away from the court, Nick was forced to spend most of his day with some less-than-wonderful people. His brother Tony had broken his right ankle at work a few days earlier and couldn't drive. He had money to pick from some of the guys he took bets from, so he needed Nick to drive him around.

Nick wasn't very thrilled about having to waste two or three hours being a chauffeur for his brother, but he did it without too much complaint. They had made four or five stops before stopping at a bar in Dyer, where they were supposed to meet three people who needed to pay up. Tony bought dinner while they waited. One guy showed up and paid Tony his $600, but a second guy came by and only had $400 of the $1,500 he owed Tony. This was the first Tony was hearing about the money problem and the two of them got into a heated argument. The guy threw the money on the table and left, and Tony was steaming. He got even angrier while they ate when the third guy didn't show at all and then didn't answer his phone. Oh, the joys of bookmaking.

Tony was pounding the beers, since he had a designated driver. As they left, he had Nick drive through the bank ATM line, where Tony pulled another thousand dollars out of his account. He hated doing that, but it had to be done.

Joey Risone had to be paid. No exceptions, no excuses.

They drove east to Chicago Heights and stopped at a seedy little bar in the rough part of town. Tony hobbled out of Nick's truck on his crutches and they walked in together.

And for the first time, Nick met mobster Joey Risone.

"Joey, this is my little brother Nick," Tony said as they walked to the bar.

"Little brother my ass. This boy is huge," Joey said as he shook Nick's hand. "I hear you're a big football star. Where you going to college?"

Nick nodded in modesty. "Haven't decided yet. Down to three, Michigan, Ohio State and Florida State. I have another month to decide." He didn't have much to say to Joey. He'd heard enough stories about him from Tony and he looked just like Tony had described him. And his bar was as dumpy as Tony had said.

"Grab a table, Nick. I'll be just a minute," Tony said and he and Joey went into a back room. "Just a little bit of business to do."

"Get him a beer," Joey shouted to the bartender. Nick waved him off, though. "Just a Coke would be good. Thanks," he said.

Nick sat at the dirty table by himself for about five minutes, a bunch of nasty people in the bar occasionally staring over at him. He was out of place and he knew it. He was glad to see Tony re-emerge and couldn't wait to get out of the place. He hated all the smoke, and the filth.

Joey reached out his hand one more time as Nick left. As they shook hands, Joey put his other big hand on Nick's shoulder. "Anytime you feel like a drink, you're always welcome, kid. We won't ID you in here."

"Thanks, but I'm good," Nick said as they left.

"Man, you were right about that place," Nick said to Tony on the ride home. "What a dump."

"Yeah, but at least you know where it is. I might need you to come back here the next couple of weeks until I can drive again."

"Oh great," Nick said, sarcastically. "Thanks a lot."

Over the next four weeks, Nick drove over to the bar every Thursday. Tony rode with him most of the time, but one night he went alone. He took Danny along for the ride, just to show him the dump and because Angelo's was on the way back home and they were going out to eat. They looked very out of place in their Crossroads letterman's jackets, but they only stayed a few minutes anyway. Nick was thrilled when Tony's cast came off.

* * * * *　　* * * * *　　* * * * *

Christmas came and went, and it was wonderful. Danny and Candice enjoyed their first Christmas together and the little break from basketball had been nice too. They got three days off for the holiday, then had two brisk practices before their prestigious holiday tournament in South Bend. They won the first two games, but lost the final to a very good team from Chicago that had three Division I recruits who could all play. Crossroads played well but just couldn't make a shot down the stretch and lost by two. So as they headed into the home stretch of their regular-season schedule, they were 10-2.

Impressive, but not without flaws.

They wouldn't lose again, winning their final eight regular season games to finish 18-2. There were some magical moments. They avenged the loss to North Hammond with an impressive 16-point victory at home in front of a sellout crowd of more than 5,000. Danny scored 44 points and just couldn't miss. They went to Ridge Central and spanked them by 20, which was nice. The basketball rivalry wasn't as intense as the football rivalry, because Ridge Central had been fairly average in basketball the past few years, but beating them at anything was always fun.

The second-to-last home game was memorable for several reasons. Danny scored 41 points to become the school's all-time leading scorer, and that was special. But what was fun was a great little recruiting ploy by the University of Michigan. Football signing day was just five days away and Nick still had Michigan, Ohio State and Florida State on his list. He wasn't talking about it publicly, but had confided to Danny that Florida State was out, reluctantly. He loved the school – and the girls – but wanted to play closer to home.

Michigan pulled out all the stops.

The Michigan recruiters teamed up with their local alumni associations to make one final statement. At the basketball game, the Michigan boosters gathered in the parking lot and then all 300 of them – dressed identically in blue jeans and blue and maize MICHIGAN sweatshirts – marched into the fieldhouse together. They sat in the top rows behind the Crossroads bench and made quite a scene, all in a good way. They loudly sang the Michigan fight song during pre-game warm-ups and gave Nick a two-minute standing ovation when the starting lineups were announced.

They cheered loudly for Crossroads the entire game and shouted 'Way to go, Nick; Way to go, Nick" every time he did anything. It was an easy win and everyone had a good time. Even Nick got a good laugh out of the gag. It was nice to be wanted.

The show of support wasn't the difference-maker in Nick's decision, but it was nice nonetheless. It was a tough decision, but in the end he liked the Michigan coaching staff a little better. He really liked that his position coach had been his primary recruiter and liked that he almost certainly would start as a freshman with their current middle linebacker graduating. He announced his decision at school the following afternoon in a made-for-TV thing on ESPNU, where a dozen of the nation's top recruits all made their choices known on live TV. Michigan it was, and Nick was glad to have it all over. He was the biggest piece of Michigan's No. 1-ranked recruiting class and the Ohio State coaches were devastated.

Danny and Coach Jackson were glad it was over, too. Nick had done a nice job of making sure the whole recruiting process didn't get in the way of basketball, other than the trip to Florida State in November, but it was nice to focus on the prize at hand. They won their last two road games and wrapped up their season at home with an easy win over South Hammond that included a nice ceremony after the game on Senior Night, when it was announced that they were going to retire Danny's number. He enjoyed the ceremony, and enjoyed it even more that he could share it with him mom and siblings, and Candice and her parents.

Everyone rushed off to Angelo's to celebrate a great regular season. They were 18-2 and ranked No. 5 in the final state poll.

It was time for the playoffs now. They were healthy, and they were ready. They were nine wins from a state title.

But they were also just one loss away from it not happening.

Sudden death is a scary thing.

14

The suit jacket was off and the tie was loosened at least two buttons down the front of Coach Will Jackson's sweat-stained shirt. His lips were pursed, his eyes narrowed as he sat at his desk. He leaned back in his chair, put his hands behind his head, and stared across the desk at three inquisitive local reporters.

"I really don't know how the heck we won that game," he said in a soft tone, his head shaking gently from side to side. "But we'll take it."

The 5,000 others who had packed into the Crossroads High School fieldhouse on a frigid Saturday night thought the same thing. Scrappy White Hawk had outplayed Crossroads in the sectional championship game most of the night, but the Marauders made just enough plays down the stretch to win the game 56-54. All year long, Danny and Nick had talked about cutting down the nets four times, and this was the first. They were sectional champs, but no one was very happy.

It wasn't a fun night.

Certainly not like it should have been.

Getting to the finals was a breeze, as expected. As the top seed, they had no problem with No. 8-seeded Newton County in Wednesday night's opener. They were small and not very athletic and really didn't have an answer for all of Crossroads' weapons. Danny scored 32 points in an easy 81-52 victory. The semifinal against Southlake should have been tougher, but it wasn't. Danny and Nick combined to score all of Crossroads' 22 points in the first quarter, and they won in another rout. The final was 77-50 and Danny scored another 32 points. He was clearly the best player on the floor, and it was nice vindication for the upset loss from a year ago.

But the White Hawk game in the final was downright strange. Danny drove to school with Candice, and he didn't see Nick until they met in the locker room. Nick was about 15 minutes late and when he got there, he was very quiet. He walked in with his headphones on and never took them off while he dressed, stretched out and got his ankles taped. Even during warm-ups he was sullen and methodical. On the first possession of the game he picked up a foul trying to block a shot. Not a minute later, scrambling for a loose ball, he dove onto a White Hawk player and what looked like should have been a jump ball was instead called a foul on Nick. The White Hawk player took umbrage with Nick's physicality and gave him a shove. Nick immediately shoved back, harmlessly, but both referees immediately stepped between the two players to ease the situation. After a brief conversation, they called technical fouls on both players. The technicals also counted as personal fouls, so less than two minutes into the game, Nick had three fouls.

He was steaming. Will Jackson had no choice but the take him out. Nick ignored his coach as he walked to the end of the bench and grabbed a seat.

"Nick, come here," Jackson said as he slapped the open chair next chair to him.

"I'm fine right here," Nick said, pulling his warm-up jacket up over his head.

Will Jackson, quite perturbed, got up to walk down and confront Nick, but an assistant stopped him. "Just let him cool down. He's done for the half anyway, so stay focused on the game. We'll talk to him at halftime."

With Nick on the bench, the Marauders seemed out of synch. Danny was being double-teamed or triple-teamed all the time and didn't get many good looks. His teammates were pressing, forcing shots, forcing passes and being a step slow on defense. At halftime, White Hawk had a nine-point lead, including a three-pointer at the buzzer, and the Crossroads players stormed off to the locker room angry and in a daze. The partisan Crossroads crowd was just as dazed.

This was not looking good. Their dream season was on the precipice of ending.

"We're playing like crap," Kenny Dockery screamed at his teammates when they got in the locker room. "We need to get our head out of our asses. We're better than this."

Everyone was on edge. Danny stepped in and calmed everyone down. Nick didn't say a word, just kept walking straight back to the bathrooms and closing a stall door behind him. He sat there for a few minutes, just staring at the door.

About five minutes had passed before Coach Jackson and the other coaches came in. The players expected some ranting and raving, but instead their coach gathered them in a circle around him.

"Sit down," he said. "Now sit back and take a deep breath."

They did.

"Take another one."

They did again.

Then he slid his chair closer and his players did the same. He grabbed the hands of the two players on either side of him and everyone followed, like some young Boy Scouts around a campfire.

"Look at me," he said, and everyone locked eyes with him.

"I know with 100 percent certainty that we are going to win this game," Coach Jackson said in a soft voice. "We are better than they are, and there is no way they can beat us on our floor, especially with a sectional championship on the line.

"All we're doing wrong right now is trying to do everything a tick too fast. Just slow down, OK? Take a deep breath, OK? Relax out there, and have fun. We are well prepared, so let's just go play our game. Let's run our offense and patiently wait for good shot. We don't need to rush anything. We've got plenty of time."

The players listened intently, nodding at each suggestion. Jackson pulled them all even closer.

"Danny, are you 100 percent convinced we're going to win this game?"

"Yes. Yes, of course," he said.

"Kenny? You?"

Dockery nodded.

"You guys? You all in?"

They nodded too.

Coach Jackson stood up, and his players followed. "Then let's go out there and play Crossroads basketball and kick their ass," he said. The players started to file out, and as they did, Coach Jackson stopped Nick and stared him right in the eyes.

"Get your head clear right now and get all that anger out of you before you walk out of this room. I need you, and I need you right now. Two damn minutes in the first half, that's it. You need to play smart and help us get back in this game."

Nick sternly stepped around his coach and glared back at him with an evil eye. "Just leave me alone," Nick snapped. "I'll be fine."

Of course, he wasn't.

Danny hit a three-pointer on the first possession to cut the lead to six and Nick rebounded a White Hawk miss on the other end. Danny then drove to the basket and put up a little floater that bounced off the back of the rim. Nick was in perfect position to grab the offensive rebound. He came down and went back up strong to the basket.

There was minimal contact on the way up, but his White Hawk defender flopped backward as if he'd been hit by a truck. The referee, not two feet away, blew his whistle and signaled an offensive foul on Nick and waved off the basket.

Nick couldn't believe it. He slammed the ball to the floor forcefully with both hands and on its way back up, it accidentally slid off his fingertips and nailed the referee right on the bottom of the chin. It only took a split second for the official to stare down Nick and blow his whistle again.

"Technical foul, 44!" he shouted on his way to the scorer's table. "Offensive foul, 44. Technical foul, 44.

Nick could certainly do the math. As the huge crowd booed away and roared its disapproval, he knew what that meant. The offensive foul was his fourth, the technical his fifth.

He had just fouled out of the game.

One minute into the second half, and he was done.

As Coach Jackson railed at the referee, trying in vain to have the technical waved off, Nick walked to the end of the bench, sat down and slammed his fist on the chair next to him. From midcourt, Danny looked on with anger at his friend, but also worried about the big picture. They were still behind and now had to play the rest of the game without their second-best player.

Jackson, of course, lost his argument. One referee walked to the far free throw line with the White Hawk shooter, but just before he handed him the ball to shoot the technicals, the referee near the scorer's table blew his whistle. The three officials huddled for a minute, then one of them walked over to Coach Jackson.

"Coach, he's out because of the five fouls, but that was also two technicals, so he can't be sitting there on the bench. He's not just disqualified; he's ejected. He needs to go to the locker room," the referee said. Jackson knew he was right, but he argued some more. The crowd watched in silence, not sure what was going on.

Coach Jackson walked over to Nick on the bench and told him what the ruling was.

"I'm not leaving," Nick shouted.

"You have to," Jackson said. "That's the rule."

"It's a bullshit rule," Nick said, getting up out of his chair and walking away from his coach.

Jackson carefully grabbed Nick's forearm. "Nick, let's go. You've got to go now. Don't make it worse"

Nick whipped his arm away and started walking across the court to the locker room. The crowd, finally, had figured out what was going on, so they roared some more. Nick ripped off his jersey and threw it against the wall before disappearing into the locker room, alone and angry.

Jackson immediately called timeout and gathered his players around them.

"I don't feel any damn different than I did in that locker room. I am 100 percent convinced we're going to win this game, so let's go do it. Forget all that. We've got 15 minutes to go and five damn good players on the floor. So let's go play." He pointed to Kenny Dockery to check in, then drew up some plays.

Going with a small lineup, they started pressing White Hawk full-court with their diamond-and-one press. Danny was at the back of the diamond and was perfect for that role. He was great at knowing when to trap and when to fill a passing lane. White Hawk wasn't ready for it and they quickly got a couple of turnovers. By the end of the third quarter, the deficit was down to three.

The teams spent most of the fourth quarter exchanging baskets. Crossroads grabbed the lead on a few occasions, but White Hawk always answered. They were killing Crossroads on the boards with Nick not around, getting easy second-chance points on offense and limiting Crossroads to one shot each trip. When the clock ticked down under a minute, Crossroads still trailed by one.

Danny, harassed all game by the double-teams, had made only 5-of-15 shots. Coach Jackson used his last timeout to set up a play as part of their motion offense, running Danny through some screens to get open and take the last shot. But when it played out, White Hawk did a great job of switching on every screen, denying Danny a good look. With 12 second left, he caught the ball and tried stepping through the double-team for a shot. A third defender emerged, so he was forced to kick it out to Kenny Dockery, his friend for years who had become nothing more than a bit player on this team for most of his senior season.

Danny had hoped to re-set the offense and get the ball back, but Dockery was open. He took the three-pointer … and hit nothing but net for a two-point lead with six seconds to go. White Hawk got a good look on the other end with three seconds left, but the shot missed. They got an offensive rebound and put up another shortie, but it hung on the rim for a second, then rolled off as the buzzer sounded.

It was a great escape.

Danny had finished with only 12 points. Nick, of course, had zero points, one rebound and five fouls in his three minutes. Kenny Dockery, with his final three, turned out to be the leading scorer with 13, his first double-digit game all season. Tony Vincent had been watching the game from the locker room door, giving Nick play-by play. He did come back out after the game, already in street clothes, but still didn't seem very happy. He quickly snipped off a piece of the net, handed it to his brother and walked right out of the fieldhouse.

When Danny and his teammates finally made it back to the locker room, he was shocked to see that Nick wasn't there. He answered one or two questions from the reporters, but immediately sent them in Kenny's direction. This was Kenny's 15 minutes of fame, after all, and he wanted him to enjoy it. Then he left, telling Coach Jackson he was leaving on the way out. They both nodded, knowing that it was up to Danny to go talk to Nick. Coach Jackson left it at that, but he wasn't happy. It was one thing for Nick to be a non-factor in the game. It was another thing to just walk away. This from a kid who was about to be under a much bigger spotlight in college? Coach Jackson wasn't going to let him get away with it.

"Let me say this first," he said to the reporters. "Kenny Dockery had a hell of a game. I am so happy for him. Here's a kid, a senior, who loses his starting job, but he never sulked. He still came to practice and worked hard every day, and when we needed him tonight he really stepped up.

"How we won this game is beyond me. I guess the best way to describe it is we persevered. We were horrible on offense, but we guarded well. And when we needed to make some plays at the end, we did. We've relied so much on Danny and Nick all year and tonight, well, you saw it. Danny did not score well, but you've got to give White Hawk credit for that. They guarded him really well and we didn't do a very good job as coaches of getting him better looks.

"As for Nick, well, he didn't come ready to play. His head wasn't in it from the get-go. He turned a bad situation into a worse situation in the first half, then lost his cool in the second half. I know that wasn't intentional, but this is an All-American-type athlete and he can't be doing that. I guarantee you his football coaches at Michigan won't put up with that kind of crap next year and I'm not putting up with it now. He let us down big-time tonight and his teammates picked him up. He owes us one now, that's for sure. But if I know Nick – and I think I do – he will be ready to practice on Monday and be ready to play next Friday."

From the school lobby, with Candice waiting, Danny quickly dialed Nick's cell phone. It rang several times, but Nick did finally answer. There was no hello, just an immediate diatribe from an angry young man.

"Look, tonight – just for tonight – I want you to leave me alone, OK? I'm still incredibly pissed off and I'm just going home. I will talk to you tomorrow. Got it?"

"Yeah, I got it, and that's fine. But you shouldn't have just walked away. We're a team, man, and you walked away from your teammates tonight. You ...'

Click.

Danny snapped his phone shut, perturbed that Nick had hung up on him. But he knew. There were times to reel Nick in, and times to let him be. He'd seen all these mood swings before. So he left him alone. He grabbed his girlfriend's hand and they walked together to the car. They met their two families at Angelo's and ate pizza and shared laughs with their family, friends and teammates for several hours. This was a team with high expectations for this season, and a sectional championship was just a step in the journey. But it was a sectional championship all the same, and Crossroads was one of only 64 schools celebrating that night across the basketball-crazed state of Indiana.

Most everyone was happy. Danny and Kenny – who used to be a busboy at Angelo's – posed for a few pictures, and Angelo promised to put one up on the wall. After a few hours, they all left. On the way home, Danny had Candice drive by Nick's house. His truck was in the driveway, but all the lights were out.

Danny went home and went to bed himself, a sectional champ.

Step One was complete, but not without some anxiety.

* * * * *   * * * * *   * * * * *

Nick **had seen the** headlights on his bedroom wall as he lay in bed. He didn't bother getting up, but he was sure it was Danny. He'd already been staring at his ceiling for hours, and there would be more of the same before he finally fell asleep. He was mad at the world, and everyone was on his list, from Coach Jackson to those horse-bleep referees to Danny.

But he was also mad at himself.

He had played poker online before on game days, and it was never a big deal. He had bet on college basketball games on game days too, and that was never an issue either. This time it was, and even Nick was seeing the correlation.

He woke up excited and happy, looking forward to a sectional championship game. He was feeling good, and feeling lucky. He had made three bets online on the early afternoon college games and decided to play some cards as well. Instead of his usual fifty-dollar poker games – which used to be ten-dollar games before that – he had decided to play in a $200 tournament because his online bankroll was fairly hefty. In the first five hands that were dealt, he'd had good cards and played three straight hands, but never hit anything. His 4,000-chip stack dwindled to about 2,700. On the fifth hand, he got the ace and two of hearts and made a decent-sized bet. Two players called. The flop came ace-two-two, and he was immediately staring at a full house. One player bet 500 chips and the second player folded. Nick looked at the board and was sure he had a winner. He pushed all-in and was surprised his opponent called. He had ace-king, so Nick was way ahead.

Until a king came on the turn and another one came on the river, and Nick's tournament was done, beaten by a better full house. He lost $220 in about 10 minutes. He said what the hell, and bought in for another tournament. This time, about six hands in, his ace-high flush was called on an all-in bet and even though he was ahead, his opponent hit runner-runner 10s to beat him with a full house. In less than a half hour, he had lost $440.

Then Maryland and Duke didn't cover their number in the basketball games either. As Nick had pulled into the school parking lot on that Saturday night before the game, he checked his phone for a score from the North Carolina game and they too had won but didn't cover the number. He was 0-for-3.

Between the poker games and the basketball, he had just lost almost $1,200 in one afternoon. So, yeah, he didn't exactly walk into the locker room in the proper frame of mind. But still, as he lay there in the dark, staring at his ceiling, he wasn't about to give anyone a pass, especially those gutless referees.

Why blame himself when there were so many others to consider first? After all, that's what gamblers do.

Still, this had been a very bad day.

* * * * *   * * * * *   * * * * *

The sun was shining on Sunday morning when Danny woke up, and it was an unseasonable 50 degrees, quite rare for an early-March morning. It was a little after 9, and as he awoke his first thoughts were of Nick.

Still in bed, he called him anyway. Again, Nick answered after several rings.

"OK, go ahead. Give it to me," Nick said.

"I'm not going to do that, Nick. Man, I woke this morning a sectional champion and so did you. Maybe we didn't contribute much to it …"

"Much? How about nothing?"

"That's why it's a team game, Nick. We found a way. Have you looked outside? It's gorgeous. Let's walk downtown and go get some doughnuts."

"Deal," Nick said, and fifteen minutes later they were walking downtown, past the park and the basketball courts, past the Dairy Queen and the dentist office, past the library and into the pastry shop. They grabbed some doughnuts and juice, and took a table in the back.

"So what was going on yesterday? It seemed like you were in a bad mood when you got to the game," Danny asked. "Weren't talking to anybody, in your own little world. Then all that stuff on the court happened. Did it all go hand in hand?"

"I'll admit I wasn't in a very good mood, but those calls were horrible, man. I let it get the best of me, and I'm sorry for that. I'll apologize to everyone else tomorrow, too. It was just a bad, bad day. Sometimes I just get mad at the world and I store it all in. No parents around, my brother hardly home and always in a bad mood when he is, no girl right now to keep me happy. Sometimes it just all sucks."

"That's all it is?"

"Yeah, that's all," Nick said, lying through his teeth.

"Well, you know I'm always here if you need me. Always," Danny said. "That's what friends are for and you know I'd do anything for you. Just reach out, OK?"

Nick nodded. They finished their doughnuts and headed for home. Danny left for Candice's, Nick just stayed home.

Stayed home … and moped some more.

15

Practices had been fresh and spirited all week, and everything that Coach Will Jackson did was geared toward looking ahead, not back. Even their Monday film session was short and sweet. Jackson had great editing skills and all he showed his team of the narrow sectional championship win over White Hawk were the plays that mattered. He used film sessions as a learning tool and that's what he did this week, too.

He did fine time for some levity at the end of the 20-minute session.

"Here's 10 mistakes that we simply cannot make again," he said before hitting the clicker button.

The room burst out in laughter as Coach Jackson showed Nick slamming the ball to the floor and it coming back up and nailing the referee right on the chin. It was just a 2-second clip, but he showed it over and over about 10 times.

Everyone laughed, including Nick.

"So I think that just about covers the abusing of referees," Jackson said with a smile.

On game day, there was a brief pep rally at school in the last period of the day, then the guys retired to the locker room to get ready to take the bus ride up to Gary. Danny was the first one in the locker room, and he already saw Coach Jackson looking at some more film of Ridge Central. It caught Danny by surprise a bit, because Coach Jackson had been confident all week. He wasn't finding anything different at the last minute, was he?

"No, I just wanted to re-watch some of their defensive sequences to confirm something. I was right. They're still horrible at playing pick and rolls. We need to take advantage of that tonight."

Crossroads had already beaten Ridge Central twice this year by comfortable margins. To see them again was a real treat, considering its upset of North Hammond might have been the most shocking sectional final in the state. Danny and the boys were big favorites tonight, but still it was a rivalry game and Ridge Central was going to give them their best shot.

Out in the distance, Nick Vincent strolled into the locker room, shouting from the rooftops. He was ready to play, and that made Danny feel good.

"I've got this one. I've got this one," he kept saying, and Danny knew exactly what he meant. He knew Nick felt horrible about letting his team down the previous weekend and it wasn't about to happen again.

It didn't.

They were the first game on this Friday night, and the 7,500-seat gym at Gary Northside was full for the 6 p.m. tipoff. Nick was everywhere from the outset. Ridge Central made only 3 of 11 shots in the first quarter and Nick rebounded all eight misses. Danny was getting open and shooting well, and by the end of the quarter they had a big 23-8 lead. Danny and Nick each had 10 points, often running "Redar Park," their two-man isolation pick-and-roll play that they'd been running together since their 2-on-2 games with the bigger kids at the park. They'd run that play a thousand times, and it still worked all the time. Every nuance of the pick-and-roll seemed to lead to a basket.

Nothing ever really changed as the game progressed. The better team was also playing better and Ridge Central didn't really have a chance. They played hard, but just weren't a very good offensive team, so they couldn't mount a rally. When it was all said and done, Crossroads won 78-48 and the starters didn't even play in the fourth quarter. That was nice, considering the championship game was just 16 hours later on a Saturday afternoon. Everyone got plenty of rest. Danny finished with 25 easy points and Nick had 18 points and 16 rebounds. They were both awesome, so it was never close.

Danny and Nick sat at the end of the bench together as the clock wound down, smiling and laughing as they came one step closer to their dream. It was a stark departure from the previous game.

"I don't care what the sport, I still love kicking their ass, the cocky bastards," Nick said.

Danny put his arm around Nick's shoulders and jostled him around. "Just another step in the journey, my friend. Just another step."

* * * * *　　* * * * *　　* * * * *

As they were walking off the floor, the Gary Northside team was coming out of their locker room for their game with Burns Harbor.

"Nice game, Danny," Tyrone Wells said. He was Northside's best player and an AAU teammate of Danny's for several years where they had become good friends. "We'll see you tomorrow."

"I hope so," Danny said. "I did my part. You do yours."

The Crossroads guys sat together to watch the second game. It wasn't as bad a blowout as their game, but it wasn't really close, either. Wells, who had already committed to Northwestern, was unstoppable. He's a 6-1 point guard who is lightning quick and has a nice little pull-up jumper. Javier Hernandez was sitting right in front of Danny and Coach Jackson. Near the end of the game, Jackson whispered into his ear.

"You hold him down, and we win," he said. "It's that simple. Just force him to his left every time and we'll be there to help. Make the other four guys beat us."

Coach Jackson reiterated the same message the following morning prior to the regional final. He didn't think Gary Northside was very disciplined on defense and his team could wear them down with their precision motion offense. He knew they could get Danny open all day long. The key to the win would be keeping Tyrone Wells at bay.

Hernandez had emerged as a steadying influence at point guard, providing the missing link to what this team needed with exceptional quickness of his own. He was only a sophomore and at this stage of their careers, Wells was clearly the better player. But Javier was surrounded by better teammates, so he didn't have to do it all like Tyrone Wells had to. All he had to be was a disruption, and the rest of the guys would help out.

As it often was with a great coach like Jackson, the game played out exactly as he had hoped. On offense, they were scoring at will. Danny was getting open jump shots practically every trip down and whenever they double-teamed him, he would easily find an open cutter heading to the basket. Defensively, Javier did his job, constantly forcing Tyrone Wells to his left and into a double-team. They forced Northside to play at a frantic pace and they didn't like that in a half-court setting. They made a lot of turnovers in the first quarter and Crossroads jumped out to a 20-11 lead.

Where Northside did have an edge though was in overall speed. With every Crossroads miss, they decided to push the ball up the court quickly and play a full-court game. They knew they didn't want to get into a set-offense slugfest, so they ran the fast break and pressed full-court. Javier held his own as a ball-handler and Danny was a huge help getting the ball up the court.

Both teams were playing as if this was a life-or-death situation. Of course, it was.

By halftime, the Crossroads lead was down to four and by the end of the third quarter it was down to two. As each minute passed, the two teams kept trading baskets. For the last six minutes of the game, neither side led by more than two. Northside was fouling often in its press and Danny was demanding the ball. He was fouled five times and made all 10 free throws. It was getting frustrating to the Northside faithful that Danny wouldn't miss. His last two free throws tied the game.

Tyrone Wells drove into the lane with about 25 seconds left, beating Javier by about a half-step. But Danny closed in from the other side and Nick stepped up with a hand in the air, forcing Tyrone to arc his shot a little higher than he wanted. It bounced off the back of the rim and Nick grabbed yet another rebound. Crossroads immediately called timeout.

Coach Jackson gathered the troops and set up a final play. "If they press, set up press-break and run the double-screen for Danny. We'll take the foul if they're giving it, but if they don't foul let's get the ball pushed up court and set up the offense. We're tied and I don't want them to have another shot, so let's plan on getting Danny through a double-screen for a jumper on the sideline. Stick to the motion, and let's get a shot off with 3 or 4 seconds left."

They all understood, because they had worked on these end-game situations in practice for months. But they also knew that if things broke down, Danny could find a way to create some sort of shot. This was, after all, a confident bunch with a very confident leader.

"If they let us run it down and they're in man, keep Redar Park in mind," Danny said to Nick. "Set me a good pick and I'll turn the corner on them. But just like always, roll hard to the basket, just in case."

Northside chose not to press, fearful of another foul and Danny draining two more, so they settled into man-to-man on the other end. Perfect, Coach Jackson thought. Perfect, Danny thought. They kicked the ball out to a wing, then back to Javier. Danny crossed the court along the baseline through two picks and caught the ball on the wing, with just a single defender staring him down. He glanced at the clock – 8 seconds – and gave a quick thrust of the fist. Javier drifted to the far side of the court and Nick raced up to set a pick. Danny dribbled hard to his right but Nick's defender had fallen off on him as well and was squaring up on him. He saw a third defender, Tyrone Wells, sprinting from across the court to help out, so Danny did what he had been doing for 10 years, shuffling a little pass to Nick, who was cutting to the rim wide open. Nick caught the pass and elevated, slamming down a ferocious dunk for a 77-75 lead. The Northside guys, stunned, hesitated for a second to get the ball in and the clock wound down.

It was over, Another win, another escape. Five wins down, four to go.

Time to cut down some more nets.

Afterward, the reporters wanted to know why Danny didn't take the final shot himself. He was, after all, their top scorer and already had poured in 30 points.

"I didn't take the shot because I didn't need to," He said. "I had two guys on me and a third one coming and without even looking I knew Nick would be there if I needed him. We've been running that pick-and-roll since we were little kids and we know how to play with each other. It didn't matter to me one bit that I made the last shot, only that we made the last shot. It was a perfect ending."

* * * * *   * * * * *   * * * * *

The euphoria around the Vincent house didn't last long. Sunday turned out to be a bad day for both Nick and his brother Tony. The NCAA basketball tournament was in its first weekend and Nick had bet a few games with his brother on Thursday and Friday, and split on them. He intentionally ignored Saturday's games because he was playing a game himself and didn't want a repeat of the previous weekend.

But he bet four Sunday games … and lost them all. For the week he was down $450 and he made sure Sunday night he hit the ATM machine to pay off Tony right away.

Tony made a mistake, though, in paying too much attention to Nick's bets. The action he was taking from his 30 or so bettors wasn't as balanced as a bookmaker would like, especially on the games that Nick liked. Instead of laying off some of the bets with Joey Risone's guys, he took a chance on hoping to win some big money himself. It didn't happen. Late Sunday night, with the betting week over, he crunched all his numbers and realized he was down about $4,500. Throw in his weekly nut to Joey, and he owed Risone about $5,000.

"That's almost a month's pay for me," Tony said. "I'm getting really tired of all this."

It wasn't just this one bad day. Tony was tired of occasionally getting stiffed by people. A few guys who refused to pay – they just couldn't, they said – Tony covered them with Joey and just cut them off, because he was afraid of what Joey and his thugs might do if they knew someone wasn't paying. And it was a pain getting around for a while with his bad ankle. This was supposed to be fun and profitable, but anymore it not only wasn't fun, it wasn't profitable.

So, just like that, Tony decided to quit.

"I'm not going to do this anymore," he told Nick. "I'm going to collect and pay out everyone this week, and that's it."

"What's your fat guy going to say about that?" Nick said. "He's going to be pissed, isn't he?"

"We'll see. His kid, Joey Junior, has been itching for a little more action. Maybe I'll just suggest he can have my list of guys and I'll just walk away from it."

"What about you yourself? You still going to play some games?"

"You know what? Probably not. I'm kind of tired of it all. I don't need it. I gamble for fun and it's just not fun anymore."

Later that night, when Nick finally got ready for Monday before going to bed, he wasn't even thinking about the big semistate weekend coming up. Only one thought kept running through his mind.

"Who am I going to place my bets with?"

* * * * *   * * * * *   * * * * *

Reaching the semistate was a huge deal for any Indiana high school basketball program, and so it was for Crossroads, as well. The three towns that fed into Crossroads High School – Schererville, St. John and Dyer – were all abuzz and, of course, the local newspapers were writing all sorts of stories. Mike Carey, who was an excellent writer and probably too good to be working at a mid-sized paper like the Star-Press, did a beautiful profile on Coach Jackson on Thursday and a huge piece on Danny on Friday, ranking him among the Region's all-time "pure shooters." Danny certainly never thought of himself in that kind of historical perspective and was almost embarrassed by the story. Still, it was nice nonetheless and both his mother and Candice had quickly clipped out the article and all the pictures and charts and added it to their ever-growing scrapbooks. It was a nice sports section.

The front page of the newspaper was nice, too. Thursday had been a big day for Ben Richardson and his friends at the recovery center. In an unprecedented and long overdue move, the Indiana state legislature had finally voted to approve funding to deal with the growing compulsive gambling issue in the state. Ben and three other directors were beneficiaries of a grant that allowed them to man a 24-hour help-line and provide marketing dollars to more readily promote their treatment options around the state. Most importantly, tax dollars collected directly from casinos, race tracks and lotteries were earmarked for direct treatment of residents in need. With the proper assessments and documentation, the state was now going to contribute approximately three-quarters of the cost of a 21-day treatment program. It was a huge step, something most states had ignored for years. It meant that Ben's program, and a few others like it around the state, could now become close to being self-sustaining. It went a long way in easing Ben's financial concerns over operating the treatment center.

The article was nice and very complimentary of Ben, who ran the only facility in the state north of Indianapolis. When Danny got home after school, his mother had pointed out the article to him and he gave Ben a quick call to congratulate him. Of course, most of the conversation quickly turned to the basketball weekend.

It was all anyone could talk about.

The team bussed the hour and a half to West Lafayette early on Friday afternoon and checked in to their hotel not far from the Purdue University campus. Danny and Nick were roommates, but they weren't in their rooms long. They had a light early dinner as a team, dressed at the hotel, then took the bus over to the arena. They were the first of two games that night.

When they got to the arena, Danny was surprised to see Indiana University coach Henry Garrison in the gym. Indiana had lost in the NCAA Tournament regional semifinals the night before, and just as quickly, there he was. On to the next year. Danny was already signed, of course, but the recruiting never ends. Bishop Blaney out of South Bend, Crossroads' opponent in the Friday night semifinal game, had an uncommitted junior that Indiana was still interested in and the two young sophomore guards at Anderson were also being heavily recruited. Seasons come and go, but recruiting never stops.

Danny thought it was nice to spend some time with Coach Garrison. They hadn't seen each other since November but had chatted on the phone several times. They talked for about five minutes before Danny joined his teammates in the locker room. Garrison congratulated him on his fine season to date and wished him well for the weekend.

"One last thing," he said to Danny. "I just wanted to tell you that I'm really glad you're coming to Bloomington next year. You've really proven to everyone that you were deserving of that scholarship. You've had a great year."

"So far," Danny said. "But we've still got plenty of work to do."

"You'll do fine. Just keep playing hard and keep your guys relaxed. I'll see you after the game."

It didn't take long for Crossroads to impose its will. Javier Hernandez had a few steals and Danny wasn't missing. He was very comfortable on the Purdue floor, really liked the sightlines, and made 7-of-10 shots in the first half as they built a 38-23 lead. It was an impressive performance. Coach Jackson had them well prepared and everyone played well. Their lead never got under double-digits in the second half and they rolled to a 72-59 win. Danny finished with 29 points and eagerly watched the nightcap, happy to see Anderson win. He could tell they had improved since that November beat-down in Indianapolis, but he also was very confident they could win again.

On Saturday morning, Danny was thrilled to see that all of his teammates were still very relaxed. They were enjoying the moment, being just a game away from their first-ever trip to the state finals, but they were also very relaxed. They belonged, and they knew it. More importantly, they were playing like they knew it.

Danny was able to have a little fun with Nick, reminding him about how easily they had beaten Anderson without him. That was the weekend Nick was on his Florida State recruiting trip, falling in love with all those beautiful girls a thousand times over.

"Anything less than a 25-point win today will be all your fault," he reminded Nick.

"You know I know that. Don't worry. I've got you covered today."

And he did. Anderson was quick, but not big, and Nick scored at will early, getting single coverage in the low post. Coach Jackson wanted the ball pushed inside early, hoping to get Anderson to pack in their defense a bit and open up the 3-point line later. When they didn't, they just kept feeding the ball to Nick and he was scoring practically every trip. Nick had 10 first-quarter points and Crossroads got an early 23-11 lead. Once again, they were playing with a lead and dictating the pace and style of play in a pressure-packed tournament game. It made it so much easier to play that way.

Anderson, always looking to push the ball up the floor, made a little run midway through the third quarter, but never got closer than nine points. When Danny responded with three straight 3-pointers, the outcome was no longer in doubt. Danny finished with 37 points and they won 85-67.

For the third weekend in the row, they all climbed a ladder and cut down the nets again.

They were getting pretty good at it.

16

Danny and Candice hadn't had the chance to spend much time together during this crazy playoff run, but they were both fine with it. It helped a lot that Candice was an athlete herself and knew what the demands could be like in the middle of something important. They'd see each other at school here and there and were glad to have Mrs. Wesson's English class together. Some nights they found an hour or so to study together or share dinner at home, his or hers.

Everyone was leaving on Friday morning for the state finals, so after practice on Thursday Danny and Candice went to Applebee's for dinner, just the two of them. It was the first time they had been out in several weeks, and it was nice.

They also got to be part of the euphoria that gripped the town. When they got to the restaurant, it was crowded and there was a 20-minute wait, they were told. There were seven or eight parties waiting, but almost immediately and older woman came over and handed them her blinking buzzer.

"You can have our table right now. Go ahead, I'm sure your time is limited," the woman said. "And thank you so much for this season. It's been so much fun."

Danny gave Candice a sheepish grin and thanked the woman. "You really don't need to do this. It's OK, we can wait."

The woman would have none of it, so Danny and Candice took their seats in a booth. Just a few minutes later, two young boys – probably around 10 – came over to their table and asked Danny if they could have his autograph. That was a first.

"Sure," Danny said, again flashing a somewhat embarrassed look on his face.

Candice couldn't help but smile herself. "You're a big star now. My big star," she said.

"It's nice everyone's so excited. It's a once-in-a-lifetime kind of thing," Danny said.

"You more excited, or more nervous?" Candice asked.

"Excited, definitely," Danny said. "That's the great thing about playing for Coach Jackson. It's just all about preparation with him, just like every other game we've played. He's watched a lot of film and we have a good game plan, and he's only focused on that first game. We can't win a state championship Friday night, so all we're focused on is Lawrence Township. He has us ready and I think every-one feels the same way. We're more excited than nervous. It also helps that we've already played down there and we'll be comfortable. At least as comfortable as we can be playing an Indianapolis team in Indianapolis, but I think we'll be OK."

"It's going to be a fun weekend," Candice said. "One of those weekends we'll remember forever."

"Yeah," Danny said. "Win a couple of games and it will rank right up there – almost – with getting married or having a child. It'll be that special.

"You think about those kind of things?"

"Sure I do. The time will come for all that. There's this girl I really like," Danny said, this time with a sly little smile.

"Oh, my" Candice said, unable to avoid smiling herself.

* * * * *   * * * * *   * * * * *

Crossroads got 3,500 tickets to distribute and they were all gone the first day. Several others were actually buying tickets online in the resale market. The event was a sellout all the time now that they had gone back to a single-class tournament and tickets were hard to come by.

And when it came time for tip-off on Friday night, it seemed like half of Schererville was there. The Fieldhouse in downtown Indianapolis was filled to the brim, each of the 18,000 seats taken. It was an incredible atmosphere.

Danny couldn't help but notice how comfortable he was warming up. He wasn't nervous at all, just focused on the task at hand. He was well prepared. So were his teammates.

But they also weren't at all over-confident.

They knew they were going to have their hands full. Lawrence Township was a perennial state powerhouse. They had won five state titles in the past 20 years. They were ranked No. 1 in the state at the beginning of the season but kind of slipped off everyone's radar at mid-season when a few injuries and an always-tough Indianapolis schedule led to four losses in five weeks. But they seemed to have their house in order again in reaching the state finals.

Lawrence Township relied heavily on Bradley Daniels, a 6-foot-10 center who had been something of a child prodigy. He was 6-foot tall in the sixth grade and even his decision on which high school to attend was a huge media circus in Indianapolis. He verbally committed to North Carolina after his sophomore year at Lawrence Township, which raised some eyebrows, but his junior season was a big disappointment. He hurt a knee first and missed 10 games. He came back, played two games but then got in a fight at school and he was suspended for three games

He hurt an ankle the week before sectionals, played through it – but not very hard – and they were upset in the first game of sectionals. During that summer he tried twice to take the SATs and both times got scores that were far too low to get in to North Carolina, especially since he was barely passing most of his high school classes. It seemed odd that he de-committed in the fall and then seemed very odd when he signed with Cincinnati in November during the early signing period, with a new SAT score that was just barely high enough for acceptance. North Carolina didn't seem to be at all disappointed to lose him. He just wasn't that star everyone expected, and was trouble waiting to happen. He was out of shape and didn't care much about working hard.

But Coach Will Jackson had watched enough film to know he was still a very good high school player and he presented Crossroads with a huge challenge. Every waking hour, he was watching film and devising a game plan. Every practice all week was very detailed, very precise. And when they finally took the court on Friday night, in front of all those people, they were ready.

The key to the game, the way Coach Jackson saw it, was making Bradley Daniels uncomfortable. Daniels was tall, but he wasn't strong and didn't like getting leaned on. So the plan was for Nick to be as physical as possible, to push him around and keep him off his spots. Daniels was a very right-handed player, so he wanted him pushed to the left and he wanted him constantly double-teamed. Daniels wasn't a very good passer and Coach Jackson knew the double-teams, especially coming from all sorts of angles, would bother him.

That was the plan on defense. On offense, he wanted to run Danny through a bunch of screens early and continue to attack that way until Lawrence Township found a way to stop them.

They never did.

Danny had the crowd on its feet from the get-go. He made his first six shots, including three three-pointers, and once again proved that he was clearly the best player on the floor. With Nick frustrating Daniels on one end, Danny was frustrating him on the other. Danny scored mostly from the perimeter but he also drew two fouls on Bradley with pump fakes in the lane. Danny scored 19 points in a fast-paced first quarter as they dashed out to a 28-13 lead. Daniels picked up his third foul early in the second quarter when he tried to plow through Nick on his way to the basket and took a seat in angry fashion, having only scored two points in 10 minutes.

Lawrence Township never got within 10 points the rest of the way. Whatever they tried, Crossroads was always prepared for. When Daniels went out, they tried pressuring full-court and trapping on defense. Coach Jackson simply went to Kenny Dockery off the bench and went small and with all those ballhandlers on the floor, they handled the pressure well. Danny continued having a game for the ages. When he was all done, with about three minutes left in the game, he had 42 points on 15-of-17 shooting and a perfect 6-for-6 from the line. The final score was 91-60, as impressive a win that Coach Jackson had ever seen.

Bradley Daniels ended his high school career with more fouls than points, five to four. He was a complete non-factor.

"To stop Daniels, you need to have somebody who can be a complete pain in his butt for a whole game and that's what we've got in Nick Vincent," Jackson told the media after the game. "Trust me, no one is more of a pain in the butt than Nick. He was certainly up for the challenge, even giving away six inches. That's just the way he's wired, football or basketball. He will do whatever it takes to win. And Danny Bridges, well, that was just another incredible performance. He knows how to score and he's the big reason why we've been so successful. He's been so good every game – especially early in every game – that we've been able to set the tone as to how we want to play. These guys are all very driven right now."

They stayed to watch the second game, a 46-42 victory by Riverside, a high school across the Ohio River from Louisville on southern edge of the state, over New Castle. It was an ugly game, so when Danny and Nick got back to their hotel room Friday night, they were very confident heading into Saturday afternoon's championship game.

"We're going to do this," Nick said. "Just like we promised each other."

* * * *   * * * *   * * * *

Promises made, promises kept.

Thousands of hours of practice, in the gym or the driveway or at the park, culminated in a state championship for Nick and Danny on that brisk Saturday afternoon in Indianapolis.

But it wasn't easy.

Riverside gave them everything they wanted, and more. They were a good team, undefeated but against a marginal schedule. They had two good players, Neil Sewell and Noah Marbury, Division I kids going to Western Kentucky and Evansville. Sewell was a 6-7 kid who could find ways to score inside, and Marbury was a 6-3 guard, very quick with a nice shot and a great defender.

Much like Coach Jackson had done the day before, Riverside coach Tim Nichols had challenged Marbury to shut down – or, at least, slow down – Danny Bridges. He knew the only way to win was to contain Danny, who had played only one bad game in this tournament, the near-debacle with Crown Point in the sectional final. He wanted someone else to beat them, so his game plan called for

Marbury to crawl inside Danny's uniform, whether he had the ball or not. He told Marbury to not concern himself with the other players on the floor, to simply deny Danny the basketball and to know that if Danny got the ball, that a double-team – or a triple-team – was coming immediately.

Their plan of attack led to a game that was not aesthetically pleasing in any way. Coach Jackson made sure his guys stayed patient, methodically working their offense in an attempt to get a good shot on each possession. It wasn't easy. Danny had a hard time shaking Marbury, who did a great job of sliding through screens and was getting plenty of help from his teammates. Crossroads, which had started quickly in practically every game during its tournament run, trailed by two at the end of the first quarter, scoring only eight points. Danny had just four, on 2-of-5 shooting. At the half, the game was tied but scoring was still hard to come by. It was just 22-all at the break. It was nothing like the fast-paced beat-down the 18,000 fans had seen the night before.

Halftime was as chaotic as Danny had ever seen, but it wasn't unexpected considering the stakes. Coach Jackson immediately went to the whiteboard, wanting to make some changes. He hurried through a few defensive changes and wanted to go ahead and use their deadly diamond-and-one press early in the third quarter, just to change up the pace.

But it was on the offensive end that he chose to get more daring. He chose to give Danny Bridges, the best player in the tournament, a new job.

Decoy.

He patiently worked through four or plays from their playbook on the whiteboard, but with a few subtle changes. Coach Jackson had noticed that when Danny crossed the floor through the screens that Marbury and at least one other player were going with him. So he wanted Danny to stay very wide and deep outside the three-point line. He wanted Javier Hernandez to attack with the dribble, then look for Nick or others in two-on-one or three-on-two situations.

Of course, it worked to perfection. Every time Danny crossed the floor, a couple of defenders went with him and Hernandez immediately attacked. They got some easy shots early and got a few steals from their press. Danny took only two shots in the quarter, both off transition plays from the press, but Coach Jackson's change-ups worked perfectly. When the fourth quarter started, they had pulled ahead by six, 40-34.

Riverside had one last trick up its sleeve. When the fourth quarter started, they went to a box-and-one defense, with four guys packed in the lane tightly in a two-two zone and the fifth guy, Marbury, shadowing Danny wherever he went. Crossroads settled for jump shots, and they were missing. With just four minutes left, the game was tied again.

Danny made a couple of tough shots in the lane over two defenders and hit a three-pointer while practically falling out of bounds, doing anything he could to keep his team in the game. But Riverside wasn't going anywhere. They hit a three-pointer of their own with 40 seconds left to tie the game and Coach Jackson called timeout.

His mind was racing. He'd seen three different defensive concepts from Riverside during the course of the game and he had no idea how they would play the last possession. But if he had to guess, he was figuring they'd go back to denying Danny the basketball.

He was right.

Danny brought the ball upcourt, but as soon as crossed midcourt he was immediately double-teamed and he passed off with about 25 seconds left. Perfect, Jackson thought, just as he had expected and just as he had instructed during the timeout. He ran Danny to the right side of the court then had him cross the lane through a pick. But Nick sent a quick second pick and Danny popped out free for a split-second back on the right side and caught the ball from Hernandez.

He didn't hesitate. As soon as the double-team approached, he attacked the basket and Nick sent a vicious pick on Marbury. With the clock ticking down, Danny drove hard at the basket with two guys still on him. With just three seconds left, he slammed on the brakes and went airborne. The hushed crowd expected a final shot, a 6-footer from just outside the lane. Four arms went up with him and 18,000 fans held their breath.

And then it happened.

Just as they had always dreamed about.

At the top of his jump, Danny got exactly what he wanted, a wide-open Nick Vincent cutting the basket after his pick. Two guys were on Danny and Marbury, after the pick, was rushing at him too. No one went with Nick. Danny hit him with a perfect pass, just as he had done a thousand times, and Nick laid it in for the lead a second ahead of the buzzer.

Crossroads had won, 61-59.

Danny jumped into Nick's arms and they fell to the floor together. Their teammates rushed into the pile too and their fans stormed onto the floor. It was pure mayhem, but all good. The celebration went on for several minutes and there wasn't a dry eye in the place. Once calm was restored, the players climbed the ladder one by one again, and snipped off a strand of the net. Nick and Danny were the only two players left to go up, but Coach Jackson stopped them and went up the ladder himself to get his piece.

Then he handed Nick a second pair of scissors and told them to go up together to get the last of the net. They did. Nick snipped off two strands for himself and Danny did the same, finally cutting down the last strand and pulling the net down over his head.

They got their state championship trophy and Danny got his MVP trophy as the cameras snapped away. Nick never left Danny's side. They posed arm in arm over and over, refusing to let go of their hardware, or each other.

For as often as they had dreamed of this moment, both of them kept thinking the same thing: This is even better than we had ever imagined.

* * * * *　　* * * * *　　* * * * *

In the half-hour after the ceremony, Danny figured he'd hugged half of Schererville on the Fieldhouse floor. The best of the hugs were saved for Candice and his mother, who, try as they might, just couldn't stop crying. The two-hour bus ride home seemed like 10 minutes and when they got back to Schererville, they all immediately headed off to Angelo's for one last postgame pizza celebration, trophies in tow. With hundreds of friends around, they celebrated well into the night, camera phones getting a hefty workout.

Ah, state champs.

It was well past midnight when they all finally left the restaurant. Danny said goodbye to Candice and rode home with Nick, who still couldn't stop smiling. When he pulled into Danny's driveway, he reached over and grabbed Danny once more. They slapped backs several times and Nick looked into Danny's eyes.

"This is the best day of my life," he told Danny. "The best."

Danny agreed with him and opened his passenger-side door. Nick looked at him, tapped his heart twice and pointed and Danny. "I love you, man. I'm really glad we could do this together."

"Wouldn't have it any other way," Danny said.

"OK, I'll see you at nine o'clock tomorrow morning," Nick said. Danny looked at him, perplexed. "I have something to do in the morning and I need your help. I'll pick you up at nine."

Danny shook his head – what's he up to, he wondered – and popped into the house. His mother was still awake, as always, and he hugged and kissed her again. They walked over to the mantel above the fireplace and put his MVP trophy in the center and they both hugged again. Danny tied his strand of net around the trophy and kissed his mother good night.

The perfect ending to a perfect day.

TOM BREW

17

What's it like to wake up a state champion? Well, it *smells* really good.

Danny had set his alarm for 8 a.m., just to be safe, and he was glad he did when it went off and rousted him from a sound sleep. He was normally an early riser, but not today. He was exhausted and had slept like a baby. There would be no early-morning run. He had certainly earned the day off.

The first thing he noticed after that alarm was the smell of fresh-baked bread coming from the kitchen. Before Danny's feet had even hit the floor, he smiled and said one thing to himself, over and over.

"I have the best mom in the world."

Danny showered quickly and threw on some jeans and a sweatshirt. And when he walked out to the kitchen, his mother had a sly smile on her face. She knew her nice surprise – four still-warm loaves of bread – would be a big hit.

"Well, you said Nick was coming by in the morning and I figured you guys would like some bread," she said, unaffected by the fact that she had to wake up before 5 a.m. just to have it ready in time.

Next to the bread was a big stack of papers. Mary already had been out to the store and couldn't help but buy ten newspapers. Danny quickly grabbed the Star-Press sports section and smiled. The two huge words – STATE CHAMPS! – jumped off the page. So did the picture of him and Nick, which ran the entire width of the page. It was a picture of them right after the award ceremony, with trophies in hand, the net still around Danny's neck and huge smiles stretching across their faces.

Danny loved it. Loved it mostly because it was him and Nick.

A few minutes before nine, Nick called to let Danny know he was on his way and to be ready to go.

"You need to come in, because my Mom has something for you."

"Bread?"

"Yep."

"Awesome. Warm me up some hot chocolate and get the toaster ready. Be there in about two minutes."

When Nick popped in the back door, Mary gave him a big hug and they went right to the kitchen. She cut slices and made toast as fast as she could while Nick and Danny buttered it up and dunked it in their hot chocolate. They went through a loaf in about 15 minutes, laughing and talking and looking over the sports section. It was the perfect start to their day. Mary enjoyed every minute of it, too, occasionally messing with Nick's hair or patting his shoulders. Her guys.

"OK, now we've got to go. I need you for about a half-hour," Nick said.

"Where we going?"

"You'll see." Nick put his coat back on and thanked Mary as she handed him two more loaves of bread to take with him.

"Hey, wait a minute!" Danny said with a grin. "How come he gets two?"

Mary just smiled. She knew. So did Danny. She had cared for these two since they were little boys. She could still remember when they just stood on her kitchen chairs and ate bread from their little hands.

And now she knew. She had no idea when – or if – she would make bread for the two of them together again.

Nick gave her an extra-long hug before they headed off. Nick asked if he could take one of the sports sections and Mary, of course, said to go ahead. When they got in Nick's truck, they took off quickly.

He drove a few miles down the road and turned into the cemetery, neither of them talking. Nick had nothing to say and Danny, staring over at his friend, wasn't sure what to say. Nick stopped his truck and pulled a bag out from under his seat. From the bag, he pulled out an old tin box. On the lid was a rendering of a mother pushing her little boy on a swing.

"My mom used to sew all the time and she kept her buttons in this tin. But when she was sick at the end, she gave it me and put some of her favorite pictures in it," Nick said to Danny, softly and slowly. "She said the picture on the lid always reminded her of me. I thought today it would be a nice time to give it back."

They got out of the truck and walked about 50 feet directly to Clara Vincent's grave. Danny stayed quiet, somewhat surprised at how Nick walked straight to the grave as if he'd done it a thousand times. Danny couldn't remember even one time where Nick had mentioned visiting his parents' gravesite. Nick got down on one knee and dug a hole with a gardener's tool, chipping away at the hard ground right next to the tombstone. He opened the tin one last time and pulled out about a half-dozen articles, things Nick had clipped from the newspaper during the football and basketball seasons. He tore off the picture of Nick and Danny from the morning's paper and then pulled something out of his coat pocket.

It was the second strand of net that Nick had cut down the night before.

Nick put the articles and the strand of net into a plastic bag and sealed it tight. He closed the lid, put it in the ground and covered it up with dirt. He tapped the dirt back in place, stood up and tapped the top of the headstone a few times.

"I come here a lot, but always by myself," Nick said to Danny, smearing some dirt across his face as he wiped away a tear. "Sometimes in the middle of the night when I've got a million things on my mind and I can't sleep, I'll just sit over there in my truck for hours. Fallen asleep here a few times."

Danny just nodded his head. He was truly at a loss for words.

"But I wanted you to come with me today. I wanted you to share this with me," he said. "In a few months, we'll be going our separate ways, on to other things. But what we did last night, we've talked about for years. Talked about it among ourselves, talked about it with your mom, talked about doing great things with my mom when we were only so big. And we did it. I just wanted you to be with me here as this chapter kind of ends."

Danny cupped his hand around the back of Nick's neck and smiled.

"Nick, it never ends, man," Danny said. "We'll be best friends forever. It won't matter that we'll be in different places in a few months. I'll still always be there for you. You'll be doing your thing and I'll be doing mine and that's all going to great. But we're still going to be able to share our successes together. That'll never change."

"Yeah, it will," Nick said. "It'll have to. It won't be like this anymore. This part is over."

"But what comes next it going to be great too. I don't know about you, but I can't wait for the next step. Can't wait to get to Indiana myself, and I can't wait to watch you play at Michigan. And we'll always have what we did last night. We'll have it forever."

"I hope so," Nick said. "It's just going to be so weird in a few months. I'm going to be all alone up there."

"The hell you are," Danny said. "You're going to make a hundred new football friends and probably two hundred new girlfriends. You'll have a blast."

"Maybe so," Nick said as they walked back to his truck. "But it'll never be the same as this. Never."

*****   *****   *****

Since Nick and Danny were both committed to head off to summer school in June, they only had a few months to go in Schererville.

And they flew right by.

About two weeks later, Danny was invited to Florida for a long weekend with Candice and her parents. They had a great time, other than his usual embarrassment on the golf course. Even Candice's mother beat him, but it was all good. They did a lot together, the four of them, but Danny and Candice also found some time to be alone. They took a nice long walk along Clearwater Beach at sunset one night, and it was beautiful. They were very happy together.

When they got back, there was one banquet after another and lots of week-end road trips for practice with the Indiana All-Star team. Danny was honored to be selected – he was Crossroads' first player to ever make the team – but the practices and exhibitions leading up to the June series with the Kentucky All-Stars took up lots of time.

Danny had always been an excellent student, but even he had to admit that focusing on his school work during this spring semester had been a challenge, first because of the pressures of the basketball season and now because the end was so close. Fighting off senioritis wasn't easy.

Danny did enough to get by and got all his A's and B's, but one project was looming over his head that he was having a hard time tackling. His final paper for Mrs. Wesson's English class was due, but he just didn't have the energy to start it, let alone finish it. The assignment seemed simple enough – 1,500 words on "Your Philosphy of Life" – but nothing really came to mind. Danny wasn't grasping any kind of philosophy. To him, he was way too young to approach any topic with that kind of perspective. It didn't help that Candice wrote hers in one weekend when Danny was off with the All-Star team. He thought about it and thought about it, but he had nothing.

So on the last Monday of the school year, Danny went to Mrs. Wesson with a question. "What happens to my grade if I don't do the final paper?"

"Well, you have an A going already, but you can't not do it, Danny," Mrs. Wesson said, this tiny old lady lecturing her big, tall student. "It's important for one, and for two, I was really looking forward to reading your paper. You're such a good writer. And with all the good things that go on in your life, I'm sure you would have plenty to write about."

"But I have moments, I don't have philosophies. I'm not a philosopher. I just try to be a good kid every day. And right now I've just got so much going on I don't think I have time to finish it. And frankly, I just don't have the motivation. And if I decide to just not do it, then I could be done and I could relax a little bit and school would be over. I seem to want to do that a lot more."

"Well, Danny, you are one of my all-time favorite students but I have to say this really disappoints me. The paper is due on Thursday and I hope you write it. And least think about it."

Danny said he would, but the next two nights he had an awards banquet in Hammond and a photo shoot and practice for the All-Star team in Indianapolis. When he got to school on Thursday, all he had for Mrs. Wesson was a nice thank-you card from Hallmark. His note was short and sweet.

"Mrs. Wesson, thanks for the nice words and I want you to know you are my all-time favorite teacher. But I just can't write that paper. Maybe there will come a time when I can write about my philosophy of life, but that time isn't right now. I just don't have a philosophy of life right now. I'm really sorry. Signed, Danny Bridges."

Later in the day, she read the card over and over. She wrote his final grade in her grade book – a B-minus – and closed it for the day, saving the other papers to be read some other time. She appreciated the card, but was really hoping for a paper instead.

She couldn't help but hide her disappointment.

* * * * *   * * * * *   * * * * *

Danny and Candice had a great time at prom. Candice, of course, was as beautiful as ever in a cranberry-colored dress and they had a great time together in a festive cap to what had been a wonderful senior year. It was nice, too, that Nick was there. He sat down with Abby Parsons a few weeks earlier and asked her to prom. Nick didn't care about all the dancing and extravagance, but he also didn't want to think he was going to miss out on anything that might be fun, especially with all his friends around.

Plus, he had still felt bad about breaking up with Abby back in the fall. He knew she wasn't long-term girlfriend material, but they also had been friends for a long time and he didn't want to leave town with her angry at him. So they talked, about just being friends, but also about having fun together when the opportunity arose. Prom was perfect, he thought, and Abby gladly said yes. They partied all night with the gang, and had fun. Abby smiled from ear to ear in all the pictures of her and Nick. If only for just one night, it was everything she had dreamed about. For Nick, living in the moment, it was just a fun night. They were both equally happy.

Nick and Danny had their graduation party together. Mary Bridges wouldn't have it any other way and Tony Vincent didn't mind acquiescing one bit. The Vincents didn't have much family around and the same kids would show up to two different parties anyway, so having one seemed wise. Mary did it up right and the kids had a great time. Candice gave Danny a professional-looking scrapbook as a gift that included every article written through the year, with the picture of the two of them from football season on the cover and a wonderful hand-written letter from Candice on the back inside cover. It was spectacular. At the end of the night, Candice gave a second copy to Mary as a gift – with its own handwritten note inside on the back cover. Mary, of course, cried and cried.

And just two weeks later, Danny and Nick were gone.

After the All-Star games in Louisville and Indianapolis – both Indiana wins – Danny headed off to Bloomington for summer school and his immediate indoctrination to college basketball. For the summer, he lived in a four-bedroom apartment across from Assembly Hall, with Michael Trickett as his roommate and mentor. They worked out early every morning, went to class for a few hours after that and played basketball as a team – minus the coaches – for several hours every afternoon. Trickett was a huge help in getting Danny settled. He'd pop back home every few weekends to see Candice and they had a nice summer together, even though it took some getting used to being apart most of the time. They were making it work, which came as no surprise to either one of them. That was the plan.

Nick left for Michigan a few days later. One of the other recruits, Dale Gerard, had invited Nick and a few other freshmen to his family's lakefront cottage for a weekend of fun before heading off to school. The lake was just south of Paw Paw, where Nick and Tony had stayed at the casino earlier in the year and had so much fun. They opted to have a little brother-bonding one more time and went up Friday morning to play cards and have a few laughs. Nick won $300 and he and Tony splurged with a huge steak dinner at the swanky restaurant in the Two Paws casino. The following morning, Tony headed back home and Nick met Dale and some of his high school friends at the cottage. They rode Jet-skis, did some tubing and had a great time. Dale and Nick, who had first met on Nick's recruiting trip to Michigan, became fast friends. On Sunday, they headed east to Ann Arbor and were glad to see they were roommates for the summer.

They were all college kids now.

* * * * *   * * * * *   * * * * *

Danny fell in love with Bloomington immediately. The rolling hills in and around campus were nice for his morning runs and he adapted quickly to his classes. He was also thrilled to have Michael Trickett to lean on. He had gotten to know him a little during his recruiting and Coach Jackson always spoke highly of him. Trickett, who was about to be a fifth-year senior, had already seen it all on the collegiate level and was more than happy to help Danny. Their workouts were interesting, only because Trickett was 50 pounds bigger than Danny and could lift much more weight. He loved being able to tease Danny about that, all in good fun, and Danny took it all in stride. Danny was just glad he had worked out so much a year earlier, or he would have never been able to keep up. But throughout every workout, Trickett made the point of how physical college basketball was, especially in Big Ten games, and how Danny needed to focus on getting stronger every day.

He noticed that when they played. The older guys were great about helping Danny and his other freshmen with learning the offense and with learning some tricks on the defensive end. But when they scrimmaged, they scrimmaged hard. Really went after it, and no one backed down. Danny would go back to the apartment exhausted every night, but he loved every minute of it.

He also felt very good in knowing that his game translated pretty well. Coach Garrison was right the day he offered him a scholarship; he did need to work on his defense. But he loved running their motion offense, which was very similar to what he had run in high school, and he spent most of his summer hitting lots of open jump shots off of screens. The coaches, who taped the scrimmages and watched them privately later, were very pleased with Danny.

They knew they had gotten a steal.

* * * * *   * * * * *   * * * * *

Nick was fitting in immediately in Ann Arbor as well, because a poker game broke out in the dorm his first night there. The stakes were very, very small, but it was a nice way for all the newcomers to bond. These other freshman might be nice guys, Nick thought, but they all sucked at cards. He won a few bucks and had lots of laughs. Dale Gerard won some money too and they talked well into the night about poker.

Workouts were fun, too. The strength and conditioning coaches were amazed that Nick had virtually no weight room training considering how strong he was. They were careful with him in setting up his routines because they didn't want to risk injury, but then they were also shocked at how easy everything came to him. During the course of the summer Nick added about 10 pounds, all muscle, and was fast as ever on the field. He could out-run all their linebackers during sprints, and even some of the defensive backs. His coaches were drooling. They couldn't wait to get him into pads in August.

* * * * *   * * * * *   * * * * *

About halfway through Nick's summer in Ann Arbor, he had a little problem. Since he wasn't placing bets through his brother anymore, most of his gambling on sports was done online, an offshore website based somewhere in Central America. He had sent them $300 by Western Union to some bizarre name in Honduras about six months earlier and reloaded his account one other time for another couple of hundred just after he got to Michigan.

But Nick did well during the NBA Finals and was on a little bit of a hot streak during baseball season, riding a handful of pitchers that he felt good about night after night. He worked his account up to about $1200 and figured he'd withdraw some of it since his bank account was dwindling a bit. But he was shocked, pissed really, when he tried to log on one day and the website was blocked. Federal authorities had shut it down as an illegal gambling operation and Nick's blood started to boil.

He did a quick Google search on the company and sure enough a federal task force found the owners and the site and with some cooperation from a few foreign governments they arrested the directors when they landed in Miami for a business trip, The government shut down the site for good and seized millions of dollars of their U.S. assets. It was illegal for U.S. citizens to gamble on these overseas websites, so it wasn't like Nick had any recourse. Just like that, his money was gone. And with being away at school instead of being home and working for his brother all summer, his bank account was getting low.

Worst of all, he needed to find a place to lay down his sports bets. He didn't like not having someone, or some thing, just a phone call or click away.

This could be a problem, he thought.

* * * * *   * * * * *   * * * * *

Summer school ended for Nick and Danny and both of them had a week free in Schererville before having to head back to school for the fall semester. They looked forward to spending some time together and had a blast. They caught a Cubs game one day, plowed through some pizza one night at Angelo's and had plenty of laughs. They shared a lot of stories about their summer workouts and their teammates and both were genuinely happy with their decisions and their upcoming seasons.

"So it's all good there, then?" Danny asked him one night when they were sitting out back on the porch, enjoying a calm summer night.

"Yeah, it's good. Made a few good friends, the coaches don't seem to act like pricks too often, and everybody's into working out pretty hard. Just about all of the freshmen were there all summer, and it's a pretty good class. Lots of diversity, that's for sure. We should be pretty good and they keep telling me I'll be starting. I plan on that."

Danny was thrilled to listen to Nick go on and on. He always worried about Nick's mental state and he was glad to see he was settling in so well. He seemed genuinely happy, and that was good enough for Danny.

The night before Nick had to go back to Ann Arbor, he was sitting at the house waiting for his brother Tony to get home from work. They were planning on heading out for one last dinner, so Nick was just biding his time.

Then the phone rang. A huffy voice on the other said "Hey, Tony,"

"No, this is his brother Nick. Tony's not home. Can I take a message?"

"Hey football star, this is Joey Risone. You met me over at my bar one time. How ya doing?"

"Oh yeah, I remember you. I'm fine."

"Hey, tell Tony to call my kid, Joey Junior. He's got a question about one of the guys in Crown Point who's been betting some big dollars lately. Joey's number is 555-8419, OK?"

"Sure, I'll let him know. He'll be home in about an hour."

Nick hung up and wrote down the number and a little note for Tony and then jumped in the shower. Before he did, he grabbed his cell phone and went to the address book.

He typed away.

Joey Junior. 555-8419.

Just in case.

TOM BREW

18

Recruiters will say anything to get a player, and everyone did that with Nick last spring. The Michigan coaches were no different. They had told Nick he'd be the first true freshman to start at middle linebacker in 30 years and they told him he'd be the guy to get them over the hump in their quest to win a Big Ten title, and maybe more.

But Nick did know better. He knew nothing was going to be handed to him, so he worked his tail off through preseason workouts and when they finally put the pads on he eliminated any and all doubt. He was fast, hit like a tank and was smart enough to pick up their intricate defense and learn all the calls. It was a no-brainer for the coaches when Michigan hosted Bowling Green in the opener. It was freshman Nick Vincent starting at middle linebacker and running out of the tunnel in front of 108,000 fans on a beautifully warm Saturday afternoon in September.

Nick didn't disappoint. He had 11 tackles in the opener, an easy victory, and did a great job of calling the plays in the huddle and being a leader. They did lose one non-conference game – a 17-13 disaster at UCLA when they gave up a long pass for a touchdown and a long punt return for another. Even in defeat, Nick played well. They crushed Notre Dame to avenge last year's loss, which Nick dearly loved, and they cruised through the Big Ten schedule as well, losing only to Wisconsin early when the offense, still breaking in a new quarterback and a young offensive line, managed only six points in a 16-6 loss. Other than that, Michigan's defense kept them in every game and even though he was only a freshman, he was clearly the best player on that side of the ball. Nick was loving his Saturdays in Ann Arbor.

He was also loving his Wednesdays.

His roommate Dale Gerard was being redshirted during his freshman year, which meant he could practice every day but not play on Saturdays. A night in the middle of the week turned into poker night and Dale was in charge of putting it all together. He'd met quite a few other freshman in the dorm who liked to play, and most of them weren't very good. Bruce Lawton, a friend of Dale's from his hometown who was a senior at Michigan, rented a house with a bunch of guys just down the street from their dorm, so Dale recruited the players and they had a game every Wednesday night, twenty players down in the basement on two tables, throwing in fifty-five dollars each, five guys getting paid with the winner making $400.00 and the house keeping five bucks a guy.

Bruce, Dale and Nick worked out a little deal among themselves. They agreed to split the five dollars from each player and split whatever they earned in prize money. Their goal was to knock out all the other players and make as much money as they could themselves. Most Wednesday nights, it worked. By the middle of November, Nick was up almost a thousand dollars. Considering where his bank account stood, the extra money came in handy.

Ah, college.

* * * * *   * * * * *   * * * * *

Life was pretty darn good in Bloomington, as well. Danny was adapting quickly to college life, excelling in his classes and enjoying every minute of his college basketball experience. All freshman athletes had to live in a dorm their first year, and it worked out well enough for Danny. The dorm was right across the street from the practice facility, and he spent most of his time there, either working out or studying, and probably spent more time hanging out at Michael Trickett's apartment than he did in his dorm room.

He and Candice talked for a half hour or so practically every night. Danny got away to Northwestern for a few weekends in September and early October, and Candice came to Bloomington later in October for Midnight Madness, Indiana's first practice that was open to the public and had become more of a show than anything. They had a dunk contest and a 3-point shooting contest and it was Danny's first night of feeling the love from the IU fans after he made 14 shots in a row and won the contest. Danny proudly introduced Candice around and they had a nice weekend together.

Candice was back four weeks later, along with Mary Bridges, for Danny's first college game against Ball State. About six minutes into the game, Danny popped off the bench and made his first appearance in an Indiana uniform. On their second possession, Michael Trickett caught the ball and wheeled into the lane but was covered. He spotted an open Danny Bridges in the corner and rifled a pass to him. Danny caught it in stride, squared up and hit a jump shot from 17 feet for his first college points. The sellout crowd roared with applause.

A few possessions later, Danny drove into the lane and pulled up for a shot just in front of the free throw lane. It hung on the rim for a second but fell in.

This was fun, he thought.

He played for about six minutes, and the game was all a blur. After a rest, he came back in with about two minutes left in the half. He hit a three-pointer, then found the ball in his hand as time was about to expire and nailed another one from about 25 feet. The crowd rose in unison to cheer and everyone in the student section was high-fiving each other left and right.

And then they chanted.

"Dan-ny Brid-ges, Dan-ny Brid-ges," they yelled as they clapped in unison. Mary and Candice just looked at each other and smiled.

Danny made two more baskets in the second half, finishing with 14 points in his first college game, an easy win. He scored 12 a week later in another romp, and the Hoosiers were 2-0 as they prepared to head off to Hawaii for a holiday tournament over Thanksgiving break.

All was well.

* * * * *   * * * * *   * * * * *

All **was well** with Nick, as well. After two early losses, the Wolverines were on a roll, winning Saturday after Saturday. Nick was happy, healthy and getting rave reviews from the press and opposing coaches alike. He was clearly the best freshman in the Big Ten and even as a freshman was a candidate for Defensive Player of the Year.

He was loving college life and handling the stresses of it all pretty well. All the film work and game preparation was daunting at times, but it was all good.

And his Wednesday night poker games were great for blowing off steam. One night in October he had fun knocking out a smart-ass rich-kid freshman from Long Island. Nick had gone all-in with kings and James Walton, an arrogant little punk who was always talking about how great he was, called him with a pair of aces. Nick hit a third king on the turn to send the kid home, and he whined like a baby. A week later, just a spot away from the money, Walton went all in with ace-king and Nick, who was the chip leader, called him just for the hell of it with a pair of twos. They held up and Nick had him again. He certainly had the kid's number.

Walton knocked his chair over in anger and then started going on a rant about how bad a player Nick was. He went on and on for a few minutes on how he hated getting beat by bad hands all the time in this basement. Nick just shook his head. They all laughed about it after Walton was gone. The kid was a real whiner.

A couple of weeks later, Nick was late getting back to his dorm room on a Wednesday night and was hurrying upstairs to grab a sweatshirt before heading over to the house for the tournament. Dale Gerard was waiting for him and as they walked through the dorm lobby, James Walton caught up with them.

"You guys going over now?" Walton said.

"Yep, starting in a few minutes."

'Cool," he said. "I'll go with you guys."

Gerard stopped walking.

"Sorry, man, but we've already got 20. There's no room for you tonight. You can't play."

"Oh, that's such bullshit. You take my money for a couple of weeks and now you won't let me win it back? That's wrong."

"Hey, there's lots of guys who want to play and it's a small room. Sorry, but that's the way it goes."

Walton stormed off, flipping both of them the bird. They laughed, and walked down the road.

* * * * *   * * * * *   * * * * *

Nick had just a couple of morning classes on Thursday, so he called a guy named Kenny Phillips and arranged to meet him for lunch. Phillips was 30 years old, a guy who had a cup of coffee as a college football player at nearby Eastern Michigan University but was too small to make it. He had become a drinking buddy of Terrance Leach, a used-car dealer who hung around the Michigan football players quite a bit. He loved to gamble and was a very small-time bookmaker. After Nick's disaster with the online site and the $1,200 that went down the drain, he was glad to hear Kenny Phillips would take his bets.

Life was grand. Football Saturdays were perfect, Wednesday night poker games were great and now he had Kenny Phillips. He could make a bet whenever he wanted to.

What else did he really need?

19

Danny's alarm went off a few minutes before 7 a.m., Hawaiian time, and he popped out of bed and pulled open the drapes. The early-morning sunshine glistening off the Pacific Ocean was too much for his roommate on the road, Michael Trickett, who covered his head with a pillow.

"Don't give me that," Danny said. "You told me you wanted to watch this game too. So quit complaining and get up. It starts in a few minutes. It's already noon back east."

Danny was glad they had the morning free after another easy win the night before in the first round of the Honolulu Invitational. Indiana was 3-0 now after a 17-point victory over Oregon State, and Danny hit double figures for the third straight game, scoring 13 points in 23 minutes. It was their first game away from Assembly Hall and they had played well, advancing to the semifinals of the country's most prestigious holiday tournament, where No. 3-ranked UCLA awaited them. But that was later in the night.

Now it was time for football; Michigan at Ohio State, college football's best rivalry. Danny couldn't wait to watch.

And Nick Vincent couldn't wait to play.

This was one of the reasons Nick had decided to go to Michigan. It was the most important, and most watched, regular-season college game in the country. It was that way every year. Millions of fans in the two states – and throughout the Midwest and beyond – lived and died for this day. There was always so much at stake beyond bragging rights, although that was usually enough. The Big Ten title was often on the line, with national title aspirations in the future as well.

This year, for the first time, there was even more at risk.

At long last, the NCAA had finally gotten control of college football and instituted a playoff system to determine the national champion on the field. For decade upon decade, conflicting interests had conspired to keep a playoff out of major college football, which never made sense. The bowl-game lobby was very strong, as was the coaching fraternity, which thought it was good for job security when 35 coaches could win a meaningless bowl game at the end of the year instead of getting run out of a playoff where only one team could win its last game.

But, finally, common sense had prevailed. The NCAA adopted a 12-team playoff, but still catered to the big conferences, which had controlled how things were done before this. In the new system, the conference champions from the five major conferences – the Big Ten, Big 12, ACC, SEC and Pac-12 – automatically earned a playoff spot and a guarantee to be seeded in the top eight. It meant a lot to be a top-four seed, because you earned a first-round bye then hosted a second-round game on your campus. Seeds five through eight hosted the first-round games, which meant every conference champion was guaranteed an extra home game … and a big piece of the millions of dollars in revenue. The other seven spots and all the seedings were chosen by an NCAA selection committee.

Ohio State versus Michigan had huge ramifications. The Buckeyes entered the game with a 10-1 record, their only loss coming against Florida State way back in September. They were 7-0 in the Big Ten. Michigan was a game behind in the conference standings, having lost to Wisconsin in October, but a win at Ohio State would force a tie and give them the tie-breaker with the head-to-head victory. The Wolverines were 9-2 overall, having lost at UCLA early before the Wisconsin upset.

Both teams were playing well and on long winning streaks on this Saturday after Thanksgiving, the last day of the regular season. Ohio State was ranked No. 2 in the country and Michigan was seventh. The winner would certainly finish in the top four in the rankings, and the bye and second-round home game was a worthy prize.

The sun was shining in Columbus, Ohio, as well, and the temperatures were unseasonably warm for late November, hovering right around 45 degrees. It was a perfect day for football.

Nick was psyched.

He had watched enough film all week to know that Ohio State was talented and deserved to be a slight favorite. They were at home, had a more experienced roster and had a senior quarterback who had been through plenty of big games already.

But he also knew they were beatable.

The game started well for the Wolverines. They marched down the field on their first possession and settled for a field goal to take a 3-0 lead. Ohio State went three-and-out, with Nick making two tackles on running plays for no gain from his middle linebacker position. Michigan again moved the ball well on its second possession, going 71 yards in 12 plays before scoring on a 1-yard run to take a 10-0 lead late in the first period.

The silence was deafening in The Horseshoe.

But the pro-Ohio State crowd of nearly 100,000 got back on its feet early in the second quarter when their offense finally got going. They put together three first downs in the row and made it into Michigan territory for the first time.

On a third-and-five from the Michigan 37, the fans rose in unison prior to the big play. Nick had done enough film work to recognize what might be going on when the Ohio State tight end went in motion across the formation. He slid a few steps to the left, and dashed in his direction on the snap. The pass came quickly and just as the ball reached the tight end's hands, Nick's helmet ripped across his jaw and his right shoulder knocked the ball loose with a hit so hard the receiver went flying, his feet sailing up in the air like a Road Runner cartoon. The ball dropped harmlessly and Nick's momentum left him straddling the grounded tight end. The taunting wasn't intentional, but satisfying all the same. What became intentional, however, was that Nick continued to hover over his opponent for several seconds, simply glaring at him with his hands on his hips and a smile on his face. A few Ohio State linemen finally shoved him away and words were exchanged before Nick and his teammates jogged over to their sideline, a job well done.

The vicious hit made for perfect TV. They showed the replay several times, including once with just the crashing noise from the hit being caught on the sideline microphones. There were high-fives all across the state of Michigan, and even in Hawaii between Danny and Michael Trickett.

"Your boy really blasted that dude," Trickett said.

"Yeah, he can bring it," Danny said.

"He ever hit you like that?"

"No, I was always very glad to be on *his* team."

With a few minutes left in the half, Ohio State got the ball back still trailing 10-0. On second-and-short, the same tight end came across the formation again in motion. Nick was reading run all the way, and that's what he got, a quick pitch to the tailback for a sweep.

Nick, taking advantage of his excellent speed, ran to the ball quickly. The tight end curled around the Michigan defensive end and looked to meet up with Nick along with his pulling guard. The guard blocked Nick high, but the tight end drove down low and crashed violently right into Nick's left knee, leading the way with the crown of his helmet. It was clearly illegal and intentionally vicious. There was no question he was trying to injure Nick, retribution for the big – but totally legal – hit that Nick had leveled on him earlier.

The hit was direct and devastating. Nick immediately crumpled to the ground, screaming in pain and grasping for his left knee. The play continued and resulted in a 34-yard touchdown run. Because the Ohio State crowd had followed the ball, it took them a while to notice Nick lying on the ground, writhing in pain. Several Michigan players were waving frantically to their trainers, who quickly dashed out on the field. When they got to Nick, the extent of the injury shocked even the veteran guys. He was screaming in pain, pounding his right fist on the ground. The head trainer put both hands around Nick's knee and could immediately tell there was nothing holding it in place. He had shredded one ligament for sure, and probably more. It was not pretty. They cut the bottom of his pant leg to get a better look, and winced at what they saw. Within minutes, they careful loaded him onto a cart and wheeled him straight to an ambulance. It didn't take long for them to speed away to a nearby hospital. The game had resumed before the ambulance even left the stadium. There was some polite applause from the Ohio State faithful as Nick was wheeled off, but there were also plenty of high-fives in the student section.

Sportsmanship didn't always win out in the Michigan-Ohio State rivalry.

* * * * *   * * * * *   * * * * *

Danny sat on the end of his bed, just staring at the television set in a daze. They showed the replay several times and it turned his stomach. It was one of the worst injuries he had ever seen in all his years of watching sports, and here it was happening to his best friend. He felt so helpless, especially from 4,500 miles away. It was hard to watch the rest of the game. He did, of course, hoping for updates, but they were few and far between. A sideline reporter mentioned the injury at halftime, but that was it.

This was sports in its purest form. Someone gets hurt, it's next man up. The game goes on.

Michigan seemed to be affected by the injury. They were horrible in the second half, on both sides of the ball. They never scored another point and lost 27-10. By the time the doctors had gotten done with Nick at the hospital, the game was long over.

Their worst fears were indeed realized. Nick had torn both his anterior cruciate ligament and his medial collateral ligament. There was also substantial cartilage damage. The injuries were so severe that a lengthy operation was going to be required, followed by a long and difficult rehabilitation.

After all the X-rays and MRIs and other tests, Nick was given quite a bit of pain medicine and he dozed off for a few hours. When he awoke, the trainers filled him in on the devastation.

"Nick, it's not good. You've completely torn two ligaments and you've got some other issues that we really won't know more about until all the swelling goes down," the team doctor said. "There's a lot of trauma there, so you'll need to stay here overnight for evaluation, and then we'll fly you home at some point tomorrow. I'll stay here with you and Coach Jefferson is going to stay too. He'll be here in a little bit. And we've called your brother. He's driving over too."

"How long?" Nick whispered through his fog.

"How long for what, Nick?" the doctor asked.

"Before I can play again?"

"Well, it's way too early to know for sure, but this is usually a 9-to-12-month recovery time. If all goes well, you'll be ready for next season."

"And if it doesn't go well?"

"Nick, let's not even think like that. I've done thousands of knees. We'll get you back together."

"But how bad is mine, comparatively speaking? You've done a thousand of those?"

"Well, let's say hundreds then. I won't belittle the situation here, Nick. It's definitely bad. But it can all be fixed and you can get healthy again. You'll be like new down the road, it's just that it's going to be a long road of rehab. But you're young and you're strong and your knee joint is pretty good."

Nick turned his head away and didn't say a word. It stayed quiet in the room for several minutes.

"Maybe we should let you rest, Nick," the doctor said as the posse headed out the door.

"That'll be good," Nick said, clicking off the light next to his bed. Just before the door closed, Nick shouted one last question to them.

"Hey," he said, "did we win?"

"No, we didn't. Lost 27-10."

"Shit," Nick said. "I already hate those bastards."

* * * * *   * * * * *   * * * * *

On the way out to the bus to go to the arena, Danny called Tony Vincent real quick and was surprised that he picked up the phone on the first ring.

"So you heard?" Tony said.

"Heard? I watched it. Just seeing those replays nearly made me sick. It looked bad."

"Apparently it is," Tony said. "I couldn't go to the game because of work but I'm driving over to Columbus now. I just talked to one of his coaches and he tore up the knee real good. They're keeping him overnight and he'll need a big operation soon. That prick hit him right square in the knee with his helmet and just ripped it apart, the coach said.

Danny couldn't talk long, but Tony agreed to call him in a couple of days when Danny got back to Indiana. He jumped on the bus and updated Trickett. Assistant coach Tony Carter, who had been watching the game and had met Nick on one of his recruiting trips to Schererville, came over and talked to Danny as well, asking a few questions about Nick. Danny didn't have many answers, certainly not any good ones.

The wait for the game to start was endless for Danny. He couldn't get his mind off Nick and it didn't help that the Kansas-Clemson semifinal that preceded their game went into double overtime.

When they finally got started, Danny made his first appearance in the game about four minutes in. On the first defensive series, he went behind a screen instead of over the top, as they had been instructed to do, and allowed an easy 3-pointer. A few possessions later, he lost his man again on backdoor cut, giving up an easy basket. On offense, his cuts weren't crisp and a few passes occasionally went astray. He missed both shots he took. On his third defensive lapse, Coach Garrison yanked him from the game after only six minutes and the team trailing by 10. As he sat down, Garrison glared down the bench at him and, for the first time in his Indiana career, Danny heard some harsh words from his head coach.

"Get your head out of your ass," he shouted.

Things weren't much better when he entered the game in the second half. His man hit a few jumpers over him and he missed a block-out, giving up an easy lay-up. He did hit a 3-pointer and scored on an offensive rebound, but he clearly was not playing well, which was seriously disappointing his head coach, especially after how well Danny had played in the first three games. He was yanked after about five minutes and never got back in the game. Danny stunk, and his teammates weren't much better. Indiana lost by 17, a thrashing by a very good UCLA team.

The cramped locker room was very quiet afterward. The players showered and got changed with barely a word mentioned. This veteran team didn't plan on winning every game, but they sure didn't plan on getting embarrassed either. No one said anything to Danny; now wasn't the time. Except for Michael Trickett, no one knew about Nick. Most just took it as a freshman learning his way, and having a bad night in his first collegiate road game.

But there was more to it than that.

As the team prepared to leave the empty arena, Tony Carter grabbed Danny and took him back to a small coach's office. Coach Garrison was waiting for them. Coach Carter closed the door, and sent the rest of the team on their way back to the hotel.

"Come with me," Garrison said, and the three of them walked out of the locker and back out to the arena, where only a few cleaning people were still around. As they walked along the baseline, Garrison put his arm around Danny's shoulders as Coach Carter trailed behind. They walked the 50 feet without a word being said, then headed up the sideline. About halfway down, the coach stopped.

"See these white lines here, Danny?" he asked, in a soft tone with his little Southern drawl that had never gone away. Danny nodded.

"Anytime you cross these white lines, your mind has to be 100 percent completely focused on basketball. During your time at Indiana, you're going to have days where you might be overloaded with academic stuff, or you might be having an argument with your girlfriend or some other friend, or you just might not be healthy. None of that matters when you cross these white lines. You have to give me your undivided attention every minute, or I have no use for you. You can't help me if you don't show up like you did tonight. Do you understand me?"

Danny nodded again.

"Now, Coach Carter told me about your friend, and I'm sorry that happened. But even so, there was nothing you could have done about that tonight. Whether you would have played well, or played like garbage, he still would have been suffering tonight. So you have to remember to keep a singular focus when you cross these white lines. It can't be any different."

"I understand, coach. I really do," Danny said. "I won't let it happen again."

"That's what I like to hear. It's all a process here, Danny. You get better when you learn from your mistakes. Hopefully, you've learned from this."

Coach Garrison waved over to Carter. He was talking on his cell phone. The three of them sat down on the first row of the bleachers. When they did, Coach Carter handed Danny the phone.

"Nick's linebackers coach John Jefferson is a friend of mine. He's with him. Say hello, but only talk for a minute or two, OK? He's kind of out of it."

"Nick? You there?" Danny said into the phone.

"Hey, man. How's Hawaii?" Nick said, his voice soft and slurring from all the drugs.

"Never mind Hawaii. What about you? You doing OK?" Danny leaned back on the bleachers as his two coaches stood up to give him some space.

"It's screwed up pretty bad, they tell me, but the drugs are good. I can't feel much. I'll have to have surgery when I get back. No football for a while. Shoot, no nothing for a while, it sounds like."

Danny could feel himself getting choked up, but he didn't want to show it. He knew his friend had to be hurting.

"You guys win tonight?" Nick asked.

"No, we didn't. Got smoked."

"Really? What happened?"

"It's a long story, man. A long, long story."

TOM BREW

20

Sunday morning turned into Sunday afternoon, and the afternoon turned into evening before the team doctor returned to Nick's room with the news that Nick had been waiting to hear all day. It was time to go home.

Good riddance, Columbus, Nick thought. He was still a bit dazed from all the pain medication, but he also knew that 28 hours in this hospital bed had been enough. He was ready to get out of there and head back to Michigan.

But first, Dr. John Stafford, the team's orthopedic surgeon, had some instructions for him. He spelled out what was going to happen in a monotonic voice and Nick didn't like hearing any of it. This was all real, and he knew it.

"We're going to get you up out of bed now and put you in this wheelchair for the trip out to the ambulance," Dr. Stafford said. "It's going to be natural for you to want to put some weight on your left leg, just to see what kind of stability you have. Let me tell you now, you have no stability, so don't even try. We've got a corporate jet waiting for us at the airport from one of our donors and we'll be back in Ann Arbor later tonight. We'll do some more tests and see how this swelling does, then we'll figure out when to do the surgery."

"Sooner the better," Nick said.

"Well, it's not that easy. This is a very serious injury and you've got an enormous amount of swelling going on. You broke a lot of blood vessels too, and we've got a lot of cleaning up to do before we can even consider going in. It could be a week or more before we operate."

"Do I need to stay in the hospital that whole time?" Nick asked.

"We'll see. A couple of days for sure, while we're doing all the tests. Let's play it by ear and make a decision Tuesday night. We'll know for sure then when we can do the surgery, so let's just wait to decide."

Nick's first flight in a corporate jet wasn't all that memorable. Dr. Stafford had given him more pain medicine and a sedative and about 15 minutes after they took off, Nick was sound asleep and didn't wake up until the wheels hit the pavement at the tiny airport in Ann Arbor. An ambulance took him to the hospital and by midnight he was back in a hospital bed once again.

He went through a battery of tests throughout the day on Monday and Tuesday and was amazed how all the strength had gone away in his knee. It hurt every time a doctor or technician moved his leg around and he was shocked as to how unstable his joint was. He quickly grew tired of all the ice packs and hated the constant interruptions to his sleep during the night. It didn't matter that several of the nurses were very cute; he just wanted some sleep. Of course, it was impossible to get comfortable anyway, with his knee the way it was, so "quality" sleep wasn't really an option. The only enjoyable time he had was watching Danny and Indiana beat Notre Dame on TV Tuesday night.

That, and a Wednesday phone call after his doctors had determined the substantial surgery would be done in five days. It was Danny on the other end.

"Well, pal, what's the verdict? They ready to start putting you back together yet?" Danny asked with plenty of energy in his voice, doing his best to cheer up his friend.

"Monday morning, 6 a.m.," Nick said. "Supposed to be three hours or so. They've turned me every way but loose the past few days and they say they're ready. Just want this swelling to go down some more."

"What's the prognosis?"

"They told me 9-to-12 months the first day and they haven't said anything differently since. They might know more after the surgery is over. I'm ready to go, that's for sure. Want to get this over and start the rehab. I've got to be ready by August. That's nine months."

"Do what they tell you and be patient," Danny said. "I know that's not your strong suit, but it's something new for you. Just don't over-do it."

"I can't imagine overdoing anything for a while. It's amazing how screwed up it is. When I have the brace off, if I'm lying in bed and want to raise my foot, I can't even do it. It's shot. But they say I'll be like new after they're done with me. And how about you? Saw your game last night. You played well."

"Yeah, thanks. It was a nice win on the road," Danny said. "Figured you'd like us beating Notre Dame."

Nick and Danny chatted for about 15 minutes until his doctors showed up again. They asked him if he wanted to go home, and Nick was all for it. He said goodbye to Danny and perked up. It's not like his dorm room was all that flashy, but it sure beat the hell out of his hospital bed. They gave him a sweatsuit early the next morning, filled his Vicodin prescription and drove him over to his dorm. Dale Gerard, his roommate, was thrilled to see him.

"I guess I'm your babysitter for a few days," Gerard said with a smile.

"What? No girls? I like girls for babysitters," Nick said with a laugh. Dale was glad to see him in a good mood, despite everything he was going through. He was just glad to be out of the hospital. Dr. Stafford, a 64-year-old surgeon who had been working with athletes for 30 years, had performed hundreds of knee reconstructions. This one, though, was about as extensive as he had ever seen. Nick's knee was a mess and it took every bit of four hours to get everything done. Nick's brother Tony took the week off to help out and be with his brother and Dr. Stafford filled him in on how it all went.

"Well, it was as bad as we expected when we got in, but all things considered it turned out well," Dr. Stafford said. "He's a got a long road ahead, though, and he'll need plenty of encouragement."

"I know the first question he's going to ask. He's going to want to know the time frame. He's going to want to hear nine months, not 12, or certainly not more than 12."

"I know. He's no different from most athletes. They never want to miss any playing time. Between you and me, being ready to play football by August might be a reach. September or October might be a reach. But we'll see. Nick's a very strong, very healthy young man and everyone heals differently. From what everyone tells me, he's got a great work ethic and I'm sure he'll adapt well to rehabilitation. We'll just keep evaluating along the way."

At the end of Day One, a groggy Nick was finally able to stay awake for a while. Tony was still there, and basically filled him in on what Stafford had said. They talked surgery for only a few minutes, with Tony hopeful to change the subject and get Nick's mind on something else. Easier said than done.

"Did you see the play?" Nick asked his older brother.

"Yeah, lots of times. Got home from work just as the game started. I taped it I watched it a few times. It didn't look pretty on TV, that's for sure."

"It didn't feel too pretty live either. That prick, I know he did it on purpose. He was still pissed about me lighting him up earlier in the game."

"Yeah, it sure looked like he was going after your knees. Replays made that look pretty clear. Of course, he denied it in the papers after the game, saying he was just trying to seal you off and he underestimated your speed. He's a lying prick."

They talked for about an hour before Nick dozed off again and Tony headed back to the hotel.

At the end of Day Two, Nick woke up a little before midnight drenched in sweat from head to toe. It had been a rough day. His doctors wanted him out of bed, up and moving. Physical therapists came by throughout the day and started working on his knee. It wasn't fun. He dozed off after dinner, but now didn't feel well at all.

He buzzed a nurse, who came quickly. "I don't feel good," Nick said. "And I'm sweating like crazy."

She checked his vitals quickly, and was shocked to see his temperature has risen above 102. By the time a doctor arrived an hour later, it was over 103 and

Nick was burning up. They drew some blood to test and ordered up some antibiotics, worried about infection. Nick got worse during the night and they amped up the treatments. In the morning, the bad news came.

"You've got a staph infection, a pretty bad one," Dr. Stafford called. "We're trying to get it under control, but it hasn't been easy. We'll keep pumping the drugs in you and monitor it very closely. Hopefully you'll start to feel better in a day or two."

It was more than like three or four days before Nick finally felt normal again. Stafford, who had been stressing over this infection as much as Nick, was relieved to see it finally under control.

Still, he had concerns.

"It's never good to have that kind of extensive infection after surgery," Stafford said. "We'll have to do some tests in a week or so, take some more pictures, and see how you're progressing, just to make sure everything's OK in there. You had us scared here for a while."

"I'm not real happy either, believe me," Nick said. "It's been two and a half weeks now since I got hurt and I'm still laying in a hospital bed. I'm getting a little stir-crazy."

"We told you it wouldn't be easy."

"Yeah, but you didn't tell me we'd have all these surprises along the way. I'm tired of hospitals and doctors and all this crappy food. I'm ready to start getting better now."

"You will, Nick. The worst is over now. We'll send you home soon."

At the end of Week One, Nick finally was released and went back to the dorm, with a hefty brace that ran from mid-thigh to mid-calf on his left leg. He mostly stayed in his room, watched basketball and placed a few NFL and NBA bets with Terrance Leach's friend in Detroit, Kenny Phillips.

It was nothing big, losing a few bets but winning a few more. He finished a couple hundred dollars ahead for the week and told Kenny Phillips just to hang on to his winnings until he got back in January. He played some cards online, too, and broke even after several hours of playing.

At the end of Week Two, Tony came to pick him up and take him home for Christmas. A couple of weeks in Schererville was going to be nice since Nick had grown very tired of hospital rooms and his cramped dorm room. It would be nice to be in his own bed. His brother brought him a few good meals from Angelo's and a few of the guys from high school stopped by now and then. Danny only got two days away for Christmas, since they were in the middle of a season, and they tried to catch up. Mary Bridges, of course, came through for Nick with some fresh bread as well. One night the Bulls were playing the Detroit Pistons and Nick called

Kenny Phillips back in Detroit to get the line. The Pistons, at home, were favored by 12 against a depleted Bulls team, Kenny said, which surprised Nick since the line was only 10 in the paper. All the Detroit locals were pushing the number up, he figured. He told Kenny he'd call him right back.

After he hung up, he looked up a number in his phone and made his first phone call to Joey Risone Jr.

"Joey, this is Nick Vincent, Tony's brother,"

"Hey, kid? Heard you got hurt. You doin' OK?"

"Getting better, little by little," Nick said. "Home for Christmas for a few weeks, so that's been nice, but I am a little bored. I've got a question for you. What's the line on the Bulls and Pistons tonight?"

"The number is 8 1/2. Why?"

"Going to watch the game and figured I'd have a little action on it. I'll take the Pistons minus the 8 1/2 for $300, OK?"

"You good for it?"

"Of course. You good for it?" Nick said with a laugh.

"Sure kid, you're in for the 8 1/2. Each betting week still runs through Sunday and we settle up on Thursdays. Got it?"

"Sure, Joey, no problem. Thanks a lot."

"No problem, kid. Call anytime."

Nick quickly called Kenny Phillips. "Give me the Bulls plus the 12 points for $300," he said. "That's a big bet for you, but I've got it. Bulls plus the points for three. See ya."

Nick didn't say a word to Tony when he got home with a pizza from Angelo's and the two of them watched the game and ate the pizza. Tony offered a beer, but Nick passed, figuring he better not while still taking the pain meds. Outwardly, he rooted for the Bulls but he was really hoping for a Pistons win between 9 and 11 points, so he'd "middle," which means winning both bets. Sure enough, the Pistons won by 10 and Nick won both bets, making $600 just like that.

Nick Vincent, the man in the middle.

* * * * *   * * * * *   * * * * *

Month One from Nick's surgery ended with a late afternoon rehab session back in Ann Arbor, and it did not go well. Nick wasn't in a very good mood anyway; it was mid-January in Ann Arbor, the weather was awful, classes had begun and getting around the campus on a bad knee was very disconcerting. He had been on a motion machine and rode a stationary bike a bit, but the healing process wasn't going as quickly as he would have liked. He could bend his knee just fine, but any extension of his knee was difficult. He still couldn't completely straighten out his knee and when the therapist got a little overly aggressive with him, he snapped.

"You've got to push yourself through this Nick," she said. "It's not easy, I know, but you should be getting more range of motion now than you have."

"You don't think I know that?" Nick snapped. "I'm the one dragging this leg around all day, not you. I don't have a baseline for how I'm supposed to feel, but I sure thought I'd feel a lot better than this. It's very frustrating."

At the end of Month Two, Nick finally got full range of motion back in his knee and he starting working a bit on a treadmill. Walking at a decent pace the was fine, because he knew where every step was going to be, smooth and level. But walking around on campus was another matter. Hills weren't fun, nor was the occasional crack in a sidewalk where he knee bent in weird ways. Around the first of March, Indiana came to Michigan for the final regular-season game in the Big Ten and Nick went over to the team hotel to see Danny. Michael Trickett, Danny's roommate on the road was also there when Nick arrived. They visited for about an hour, and talked mostly about Nick's knee.

"It's just weird, man. I keep feeling a little better every day, but anytime I add any weight to any exercises, it's just really a struggle. And I can't last long doing much," Nick told them. "In controlled environments, it feels OK but if I'm walking down the side of a hill or something, it just doesn't feel real stable, like it's too loose or something."

"And it's been three months?" Michael Trickett asked, somewhat per-plexed since he'd been through an ACL rehab once before himself.

"Yeah, just about three months." Nick said. "They had me try to jump rope yesterday and I couldn't do it for more than about ten seconds. I wasn't ready for that. The workouts in the pool go fine and they want me to start doing some light jogging starting next week, so we'll see how that goes."

They had a nice visit and Nick enjoyed watching Danny play later that night, the first time he'd seen him play a college game in person. Danny played well, scoring 13 points, and Indiana won comfortably. It was a nice day for Nick, a nice reprieve from his boring, painful days of rehab.

* * * *   * * * *   * * * *

Nick found other ways to keep himself entertained. He played plenty of poker online, and he was betting on the NBA a little, twenty-five dollars here or fifty dollars there and he took a shot a middling a few games with an extra call to Joey Risone Jr. now and then. He didn't hit any more but did OK overall, especially on a few of his bets during the NCAA Tournament. He was just as happy about one bet he didn't make. He never bet on any of the Indiana games but thought about it in the tournament. He backed off when the line got too high and was glad he did when Indiana lost outright in an upset to end its season.

As April rolled around, Kenny Phillips owed him about $400 and he owed Joey $200, which was the limit they had set for each other for settling up. He collected from Kenny and went to a check-cashing store to get a prepaid credit card. He got two cards for the same account, and threw one in an envelope and mailed it off to Joey at his father's bar.

"Not sure when I'll be back in town so I thought this might be easier. Just swipe the card at any ATM and take your $200."

When Joey got the card he walked across the street to an ATM machine and swiped the card. He withdrew the $200 and stuck it in his pocket.

Simple enough.

TOM BREW

21

Spring turned into summer and Nick kept pushing himself every day. The Michigan staff wanted him to stay in Ann Arbor for the summer to maximize his rehabilitation and he reluctantly agreed. He got out of his dorm room and into a more spacious apartment, and he did his thing, although he really missed Scher-erville and all his friends back there. Still, he tried to make the most of it, pushing hard toward his goal of being ready for the football season.

On the whiteboard in his bedroom, he had five dates listed for motivation.

August 8 – team reports

August 15 – first practice in pads

September 6 – first game

October 4 – first Big Ten game

November 29 – Ohio State!!!

As each day of his rehabilitation passed, the good days and the bad, he counted down the days until August 8.

In many ways, he started at the back. His goal for the home game with Ohio State was to be 100 percent healthy and be ready to wreak havoc in the arch-rival game that would likely once again be for the Big Ten title. After being carted off in last year's game, he wasn't about to miss this one. The Big Ten opener on October 4th at Northwestern wasn't going to be missed either. In doing all the math for recovery time from his elaborate surgery, being ready to play football by October 4th was a worst-case scenario. In Nick's mind, playing in that game was a 100 percent certainty as well. As far as he was concerned, being ready for the first game on September 6th was something he really wanted to do, but he also could agree and understand what his doctors, trainers and coaches were saying, that the first four non-conference games were nowhere near as important as the eight Big Ten games.

"If it wasn't for the Notre Dame game in there, on September 20th," Nick would always remind them. That game meant a lot to Nick, and it was the third of the four games. He really didn't want to miss it.

So he worked and worked. There were days he felt good, where a full day of workouts and treatments would go well, that the strength was there in his knee and the pain and recovery time afterward were minimal. But there were bad days as well. It always seemed as though he was behind in his progression, which

151

was incredibly aggravating. Things he should have been able to do at four weeks really didn't happen until the sixth or seventh week. Any time they added weight to any of his exercises, Nick was always shocked as to how poorly the joint would respond to the additional workload. Even when he started to do very light jogging on a treadmill, he found himself favoring his other leg quite a bit. Pain medicine, usually something strong like Vicodin, was a must after most every workout.

It was all tough to deal with mentally, primarily because Nick had never had a major injury before. He'd shaken off a few sprained ankles in high school and played hurt a few games with a sprained shoulder, but those injuries never slowed him down.

This was different. Very different.

Recovery from major knee surgery requires an enormous amount of patience, but that wasn't a strong suit of Nick's. Never was. And since the best-case scenario for a complete recovery was nine months, that September window mattered a lot to Nick. Being behind schedule at all just wasn't an option.

So he worked hard every day. From the waist up, he felt great. He had never worked out so hard, and he was as big and as strong as he had ever been. His legs were another matter. His trainers were careful not to push the lateral movement exercises. Those are the last to come, because they are so reliant on a strong ligament to keep the joint in place. Simply running out on the field in July instead of the treadmill was a big step up, but they were very forceful with Nick to remind him that everything, for now, was straight ahead. No cutting, especially on the bad knee, for now.

When August rolled around, Nick knew he wasn't going to be ready to run 100 percent with his teammates when conditioning started in a week. But he also didn't want to be too far behind. He figured if he could run and cut while wearing a brace by mid-August, that two weeks of practice would have him ready for the season opener.

The doctors weren't so sure that was a good idea. In their mind, targeting an October return to the field seemed more realistic. The coaches, like Nick, preferred the September date. He was, after all, their best defensive player and their team leader on that side of the ball. The sooner the better, they thought. Physically, he looked great to them.

So that first week of August, they decided to push Nick a bit more. His morning rehab sessions went fine, and in the hot, steamy afternoons they altered his routine a bit. They added some cones to Nick's running routine, but they weren't set are severe angles. Nick would jog, at a very leisurely pace, from one goal line to the other, weaving gently through the cones, all set 10 yards apart and just two yards off-line. He did six of those, took a little break, and then did his usual 40-yard sprints, at about 80 percent of what he used to do pre-injury. He did six of those, took another little break, then did six more jogs through the cones.

They did this for three days and everything was fine.

Nick woke up on Thursday morning, August 7, with just the usual pain and stiffness. He stretched out a bit and headed to the weight room. He did his entire morning workout without incident, rested for a few hours, had some lunch and headed back to the facility to get changed. About 3 p.m., he laced up his spikes, tied the drawstring on his shorts, stretched out some more and got ready to start his afternoon running.

It all seemed so normal.

It was pushing 90 degrees again, the mid-day sun pounding down on the lush green grass. There was a trainer on the field, three assistant coaches and about a dozen other players, all getting in some running. The trainer set up Nick's cones, a yard wider this time, and after he set a cone at the 50-yard line, he jogged back to the other side himself.

"OK, Nick, here's the plan for today," he said. "We're going fifty yards instead of 100, and let's pick up the pace a bit. Not a flat-out sprint, but not a jog either. Put some pace to it and keep your weight balanced. Let's start to get some more cutting and movement into this. Fifty yards down, catch your breath and fifty back, OK?"

Nick nodded and took his usual slow jog around the perimeter of the field to get loose. He got back, took a sip of water, re-tied a shoelace and sauntered up to the goal-line.

The whistle blew and off he went. He planted his right foot around the first cone and cut around it. As he approached the second cone he slowed down a bit, planted with his left foot and continued on. Right, left, right and at midfield he stopped. The trainer stared at him.

"Was that on purpose, slowing down? Does it hurt?"

"No, I'm fine. You said no sprint, so I just slowed down a bit."

"You pushed pretty good off your right. Can you do the same with your left? Did it feel alright?"

"Yeah, it was fine. Just going easy."

"Well, let's get after it a bit and see where we are. You've felt fine every day, so let's take the next step. We have a game in 30 days that you keep saying you want to play in. Let's crank it up a notch."

The trainer jogged down the goal line and gave his whistle a blast. Nick burst past the first cone, and then the second, sprinting a bit quicker this time. He curled around the third cone, then veered to the left. As he got to the fourth cone, he stuck his left cleat into the ground.

In an instant, he felt it. His knee buckled beneath him, and he fell to the ground. The pain shot through his leg and shot up through his body, Nick grabbed his knee with both hands and let out a scream.

His ACL, once again, had been torn to shreds.

The trainer immediately ran over to him, as did every coach and player on the field. It was the last thing anyone wanted to see. There he was, Nick Vincent, down the field again, eight months after that horrific injury in Columbus.

Nick's screams eerily carried across the campus.

The team doctor was at the hospital, about a mile away, but he got out to the field in a matter of minutes. They brought the cart out and loaded Nick onto it. Within 15 minutes he was in an ambulance, again, and off to the hospital. The MRI confirmed the ACL tear, which was totally unnecessary for Nick. He knew what had happened.

"It's the ACL. Everything else is fine," the doctor said. "We're going to have to go back in and do it again."

"The hell you are," an agitated Nick screamed at the gray-haired surgeon, three times his age. "This knee has not been right since the day you operated. I've fought through this and fought through this for eight months and it's never seemed right. The first time I push it much at all, boom, it tears again. You're freaking crazy if you think I'll ever let you cut on me again."

"Now, Nick, take it easy. I know …"

"Just please leave. Right now. I don't want anything to do with you right now. Get the hell out of here."

The doctor left, giving Nick some space. The trainer, who had been at Nick's side for eight months of rehab, remained behind, as did the nurse, who was checking Nick's vitals.

"Nick, I know you're pissed and I know you're hurting, but you don't need to be taking it out on him," the trainer said.

"The hell I don't," Nick said, loud and angrily. "He screwed up the first surgery and he knows it. He'll never admit it, but he knows it. Most importantly, I know it. I don't want that dumb ass anywhere near me. I'm going to want a second opinion, and someone who knows what the hell they're doing is going to do the damn surgery."

Nick slammed his fist against the bar alongside his bed. The nurse, sensing the need to calm Nick down, stepped alongside him and quickly said "Whatever you need, Nick. Whatever you need." She said it softly, yet confidently. "We can get someone else to look at it for you. Now just lay back and relax, OK? No sense in getting upset. It's not going to help anything right now."

Nick laid his head on his pillow and the nurse upped his pain medication a bit. The trainer remained quiet.

"I need my phone. It's in my locker. Would you mind going over there and getting it?" Nick asked the trainer. He nodded and left.

"Can I make a long-distance call from this phone? I need to call my brother," Nick asked the nurse.

"Of course, Nick," she said. "Just dial nine first."

Nick banged in the digits to Tony's cell phone and his brother picked up right away.

"You're not going to believe this. I just tore my ACL again," Nick said. Tony was shocked.

"This doctor here, he's a freaking fool and I don't want him around my knee ever again. You need to get me out of here. I want to come home and go see a doctor in Chicago, someone who knows what the hell they're doing. Call Coach Bowen at Crossroads High School. He knows that orthopedic surgeon from the Bears. He's done a lot of pros. Make some calls and see if you can get me in to see him."

"I'll get to Bowen tonight. Don't know if I can get to the doctor this late, but we'll try. Get some sleep and I'll drive up real early in the morning and hopefully we'll have some answers by then. Just rest, OK?"

Nick said goodbye and hung up the phone.

"Comfortable?" he nurse asked.

"Yeah, I feel a little better. Wouldn't mind sleeping now, I guess."

"I'll take care of that for you. Give me a minute," she said. She strolled off to get a sleeping pill, but by the time she came back, Nick was sound asleep. The trainer came back about the same time, and left Nick's phone on the table next to his bed.

* * * * *   * * * * *   * * * * *

On Tony's ride home, he talked to Jack Bowen for a while, and Jack was more than willing to lend a hand. Jack still spent plenty of time around the Bears organization and was happy to help. Nick was always one of his favorites.

As Tony got close to home, he was surprised to see Danny sitting out on his front porch, drinking some iced tea with Candice. Both were home for a week before the fall semester of their sophomore years started. Tony hit his breaks quickly, parked his truck in front of Danny's house and walked up to the porch.

They shook hands, glad to see each other. It had been a while.

"Did you hear from Nick tonight," Tony asked.

"No," Danny said. "I haven't talked to him since Sunday. Why?"

Tony paused for a moment, his voice cracking. He tried to speak, but couldn't. He tried again.

"Nick tore his ACL again this afternoon. Just running, no one around him on the practice field, and it gave way again. I'm going up to get him in the morning and take him to a doctor in Chicago."

Danny was speechless. Candice too. Danny just shook him head in amazement. He couldn't believe it.

"So he'll be here tomorrow night?"

"Yeah, probably," Tony said.

"Good," Danny said. "I'm not leaving until Sunday, so just have him call me tomorrow whenever he's up to it. And if there's anything I can do, just call."

Tony left and Danny and Candice just sat quietly on the porch swing for several minutes.

"I just can't believe that," Danny said. "It's unbelievable."

Candice took his hand and held on tight. There was nothing she could say.

* * * *   * * * *   * * * *

Tony left at 5 a.m. and was in Ann Arbor by 10. As he walked down the hallway to Nick's room, the surgeon who had performed the original operation was walking toward the room from the other direction. They shook hands, and chatted briefly before entering Nick's room.

"So what happened?" Tony asked.

"If I had to guess – and it would really only be a guess at this point – I'd think maybe the allograft wasn't as good as we'd hoped and that staph infection probably didn't help either. It just wasn't as tight as we would have hoped. It just didn't have the time to heal properly. This is very rare, but it happens. Nick is upset, I know …"

"That's an understatement," Tony quickly interjected.

"I know, but he has to look at it this way. In our original worst-case scenario, we thought he might need 12 months to fully recover and that would have meant missing the season. It's not much of a consolation, I know, but now he'll have that 12 full months to be 100 percent for next year. He's still got a great future ahead of him."

"Needless to say, though, he's going to want a second opinion and I'm not going to talk him out of that. Probably couldn't anyway, even if I tried. I hope you understand. We're going to see a doctor in Chicago."

"I figured that, after yesterday. That's not a problem. Nick's health has always been my primary concern and that will always be the case. I brought all his films for you to take with you, and please give the doctor my card. I'll be happy to talk to him and I'll look forward to hearing what he has to say. And any follow-up, we're here."

"Thanks, I appreciate it. I know Nick's mad, but don't take it personal. I certainly don't. He's just really disappointed in losing a season. That's just not the way he's wired."

"None of them are."

"Nick's different than most, though. Football means everything to him. He'll hate not being able to play all year. He will go crazy. And that doesn't even count all the pain and suffering he just went through with rehab. That's all wasted. He'll have to start all over again."

Tony got Nick checked out a few hours later and they headed back to Schererville. They had a Saturday appointment in Chicago that lasted all day. They didn't get back home until about seven Saturday night, and Danny stopped by.

He didn't stay long. Nick was tired, and he didn't have much to say. He was in a mood, a bad one, and Danny had seen it many times. He understood.

"I was thinking, on the ride over here yesterday, about just leaving Michigan, maybe going somewhere else," Nick said. "Tony talked me out of it right away, and he's right. I picked that place for a reason, love my teammates and what it's all about. So the doc probably did a crappy job, but even this doctor told me I can't really blame him. Just a bad situation, I guess, and I'll have to start all over. So be it. I'm just really not looking forward to going through all that rehab again. It's a bitch."

"So you're going to have the doctor in Chicago do the surgery?"

"Yeah, I feel more comfortable with him. We're going to do it in two weeks. That way I can get classes started, plan for a week off for the surgery without getting too far behind. I'll come back and forth now and then for check-ups, but I can do all the rehab in Ann Arbor. I like our trainer. And I'll know more of what to expect this time."

"Well, Candice won't be far away in Evanston, if you need anything while you're here. You have her cell phone, right?"

"Yeah, not sure I've ever called it, but I've got it."

"Anything you need, just let us know," Danny said as he got up to leave. "Just hang in there, man. We're all rooting for you."

* * * * *　　* * * * *　　* * * * *

Nick was back in Chicago two weeks later. The surgery went well, there were no infection issues and everyone was happy.

So it was off to Ann Arbor, crutches and brace in hand, to start on his rehab. Again.

22

Nick had two things going for him this go-round. He felt more confident that this surgery had gone well and it was much easier to get around the Michigan campus on crutches on warm September days than it had been in the dead of winter.

His first visit back to the physical therapist snapped any good thoughts away. The pain, again, was incredible. And the pain, again, was going to be that way for several months.

Not fun.

His days would start with a few hours of therapy and then he would trudge back to his empty apartment, depressed, sullen and irritable. Vicodin became a daily ritual. He didn't leave his apartment much. He'd go to each class once a week, but skip the rest of the time; no big deal, he thought, since he could always use his ripped-up knee as an excuse. He'd play poker online, he'd study his baseball matchups and he'd gamble on a little football, pro and college. Every day he'd make a call to either Joey Risone Jr., or Kenny Phillips, and he'd place his bets. It still wasn't much, three or four games a day, $25 or $50 a pop. He'd win more they he'd lose, but not by much.

And he needed to win. After a second consecutive summer of not being able to work for his brother Tony, Nick's bank account was dwindling. For the first time since he was about 14 years old, it was under $1,000. He didn't have much debt since his scholarship covered most everything in Ann Arbor, but the little incidentals always added up. He got a little concerned in mid-September when he had to drop $400 on a couple new tires for his paid-for pick-up truck. Not having money always stressed him out, affecting his sleep habits and certainly his mood.

So he made a phone call.

To Joey Risone, Jr.

It was an unusually warm Thursday afternoon in September, so Joey was sitting outside his father's bar in Chicago Heights, eating an Italian sub sandwich and washing it down with an ice-cold Molson Golden.

"What's up, Nick?" he said between bites, always happy to hear from one of his favorite clients. "Looking for your money?"

"No, no," Nick said. "Just checking in with you."

"I was just having lunch and was going to walk across the street afterward to throw your $200 on the card," Joey said. "Why is it I'm always paying you? That's like seven weeks in a row."

"Yeah, but it's just scraps. Barely finishing over .500 every week. Hey, Joe, I've got a question for you. My scholarship money still isn't here and things are a little tight. If I needed to borrow two grand to get some work done on my truck, how much would you charge me in interest, if I needed it for like two or three weeks?"

Joey thought for a minute. "Two grand?"

"Yeah."

"I can do that for three points a week, but on the two-grand total each week until it's paid off. That's sixty bucks on the interest, every week, and no more than three weeks, OK?"

"No, three weeks is plenty. Two's probably more realistic. Should happen anytime. But that's fair. Thanks for the help."

Joey took a big bite of his sandwich and finished off his beer. Then he reached down into his pocket and peeled off several hundred dollar bills. He counted out only 12, then stuck them back in his pocket.

"How soon you need it? Tomorrow soon enough? Don't have it all with me right now and I've got lots of collections to make today."

"Yeah, tomorrow's fine. I do want to take my truck in though, so I'll go ahead and do that in the morning and try to grab the money off the card by noon or so. Is that OK?"

"Sure, noon won't be a problem. Meeting a few guys here tomorrow for lunch anyway, so I'll do it right before then. Just make sure I get it all back in three weeks though, OK? Don't want this to be a long-term thing."

"No problem. Consider it done. I appreciate it."

The next day, sure enough, the balance on the credit card was $2,200. Nick took out $1500 in cash and hid it in a drawer in his apartment, all but a hundred. He called Kenny Phillips about hooking up on Friday night, since he owed Kenny about $120. They didn't usually settle up unless one of the two was over $200, but he called him anyway. Kenny, a big Michigan football fan, knew all about Nick's second surgery.

"I need to get out of this apartment," Nick said, a total lie. "Want to meet at PT's for some pizza and I'll pay you what I owe you?

"Sure," Kenny said. "See you about 7?"

Perfect, Nick thought.

They ate their pizza and watched a little baseball. Nick had the Tigers and Red Sox that night with Kenny, just a few little $25 bets. Then Nick had a question, the same one he asked Joey Risone earlier.

"Kenny, I was wondering. I haven't gotten my scholarship money yet and I need to get some stuff done on my truck. Can I borrow two grand at say three points for a couple of weeks tops? That's all the time I need."

"I don't know, Nick. Things are a little tight with me right now, but I'm sure Terrance Leach could do it. Let me call him later and I'll get back to you tomorrow."

"OK, that'll work," Nick said. "Just call me tomorrow so I know."

Sure enough, the next day Kenny called.

"Where are you?" Kenny asked.

"At my apartment. Why?"

"I thought so. I'm right down the street. I've got your money from Leach, two grand. He said no interest from you as long as he gets it back in two weeks. If it's past two weeks from today, then add $200 to the total, OK?"

"Sure. Great," Nick said. "No interest? Tell him I appreciate it. Why don't you come on up so I don't have to navigate these steps on crutches again."

Kenny popped up, but didn't stay long. Nick gave him a hundred dollar bill.

"For you," he said, "for helping me get this done. Thanks a lot."

For the first time in a week, Nick slept like a baby. It's amazing how relaxed you can get when you've got some money in your pocket. Especially since it was so easy to get.

Just a few quick lics and that was that.

He had a pretty good weekend, as well, especially with baseball and college football. So by Sunday night he was $460 ahead with Joey and $200 ahead with Kenny. He called Joey on Monday.

"Hey man, take the $460 I won and put it toward the two grand," Nick said. "And then take another $500 off the card. That'll make it an even eleven hundred I owe you, with the interest."

"That's good news," Joey said.

"Yeah, the truck repairs weren't as bad as I thought, so I had some left over. And I heard from the financial aid office. My check should hit my bank any day."

Nick was lying through his teeth, of course, but he didn't care. He didn't bet much all week and by the following Friday he was up about $170. He took $1,000 out of his drawer and drove over to the check-cashing place. He put the $1,000 on the card and called Joey.

"Hey man, going away for the weekend, so I won't be calling. Got my check and put the money on the card. There's a thousand there, plus the $170 you owe me. Take it all and we're all even on the two-grand, OK?"

"Sure, kid. Glad it worked out. Happy to help."

Nick didn't bet at all with Joey all weekend but he rode some hot pitchers and a few college football upsets to finish about $300 up with Kenny. He met him on Monday and handed him back 17 of the $100 bills he had just given him a week earlier.

"Will you be seeing Leach today?" Nick asked.

"Yeah, especially now. He'll like that he didn't have to worry about this."

"No, never. I just appreciate the help. Got a little tight there. But have Terrance call me after you've paid him the two thousand. I'd like to thank him."

Nick had a nice chat with Leach late on Monday night, then went to bed. He couldn't help but laugh that he bet with his bookies' money for two weeks, came out way ahead, paid them off with his winnings and all was good. He still had $200 on the card and $700 in his drawer.

That was so easy. He slept 12 hours.

* * * * * * * * * * * * * * *

Saturdays weren't much fun for Nick, but Wednesday poker nights were still great. He didn't travel on the road with the football team, but he went to the home games, first on crutches in September and then in his bulky brace in October. Nick hated being there; not being able to play ate away at him. One of the Detroit columnists wanted to spend an entire game day with him, but Nick politely refused. He did agree to a 15-minute interview prior to a home game in late October but that was it. During the game Nick was more preoccupied with checking scores – and his bets – on his cell phone than he was the action on the field. He hated being there, and couldn't wait to leave. He felt completely disconnected from this team.

Wednesday nights were a different story. The guys from his freshman year still had the rental house with the basement and they'd get 20 guys for a poker tournament every week. There was so much interest in the tournament, they were always turning down people. One week they wedged a third table in and the whiny James Walton got a chance to play, but everyone else really hated it. It was just too crowded, and too uncomfortable. James Walton hated it even more when he got placed at the same table as Nick and lost early when he hit a straight on the river and went all-in. The same card gave Nick a flush and James stormed out of the house bitching. Nick just laughed and laughed. In the first six tournaments, Nick turned his $300 in entry fees into about $600 and he loved every night of play. He just loved playing tournament poker.

A week later they went back to two tables and everyone was happy. Everyone but James Walton, the whiny New Yorker from Long Island. He wanted to win his money back and wasn't happy when Nick told him there wasn't going to be any room for him.

The following day, a Thursday, Kenny Phillips owed Nick a few hundred dollars and they met for lunch. Kenny was whining about his money problems to Nick. He owned part of an equipment and party rental company and sales were stagnant. Kenny also owned the small strip center the rental company was in, and it was currently about a third empty. Kenny had to check on one of the empty spots that day because a tenant had just moved out. Nick came along for the ride.

The spot was about 1,200 square feet and there was a small reception area in the front. The back, though, was wide open and spacious.

Nick had an idea. This seemed like a perfect place to host expanded poker tournaments. He knew he could find the players and his roommate Dale Gerard and his buddies would certainly want to be partners. And he knew Kenny, who was always broke but liked to play poker himself, could use the money.

"Hey, let me ask you a question," Nick said to Kenny. "You haven't re-rented this space yet, have you?"

"No. Hell no," Kenny said. "And in this market, it could be empty for a while. Why?"

"You know how I play poker on Wednesday nights down the road? We've always got a lot of guys who want to play and we don't have room for them. What if we played here? There's room for eight or ten tables easy. I could give you say $100 a night, plus a free seat in the tournament, either $50 or $100 entry fee, and with that kitchen there and refrigerator you could buy beer and pop and sell them for a couple bucks each and keep that profit too. Make sense?"

"Done," Kenny said. "Put it together. I need the money"

"Might take a few weeks to get it set up, but let's do it. Could be fun."

Nick made a few phone calls, to Dale Gerard and his friend Bruce Lawton, who ran the crowded Wednesday night game like he'd been doing it for decades, and they loved the idea of being young entrepreneurs. Nick had seen an ad in the sports section about a Detroit casino doing some remodeling and they were selling off their old temporary tables cheap. He bought eight over the phone, for $500 total, and he and Kenny grabbed the box truck from Kenny's rental company and they went to pick them up. They set them up back at the strip mall space and there was plenty of room for even a few more if they wanted. They decided eight would be plenty; no sense in making it overcrowded. Kenny had hundreds of chairs for party rentals, so they walked down with about a hundred, just in case.

Then Nick picked up the phone again.

And, once again, he lied through his teeth.

"Hello, Joey," Nick said, finding young Joey Risone Jr., at his father's bar. They talked betting lines for a few minutes, Nick made four or five bets, and then he popped the question.

"OK, Joey, here's the deal. I've got this little poker tournament thing going up here and we're about ready to make it a big thing. Got a big space we can rent cheap and got plenty of bad players who want to play. But I don't want to just play; I want to be a partner with these other two guys. I need to buy 15-20 tables, a couple hundred chairs, chips and stuff. The way I'm looking at it, it might be worth a grand a week to me. Can I borrow ten grand from you and pay you back over, like, I don't know, six months?"

"Ten grand? That's a little steep,"

"Oh, you can handle it," Nick said. "And this could be a really sweet deal. I know you've got it."

"The hell I do, but I can get it. Three points a week again?"

"I was thinking two."

"Give me a few minutes, and I'll call you back."

About 30 minutes later, Nick heard Joey's voice again, but this time it was muted. He was on a speaker phone in his father's office. Joey Risone, Sr., jumped in, too.

"OK kid, you really think you can make a grand a week off this? Can you pay me back that quick if I loan you this money?"

Nick thought for a moment. "Well, it might take a little while to really get it rolling, but I figure $500 a week would be no problem. Can we start there, $500, plus the interest, the two points?"

"We'd need three points to do it," Senior said.

"Three's a lot," Nick said. "How about two points the first three months, only on the balance, and three points after that if it's not already paid off? That's fair, isn't it?"

Nick could hear the two of them whispering back and forth. Then he heared a chair squeak, and a door close. Then he heard Joey Risone Jr., speak, clear as a bell.

"OK, we'll do it. I will throw the money on your card tomorrow. Two points a week for four months, four points a week after that. A little less up front, a little more later to hurry you along. Let's have it done in four months, OK?"

"Sure," Nick said. "I can do that. Thanks."

Nick hung up the phone, sat back and smiled. Now he was set. This was so easy.

He was becoming an excellent liar.

* * * * *   * * * * *   * * * * *

Nick had such a good baseball season that he got a little cocky in the playoffs. He liked the Red Sox and the Angels in the American League and they both lost. He lost his bets on the series and eight of the 11 individual bets on the games. He was right on the Cardinals in the National League, but missed out on the Braves. Some of his bets on the series were big, $200 or more, and with all the games he lost, he owed Kenny $900 and Joey $500.

It was no big deal, because he had the money he borrowed from Joey, so he paid up and paid the nut on the loan, religiously, every week. November came and went, and he lost three weeks out of four. He was getting consumed with it all, betting on more games each night and betting more money on each game. For months and months, he'd bet $25 a game, sometimes $50. Now it was more like $100 a game, sometimes $200 if he really liked it. He went nuts on one game he loved, betting $400 straight-up.

There was some crazy college football Saturdays where he'd bet on four or five noon games, four or five more in the late afternoon and four or five more at night. He'd win some, lose some, but for the first time in more than six months, he was losing more than he was winning. He looked at his sheet one Saturday and he had had 19 different straight-up bets, plus another dozen parlays and teaser bets. Had he lost them all, it would have been $17,000.

That was impossible, of course, but one thing was blatantly obvious: He was clearly addicted now. Gambling was becoming all-consuming.

Three or four games a day at $25 or $50 a shot was a distant thing of the past. By December, the $10,000 was almost gone after he jinxed himself and really did need to put about $1,200 into his truck and he still owed Joey close to $3,000.

He wasn't winning much at poker either. He was a little stressed out making sure everything went well each night, and when college football ended they moved the games to Friday night to get more players. They were getting 60 or 70 players each night and it was fun. Nick wasn't cashing very often, but Dale won a $100 entry tournament one night, raking in almost $2,500. He took Kenny and the boys to a strip joint late that night and they partied it up. Terrance Leach was there too, and everyone had fun.

On the last Friday before the students were all dispersing for Christmas break, James Walton laid down his money once again. He'd been there six weeks in a row and hadn't made a nickel, always blaming someone else for a bad beat. He peeled out his $100 entry, plus $20 for the house and $10 to the dealer for an extra

2,000 chips. He sat down with his 8,000 chips, convinced he was finally going to win before jetting back east to New York.

Of course, as usual, James got whacked. He was actually just a table away from cashing, four hours into the event with a pretty thick chip stack when he got a pair of aces. He made a sizable bet pre-flop and got two calls, including one from Dale Gerard, who was at his table and had a slightly larger chip stack.

The flop came ace of diamonds and two black nines. James tried to play it coy, checking his full house. There was another call, but Dale Gerard wanted to play. He shuffled through his chips quickly – 55,000, he counted – and looked over at James. After a few seconds, he laid out 15,000 chips. James just called, looking for more, and the third player folded.

The next card was a meaningless three of diamonds. James checked again.

Nick and a few players from the other table, which was just getting ready to take a break, turned and noticed the big pot. They stood to watch; Nick was standing right behind James. Dale pondered and pondered, then said the words Jimmy was hoping to hear.

"All-in" Dale said as he slid the rest of his chips forward.

"I call," James Walton quickly shouted as he stood up and flipped over his cards. "Full house, aces over nines!"

Dale sat quietly for about 10 seconds, for effect. Then he flipped over the two red nines and the blood immediately flowed out of James' face. The last card was a worthless five and Jimmy was done. Knocked out by four nines.

"Oh, this is such bullshit," James screamed as he slammed his fist on the table, scattering everyone's chips all about.

"It's like this here every time," The rant continued. He turned and saw Nick standing right behind him, and got even madder. "You saw my cards and signaled him, didn't you? Cheating pricks. You do it all the time."

"I didn't see your cards," Nick said. "Shut up. You lost to four of a kind. It happens. Now get the hell out of here. And don't come back. We're all so tired of your constant whining. Go home, you little New York crybaby."

James stormed out and everyone got a good laugh. No one liked that kid. After a five-minute break they started back up. Nick, who was short-stacked, got knocked out in eighth place and made a few dollars. Dale was still alive 30 minutes later when the last five players were at the final table.

And then … boom.

The back door went flying off its hinges when the two police officers slammed it with their battering ram. Behind those two officers came four more, with guns drawn.

"No one move. Hands up!" an officer shouted. "Hands up now."

Everyone obliged immediately, the five players, Nick, Kenny Phillips and about a dozen other guys who had been knocked out and were sipping on two-dollar beers while watching the action at the final table.

In walked James Walton, through the back door. The police officer looked at him and asked "Which ones?"

James pointed to Dale Gerard. "Him!" he said. "And those two right there," he shouted as he pointed to Nick and Kenny Phillips. "It's their game."

The officers quickly approached Nick, Dale and Kenny, handcuffed them and led them out to squad cars. After a search of the premises, they confiscated the cash box – which had more than $7,000 in it – and all the alcohol. The other players, after providing identification, were allowed to leave.

Nick sat quietly alone in the back of the squad car. The three-mile ride to the police station was the longest ride of his life.

One thought kept running through his head, over and over:

"What the hell is going on with my life?"

TOM BREW

23

What a mess. Nick and Dale were escorted into the police station, still in handcuffs, and Kenny Phillips was a few minutes behind them in another police car. As they strolled by the police sergeant, they turned some heads.

"What did they do?" the sergeant asked the officer.

"Illegal gambling operation. Cheated a kid out of some money."

"Do you know who they are?" the sergeant asked.

"No. Why?"

The sergeant came around the desk and walked over the corner of the room, out of sight of most everyone, with Nick, Dale and the officer.

"You're Nick Vincent, right? Play for Michigan? I work security on the sideline and I've seen you there." He looked at Dale. "You play too, right?"

"Yes, sir," Dale said politely. "I'm Dale Gerard. Nice to meet you."

"C'mon, follow me," the sergeant said to the officer. He brought his two prisoners along with him to a private interrogation room in the back and took off their handcuffs. "You guys wait here," he said to Nick and Dale as he stepped outside to talk to the officer.

"You sure you've got a good arrest here? That's two Michigan football players there." The sergeant said.

"Caught them red-handed. There was a big poker game going when we got there. The third guy, an older guy, we caught him with nearly ten grand in cash."

"Well, before we start the booking process, let's talk to them. No sense in causing any problem for the boys if we're wrong."

They walked back in. "So, explain yourselves," the sergeant said. "What was going on in there?"

Dale spoke up quickly. "Hey, we were just playing cards. That was all. Just a little poker tournament among friends." Nick nodded.

"How'd you get into that office space?"

Dale again jumped in quickly. "That other guy you've got, Kenny Phillips, it's his space. He owns that building, has a business in that building. He let us in, he's got all the chairs and he runs the show. We were just playing."

The arresting officer wasn't hearing any of it.

"That kid told us it was your show."

Nick finally spoke up. "That kid is a smart-aleck little punk from New

York. He's just mad that he always loses at poker. He never wins, and then every time he gets knocked out, he complains. Tonight he just complained to you guys. That's all there is to it."

The sergeant looked at the officer. "Does anyone know they're here?"

"Nope. You're the first."

"Well, I think we should let them go now. If anything, it's just a little misdemeanor charge and there's no sense in dragging them through all that bad publicity. It's not worth all the headaches, for them or for us. Just let them go."

The officer wasn't real happy about it, but he was young and inexperienced, so he agreed with the sergeant, a 30-year veteran.

"How do you know Phillips?" the sergeant asked. "I don't, really," Dale interjected immediately. "Just met him when we started playing cards and he had a big, empty space in that building that could hold a lot of people."

He didn't ask Nick and Nick didn't offer anything. It was a good thing. Fifteen minutes later they were walking out the door, no arrest, no warning, no nothing. Kenny Phillips wasn't so lucky. He was booked, charged with a few things and spent the entire night in jail. He couldn't get out until late the next morning, when his brother finally bailed him out.

He did it with a thousand dollars from the stash in Nick's dresser drawer. It was the least Nick could do, since he and Dale sort of sold him out to the cops to protect their own tails. He pled out a few weeks later, avoiding any jail time by agreeing to probation and a substantial fine. The amount? Eight thousand dollars, the same amount confiscated, practically to the dollar. The cops certainly knew what they were doing.

Nick and Dale knew they were lucky to get a break with the cops. No one had to know about this, and that was a good thing. The only other issue were the others at that final table. Would any of them cause a problem? Dale didn't think so, but just to be sure he and Nick worked out a plan, to give them all their money back, plus a couple of hundred dollars for what they might have won. They would understand all the money was confiscated and this was coming out of Nick and Dale's pocket. No one complained, really. It wasn't like they had any recourse. Dale passed on his share, of course, and Nick paid for most of it out of his stash.

The stash, though, was just about gone. He had less than a thousand dollars and he still owed the Risones about $2,000. He used just about all of it to make another on-time payment to them and then he thought … and thought ... and thought.

And then he made another phone call, just a week before Christmas.

It was a doozy.

* * * * *   * * * * *   * * * * *

Nick was a nervous. He had only slept a few hours the night before and his heart was pounding in his chest.

He had a big question to ask Joey Risone, and he rehearsed his spiel over and over. He thought back to September, when he asked to borrow $2,000 and Risone didn't even blink. He thought back to a few months later, when he asked for $10,000 and the older Joey Risone got involved but he still got the loan. He paid the first one off quickly, just like he said he would, and he had been paying them something every week on the second loan, which was almost paid off.

If anything, he was a qualified borrower, he thought.

So he waited until a little after noon and called Joey Junior on his cell. He didn't answer and Nick left a brief message, but Joey called right back about 15 minutes later.

"What's up, kiddo? Merry Christmas," Joey said.

"Not much. Wanted to get out of here and go home for Christmas a couple of days ago but I've got an issue that's come up here and I can't leave," Nick said, talking slowly and softly. "It's a huge problem, and I need your help."

"What's wrong, something with your poker thing?" Joey asked

"No, that's going great. Making lots of money," Nick said, lying like crazy. Joey knew nothing of the near-arrest, the game getting shut down and Nick doling out a lot of money – Joey's money – to keep people quiet.

Nick continued, sweating like crazy and nervous as hell.

"There's this girl here. Man, you should see her, just smokin' hot," Nick said. "I met her one day at this fraternity party and we hit it off. Well, I've been sleeping with her for a while now and a few days ago she told me she was pregnant. That's bad enough, but then she told me she was still in high school, that she was 17, not 19 like she told me. I couldn't believe it. Now, that's a problem, that she's pregnant, but here's the real issue. She told her parents and her father is this prick big-shot lawyer in town, and he is pissed. When she told him that I got her pregnant, and that I was a football player, he went through the roof and wanted to come after me."

"What, he wants to kill you?"

"Worse."

"There is no worse, Nick. Trust me on that one."

"Well, it seems worse. He wants to go to the police and have me arrested for statutory rape. And then he wants to go the school and the newspapers and make it all public. Man, she's 17. She lied to me and she sure as hell doesn't look

17, but she's got me now. I really need to make this go away."

"What's he want?"

"Twenty thousand dollars, for an abortion, whatever else she needs, a place to go somewhere away from here. He says if I pay, he'll keep it all quiet. If not, he goes right down to the police station."

"God damn," Joey said. "Sounds like a real prick."

"Well, yeah, he is. But it's his daughter, you know. You don't mess with some guy's little girl. I'm in a real bind here, and I really don't see any recourse other than paying them to keep quiet."

"How the hell are you going to pay me back 20-grand?"

"Same way I paid you back the two-grand, and most of this 10-grand. Every week, a big chunk at a time. You know I'm good for it. I've paid you every week, right on time. I'll keep doing it. Joey, this poker thing is going great and come January we're going to start playing two nights a week instead of one. It'll be great."

That, of course, was a huge lie, but it was worth telling, especially since Joey hadn't said no yet.

"Well, I'd have to talk to my dad about that. That's a lot of money and I don't have it. He may not have that much either. It gets a lot slower around here when football slows down. But let me talk to him. How soon do you need it?"

"Right away. Hell, he could change him mind and go to the cops any minute now."

"And you think you can trust him about keeping quiet?"

"Yeah, I think so. I don't think he wants this to be public, but he damn sure doesn't want me skating on it either. He wants to get his girl out of town and away from me."

"Let me talk to some people and we'll see what we can do. I'll get back to you."

"When?"

"Today, for sure."

"OK, thanks. Please make it happen, Joey. I really need your help and I've got nowhere to turn. I'm done if you don't do this for me. I'll be off to jail for years."

"Try to hang in there. I'll call you as soon as I can."

Nick hung up the phone and smiled a sly smile.

A job well done.

Or so he hoped

* * * * *   * * * * *   * * * * *

It **was only** a couple of hours later when Joey Junior called back. Nick answered promptly.

"Well, I am very nervous about this and so is Big Joey, but we'll do it for you." Joey said. "We like you, kid, and we don't want to see you get in trouble."

"Oh, thanks Joey. Thanks so much," Nick said. "You just don't know how much this means to me."

"We're only going to charge you a point-and-a-half a week, but we want you to pay at least a grand a week if you can. Five hundred minimum. And we want it all back in six months. If not, it goes up to three points after that. And if you miss a payment one week, it goes to three immediately. Got it? We've got to borrow some of this money just to give it to you, so these are the terms, and it's take it or leave it."

"I'll take it. No question," Nick said. "And I'll shoot for the grand a week, but the five-hundred is a lock. I've already been doing that and I can keep doing it. I'll shoot hard for the six months."

"OK, tomorrow's Christmas Eve, so this guy's not going to mess with you for a couple of days. You're coming home anyway, right? So enjoy Christmas with your brother and come by the bar at noon on the 26th. We'll have a briefcase ready for you and you can go back to Michigan and get this taken care of."

"Works for me. Thanks again."

"Tell your brother I said hello."

"Yeah, right," Nick said with a laugh. "He'd kill me if he knew all this was going on. I can't tell him any of this."

"Probably a good thing. I'll keep it between you and me," Joey said. "See you in a couple of days."

Nick packed a bag with some clothes, took a shower and ran out to get some food. He called his brother Tony and gave him the change in plans, that he'd be home for a couple of days after all, and that he'd see him the next day when he got home from work. Nick got a good night's sleep, again, and headed to Schererville about noon, thinking about nice, hot pizza from Angelo's the whole ride.

* * * * *   * * * * *   * * * * *

A **couple days** with his brother was good for Nick, even though he had to keep a whole lot of things quiet. He did tell him about the poker games, but not the bust, so he could at least put a good thought in Tony's head about having enough money all the time. He filled him in on his second round of rehab – "hurts like hell but the Vicodin is a savior" Nick said. Danny wasn't home – Indiana had a holiday tournament they were leaving for on Christmas night – so Nick made sure to be a homebody. He watched some football on Tony's tiny 20-year-old television and other than running into Kenny Dockery at Angelo's, he really didn't see anyone. He said goodbye to Tony on the morning of the 26th and drove over to Chicago Heights, all excited.

He called Joey on his way and walked through the door of Joey's bar right at noon. He quickly was summoned back to Big Joey's office and he took a seat. Both Joeys were there and Big Joey pulled a duffel bag out from under his desk. He unzipped it and pulled out a briefcase. He opened the briefcase and Nick couldn't believe his eyes.

It was full of $100 bills.

"There's twenty in a stack, ten stacks all told," Big Joey said. "I'm even more nervous about this today than I was two days ago, but I'll do it for you. But let me remind you of one thing. If you think you have trouble with this guy, just triple it and that'll be the kind of trouble you'll be in with me if I don't get this money back. Got it?"

"Of course. Absolutely," Nick said. "Believe me, I wish I didn't need it. But I've paid you every week, right?"

"Yes, you have. It's the only reason why you're getting this money."

"So you're good with the points and you're good with the six months, so make that happen, OK?" Joey said. "And one other thing. We need some help from you too. Look, you've been killing us on college football all year and we want to know who you like a day in advance, or at least several hours before the games start. That way we can adjust our lines for everyone else if we have to, and we can lay some of this money off. We help you, you help us. Deal?"

"I don't care about that. That's fine. As long as I get fair lines, right?"

"Of course."

Joey closed the briefcase and slid it back in the duffel bag.

"It's all yours, kid. Go pay off your problem as soon as you can."

Nick shook their hands and thanked them again. He threw the bag over his shoulder and headed east. He stopped at a rest stop on the interstate and parked far away from any other cars, took the money out of the briefcase and stuck nine stacks in the glove box and locked it.

He kept one stack and went to the Best Buy in Schererville. He spent about $1,400 on a nice 50-inch high definition TV, loaded it into his truck and drove it to Tony's house. He spent 20 minutes hooking it up, left his brother a nice note, and drove off to Ann Arbor, sticking the other $600 in his wallet.

One stack down.

* * * * *   * * * * *   * * * * *

As soon as he got back to Ann Arbor, he took the money out of the glove box and found a good hiding space in his bedroom. He took another stack of cash and drove over to the check-cashing store and put $1,000 on his credit card, figuring he was going to be sending it back to Joey that way the next week anyway. He called Joey in a few days and let him know about the deposit and that all was good with the girlfriend and the crazy father. She had her abortion and was long gone to live with an aunt for a while, he said. It was all a total lie, of course. Nick bought some nice clothes, paid lots of bills and had a nice lunch with Dale Gerard and some of the guys like it was nothing. Nick, of course, picked up the tab.

A second stack down.

While he was running all these errands, his truck kept acting up, slipping every time he pulled away from an intersection. His transmission was falling apart. So after lunch he drove over to the Chevy dealership and had it checked out. The bad news: his transmission was shot. It would take $2,700 to replace it.

Nick drove it back to his apartment, but was right back at the dealership in the morning. He had his eye on a newer black pick-up, a lot like his but six years newer with 80,000 fewer miles. His baby had served him well, he thought, but it was time for something better. They worked out a deal, he gave them his truck and $8,000 in cash, and off he drove in another shiny black pick-up with only 36,000 miles on it.

Four more stacks down.

But still, it was a good day.

True to his word, Nick talked to Joey about the college bowl games he liked a lot, and the two college football playoff semifinals, which he wasn't leaning toward either way. He made five bets, including a big one with Clemson over Michigan State because he had heard that Michigan State had suspended a few players and none of them wanted to be in chilly Charlotte for a bowl game anyway.

New Year's Day came and went and Nick was right about Michigan State. They lost big, but Nick missed his other four games. He lost money with Joey and with Kenny, who was back in the bookmaking business again after his little arrest, but was being careful. Nick paid him $700 and threw another $1,300 on his credit card for Joey. He told Joey to take the whole $2,000 for his losses and the repayment. It hurt, but it had to be done.

Down goes the seventh stack.

The next week wasn't any better. He got screwed with three half-point

175

losses in the NBA and lost $800 in one night. In the college football national championship game, he loved Florida State over USC, but thought the line was too high. He made all sorts of exotic parlay and teaser bets, trying to buy the line down on Florida State, and he added an over bet with it all. Just as he thought, Florida State won big but their defense was so sound, USC couldn't score at all. Their 31-3 victory was way under the over/under line. Nick was mad at himself. He should have just bet them straight up instead of trying to get cute. He tried to make up for his losses, but his chasing didn't work. He owed Joey about $500 and Kenny a little more than $1,000. He paid Kenny right on schedule, and Kenny tried not to gloat but he was glad Nick lost. He had a good week with all his clients and really needed the money. Nick put a thousand on the card, and sent that off to Joey. He called Joey and pretended to be in a good mood, thankful that he had won a poker tournament for a grand. All lies, of course.

Stack No. 8, out the door.

By now, Nick was craving massive gambling action every night. He played poker online all day, but never won. He was too stressed and over-the-top aggressive. He was betting on NBA games he didn't care about, betting on college basketball games that weren't even on TV. He was down again when the last Sunday in January rolled around, but he was sure he was going to get it all back on the NFC and AFC championship games. He'd made a fortune through the years on the 49ers and Dolphins and both were favored again. He bet them straight up, bet them in parlays, bet them in a few over/under teasers.

And they all lost.

He took Stack No. 9 and Stack No. 10, paid Kenny the next week and shipped off more money to the Risones. He paid the insurance on his new truck – he couldn't believe how much it went up – and he went home to his apartment. He checked his bank account online, counted what he had in his wallet … and then punched a hole in the door to his closet.

He was down to just over three hundred dollars – just two months after driving back to Ann Arbor with $20,000 in cash.

This was not good.

He got about three hour of sleep that night, never more than an hour at a time. He even took a couple Vicodin, but that didn't even help.

This would become a nightly occurrence.

* * * ** * * * * * * * * * *

It was the bye week before the Super Bowl, so it was a pretty dead week for gamblers. Nick never called Joey all week, and made only a few small bets with Kenny, breaking even. Friday rolled around, and he had to muster up the nerve to call Joey.

It wasn't going to be easy.

He dialed the number, and spoke softly.

"Joey, I don't have your money this week," Nick said. "We had a problem with the cops and our poker game. They shut it down and they confiscated all our money. I'll have to double up with you next week."

There was nothing but silence on the other end of the phone. Five seconds passed, then ten, then fifteen …

And then, finally, a click.

Joey had hung up, without saying a word.

TOM BREW

24

By **design, Nick** slept through his Thursday morning history class, waking up about 11. His knee was killing him, so he took a long, hot shower, then packed a bag and had his usual breakfast: two bowls of cereal and a Vicodin washed down with orange juice.

It was another brutal late February morning in Ann Arbor. For the fifth straight day, temperatures were hovering in the single digits and a biting wind was blowing hard and steady out of the north. Winter was wearing Nick down, slowly but surely. It had been 16 months since his original knee injury and the subsequent procedures to clean things up after the staph infection. It had been another five months since the second ACL surgery and in all that time, Nick didn't have a single day when he could say he felt good. It was especially tough when the weather was cold. His knee was stiff, it was sore and it hurt to do anything. Vicodin was fast becoming his new best friend. Just walking here and there and getting in and out of a chair was still painful. Running or working out – still – was out of the question.

There was no such thing as a good day in the life of Nick Vincent.

Not now.

Of course, this mess he had on his hands with Joey Risone was wearing on him, too. It was one thing to have been on a long losing streak with his gambling, but it was even worse that he kept borrowing money from Joey Risone under false pretenses and now all that cash was gone. He borrowed the $2,000 in September and paid that back quickly, but then he borrowed the $10,000 in October, claiming he needed it to set up the poker game, and paid most of it back, but not all of it. Then he borrowed $20,000 more in December with the pregnancy lie and had only been paying the interest he owed Joey. He hadn't touched the principal yet and now had gone two weeks without sending him any money. Risone's patience was wearing thin. He wanted his money back.

Of course, Nick didn't have it.

His bank account was finally empty. He couldn't ask his brother for help – Tony didn't know how deep his gambling problems had become and he didn't have that kind of money laying around anyway. Nick had nowhere to turn. He was desperate and hated the predicament he was in. This was his life now, which wasn't much. His football-star days seemed long gone. He was just a deadbeat gambler now, an after-thought to most people, the worst thing possible.

No one cared about Nick Vincent anymore.

No one but Joey Risone.

Joey Risone and his son had stopped taking bets from him, but Nick was still making small bets – and losing like crazy – with Kenny Phillips in Detroit. Risone started yelling and screaming at Nick during their cell phone conversations the previous week and Nick did a dumb thing, yelling right back. It went back and forth for about 10 minutes and the conversation went nowhere. Every time Nick saw Joey's cell phone number pop up on his cell phone, he cringed, usually ignoring the call. It was getting very ugly. Finally, a few days later, Joey Risone called Nick back from his cell phone and said he wanted all $20,000 in a week or two, or there would be problems. Nick knew not to yell this time, but he tried to buy himself some time by telling Joey he was working on it in Ann Arbor and would be back in Indiana in a few weeks.

Well, those few weeks were up. Nick had to do something with Joey this weekend, or there would be problems. Nick knew Joey was a pretty unstable guy, and he had heard a lot of his brother's stories about Joey. He didn't want to mess with him, but at the same token, he didn't have the money and wasn't about to let someone push him around. It was not a good situation to be in.

Still, he was going to try to fix this mess. Nick, certainly a sick compulsive gambler by now, followed the first rule of Gambler's Code of Finance: Rob Peter to pay Paul. He left his apartment and drove east to Dearborn Heights to meet Terrance Leach. Terrance was a sleeze-ball who owned about a dozen "Buy-Here, Pay-Here" used car lots. He sold overpriced cars, charged ridiculous interest rates and late fees, and had a quick hook with repossessions. He owned the repo company too, so he was always making money, coming and going. Leach made lots of money and loved flashing cash around the Michigan athletes.

During Nick's freshman year, he ran into Leach about four or five times, and each time there was a little handout, sometimes a hundred, sometimes just a couple of twenties. He put Nick and a few other players on the payroll during that first summer in Ann Arbor, cleaning cars and shuffling vehicles from lot to lot. They got real paychecks, but plenty of cash on the side for untraceable little favors. One day he asked Nick to run and get a couple of sandwiches at Subway. The bill was twelve dollars, but Leach gave him a $100 bill and when Nick got back, he told him to keep the change. Those were nice little favors.

Now Nick needed a big favor. In mid-afternoon, he found Leach in his office. He hobbled in, and closed the door.

"Hey Nick, I was just talking about you a few days ago," Leach said. "Some of us were wondering how you were doing. How's the knee?"

Nick wasn't about to tell him the truth. He wasn't about to talk about the pain, or lack of strength, or all the Vicodin. Telling that tale wouldn't help with his current dilemma.

"It's good, Terrance. It's good. Coming along nice," Nick said. "We got some good reports last week when I went to the doctor. They did another MRI and everything is really healing up nicely. I'm working out a little now, and we're going to keep adding to it a week at a time, with the goal of being ready to go by September 1. We're all confident that's going to happen, especially since we're not rushing the rehab like last time."

Nick was putting on a good front. He was lying through his teeth, but that was fast becoming a common occurrence. Even so, talking about playing football again by September was really difficult. Nick was losing hours of sleep every night, writhing in pain and wondering if he'd ever play football again. But he had become so good at lying, that when he said it he felt like even he could believe it.

That's the second rule of the Gambler's Code: Keep telling the same lie long enough and people will believe it. More importantly, you start to believe it yourself. And he was sure hoping Terrance Leach was going to believe it, too.

"Terrance, I've got a problem and I wanted to come to talk to you about it to see if you can help me," Nick said, squirming in his chair and trying not to look nervous. He had rehearsed this tale a dozen times over the past few days, but still the words were tough to get through. He was having to tell his pregnant-girl lie again, and this time he had to really lay it on thick. It worked on Joey Risone a few months back and now it was critical that it worked on Terrance Leach.

"There's this girl in town I've been screwing, a local girl. Here's the bad thing; three bad things, really. She's only 17, she's pregnant and her dad's a lawyer. They want 20-grand and want me to pay for the abortion and send her out of town for a while, and they want the money right now. He said if I don't do it, he'll call the newspapers and call the cops and have them arrest me on statutory rape charges. It's a mess, and I really need this to go away. I don't have that kind of money and I have nowhere else to turn."

Terrance Leach was startled. And uncaring. It's one thing to be the high-roller fan, hanging around with the players, buying them drinks. But this was different. Here was Nick asking for a huge amount of money, and all Leach could think about was this one-legged gimp whose career was probably over had the audacity to sit in his office and ask for that kind of cash.

"Jesus, Nick. I feel really bad that you're in this mess, but I can't help you with money like that. I don't have that kind of money. Business has been bad and I've got to watch it a little. It's one thing to be out buying some drinks and stuff, but hell, that's all just a write-off for me. I don't have that kind of money."

Nick was speechless. He was hoping this was going to be easy, but it wasn't turning out that way. He thought his story sounded severe enough that Leach would bite, but it wasn't happening.

"How much would the quickie abortion cost, like five-hundred dollars or so? Maybe I could help with that. And how serious is this guy about going to the cops? Who is he? What's his name? Maybe I can talk to him."

"No, no, no." Nick said. "I wouldn't want you to do that. That just might make it worse. I just want to be able to have them go away, and have this all behind me."

"Well, screw him, Nick. Threaten him right back. Tell him you're going to go to the papers that he's trying to blackmail you. Hell, he will get disbarred."

"But I can't take that chance. He calls the cops and I'm going to jail. I'm ruined. She lied to me. She told me she was nineteen, but she's only seventeen."

"Let me take care of this son of a bitch then. Give me his name," Leach said.

"I can't let you do that, Terrance. It'll just make it worse. Just please help me make all this go away."

Leach stood up and opened a drawer in his file cabinets. He pulled out a bag, and started peeling off some hundreds. "Here's some money for the doctor, and a little more. Go tell them you'll pay for that, but you can't do anything else. Just tell him the truth, that you're just a college kid with no money. Take this; here's eight hundred dollars. Just tell him that's every dollar you have, and that you'll give that to them, but that's it."

Nick took a deep breath, and sighed. His plan wasn't working. He had hoped to walk out with a plan to get his hands on $20,000, but instead was looking at eight measly $100 bills.

This was not good.

Nick paused for a moment, and stood up. He stretched out his hand and shook with Leach. He picked up the money and thanked him. "I really appreciate it, and I'll let you know how it goes," Nick said. Nick was trying to seem polite, but underneath he was seething. He was hoping he was going to be able to get out of this mess, and now he was basically back at square one.

"So I'll need that $800 back, whenever you can, OK?" Leach said, which startled Nick a bit. "And when you can, bring me some autographed helmets. They always make nice gifts."

Nick nodded and headed out the door, doing his best to not display his anger. He jumped in his truck and started heading west to Indiana, not sure what to do next. Best case scenario? Maybe he could give Joey Risone another $500 and buy another week or two. Maybe Leach would help with a few of those payments, if need be.

In any case, there were no clear alternatives.

His stomach tossed and turned the entire five-hour ride.

* * * *   * * * *   * * * *

Nick's next dilemma was figuring out where to stay when he got home to Schererville. Since his brother Tony had stopped gambling and book-making more than a year ago and severed his relationship in a friendly way with Joey Risone, the brothers never shared any conversations about gambling. Tony knew he had been getting consumed by all the betting and book-making and it affected his regular construction business, so he simply stopped. It was no big deal to him. He didn't gamble compulsively; he just bet like most normal people without it being all-consuming. There's a huge difference between gambling and gambling compulsively and Tony Vincent never crossed that threshold. He worked too hard for his money and hated the thought of losing it.

If he knew Nick was in so deep, he probably would have beaten the hell out of him. Nick wanted to be sure Tony didn't know what was going on and he definitely didn't want Joey Risone coming after his big brother, too.

Still, home was home and it was just a couple of days. Tony wasn't even home much anyway, so Nick decided to stay there after all. He called his brother and let him know he was on his way, and they agreed to go have dinner together.

They went to Angelo's for some pizza and talked about Nick's knee, his school work, Tony's construction business and the long, dreadful winter weather. Gambling never came up, nor did the name of Joey Risone or any outstanding $20,000 debt that was growing by the days with interest. Nick was uncomfortable the whole time, but it was good to see his older brother. They had fun.

When they got back to the house about 7, Tony had to run out to take care of some things. Nick needed to charge his dying cell phone, so he picked up the home phone and called Joey Risone. Joey answered on the first ring.

"Haven't seen that number in a long time. What's up, Tony?" Joey said.

"It's not Tony, it's me, Nick. I'm in town, like I told you I would be," Nick said. There was silence on the other end of the line.

"Well, good. I'm glad you came home. You bringing me my money tonight?" Joey asked.

"Are you going to be at the bar? I can be there in about an hour," Nick said.

"Yeah, I'm here all night. Come on over."

Nick made sure he didn't say anything about the cash shortage on the phone, because he wanted to have that conversation in person, and in public. He

183

figured his chances with Joey were best that way. He put five of the $100 bills in his wallet, waited for cell phone to fully charge and then took off. He hid the other $300 in his truck, just in case.

Risone's bar was definitely a dingy place. It was small and dirty, with a long bar and about eight booths. It had a couple of pool tables, some poker machines and a juke-box right out of the '70s in the back of the bar. Nick remembered thinking it was a dump the first time he went there with his brother to drop off some money, but now that he'd seen a little nightlife himself, he knew with certainly that this place was a hell-hole. He wasn't looking forward to walking through the front door, but he knew he had to do it. He got out of his truck, stepped over some construction debris from a sidewalk repair, then walked into the bar.

It was awkward. For starters, Joey Risone was a sports fan and thought it was cool that he knew of Nick, this highly-regarded football stud. He genuinely liked Nick, but now this money thing had gotten way out of hand and he was legitimately pissed. He could care less now that Nick Vincent was a Michigan linebacker. In his eyes, Nick was just another low-life gambler who owed him money. A lot of money.

Still, when Nick walked in the door on this chilly Thursday night, Joey was behind the bar, pouring himself a drink. He came around the bar, gave Nick a big hug and a hearty slap on the back. "Our big football star!" he said, loud enough for everyone in the bar to hear. The place was filled with regulars, all friends of Joey.

"Come on back," Joey said tersely, and Nick followed him into the back room, where all the book-making took place. Joey's younger brother Paulie and Joey Junior came with them, and the four of them walked into Joey's tiny and cluttered private office.

"Got my money?" Joey said, the smile suddenly leaving his face.

"I've got your $500 Joey and I can get you a couple thousand more in a couple of weeks. That's the best I can do. You need to give me some time," Nick said. He was nervous as hell. Here he was, twenty years old and in a big mess and he was telling a fifty-year-old known killer how this was going to play out.

"Not acceptable. Totally not acceptable," Joey yelled as he rose out of his chair and put his hands on the desk. "That was not our deal. I need that money and I need it now. I borrowed it to give it to you and now the people I owe want their money back. You're putting me in a hell of a mess. I am not going to get my ass kicked because of you. If anyone's going to get their ass kicked, it's you."

Joey's cheeks were getting red and it was obvious his blood-pressure was boiling over. His brother locked the office door behind Nick.

"So you've got $500? That's it? Where is it?"

Nick opened his wallet and handed him the five $100 bills. Joey grabbed the wallet out of his hand, looked inside and saw a twenty and a couple of singles. That was all. The other $300 was hiding in the truck, and Nick wasn't going to tell him about that money unless he absolutely had to.

"This is it? You don't have anything else?"

"No," Nick said. "But I'm trying to get more. You just have to give me some time."

"Bullshit. I don't have to give you anything. Pay me. Pay me now. Look, I've already borrowed money from my uncle once and now I need to pay them the rest. I have until Saturday, so you have until Saturday. I want the entire twenty-grand by noon on Saturday, or I'm going to stick this pole right up your ass. You'll be sorry you ever met me. Now get the fuck out of here before I kick your ass right here. I don't care how big you are. I'll still kick the shit out of you."

Nick was a couple inches taller than Joey, about the same weight and certainly much more fit, even with one knee. But still, he wasn't about to throw punches with him, not with his goon of a brother right there and a dozen friends right outside the door. Joey's brother opened the office door and Nick walked toward the front door of the bar. As he reached for the handle, Joey yelled out to him, from about 30 feet away. "Hey, asshole!" he screamed.

Nick turned around quickly and saw Joey, a pistol in hand. He was aiming right between Nick's eyes.

"Listen, you worthless prick. You have until noon Saturday or you will be seeing my little friend here again, got it? I don't care where you get it. You know, that's what's pissing me off right now. I know you can get it."

Nick was scared, but he was also very upset as well.

"If I could get it, I would. But I can't," Nick yelled, his voice cracking from fear. "I don't know anyone with that kind of money, no one at all. You know that. So don't threaten me. How dare you point a gun at me? That's total bullshit."

"Get out of here. Now! Noon Saturday, you be back. Got it?"

Nick didn't say a word, just walked out the door, as angry as he'd ever been, even angrier than that day in Columbus when his knee got blown out. Even angrier than when the morphine would run low at the hospital or when a late field goal would cost him a $500 bet or a big four-figure parlay. If he had his way, he'd go back in there and beat the living daylights out of that fat punk Joey Risone. Instead, he started his truck and stared ahead in anger for a few seconds.

Then he got back out of the truck, picked up a brick from the mess outside the bar and fired it through Joey's huge picture window, glass shattering every-where.

He sped off, wheels spinning on the ice.

TOM BREW

25

The frigid winter air blowing through the front window of Joey Risone's bar was doing nothing to stop the steam blowing from his ears. He was hot; just livid. He couldn't believe that Nick Vincent, this 20-year-old sudden pain in his ass who owed him $20,000 and counting, just threw a brick through his window. Glass had shattered everywhere, even cutting a few customers. Joey's younger brother Paulie, whose temper was even worse than Joey's, wanted to chase after Nick, but Joey told him no.

"Let him go. We can't accomplish anything right now," Joey said. Joey Junior agreed. "That little prick is smart enough to know that he just did a very stupid thing. Let him stew in his own juices for a while. He's not going anywhere. He can't. Everyone knows who he is."

Joey might be an uneducated mob thug, but he was certainly reading this situation right. Nick couldn't just run and hide. That was not an option. He was a high profile college football player, well known throughout the Big Ten geographic area, and even though he was hobbling around on one good leg, people were still going to know who he was. Taking off in his truck to hide could never be an option. It was one thing to skip a few classes on some blustery winter days, but Nick certainly had to be back on campus by Monday or Tuesday, or some major red flags would be flying.

Joey knew this.

Even worse, Nick knew this, too.

In the hour or so it took Joey and his pals to board up the front window, Nick was dashing west, hurrying to get out of town. He knew he couldn't go home. He was going to need to come up with a plan and he was sure he was going to need to give Joey some time to cool off. He'd done something really dumb and he knew it. He was going to have to deal with it; just not tonight.

He got as far west as Joliet, and needed gas. He pulled into a gas station, got out of his truck, and looked around. He didn't see anything suspicious, but didn't expect to. He didn't see anyone follow him when he ripped away from the bar and he hadn't seen anyone hanging around in his rear-view mirror since then. Joliet was about 35 miles away and the opposite direction of where anyone would expect Nick to go. Schererville was to the east, and so was Michigan. It was very much a spur-of-the-moment decision by Nick to dash westward, but he was glad he had. He looked around some more before pumping his gas and felt safe. For now he could breathe, at least for a few hours,

And then his cell phone rang.

He looked down at the caller ID, and saw it was Joey Risone calling from his cell phone. He didn't answer it, of course. It rang again. And then again. About two minutes later, finally, he got a "New Voicemail" notification, so he dialed and listened in to a three-minute rant from Joey. He heard it all, then saved the message, and would listen to it again and again through the night. About the fifth time he listened to the message, he counted 34 "mother-fuckers" from Joey, all either starting a sentence or ending one, sometimes both. Nick's life was threatened 10 times.

A mile or so down the road was a casino, one owned by the same company that always took care of Nick and his brother in Michigan. He figured he could get a room cheap, or free, with his VIP card and that sounded like a good place to hide out for the night, until he could figure out his next step. He wheeled his truck into the parking garage, parked in a crowded area, and checked in. Turns out he was right; they comped his room and gave him a voucher for the late-night buffet. He went up to his room, took a long, hot shower and crashed down onto the bed, listening to Joey's message again with his speakerphone on.

This time he had to laugh.

* * * * *   * * * * *   * * * * *

Inside the Chicago offices of FBI agent Mark DiPolitto, the tapes were rolling. Four agents were listening to Joey's voicemail message too, but they weren't laughing. Their investigation into Joey Risone hadn't produced much in the first two weeks, but on this quiet, wintry Thursday night, that was all changing.

About two months earlier, a low-life in the Calabria crime family got busted trying to sell a lot of heroin to an undercover cop. Facing 25 years in jail, this grunt was ready to start ratting out some people in order to save his own hide. What he told the FBI investigators was mostly garbage, until late into his second interview. Then he had this little tidbit.

"I know about two murders that were never solved. I know who did it, both times."

With that little nugget, the interrogators' ears perked up. This low-life grunt wanted a sweet deal in exchange for the information, but that was really fine with the agents. This guy meant nothing to them. He was just another helpless and hapless drug dealer, a dime-a-dozen thug at the bottom of the Calabria crime family food chain. They were always looking for higher-ups in the organized crime families, and this might be worth something, a step in the right direction. A few hours later, they came back with his signed deal – two years in jail under an assumed name in California, then witness protection – in exchange for a name that panned out and testimony at trial when the time came.

Who was murdered, they asked? And who committed the murders?

"I don't know the names of the guys who got whacked for sure, but I can tell you where they happened and you guys can figure it out, because I know they found the bodies. I was just driving that night. But I know the guy who did it, the guy who pulled the trigger."

Who, they asked?

"A big dumb shit named Joey Risone."

In a matter of days, the FBI had all its research on Joey. They knew all about his previous run-ins with the law, about his drug-dealing, book-making, loan-sharking and prostitution interests. They knew all about his Chicago Heights bar, which was a front for everything. A few days later, they snuck into the joint in the middle of the night and planted bugs everywhere. There was one in a Miller Lite sign behind the bar, another by a light near the front door. Joey's office had a bug in the lamp on his desk, and there were two more near the desks where the bets were taken. There were cameras in every room and every phone line was bugged, including the private line in Joey's office. It took a few days to get the warrant, but they also had Joey's cell phone calls being recorded as well.

It was wall-to-wall Joey on the recorders.

And for the bored investigators, who hadn't heard much of anything good the first two weeks, Thursday night was fun. They had heard it all. Nick's call from Tony's home phone to Joey earlier in the night, their entire conversation in the bar and in Joey's office, the screaming between the two of them while Joey pointed the gun at Nick and the brick coming through the window. And, of course, Joey's call to Nick on the cell phone after he had left. They laughed that any man could use the word "mother-fucker" 34 times in a three-minute message, but they also smiled with glee when they counted the 10 death threats.

They had something there.

They confirmed everything had recorded properly, which was great because that didn't always happen. Every word, the sound quality was perfect. On every video feed, Joey's face was clearly visible in every frame, including the short time he was pointing a gun at Nick. They couldn't have asked for anything more.

A few things didn't make sense though, so they had some extra work on their hands. First off, working backward, they didn't recognize Nick on the video. He had never been in the bar before while it was under surveillance, and Nick's cell phone number didn't pop up on their hot list when they tracked that call. They did find one call from Nick's cell phone to Joey a week earlier when they dug deeper, but that was it, and it had been only a minute long. And they totally didn't recognize Tony Vincent's home number either, the one Nick had called from earlier in the night. Impressed with their quick homework, they went to their boss Di-Politto.

"Here's what we know so far," the agent said, standing in front of his boss's desk. "Risone called a kid named Nick Vincent and threatened to kill him 10 times in a three-minute message left on Vincent's cell phone. We didn't know who this Vincent was, but we checked him out and he's a 20-year-old college student at the University of Michigan. He plays football there, and grew up in Schererville, Indiana, born and raised there and went to school at Crossroads High School. He made a call to Risone earlier in the night from a land-line, which belongs to his brother, Anthony Vincent, from a home he owns in Schererville. Nick Vincent has no criminal record, just a couple of speeding tickets. Anthony Vincent, also no record. Got sued once over a construction bill, but he won the case. This kid Nick Vincent is clean, other than our boy Risone wanting him expired. He must have done something wrong. He showed up in the bar about an hour after the first phone call, and we have it all, the call, the whole time in the bar, and the call afterward threatening to kill him."

"And we don't know anything about this Nick Vincent kid?"

"No, other than from the tapes tonight. It sounds like he owes our boy Risone some money. We don't have any calls these first few weeks about Vincent making any bets and we've got nothing ever coming in from either the home number or his cell phone since we started our surveillance here, other than one quick one-minute call the first day we were recording. It said nothing. Tonight Risone said he wanted $20,000 in a week when they were arguing and Risone said something about borrowing money from his uncle to give it to this kid, so Albert Calabria might be involved down the road here too. I'm sure if Risone owes Albert Calabria money and he's not paying, then there's trouble there too, blood or no blood."

DiPolitto was certainly intrigued. He liked that he had something new on Risone, because he didn't like their original witness much, not enough to go to bat with him at trial as the only witness. But he also knew they didn't have much here yet either.

At least not yet.

"This kid, Nick Vincent, that name sounds real familiar to me. You find anything on him?"

"Hell, yes, there's like hundreds of articles that pop up when I did a Google search," the junior investigator said. He got all the grunt-work, including the website searching. "That paper there in the south suburbs, the Star-Press, named him their football player of the year two years ago. He was first-team all-state, second in Mr. Football voting and also was on their state-championship basketball team. Hell, they even retired his number in some big ceremony that last football game of the year. Sounds like he was one of those high school legends over there. Played one year at Michigan and he was awesome, but he got hurt and didn't play this year."

"Looks like he found something else to do if he's run up 20-grand worth of gambling debts to our boy," DiPolitto said. "Let's find out more about him – discreetly – and let's start tracking his cell phone calls, too. Track it starting right this second. The boy's life is in danger. I actually know someone over in Schererville. Runs a treatment clinic over there. I'll call him myself and ask him what he knows about this Vincent kid. I just talked to him about a month or so ago, so it won't seem odd to him that I'm calling him again.

"And keep your eye on that bar and Risone. We need live eyes on him now, too. Don't let him out of our sight, and let's see what his next move is."

* * * * *   * * * * *   * * * * *

Two-hundred miles and change to the south, the crowd inside Assembly Hall in Bloomington had been erupting with applause after each made three-pointer on this wintry Thursday night. In and out of each timeout, the chants of "Danny, Danny" reverberated off the walls in the second half.

Danny Bridges was having the night of his life, his best game yet at Indiana, and the fans were loving it.

It was the final home game of the season, Senior Night, but it was the sophomore Danny Bridges who was stealing the show. Penn State was the opponent, and it was a night that mattered. Indiana needed a win to stay on Michigan State's heels for the conference title, but they also wanted to win for the seniors. It was always much easier for them to say goodbye to the fans after a win.

Penn State, in the bottom third of the standings, was giving Indiana a game in the first half. The Hoosiers were up only four at the half. Danny had played well, making three baskets, including a three-pointer, and a couple of free throws, but the rest of the team was struggling.

The second half was completely different.

On Indiana's first seven possessions against Penn State's pack-it-in zone defense, Danny made five three-pointers. He was on fire. The Indiana lead quickly grew to 12 and Penn State abandoned the zone but they still couldn't keep track of Danny through all the picks and he nailed a few more long balls. By the time the game ended, Indiana had won comfortably, by 22 points, and Danny had finished with 38 points, by far a career high. He was 9-for-9 from beyond the arc, 3-for-5 otherwise and a perfect 5-for-5 from the free-throw line as well. With the win, they moved to 14-3 in the Big Ten and 22-4 overall. One more win at Northwestern on Saturday and they could tie for the Big Ten title if Michigan State lost its last game on Sunday. It was a perfect night for everyone. The seniors said goodbye, and there were lots of smiles in the locker room afterward. Reporters along press row banged out their stories, extolling the virtues of Danny Bridges, who now was the team's leading scorer and had become their most important player during the last half of the season.

Danny did all his newspaper and TV interviews and showered quickly. As much as he wanted to celebrate the big win, an economics test was awaiting him in the morning and he wanted to study some more. He called his mother first on his way home – she couldn't make it down for a mid-week game and still get to work the next morning – and then talked to Candice for about 20 minutes while he ate something. After the food was gone and the books were out just past midnight, as Thursday was turning into Friday, he decided he'd make one more call before he started studying.

He called Nick Vincent.

It went straight to his voicemail.

"You're probably sleeping, but I hope you saw the game tonight," Danny said. "It was the most fun I've had since the state finals. Say hello sometime, stranger. I miss chatting with you."

He hung up and started studying, never thinking twice about what might be going on with his best friend.

* * * *   * * * *   * * * *

As midnight came and went, Joey's bar was mostly empty. He and his bartender and a few patrons were watching re-runs of the sports highlights from the local NBC station in Chicago. Their little three-minute segment started with highlights of the Indiana-Penn State game. They showed every one of Danny Bridges nine 3-pointers and talked about his brilliant 38-point night. They also mentioned Danny's connection to Crossroads High School just across the state line in northwest Indiana and that Indiana would be in town Saturday night to conclude the regular season at Northwestern, with the Big Ten title and conference tournament seeding still on the line.

"Hey, I know that kid," the bartender said. "Big, tall, skinny kid. I remember he came in here one night a few years ago, with that punk Nick when he was dropping off some money for you from his brother. They were only here for a couple of minutes, but I remember it because it was so weird seeing someone that tall walk in here with a high school letterman's jacket on."

Joey just shook his head. "I don't remember that. Two years ago? That was a lot of vodka and a whole lot of cocaine ago for my brain cells."

Joey took another sip of his drink. He hadn't really been paying close attention to the TV.

"What did the kid do?" he said, in an uncaring way.

"He scored 38 tonight against Penn State, totally killed him single-handedly. They won by 22."

Joey got up off his bar stool and walked around for a minute before walking back to his office. He banged on his computer quickly, printed out the night's numbers and walked back to the bar.

"Indiana won by 22 and they were favored by 16. We took in $7,500 on them, and $8,600 on Penn State and the points, so it was a good night for us, too. Almost a couple grand on that game, with the vig. And the Bridges kid had 38?"

"He sure did, the prick," one of the patrons said. "Four hundred of that $8,600 on Penn State was mine. Figured that'd be way too many points. I watched most of that second half on the little TV over there and that prick never missed. Made a bunch of three-pointers in a row in the second half, one right after another. They couldn't stop him."

Joey walked around some more, his mind wandering, then carried the sheet back to his office. He looked through the whole season, and saw the action on Indiana. It was always a lot. They were popular, on TV all the time, and nearby.

About 10 minutes later, he sat back down at the bar and poured another drink, vodka on the rocks, with a splash of cranberry, same as the first dozen he had tossed down that evening.

"Interesting," he said, to no one in particular. "Very interesting"

* * * * * * * * * * * * * * *

Nick blew through the late-night buffet quickly, then headed to the tables, having no interest whatsoever in going to sleep. He had $300 left and figured spending a $100 to make some more wouldn't be a bad thing. No one, not even Joey Risone, knew he had the $300 anyway, so what the hell? Might as well give it a shot. He figured he would play poker in a cash game for two hours then get some sleep, and that's exactly what he did. His stomach was full, his gas tank was full, so he had no other pressing needs. And when it was all said and done, he had turned his $100 into $560 and, right on the button, he got up and walked away right at his two-hour mark. He was a good poker player, and he felt good to finally win some money gambling.

It had been months.

He peeled off the hundreds when he got back to his room, and clipped three of them back with the other two from before, and buried them behind some pictures in his wallet. His first thought was that at least now he had another $500 for Joey, and that might buy him another week. He needed $20,000, but that wasn't going to happen. And turning $500 into $20,000 wasn't going to happen either. Even as sick as Nick was, even he didn't believe that. So he hid the $500, and figured at least he had another week covered.

Well past 2 a.m., he turned off his hotel room light, crawled into bed and flipped on SportsCenter. He checked his phone and was thrilled to see no more calls from Joey. He had just the one missed call, from Danny, and he listened to the short message, smiling. He waited for the Indiana highlights on TV, but fell sound asleep before they came on.

Another day done.

Another week bought.

26

Danny arrived at the business school a few minutes before 10 and was greeted to with a round of applause from his classmates when he walked into the room. That's what scoring 38 points will do for you. That, and being a really nice guy who was truly liked by all of his business school colleagues. Some students-athletes didn't put much thought into being students, but Danny did. His fellow students appreciated his efforts in the classroom, especially when they were doing group projects, knowing full well how busy he was with basketball.

Applause aside, the reality of the morning was that he had a bear of an economics test to get through before his good times could start. He was looking forward to this weekend. It was the last regular-season game of the year, but it was also at Northwestern, which meant he'd get to see Candice and his family, and several other friends – including his high school coach, Will Jackson, and Ben Richardson – would be able to make the short drive up from Schererville to the game. The team was traveling to Evanston early in the afternoon on Friday, so he was really hoping he'd be able to have dinner with Candice Friday night.

The test took about an hour and went well, and when he was done he quickly walked back to his apartment. He smiled when he turned on his cell phone, because he saw two missed calls – and two voicemail messages. Candice had called first, about an hour earlier, and the other call was from his buddy, Nick Vincent. Looking at the time, just before noon, he could tell that he just missed Nick's call. Candice's message was quick – "thinking of you, busy until 4, call when you can, etc." – but Nick left a lengthy message. Even in voicemail form, Danny was thrilled to hear Nick's voice. They hadn't talked in about three weeks.

Nick was apologetic about not calling more often. He got Danny updated on what was going on with him – leaving out all the important stuff, of course. He repeated the lie about his knee getting better and the good reports from the doctor, making a point to emphasize that he planned on being ready to play football by September. He complimented Danny on his big game the night before and said he felt bad about not seeing it, but glad he got to see all the highlights. He told Danny he hoped Indiana would be sent to Detroit for the first two rounds of the NCAA Tournament, and if not they'd probably have to wait until April to see each other. He said his goodbyes and told Danny he had a busy day, so don't bother calling back.

Danny didn't think twice about that. He was just glad to hear from him, and assumed he was at school in Ann Arbor and not shacked up in a casino hotel, hiding from a mobster. He knew Nick was really struggling with his rehab, and wasn't very happy. But there wasn't much he could do about it now. He was fully engrossed in the basketball season and Nick was 300 miles away. His focus was where it was supposed to be, but he still felt bad that he couldn't be doing more for his friend.

* * * * *   * * * * *   * * * * *

Once all the vodka started to wear off, Joey Risone finally got up and started his day about 2 in the afternoon. He got dressed and headed down to the bar, picking up a newspaper on the way and ordering a burger and fries when he got there. When he went back to his office, his brother Paulie was waiting for him, all smiles.

"What's wrong with you, with the goofy grin?" Joey said.

"Here, look at this," Paulie said as he dropped about a dozen sheets of paper on Joey's desk, all neat and organized. On the front page was a big picture and some headlines, the start of a newspaper story printed out from the newspaper's website.

"The kid on the left, holding the trophy, that's our little pain-in-the-ass Nick. The kid on the right, with the net around his neck, that's the kid Danny Bridges we watched last night on the basketball highlights. The story was written about two years ago after they won the state championship and it's all about how close they are and how good of friends they are. They've been best friends since they were little kids."

"So," Joey wondered, "what's your point?"

"Well, if we're looking for Nick, maybe we start by keeping an eye on this other kid. If he's playing a game up here in Evanston on Saturday, maybe Nick's stupid enough to show up to see him. Doesn't sound to me like Nick has a whole lot of friends right now. Maybe he'd want to see this friend."

Joey soaked it all in, but the more he thought about it, the more he realized once again that Paulie never really sees the big picture. The game wasn't until Saturday night, and this was Friday afternoon. Joey wanted to find Nick now. He wasn't about to wait.

"I'm not waiting until Saturday night to track down this piece of shit," Joey said. "Let's do this. Call Doyle, the cop, and tell him I need to see him right away. Tell him it's urgent and to get down here to the bar. Tell him there's free food. That'll get him here in a hurry."

Charles Doyle was a dirty cop on the take, and had been for years. He kept Joey out of trouble and the local cops away from his door, in exchange for a handful of hundreds, a few free drinks and the occasional twenty minutes with one of the hookers Joey knew. When Joey beckoned, he usually came a running. He wasn't working anyway on Friday, so he came right down. Joey greeted him with a bottle of scotch and ten $100 bills folded neatly in his hand.

"Doyle, I need you to track a cell phone for me today and tell me where this kid is. He tore up my bar last night, threw a brick right through the freaking front window, and dashed out of here."

"I saw that when I walked in. Was wondering what happened," he said. "Who we tracing? Someone I know? Someone I want to know?"

"No, you don't know him and you don't need to. He hasn't done anything wrong other than not paying me some money he owes me and then breaking my window. Just need to do some collecting, that's all. That's all there is to it, and all you need to know. I just need you to track his phone when I call him and tell me where he is. I'll take it from there."

This wasn't the first time Joey had asked Doyle to do this, and it was no problem for him. Back at the station, they had all the technology to eavesdrop on anyone, especially someone with a live cell phone. As long as he had the number and the carrier, it didn't take much to find someone. After Doyle wolfed down a sandwich and a couple of scotches, he loaded his mouth with gum and headed to the station. Within an hour he was up and running and ready to go.

"OK, Joey, I'm all set on this end. Go ahead and call and I'll see what we can find out. And do your best to keep him on the line for at least two minutes, OK?"

Joey sat down at his desk and punched Nick's number onto his phone pad. It rang only once, and went straight to voicemail. "Shit," Joey said, banging his hand on his desk. He hung up.

Doyle was still on his cell phone. "Nothing," he said. "Must be turned off, and unless we can track a signal, we've got nothing."

"Let me do this, then," Joey said. "I'm going to play nice, and leave him a voicemail message telling him I'd be willing to work with him on a payment. I'll tell him some shit about buying some time myself, so I could give him some time. I'll just tell him to call me back, and then when he does, then we can track it."

Nick's phone was off only because he had forgotten to bring his wall charger, and it died while he was sleeping in his Joliet hotel room. He had decided this was a good place to hang out for the weekend, and had already extended his stay two more nights with the front desk. Without a charger in his room, he plugged it into his car charger in the early afternoon when he ran out to get some lunch, but he hadn't powered it up yet. A few minutes later he did, to call his roommate Dale Gerard back at Michigan to let him know he'd be gone the entire weekend.

A few minutes after that, Joey called again.

Nick, of course, wasn't about to answer it when he saw the number. It rang four times, then went to voicemail. On the back end, Joey was thrilled, because he could tell Nick's phone was on. He left the nicest, sweetest message any pissed-off thug could ever muster. It lasted a couple of minutes, with the point being made over and over that they could work something out, only if Nick would call him back right away to make some arrangements.

Nick walked into a fast-food burger joint and ordered, then sat in the corner by himself. He listened to Joey's voicemail message and was pleasantly surprised. His first thought was, "Great, I've got his $500 for next week already." Time was his ally, and this was very good news. He was also surprised that Joey was being so calm, somewhat shocked that the broken window never came up. It could only mean one thing, Nick thought. He figured Joey knew he couldn't get all this money at once and that it was in his best interest to get it over time. That was totally fine with Nick. He was sure the window would come up when he called Joey back, and he figured he had to be proactive about that and get his apologies in quickly. As he finished his cheeseburger and fries, he was as happy as he'd been in a while. It sounded like he had Joey off his back, he was glad he had a few dollars in his pocket, and he was glad he had a nice hotel room and a casino just down the hall. It didn't take much to make him happy, not with all the crap going on in his life, but this was working. There was a $100-entry poker tournament that started at 7 that night, and that sounded like fun.

After he got back to his hotel room, he collected his thoughts and prepared to call Joey. He knew he wanted to talk about the window first, to get his apologies in. He wanted to tell Joey right away that he'd have his $500 next week for sure and he figured he could get his hands on another $500, which should be more than enough to fix the window. A promise to come up with more than $500 each week would probably help, too, and he figured it was something Joey might want to hear.

He plopped down on the bed and hit the redial button on Joey's office line. Joey picked up on the first ring.

The clock started ticking. Joey glanced at his watch, and so did Doyle.

"Hey, Nick, thanks for calling back," Joey said, doing his best to sound upbeat. "Look, you've got to know I'm still a little pissed at you, but we're in this together, man, and we can work something out. Let's do that, OK?"

Nick answered right away. "Sure, Joey. That's what I want; you know that. I want to pay you, believe me, it's just not easy for me right now. I don't have any money and I've got no one to borrow it from. But I'll get you some money next

198

week for sure, the $500 I owe you plus something for the window. Is that fair?"

Joey paused for a moment, looking at his watch. "That ought to be enough, but there's more to it than just that, Nick. A couple of guys who were sitting by the window got cut up pretty good from the glass. I think a few hundreds bucks for them isn't unreasonable, either. So I want a thousand next week, then another thousand the week after that, with the other $500 going to those guys. And then once you're used to paying a grand a week, I want you to keep doing that so we can make a dent into this balance. I think that's only fair, Nick. It's only fair. Would you agree?"

Hell yes, it's fair, Nick thought to himself. Time was what he needed, and he was getting it. Finding a few extra bucks wasn't going to be easy, but at least now he had the time to find them.

While Nick was talking, Joey's cell phone beeped. It was a text message from Doyle. "GOT HIM!" it said. Joey did his best to not show his hand.

"OK, Nick, I've got to run, but you get me the money on Friday next week, a grand a week until we're caught up, OK?"

"Thanks, Joey, I appreciate you working with me here," Nick said. He was breathing easy now.

Joey was having a hard time hiding his glee. "So, where are you?"

Nick didn't think twice about it. "In Michigan, driving back to school," Nick said, lying once again like it was no big deal at all.

Joey shook his head and covered the phone with his hand. "Bet you anything he's lying," Joey said. "But Doyle will know for sure."

They said their goodbyes, Nick happy to get off the phone and get on with his weekend, Joey to get to Doyle. He hung up his office line and grabbed his cell phone.

"Where is he?" Joey shouted, "Where is that prick?"

Doyle was succinct, and confident. Oh, the joys of modern technology. "He's in Joliet, Illinois, right down the road." Doyle said.

"I'll bet you a million dollars I know exactly where that prick is," Joey said as he bounced out of his chair. "He's at the casino. Call Ralphie and Johnny and tell them to get the big van ready. We're getting ready for a little road trip."

* * * * *　　* * * * *　　* * * * *

F**BI agent Mark DiPolitto** was on a road trip of his own, driving the 45 minutes or so from his downtown Chicago office to Schererville, Indiana to see his old friend, Ben Richardson. He had called Ben in the morning, to be sure he'd be at the house, and was glad he was in town. He had some questions, and he was hoping Ben had some answers. He wanted to snoop around Schererville anyway, and he could at least be inconspicuous meeting with Ben.

Before he met with Ben, he called his office one more time to get the latest update. His minions were giddy, because they had all the calls on tape and actually had been listening in live to Joey's conversation with Nick. They had heard it all, that conversation and the interaction with the cop who was helping Joey find Nick. This was getting very juicy. Dangerous, and juicy. They heard it all that Joey knew where Nick was, and they were very concerned about Joey's next move. They had someone watching the bar, and the agents were on red-alert to follow Joey and his guys when they left.

Ben greeted DiPolitto with a hearty hug, as he did with everyone, and they sat down in the living room, just the two of them. Ben figured DiPolitto was coming to see him with some kind of update on the Aaron Maxwell murder. They had first talked about it three weeks ago when the snitch first emerged, but hadn't talked since then.

Needless to say, Ben was totally floored when DiPolitto asked his first question. He expected to hear the name of a murderer.

"Do you know Nick Vincent?" DiPolitto asked.

"Yeah, I know Nick Vincent. He lives a few blocks from here. He's been here to the house before, because his best friend used to work for me. I've watched him play a ton of high school football and basketball games. He's a great kid, a great athlete. Why do you ask?"

"Ever known him to be in any trouble?" DiPolitto asked.

"No. Why?"

"Ever known him to deal with unsavory people?"

"No. Why? Why are you asking me about Nick Vincent? He's a great kid."

Ben and DiPolitto might have been friends, but he was acting more like a cop now. He was being careful not to say too much. He wanted to gather more information before he wanted to start giving any away.

"Ever known him to have a gambling problem, or a money problem? Or anyone else in his family?"

"Jesus, Mark, that's enough. Tell me why you're asking all these questions. All I know of Nick Vincent is that he's a hell of a football player and a really good kid, and I don't know that he's ever been in trouble. I've never heard of anything like that. And I've met his older brother. He's a good guy, owns a concrete company. Does a lot of construction work. Hell, they poured my slab here for the deck and helped me re-do the basketball court out back. I know his brother Tony used to gamble, sports mostly, but nothing major and I've never heard that he was in any kind of trouble either. As far as I know, they're a great family.

"So why in the hell is an FBI agent – my friend, for Christ's sake – asking me questions about them?"

"I have reason to believe that Nick Vincent's life might be in danger," DiPolitto said. "And I have even more reason to believe that he has no idea how much danger he's in."

The color drained out of Ben's face. He had watched Nick play 15 or so football games and probably 40 basketball games at Crossroads HIgh School . Nick had played basketball on his own court with all the kids and had sat on his back porch and eaten sandwiches while visiting Danny when he was working. This made absolutely no sense to him.

"What can you tell me then, Mark? This just totally shocks me."

"Well, I can't say much, other than to tell you this gangster we're following on the Aaron Maxwell murder apparently is owed about $20,000 or more from this Vincent kid. On tape last night in his bar, we watched them talk about the money, how the kid can't pay and we watched – it's all on tape – this gangster point a gun at him and threaten to kill him and then we watched this kid have the balls to throw a brick through the front window of his bar. And then we just intercepted a phone call from the kid's cell phone. We've been listening. They know where he is now and I'm sure they're going to go looking for him."

"What are you going to do about it? Anything I can do to help?" Ben said.

"What about his brother? Maybe we need to talk to him. Do you know where I can find him?"

"Sure," Ben said. "He lives right around the corner. Let's go."

They jumped into DiPolitto's car and sped off, the FBI agent and the gambling treatment counselor.

DiPolitto had one more question.

"Do you know who Danny Bridges is?"

Ben nearly lost his breath.

* * * * *   * * * * *   * * * * *

Joey Risone decided to have his first vodka of the day as he surfed the web, reading up on Indiana's basketball season. Paulie was looking over his shoulder.

Joey leaned back far in his chair, and smiled as he stared at a picture of Danny Bridges draining a three-pointer.

"I'm thinking what you're thinking, Paulie," he said. " If we need to get our money back, maybe there's a way we can put some pressure on the kid to help us. If they're best friends and this kid Bridges knew his friend was in a life-or-death situation, maybe he can be pressured to do something for us."

Paulie shrugged his shoulders and continued. "Look, Indiana's a big favorite Saturday and this kid is their best player, with the ball in his hands most of the time. Maybe we can get to him to make sure they don't win by too much, if you know what I mean."

"One kid can't fix a basketball game," Joey said. "Not by himself."

"You don't think so? I do. We don't need him to lose, just not win by so much. And if we get our hands on Nick and rough him up a little bit, maybe the other kid might be scared enough to make sure it happens with another guy or two on his team."

Joey's mind was racing. It was more than just getting his money back. If he could pull off something like this, he'd really get in good graces with the higher-ups in the family.

Some serious cash wouldn't hurt either. Neither would the street cred. Could it be done? Maybe.

It was definitely something to consider.

"I'm going to go sit in the sauna and think a little bit," Joey said. "I'll be back before the phones start ringing, but make sure everyone's still here by 7, in case we decide to take that little road trip."

The wheels were turning.

27

Shortly **before seven o'clock**, Ben Richardson and Mark DiPolitto wheeled into Tony Vincent's driveway, but there were no signs of activity. There were no vehicles in the driveway, and no lights on inside, not even the porch light.

"It doesn't look like he's home, but let's check," Ben said as they got out of the car. "If not, then what, Mark? I don't have a cell phone number for him. Do we just leave him a note?"

Mark thought for a moment. He had to be careful here. He didn't want anyone knowing what was going on who didn't need to know. He certainly couldn't leave a card, and didn't want to leave a voicemail message inside either. He wanted to talk with Tony face to face, to see what he knew, if anything.

"Do this, Ben. Call his home phone and leave him a message. Tell him you need to talk to him about Nick and leave it at that. He won't know why you'd be calling. That will give us our opening, at least. Hopefully, he'll come home soon and get the message."

They were nervous.

* * * *   * * * *   * * * *

Shortly **before seven o'clock**, Joey Risone wandered back into the bar. He was refreshed, his mind clear, his game plan set. He strolled back to his office, and closed the door behind him, shooing away his son and brother on the way in, and locking his door. He had to call his uncle, Albert Calabria, the boss of the family, and discuss this plan with him. Albert, of course, didn't talk on the phone, not with anyone, not even family. He had people to do that and, for obvious reasons, he never wanted to be heard talking about any business on the phone anyway. But Joey called up to the compound, told one of Albert's minions that he had something cooking and needed to see Albert right away. After a few minutes of silence, Joey was told to drive over to Albert's sprawling mansion in the city, and Albert would see him.

Joey was nervous, too.

* * * * *   * * * * *   * * * * *

Shortly before seven o'clock, Danny Bridges wasn't the least bit nervous. After a light practice in Bloomington, the team jumped on their private plane and flew the hour and change to Evanston. They bussed over to the Hyatt Regency and got settled in. A team dinner was planned, but it was optional and Danny, like several other players who had family in the area, already had permission to leave the hotel for dinner with Candice. It was great to see her. It had been a few weeks, and they shared a nice kiss and a hug when Candice picked him up at the hotel door-front. They drove off to a quiet Mexican restaurant on the north side of the Chicago, and grabbed a booth in the back for a couple of hours. They had a nice visit and talked about school, how much they missed each other and how much they were looking forward to spring break in a month, when Candice could spend a full week with him.

And then she asked about Nick.

"How's he doing? Have you talked to him lately?" she asked.

"No, we haven't talked, but we swapped some voicemail messages yesterday. He's doing better, I guess. Said his knee is coming along and the rehab is going good. He said something about hoping we'd go to Detroit for the first weekend of the NCAA Tournament, but I don't see that happening. Michigan State's going to finish ahead of us, because I just can't see them losing at home to Iowa on Sunday, and as long as they win the Big Ten, they're going to get that top seed and get to stay home. I'm not sure where we'll end up, but I don't care. We're really playing well now and I think we can win anywhere. But Chicago would be nice."

They finished their meal and talked about Saturday. Danny would have a little time in the afternoon after their morning shootaround, so they planned on having lunch together with Danny's mom, who was coming up for the game and bringing Michael and Kathy along. It would be game day, so time – and focus away from basketball – would be limited, but it would be a nice short-term distraction. On game days, Danny liked to zero in on the task at hand, and get ready for a big game.

He'd be nervous, too.

A good nervous, but nervous all the same.

* * * * *   * * * * *   * * * * *

And then there was Nick Vincent.

On this Friday night shortly before seven o'clock, he was the one who should have been the most nervous, but he was happy as a lark. While he was on the mind of many others, he was very content. His head was clear. He had some money stashed away to buy himself another week with Joey, so in his mind he had no worries. He was chilling out for the weekend, and enjoying his leisurely stay in Joliet. A poker tournament was about to start, and he was excited. He'd won some money the day before and felt like his luck was changing. He was looking forward to walking down to the casino and kicking some butt.

Such is the mind of a compulsive gambler. Nick loved the action and that, of course, is what got him in this huge hole to begin with. But like most compulsive gamblers, he knew losing streaks were meant to end, and they'd always be followed by some good things. Win or lose, it's the action itself that provides the juice.

There's that old phrase, "Better to have loved and lost, then to never have loved at all." It's the same for the sick gambler. In their mind, it better to play and lose than to not be able to play at all. While you're playing, whether it's cards or a bet on a ballgame, during that time you're playing, nothing else matters. All the bad things going on simply disappear from your mind during that time when you're gambling, and that was certainly the case for Nick on this night. He had no idea what Joey was scheming, and had no idea others were looking for him. He was gambling, and that was all he needed. He was focused on winning some serious cash, so he tossed the cell phone on the bed, and headed downstairs to take his seat. There was no one he needed to talk to anyway.

Shortly before 7, with all this swirling around, Nick wasn't the least bit nervous. He was the happiest guy in the poker room when he sat down in Seat 4 at Table 2.

It was a time to play cards. What could be better?

Ten hands in, he'd seen some nice cards. A pair of aces once, a king-queen suited that he played well and a pair of tens that turned into quads and won him a big pot. The button took one lap around the table, and Nick had already turned his 3,000 chips into a stack of about 9,000. There were a little over 100 players in the tournament, and Nick was ready to beat them all. He was well on his way.

Without a care in the world.

* * * * *   * * * * *   * * * * *

Joey Risone pulled through the gates toward his uncle's spacious mansion just south of downtown Chicago. Once inside, his uncle found him a few minutes later and they shared a hug. Albert was a big man, 6-4 or so and still a relatively fit 225 pounds. He looked good for 70, and he met Joey still dressed in a sharp suit after a dinner out downtown. His hair was gray, and he was aging, but he was still sharp as a tack and ran the family with a firm hand. Rules were rules and he had no patience for anyone who didn't follow them. He'd lived the life, this thing of theirs, for nearly five decades now and had been running the Southside crime family for more than twenty years. He'd made millions off his illegal activities through the years, but did it in a very organized and business-like fashion, whether it was gambling or prostitution, garbage or trucking, loan-sharking or flat-out stealing. Albert had a good life and understood how it could continue without interruption. He didn't want any cowboys shining a spotlight on the family unfavorably. Thugs were thugs, and occasionally guys in his crew would make a mistake, and he had little tolerance for it. He ruled with an iron hand, but also protected his crew. He'd had his problems with Joey through the years, usually when he wasn't careful enough roughing someone up, but bygones were quickly bygones. Joey was his little sister's only son after all, and Joey's father had been gone now for more than 20 years. Joey was like a son to him, so he got plenty of leeway.

Still, Joey's first thoughts were always of pleasing his uncle. He made his money through the years, especially with the gambling and loan-sharking, and kicked up quite a bit to Albert. Joey's problem – always – was that he never could hang on to his own money very well, blowing it on booze, cocaine, women, fancy cars and jewelry. He was always chasing the next buck, and it would get him into trouble often, even with his uncle. There were times he'd hit it big, and made Albert happy. He was part of some inside information on harness racing for a winter, and cleared all sorts of cash. He got tipped off to some truckloads of TVs and stereo equipment and made a big hit. All the time, he took good care of Albert on every score.

This plan, though, could be huge. Joey had thought about this all day, had done his homework, and thought he had a good plan. The game seemed right, the timing right. Nick was the key, of course, but he was pretty sure he knew where to find him and he was convinced that roughing him up would put enough pressure on his dear friend Danny Bridges coming to his rescue.

They could throw a game, control the outcome, and make some very serious money.

He laid out the plan to his uncle.

"I have this kid who owes me 20-grand and change, the kid I bailed out several months ago when I borrowed some money from you." Joey said. "He's about to crack now and knows I'm ready to put some pressure on him. I played him like a fiddle a few days ago on the phone, but he's got nowhere to turn now and I can put a ton of pressure on him. His best friend is in a position to control a game for us. He plays basketball at Indiana, a big star, and they play at Northwestern tomorrow night. They are a big favorite, so we've got some room for them to still win, just not make the number. If this kid really wants to see his best friend stay alive, he'll help us."

Albert seemed intrigued. "So what do you need from me?" he said.

"Well, I've got all the guys to pull it off locally, I just need to be able to spread enough cash around on the bets to make the money. I need you to give me the OK with our guys in Vegas to walk into all the sports books and put down some decent-sized bets on Northwestern and the points. I'll need your cash for that. We can do it through the legal means there, and we can also do it with several phone calls to our usual guys in Philly and Cleveland and New York, the guys we use to lay things off on all the time. We can probably spread around $200,000 or so in Vegas without raising any red flags, especially if we do it late, and between our other guys and some offshore stuff, we can probably make another $100,000 more. At least. The kid owes me more than $20,000, and if I tell this kid at Indiana that we'll forgive that debt and let his friend live in exchange for throwing this game, then that works for me. I still owe you $10,000 from that loan. Give me access to the $200,000 and I'll make it all happen. When it all comes down, you get your $200,000 back, you get your loan paid and I'll give you a third of what we make. It could be huge and it's an immediate payday. No waiting around to get paid back any money."

Albert wasn't a wealthy businessman for nothing, so he was quickly analyzing the entire thing. His questions came in a flurry.

"What if you can't get the Vincent kid?"

"Then we don't do it. Nothing ventured, nothing gained," Joey said.

"What if his friend says no?"

"Then, right in front of him, we beat the crap out of his friend within an inch of his life and ask him to reconsider. These kids have been tight since they were babies. He'll do it when he knows it's life or death."

"And how do we know he's capable of throwing a game?"

"He's their best player and everything runs through him. He shuts it down and we're fine, but it's also a game that doesn't really matter to them a whole lot and they've got a couple of other really good players who are nursing injuries and they might not play a whole lot anyway. Just from a gamblers' standpoint, Northwestern and the points at home is a good bet anyway. They always play Indiana tough at home. This would just make it a lock."

Albert liked a good drama, and this sounded like fun.

"OK, let's do it. But factor in throwing something Arturo's way in Vegas, for getting his guys to do all the running. You do have to be careful to not over-do it out there, so you tell him that we limit it to $200,000 out there, and no one adds to any of the bets on their own. Cut him in for $5,000 and we should be good."

"Great. Thank you, Uncle Albert, thank you." Joey said, barely able to contain his excitement. "This could be a big one."

"It better be," Albert said. "You lose any of this money and you get charged two points a week, got it?"

"Sure, but I'm not worried. This is a guarantee."

Albert excused himself from the den to get a drink. As he left, Joey pulled out his cell phone and told him he was going to call Arturo in Las Vegas. He ran Albert's operations in Las Vegas and were their chief money launderer. He always had plenty of cash on hand, at least a million at a time, so doing this was a simple thing. "Sure, go ahead, and tell him I said we're good to go."

Joey dialed the number and, after a few rings, Arturo answered. Joey kept it short and to the point.

"Arturo, it's Joey Risone in Chicago. I'm here with my uncle, and we've got something cooking for tomorrow and you'll need to spring into action for us. We'll need about eight or ten guys we can trust, guys who can go in and out of the casino sports books without any trouble, and we'll need to have about $200,000 in non-traceable cash ready to go. Need it all set by tomorrow afternoon."

Arturo was stunned by the call. He'd only met Joey a few times, on some trips to Vegas with his uncle, and they had never done any big business together. Their only calls were as last-resort things in laying off some gambling action. That usually never involved more than $5,000 or $10,000 at a time, so talking about $200,000 or more was another story.

"And you're telling me I'm doing this on Albert's authority? I hope so, because I'm not doing this just because you're telling me."

Joey understood, and remained calm. It was a slap in his face, but he knew where it was coming from. Business is business, after all, even when it's dirty business. There is a chain of command to follow, after all, and he knew that was just the way it had to be.

"Arturo, he's totally involved and approves this. I'm at his house right now. He told me to call you. Even told me to tell you hello."

"Well, I don't know. I'll have to talk to him," Arturo said. "This is a lot of money."

Joey pulled the phone from his ear and rolled his eyes as his uncle walked back into the room. He covered the receiver and told Albert that Arturo was hesitating, that he needed to know for sure Albert was on board.

Albert took the phone and said hello to Arturo, asked him about the weather and his golf game. Then he got down to business.

"This thing here, it's OK. You have my blessing on what Joey needs and you get your cut. Just execute the plan like Joey tells you and we'll all make some money. And I'll talk to you soon. I'm coming to Vegas next month."

"So you OK the 200-grand?" Arturo asked.

"I OK the 200-grand. It's a go," Albert said.

He handed the phone back to Joey, who told Arturo to be ready and he'd call him in the morning. He hung up, said goodbye to his uncle and headed out to the car. As he drove through the gates to head back to Chicago Heights, the black sedan pulled in behind him. Joey didn't notice at all, instead calling his brother from his cell phone.

"It's a go," Joey said. "Have Ralphie and Johnny at the bar by 10 and we'll come up with the next step."

"They're already here," Paulie said. "Been here for a while."

The FBI agent in the black sedan following Joey in Chicago laid back safely and stayed inconspicuous. Five minutes later, his phone rang. It was a colleague back at the FBI office in Chicago, one who was monitoring all the Risone wiretaps.

"Don't lose him," the agent said. "Something's about to explode. Just recorded a call on his cell phone to a guy in Las Vegas and we even got Albert Calabria on the phone, approving the whole thing. We just struck gold. But keep an eye on him. He also just called his brother and he's heading back to the bar, setting up something for tonight. We need to call in back-up and be ready to follow the whole crew. I don't know what they're up to yet, but they're up to something. Hopefully when they're back at the bar they'll tell us the whole thing. They still have no clue about the bugs. No one's suspicious at all."

Neither agent could hide his glee. Their investigation was starting to reap dividends. They had no idea where this was going, but something was clearly about to explode and they were going to be ready to pick up all the scraps.

Little did they know – not yet, anyway – that the plan to kidnap Nick Vincent and beat him to a pulp was now in place.

Nick Vincent knew nothing.

* * * * *　　* * * * *　　* * * * *

Well, **Nick knew** something. He knew how to keep stacking his bounty. About two hours into the tournament his chip stack had grown ten-fold. The field had been cut in half and he was cruising along. A few guys had more chips than he did, but not many. Nick was having a blast, without a care in the world. He was getting good cards and playing mistake-free poker. As he sipped on a Coke at the bar during a break in the action, he couldn't help but think how much fun this was. He even thought his knee was feeling better.

About an hour later, the field was down to about twenty players and Nick had 35,000 chips. He was sitting in the big blind and was dealt an ace and queen of diamonds. Two players called, but then someone bet 5,000 chips. Nick called, but then the other two folded.

The flop came, and Nick remained stone-faced when the ace of clubs, queen of spades and three of diamonds rolled over. He had a great hand, but opted to play it slow, and checked. His opponent bet another 5,000 chips, and now had about half his chips in the pot. Nick looked at his stack and quickly surveyed the situation. "Does he have aces, or queens?" Unlikely, very unlikely with Nick holding one of each already, but possible. "Does he have a set of threes now? Doubtful, because he wouldn't have bet so much off the bat with such a small pair. Maybe he's got an ace with a big kicker, like a king. They had been sitting at the same table for thirty or so hands now, and Nick thought he had him figured out. He pegged him as having Ace-King.

"I'm all in," Nick said.

A conservative player wouldn't have been so bold, but that wasn't Nick. He was a very good poker player, tight most of the time when he needed to be, but occasionally the compulsive gambler in him couldn't always maintain that self-control. He had a few hands that could beat him – not many, but a few – and he was taking a big chance. If he lost, he'd be back down to about 15,000 chips.

He didn't care.

"All in," he said again, a few seconds later, as he slid the rest of his chips across the line.

His opponent, an old, scrawny guy dressed in overalls and probably straight off an Illinois farm, looked at this young buck Nick and figured he was bluffing. He wasn't, but that was the look. The sagacious old codger went all-in too, and flipped over his cards.

Nick was right: An ace and a king.

"You prick," the old man said when Nick flipped over his Ace-Queen. "I thought you were bluffing me."

Nick stood up with a big smile and a fist-pump. There was close to 25,000 additional chips in the pot now and a win was going to put him at about 60,000, which meant he could probably put it on cruise control to the final table and some sort of payday. He was already thinking ahead, and smiling.

Nick's smile went away, though, when the dealer peeled over the king of diamonds on fourth street. Now his two pair, aces and queens, suddenly went from a likely winner to a likely loser, just like that. It sucked the wind right out of him. At this stage in the tournament, having 15,000 chips or 60,000 was a huge difference. It was a quite a gut-shot for him.

But he still had outs. The last ace in the deck didn't help him anymore, but the last queen would. So would any diamond, which would make his flush the hard way.

"I'll take either," Nick thought.

Both players were standing up now, and the other players at the table were watching intently, as were a few bystanders. The river card came, and Nick let out a loud yell.

"Yes!" he said, staring at the eight of diamonds, the beautiful eight of diamonds. The hand was his, and the 60,000 chips.

"Time for a break," the poker manager said. "And you're all moving tables when we get back, so take your time stacking all those chips, kid."

Nick leaned back in his chair, and took another sip of his Coke. There were eighteen players left now, and twelve were going to make money. Someone was going to win, and make about $3,000. Might as well be me, Nick thought. There was still some work to do, but he was feeling good.

Life couldn't get any better than this, he thought.

If he only knew.

TOM BREW

28

Joey Risone walked into the bar, and a vodka and cranberry was waiting for him. He ordered a sandwich, sausage and peppers, grabbed a bottle of hot sauce and headed toward his office. He beckoned his brother Paulie to the back room. Two thugs, the Cerretta brothers Ralphie and Johnny, soon followed them.

"OK, we're all set with the plan and we need to go grab the Vincent kid. First thing I need to do is check with Doyle and have him trace the cell phone again, but if I'm guessing, he's still at the casino in Joliet."

Joey was talking fast now. He was excited, and eager to get things going. He had called Doyle on the way and told him to go straight to the police station. Joey wanted all this to happen, and for the plan to work, they had to get their hands on Nick. He was sure they could find him, but he wasn't going to rest until he knew for sure that Step One was complete.

He called Doyle from his cell phone, and he was at the station, ready to go. So Joey punched Nick's cell phone number into his office phone and smiled when he heard a ring, and then another. After a few more rings, it went to voicemail. He didn't leave a message.

"Well," he said to Doyle. "Anything?"

"You're good," Doyle said. "The call's bouncing off that same tower in Joliet, Illinois. Anything else?"

Joey smiled at the boys. "Nah, you're good. Go home now. I'll call you in a couple of days and bring you a little present."

"OK, be a good boy now, Joey," Doyle said. "I know nothing, and let's keep it that way. I'm going to go get drunk now, and maybe get laid if I get lucky."

Joey grew focused now as the sandwich plate landed on his desk.

"Van ready? Gassed up and good to go?" he said.

"Yeah," Johnny said. "What about toys? What kind of toys we need?"

"Now you guys listen very closely right now, OK," Joey said. "Bring some pistols, but they are only to scare this kid. I do not want anyone shooting this kid. We need him alive and we need him to help us. Bring some pipes; we may want to beat on him a bit, if he's not cooperating, but under no circumstances do we send him to the hospital or worse, got it? We need him to be coherent. We need him to become our best friend right now."

"Got it, boss," Johnny said, and a few minutes later the four of them

213

headed out the door, into the van and down the road west toward Joliet.

"Where to, boss? The casino?"

"Yeah," Joey said. "We'll look for that black truck of his in the parking lot first. Can't be that many black trucks there with Indiana plates and a Michigan football sticker on the back. Find the truck, and we'll find him. I might call his cell phone again, too, but let's get there first."

Within 30 minutes, they were in the casino parking lot. They slowly drove up and down each row outside and saw nothing, then entered the parking garage. Up they went, through the first level, back and forth, and then the second level. Nothing.

As they pulled off the up ramp onto the third level, there it was, a row over just to their left. A shiny black truck, Indiana plates with the Michigan football sticker on the back.

Nick Vincent's truck.

"Bingo," Joey said. "That's our boy's truck. Stop here, and park in this spot where you can keep a good eye on the truck and follow him out, if need be. Paulie, you and Ralphie need to go inside and look around for him. I'll stay here in the van with Johnny, because I don't want him seeing me. But keep your phone handy. You see him, you call me immediately. We see him, we'll call you. Got it?"

They nodded.

"Good. But be smart for a change. Just spot him and keep a low profile. Once you see him, call me and we'll go from there."

Joey smiled a big smile. "This is going to be fun," he said to no one in particular.

* * * * *   * * * * *   * * * * *

A row over in the parking garage, about fifteen spaces down, the FBI agents backed their inconspicuous black sedan into a parking spot. The agent cut the engine and pulled out his binoculars. The Risone van was about 100 feet away, and he could see Johnny sitting behind the wheel and Joey next to him in the passenger seat. He also had a clear view of Nick's truck a few down spots down from the van. He had good eyes on both vehicles, and was prepared to settle in for a very boring Friday night. The agents knew they could be sitting here for hours. Their boss, Mark DiPolitto, wanted an update, so they called him. They told him where they were, that they had eyes on Risone and his guys and were parked in the casino garage a few spots down from Nick's truck. They seemed to be waiting for Nick to come back to his truck.

"OK, good job. Just keep an eye on them. One of you go inside and see if you can find the kid. We need to make sure he's safe without letting Risone and his boys know that we're watching them too. Remember, we've got nothing right now, or at least nowhere near enough information. We need to let them make the next step, and then go from there. Someone needs to stay with the van, though. If it leaves, we follow it, and if something comes up and you need back-up, just call and we'll get more eyes on the prize."

One of the agents, Marion Hamilton, volunteered to take the casino stroll. He was a high-energy guy and always complained that sitting around on stakeouts was his least favorite part of the job. He had studied the video from the bar, the one where Nick's face was clearly in view of their cameras while Joey was threatening to shoot him between the eyes. If Nick was inside and in sight, he was sure he could find him.

His partner stayed in the car, eyes fixed on the van and the two guys in the front seat, Joey and Johnny. Even though he was paying attention, from the angle he was at, he never saw Paulie and Ralphie slide open the back door on the passenger side and start to walk to the elevators. His view of that door was blocked – he could only see the driver's side – so when they walked past the van and eventually within 20 feet of his car toward the elevators, they just looked like two other casino patrons walking through the parking lot. They meant nothing to him.

They went down the elevator and onto the casino floor, Paulie looking forward to finding Nick and getting this plan in action. He was still livid about the whole brick-through-the-window incident, and would have gladly grabbed Nick that night. He couldn't wait to take the next step here. He knew they were close.

They were.

Very close.

As they were walking around, looking for Nick, so was agent Marion Hamilton, the three of them walking through the same huge casino and, amazingly, totally unaware of each other.

Nick, of course, was totally unaware as well. He was focused on the matters at hand, working his way through the last few players at the final table. Back in the tournament poker room, Nick was sitting at the final table with five other players. The field had dwindled from 105 to six, and Nick was still standing. He was doing the math in his head. He already had won enough to buy another week with Joey, and now he wanted more. His chip stack had grown from 60,000 to 90,000 and only one other player had more than he did. He was looking at a big payday. Beat a couple more players, and he'd have another week or two for Joey. That's how his mind worked, and he was different that way from many sick compulsive gamblers. Most severely addicted gamblers would want to take their winnings and gamble hoping to win more. Nick was more into reality. He knew the priority at hand was getting Joey taken care of, even if it meant little by little, and he was going to do it the right way. But he had a good chance at winning some serious money here, and he was focused on doing so. He was thrilled when a hand he had folded played out, and an all-in player got knocked out. Now they were down to five.

Another week in the bank.

Paulie and his pal wandered through row after row of slot machines, and didn't see a huge, hulking football player among all the retired ladies pulling the arm of a slot machine over and over. Fifteen minutes later, they wandered through the blackjack tables and roulette wheels, and still didn't see anything. They checked the restaurants and bars. Nothing. Everywhere they went, they saw lots of people, but not the one kid they were looking for. When they had walked left-to-right through the rows of blackjack tables, they walked right past Marion Hamilton, two ships passing in the night. Nothing. Lastly, they walked through the poker room and didn't see their boy either. But the main poker room was filled with the single-table cash games at different levels, which is why they didn't see Nick. Nick was in the poker tournament room around the corner, a 20-table room behind closed doors with its own bar that was often used for private VIP parties. Paulie didn't know any better, so when they strolled through the poker room and didn't see Nick, they were afraid they were striking out. They got out of the noise and walked back into the hotel lobby, hoping to make a phone call and give Joey the update.

Agent Marion Hamilton did know better, however, and when he was wandering through the poker room and heard a roar from around the corner, he decided to check it out. Just as he opened the door, he saw Nick Vincent standing over the table, shouting out another yell as he was knocking out another player. Nick drew a pair of aces, his opponent had kings and went all-in. Nick called, and his aces stood up.

It was that kind of night for Nick. A good, perfect night.

The field was now down to four and Nick – big, tall, strapping Nick – was standing over the table, raking his chips toward his stack. Agent Hamilton stared at him, got a good look at his face, and was sure it was Nick. He quickly scanned the room, from edge to edge, to see if he recognized anyone else, or saw any potential troublemakers.

He didn't. He called his partner.

"I found Nick Vincent. He's playing poker. What's going on up there?"

"Not a damn thing," his partner said. "Still sitting here, and they're still sitting in the van. Nothing's going on."

"I figured that. I don't see anyone here out of the ordinary. Let me find out what's going on and I'll call you back. Keep an eye on those guys in the van and I'll keep my eye on the kid. We'll just see how it plays out."

Agent Hamilton scanned the room again. There were about 10 people around the final table, and another dozen or so at the bar, drinking and watching sports on TV. No one looked familiar, or suspicious. He grabbed a calendar off the counter and looked at Friday night's schedule. He saw the action, and the 7 p.m. $100 tournament, and glanced at his watch. It was close to midnight now, so this made sense. All the hooting and hollering was over the action at a final table. There was some big money at stake now, and the boy he was supposed to find was right there, ready to collect. Lucky him, the agent thought. This kid's sitting here having a blast, the agent thought, and he doesn't even know four thugs from a crime family were sitting upstairs in the parking garage waiting for him. The agent spotted someone talking on a cell phone in the corner, wearing a casino ID badge. When he got off the phone, he strolled over.

"Are you the manager?" Hamilton asked.

"One of them," he said. "Can I help you?"

"Who's your boss? Is he here?"

"Again, I ask. Can I help you?" he said, with a sarcastic tone.

Hamilton lightly grabbed him by the arm, and pulled his badge out of his pocket.

"I am Marion Hamilton, an agent with the FBI and we have a problem here that needs to be handled very delicately. Now, can you help me with that, or do I need to talk to your boss?"

The casino manager was apologetic, and concerned. Even though this explosion of legalized gambling was closely monitored and run above-board – at least most of the time – having an FBI agent hovering couldn't be a good thing. His first thought was that something was going wrong at the casino, and he wasn't about to deal with this by himself.

"My boss is in his office. It's right over there, on the other side of the bar. Come with me."

They walked toward the bar, then Hamilton stopped. "See that kid over there, at the poker table? The kid in the blue sweatshirt? You know him?"

"No," the manager said. "I've never seen him before and he didn't swipe a players' card when we started. I don't know who he is, but he's got a hell of a lot of chips. There's only four guys left over there, so he's going to win at least $1,000. Could be about $3,000 if he wins. Is there a problem?"

Hamilton stayed quiet and started walking again as the manager followed. "Let's go talk to your boss."

They walked into the office and Hamilton was introduced to the poker room director, Gary Jeffries. They exchanged quick pleasantries, then Hamilton got right to it.

"There's a kid out there playing poker. I pointed him out to your guy here, but he said he didn't know who he was. Do you?"

The director shook his head. He had no idea what Hamilton was talking about. He looked at his assistant and shrugged his shoulders.

"I don't know anything. Do you?" he asked of his assistant, looking for some guidance.

"I already told him what I know, which is very little. I've never seen him before tonight. I don't think he's ever been in here before and he doesn't have one of our players' cards. Especially now that he's going to win some serious cash, he definitely would have used his card, so he must not have one. If he did, he'd use it to get the points and the bonus money. He must be from out of town."

"So you don't know his name?" Hamilton asked and both guys shook their head no.

"Well, I know his name and he's been here for two days. And you're trying to tell me this is the first you've seen of him?"

"Hey, look, I left about 6:30 yesterday, so if he came in late last night I wouldn't have known," Jeffries said as he flipped on a large television monitor. He hit a few buttons and the camera on that table showed the four players still in the tournament. Nick Vincent was sitting there, in plain view. "Looks to me like he's been here all night, but apparently the kid's been sitting in here for about four hours or so, winning lots of poker hands. We get hundreds of players in here every day and I don't profess to know everyone who walks in the door. But tell me what you need. We're happy to help. We've got nothing to hide."

Agent Hamilton paused for a moment.

"I need to talk to that kid, but I need to do it very quietly and out of view of anyone else. Is there any way you can get him in here without raising any red flags?"

The two poker room executives looked at each other and stared. This was very bizarre. It was a request they'd certainly never heard before. They didn't like the idea of an FBI agent hanging around their office one bit, but there was also no reason to get their feathers ruffled. After all, the agent was interested in the kid, not them. They hadn't done anything wrong. At least not that they knew of.

The floor manager had an idea. He could probably buy the agent six or seven minutes alone with Nick without anyone noticing.

"We're a few hands away from taking a break anyway, so what I can do is go ask him why he doesn't have a players' card and that he needs to sign up for one. Now that he's close to winning, he'd be eligible for some prizes and some free entries to some other tournaments. I can tell him to follow me into the office to fill out the form and get him a card. It would make sense and the other people at the table wouldn't think anything of it. The breaks are ten minutes long, so you can talk to him in here, about whatever the hell it is you need to talk to him about. Is this something we need to be worrying about?"

"No concern of yours whatsoever," Agent Hamilton said. "It's got nothing to do with you, or your casino. Just get him in here."

Hamilton took a seat while the two execs went back out on the floor. For a minute, they watched the action. The cards were dealt, but no one played. They posted their blinds and antes again, and the dealer doled out a new hand. Nick folded and leaned back in his chair, but two others went head-to-head. They played for a few minutes, with few chips at stake, and the hand finished. When it did, the manager stood behind the dealer and said "OK, one more hand and we'll take our last break."

One more hand was dealt and Nick stared down at and ace and four of clubs. It wasn't his favorite hand, but he raised 5,000 chips anyway and got one call. The flop came king-four-four. He thought about checking, playing the hand slowly, but opted to bet another 15,000 chips. His opponent folded, and Nick was pissed. He played that wrong, he thought, and leaned back in his chair again.

"OK, break time. Ten minutes," the dealer said. Two players left the table and headed to the bathroom, and Nick thought about wandering up to the bar for another Coke. Before he did, the manager sat down next to him.

"Hi, I'm Gary Jeffries, the manager here. Nice tournament so far," he said.

"Thanks," Nick said. "It's going pretty good, but it's not over yet. I really need a win."

Jeffries continued. "I noticed you didn't swipe one of our players' cards here. Don't you have one?"

Nick said no. "I'm never over here. I have one from your Michigan casino, but I'm just passing through here."

"Yeah, but even finishing fourth is worth a bunch of perks for you. You get some freebies and a ton of points you can use at any of our casinos. Top three or better gets you a free seat to our monthly tournament of champions, which is worth coming back for. You should have a card. It only takes a minute to get your registered.

"Not sure I really need it," Nick said. "I don't know when I'd be back over this way."

Jeffries was surprised that Nick didn't take the bait. The last thing he needed was having to walk back into his office without Nick, so he sweetened the pot.

"Sign up today and you get a hundred-dollar credit to our restaurant. Steak and lobster probably sounds pretty good tonight, doesn't it?"

Nick was getting bored by the whole conversation. But what could it hurt? The idea of a steak and lobster actually did sound pretty good.

"Sure, sign me up," Nick said. "Bring me the papers."

"Actually, I can just sign you up online. Come into my office. It only takes a minute."

"Do we have time? We're starting back up again in a few minutes," Nick said.

"It literally just takes a minute. Come on in and we'll do it now, and get you right back out here."

"OK, I guess," Nick said. He stood up and followed Jeffries. They walked into Jeffries' office and saw Hamilton standing at the edge of Jeffries' desk.

"You can go now," the agent said to Jeffries. "Just me and him."

Nick was perplexed as Jeffries walked out the door. His only thought was getting back to the table and his tournament.

"Sit down, Nick. I have to talk to you."

"How do you know my name? Who are you, and why would I want to talk to you?"

"Sit down," Hamilton said, with a stern voice.

"Fuck you," Nick said, as he turned and walked toward the door. Before he could reach for the door handle, Hamilton raised his voice a little more.

"Do you know Joey Risone?" he asked. Nick stopped and turned to look at Hamilton.

"Yeah. So what?" Nick said. "What the fuck is this?"

"My name is Marion Hamilton and I'm an agent with the FBI. We have reason to believe you've been doing some business with Joey Risone and …"

"Business?" Nick was angry now. His mind was racing. What would the FBI possibly want with him? Why did they have him cornered in this small office now? What would happen if this got out, that he was in some kind of trouble? It was the last thing he needed.

"So I know who Joey Risone is but I don't do any business with him. I've met him twice in my life. I'm a college kid, just here to play some poker. So, if you don't mind, I'd like to get back out there."

"You need to listen to me for one minute. We have reason to believe that Joey Risone is following you."

"Bullshit," Nick said.

"We have reason to believe that he's attempting to grab you over a gambling debt you owe him."

"Bullshit. Total bullshit."

"And we have reason to believe they want to hurt you."

"You're just totally full of shit," Nick said, his blood boiling. "You're lying to me."

"No, I'm not. You have a black truck parked up in the garage, right? Third floor, against the wall?"

"Yeah, so what?"

"Well, he's parked in a van a few spots down from you. They're waiting for you."

"I'm tired of this shit," Nick said. "I'm leaving."

Nick got to the door, but Hamilton stopped him, and went right up to him, nose to nose. He had a point to make, and now was the time to make it. He was running out of time, at least for now.

"We know he wants to hurt you. We have it on tape. We know it for an absolute fact. You need to take this seriously."

"Bullshit," Nick said. "You're lying. What the hell do you want from me?"

"If I'm lying, then answer one question for me. Why were you in his bar two nights ago and why did he point a gun at you? And why did you throw a brick through his window? I've got the whole thing on tape. Now you think I'm lying?"

Nick and Hamilton were nose to nose, but Nick quickly backed off. He had no answer for that rant, that's for sure. He couldn't lie about that, and why should he anyway? He hadn't done anything wrong, other than tell a few lies and not pay back a loan. And, yes, he probably shouldn't have thrown that brick.

"I can take care of myself," Nick said. "I don't need your help."

"Listen here, punk, I'm getting kind of tired of your crap. I'm here to help you. He wants to hurt you. And if he doesn't hurt you, then he's going to hurt one of your friends. I know this for an absolute fact. I have it on tape."

"See, you're lying. He doesn't even know any of my friends. Not one."

"Yes he does. Danny Bridges. He's your friend, right?"

The color immediately disappeared from Nick's face.

Danny? Why?

Danny knew nothing about Nick's problems. He didn't have any money. What could this possibly be about?

"Hey, you need to get back out there, but I'm staying around here to keep an eye on you. I don't know what they're planning, but they are here and I need to keep you safe."

"I can keep myself safe," Nick said.

"Maybe you can, tough guy, but I'm not sure you know who you're dealing with here. Put this on, so we can at least keep track of you tonight."

221

Hamilton handed Nick a watch, a very simple-looking runner's watch, nothing fancy to the naked eye.

"It's got a microphone in it and a GPS device where we can check your whereabouts. Go finish playing and act totally normal. When you're done, come back in here and we'll talk some more. I'll show you how to work this watch."

"You're really pissing me off," Nick said. His mind was spinning.

But he grabbed the watch, strapped it on his left wrist and walked out the door.

"You're really, really pissing me off," Nick said.

Hamilton just shook his head. Why am I helping this pain-in-the-ass, he thought.

He didn't have a good answer for that.

29

Joey Risone certainly had nothing in common with FBI agents, but one thing he was sure of: He also hated sitting around in a vehicle for hours on end waiting for something to happen. He made a few phone calls, but his cell phone service was spotty in the parking garage, so he spent most of the hour just leafing through the newspaper and sipping on a cup of coffee. Obviously, this was not his idea of fun. No vodka to sip on, no cocaine to snort, no games to watch or bets to take. This was flat-out boring.

His brother Paulie wasn't having much fun either. He thought he would have found Nick by now, but he was striking out. They'd walked just about every inch of the casino – or so they thought – and hadn't found their boy. He was getting frustrated. He thought about calling Joey to give him an update, but his cell phone reception wasn't good either and he also knew that telling Joey any bad news just meant getting yelled at anyway, so he didn't bother. Paulie was by no means a genius, but his frustrations did lead to a good idea.

"Come with me," he told Ralphie as he walked through the lobby from the casino entryway over toward the hotel. "If he's not in the casino, maybe he's in the hotel. It's worth a shot to check. Just don't say anything; let me do all the talking."

He wandered over to the hotel registration desk and was greeted by a young woman behind the counter, probably mid-20s, not particularly attractive, but perky and attentive with a nice smile.

"Hey sweetie, I was thinking about staying here tonight. It's getting pretty late and I'm getting tired. You have rooms, don't you?"

"Yes sir, we do. I can certainly help you," she said with a smile.

"Good. That's good," Paulie said. "My friend has already checked in, so maybe you can get me a room close to his. His name is Nick Vincent."

The girl punched Nick's name into the computer and, of course, his name immediately popped up. "Oh yes, Mr. Vincent. He's in room 644. I have 645 available, right across the hall. Would you like that room?"

That was too easy, Paulie thought. He gave the girl a pleasant smile, and thought for a moment. "You know what," he said. "Let me talk to Nick first, to make sure he's staying and then I'll come right back to you, OK?"

"Well, I'm sure he's staying because he hasn't checked out. The room's already been paid for. There's a house phone right over there on the wall, if you want to call his room," she said.

Again, Paulie smiled. This really was too easy.

"I'll do that. Thanks, sweetie. I'll give him a call and then come back to you."

Paulie walked over to the phone and punched in 644. The phone rang and rang; no answer. Of course not. Nick wasn't there. He turned toward the desk and the girl behind the counter looked over at him. He put his hands up in the air and shook his head no. Paulie decided to walk back over to the counter and milk this for all he could.

"He's not in his room, so I'm going to go outside and call him. My cell phone's not working too well in here."

"Oh, I know. That happens. Well, just let me know if I can help you in any way. I'd be happy to help."

Paulie smiled at her, and looked down at her name tag.

"Thanks, Cassie. I appreciate your help. I'll be right back."

Paulie and Ralphie walked outside the lobby into the brisk February air. Ralphie was not used to Paulie thinking so quickly on his feet, and he was impressed. "What's next?" he said.

"Let's pretend to be on the phone out here for a few minutes, then we'll go upstairs to the sixth floor and check out where his room is. Get a feel for where things are so when we find him we can get him out of here without too many people seeing us. Paulie put his cell phone to his ear and pretended to talk for a few minutes. When he was done, they walked back into the lobby and about 20 feet past the front desk. He looked over at Cassie, and winked, giving her a sly smile.

"I got a hold of him. He's at some club. Said he'd be back in about a half-hour," Paulie said, lying through his teeth, of course. "We'll just wait for him."

Cassie nodded and said OK, then they walked away toward the elevators. They went up to the sixth floor, got off and read the signs. Room 644 was to the left, and they walked and walked down the hallway. It was the last room on the left, all the way down near the stairway. Sure enough, 645 was right across the hall. Paulie peeked his head in the stairwell and pointed to Ralphie.

"You need to walk down there and see where this lets out. See if there's parking there, if we need to move the van when we're ready to go.

"Six floors? You want me to walk back up six floors?" Ralphie said.

"No, dumb ass, just walk down, see where it exits, then walk back to the elevators from the first floor if you want. You can handle that, can't you?"

Ralphie headed downstairs and when he got to the first floor, he saw the door did open right up to the back parking lot. It was dark back there, mostly secluded, only a handful of cars. He thought for sure that they could come and go from this door and leave totally unnoticed. He was happy, and he knew Paulie would be happy too. He rushed down the hall, back up the elevators and gave Paulie the good news.

This was turning out well, Paulie thought. No Nick yet, but at least they were making progress.

* * * * *   * * * * *   * * * * *

Nick was making progress, as well. He wasn't getting any cards to play, but still one more player had been knocked out. They were down to three now. Nick had about 100,000 chips, the leader had about 140,000 and the short stack had about 70,000. There was still some work to be done.

Nick kept throwing bad cards into the muck which was probably a good thing that he didn't have to think. He was still steaming over his short, quick meeting with FBI agent Marion Hamilton. What was all this anyway? He still wasn't sure he could believe him. First off, he had just given Joey some money. And he was about to give him more, maybe much more. He knew Joey was mad about the money, but he wasn't this stupid. Or maybe he was if he thought someone else, someone like Danny, would pay his debt for him. That just wasn't going to happen.

Nick's mind was wandering, but he snapped out of it for a second when the new hand was dealt. First he saw the ace of hearts, then the ten of hearts followed behind. Now, there's a hand to play.

He was first to bet, and thought he'd play them slow. He called the big blind, which was 8,000 chips now. The small blind got out, the big blind – the chip leader – simply called.

The flop came and Nick perked up. King of hearts and a couple of black tens. He had three of a kind, and a nice kicker if he needed it.

This looked familiar, he thought. Just before the last break he hit trips, but everyone folded when he made a decent-sized bet. This time, he checked.

His opponent stared him down for a minute or so, then slid some chips across the line.

"Twenty-four thousand," he said, staring right at Nick.

In a normal world, Nick would have calmly evaluated his options, figured his odds of winning, reviewed his mental notes on the opponent and then made a wise decision. But Nick, whose compulsions could be strong especially with his mind being filled with other things like this run-in with Hamilton, couldn't always be that analytical.

Sometimes, the impulses – and the compulsions – just take over.

"I'm all in," Nick said, standing up quickly out of his chair.

He pushed his stack of chips across the line. Agent Hamilton, from across the room, saw Nick stand up, so he started to pay attention as well.

His opponent asked the dealer for a chip count on Nick. He had him covered and knew it, but was buying some time to make a decision himself. Nick just stood there waiting, confident that his trips, his three pretty tens, were enough to win. This was his tournament now.

And then it wasn't.

"I'll call," the other player said, flipping over his two kings. Not only were his trips were better than Nick's trips, but he already had his full house too, with the two tens on the board. Nick was in big trouble.

"Shit," Nick said, banging his hand on the back of his chair. He needed a miracle now. The fourth ten would do it, but that was it. The other two cards flipped over, a meaningless seven and an even more meaningless three.

Nick was out.

Five hours of solid playing and it was over, just like that. One wrong all-in, and it's done. That's the game. It can be treacherous for someone who can't control his impulses. That was Nick, as much as he tried not to be.

He finished third and won about $1,300, but that was not the point. In every poker tournament, every player but one gets knocked out and when you do, you're never happy about it. Nick certainly wasn't. He flashed an evil glare at Agent Hamilton, like he had anything to do with it, but Nick wanted to blame someone. Maybe if he wasn't so worked up over all this stuff, he would have played it differently. It's a gambler's trait too: It's much easier to blame someone else besides yourself when you lose.

Nick shook the hand of his opponent and congratulated him. He did the same with the other player, and nodded to the dealer. Jeffries, the poker room manager, came over to Nick and congratulated him. "Come with me, and I'll give you your money," he said. "That was nice playing."

"Yeah, right," Nick said. "Great playing, right up until the end when I shot myself right between the eyes. Never saw those kings coming."

On most days Nick would have considered finishing third in a big tournament a smashing success. But not now.

The tournament was over. There were no more hands to play.

It was time, once again, for life to go on.

And what was fun about that?

* * * * *　　* * * * *　　* * * * *

When Ralphie made it back upstairs, Paulie, who was suddenly having a great thinking day, had another plan. "I bet that girl will give me a key to his room if we play it out right," he said. "Here's what we do. You call the hotel number on your cell phone and ask for Cassie at the front desk. You tell her that you're Nick Vincent and you're about a half-hour away but your friend is really tired and you'd like her to give him a key to your room, so he can get some rest. We'll see if she bites."

Shockingly, the plan worked. He made the call, it got transferred to Cassie and Ralphie said everything he was supposed to. Cassie had absolutely no reason to believe she wasn't talking to Nick Vincent, so she said sure, and Paulie hurried to the elevators and went downstairs. He put this dreary look on his face and walked up to the desk. Cassie was there, and he gave her another sly smile.

"Thanks for the key, Cassie. I'm just exhausted," Paulie said, slipping her a folded twenty as a tip. "I'll just wait for him upstairs in his room now."

"Oh, I can't take that, but thank you. I'm just glad I could help."

"So am I," Paulie said to himself as he walked toward the elevators. He went back upstairs and walked to Nick's door with Ralphie. He opened it quickly, just in case, but saw no one. He was ready for action, just in case, but the room was empty. They looked in the bathroom and the closet, and nothing. Nick's small bag was on the chair, and his cell phone was on the bed. Paulie picked it up, and it was still turned on.

This is good, Paulie said. He's got to come back here eventually. He tried to call Joey from his own cell phone, but the call kept going to his voicemail. So he called Frankie's cell and got him, and told him to bring the van around to the back of the hotel, the last entryway way back on the corner of the parking lot. He told him to tell Joey they were good and he'd meet him at the back of the hotel.

Paulie was proud of himself. They were getting close. The van pulled out of the garage and the FBI agent was surprised. He had been watching the van for a long time, and no one had come and gone, at least no one he could see. It was just the two of them still in the front seat, and now they were leaving.

Maybe they were giving up for the night, he thought. His partner, Hamilton, was still downstairs, so he let the van go and he called Hamilton to tell him they were leaving. Threat diminished, for now.

Or so they thought.

* * * * *   * * * * *   * * * * *

It was well past midnight as Nick headed into the manager's office to get his money. Hamilton was waiting there for him as well, which perturbed Nick. Jeffries opened the envelope with his winnings, thirteen crisp hundred-dollar bills, and handed them over. Nick should have been happy, but he wasn't.

"OK, so why are you still here? I told you I can take care of myself," Nick said.

"It's just not that easy, Nick. I'm not sure you understand how serious this is. Joey Risone is up to something and I feel very confident that he wants to – needs to – involve you."

"But I think you're wrong. Look, I just gave him some money, and I've got more to give him now. That's all this is about with him. I owe him money and he wants it. But he knows he's going to get it. If he's done something wrong, then arrest him. But it doesn't involve me, OK? I just want to go now. I'm hungry."

"I need to keep an eye on you, OK. We're following him already, and we'd feel better following you too. We want to keep you safe."

"Man, you just don't get it, do you?" Nick said. "I can take care of myself. I'm going to eat some dinner, then go to sleep. And in the morning I'm going to drive back to school. I don't need you for any of that. There's nothing going on."

Hamilton thought for a moment. This was awkward. His partner had already told him about the van leaving and the guys back at the office had nothing on Joey's cell phone calls, just some long conversations with a woman he wanted to see later. The van was gone, and Nick was here. It seemed innocuous enough.

"You're eating here? Sleeping here? Leaving in the morning? OK, but I'm sticking around and I want you to keep that watch on, so we can help you if we need to. We've been tapping his phones for weeks, so if he's up to something we'll probably hear it. I've heard you on those tapes, remember, and I've seen you on the videos in his bar. So, quit looking at me like I'm an idiot. I'm trying to help you."

"Do whatever you need to, but I can handle myself, OK?" Nick said. "I'm going to go upstairs and get my phone and then come down here to eat. I'll be in that restaurant right there in five minutes, and you can watch me eat all you want. I don't care."

"I'll go with you. I don't want you out of my sight."

Whatever, Nick thought. He was hungry and he was tired. "OK, if you must, but this is totally ridiculous."

As Nick and Hamilton went upstairs on the elevator, Paulie had left Ralphie in the room alone while he went down the stairs to talk to Joey and make sure the van was parked in the right spot. They had just pulled up as he got there, so he filled Joey in on what was going on.

"He's got to come back soon. His phone's there, and it's still turned on. We'll just wait for him and grab him. But I've got to get back up there. I don't want Ralphie there by himself if Nick comes back."

Too late.

Nick and Hamilton got off the elevator and walked down the empty hallway. When they got to the door, they were still talking while Nick fumbled for his room key and Ralphie could hear them from inside the door. He looked through the peephole and saw Nick with some other man he didn't know.

Panic set it immediately. He wasn't prepared for this and he didn't have Paulie around to think for him.

Nick finally unlocked the door and when he and Hamilton walked in, Ralphie quickly pounced. He had his pistol in the palm of his hand and he took a quick swing at an unknowing and unprepared Hamilton, striking him right across the face and busting open a huge gash above the corner of his eye when the handle of the pistol slammed into his head. He crumbled quickly to the floor, hitting the other side of his head on a coffee table on his way down. With one fell swoop, he was knocked unconscious, lying on the floor in a pool of blood.

Nick reacted quickly and lunged for Ralphie. The burly mobster took a mighty kick at Nick and nailed him directly in his left knee, the one that had been torn up on a football field in Columbus and reconstructed on two occasions. Nick buckled, and went to the floor, not even able to get a punch off. Ralphie kicked him again, this time in the ribs, then stood over him, gun pointed right between his eyes.

He could not pull the trigger, Ralphie knew. Those were the orders. They needed Nick, needed him alive and well. So he controlled himself and stared down at Nick, who was writhing in pain on the floor.

"I'm not going to kill you. I just want to talk to you. Just don't move, OK. Stay right there."

Nick wasn't about to move. His knee suddenly hurt like hell again, as bad as it did that day in Columbus. His ribs didn't feel much better. He didn't recognize Ralphie, not right away, but he certainly figured he was one of Joey's boys. He didn't move, just stared at him.

"What do you want?" Nick said, clearly fearing for his life.

"I want you to be quiet right now, got it? And I want you to lay on your stomach and put your hands behind your back."

Nick followed orders, rolling onto his stomach. Ralphie pulled a small length of rope out of his coat pocket and tied Nick's hands tightly behind him.

When he was done, he pulled the rope tight and it dug into Nick's skin. He winced. "Now," Ralphie said. "I want you to get up and sit right there in that chair. You don't move and you don't say a word. Got it?"

Nick didn't say anything as he slowly and carefully got up off the floor, pain shooting through his knee. He braced himself on the edge of the bed as he stood up and sat in the chair next to the bed.

Ralphie stepped forward and pointed the gun at Nick one more time.

"I don't want to kill you, but I will if I have to. So don't make me have to pop you one. Got it?"

Nick didn't say a word.

"Got it?" Ralphie said a little louder.

"Yeah, I got it. But I have a hard time believing you won't kill me. Looks like you already killed him."

Ralphie reached down and felt a heartbeat still coming from Hamilton, but he was definitely out cold.

"He's not dead, but he can be. You too. Just sit there and keep quiet."

Ralphie pulled his cell phone out of his pocket and called Paulie. He answered on the first ring just before he got on the elevator, and Ralphie told him to get to the room in a hurry. He told him he had Nick.

Paulie hurried to the sixth floor. He knocked quietly on the door and Ralphie opened it. He smiled a big smile when he saw Nick sitting across the room, but nearly fainted when he saw someone else lying on the floor, bleeding like crazy and looking like a dead man.

"Who the hell is that?" Paulie said.

"I don't know," Ralphie said. "He walked in with him and I hit him with my gun. Knocked him out cold, one shot and down he went."

"Hey, jerk," he said to Nick. "Who is this?"

Despite the pain, Nick's mind was working well enough to know that he couldn't tell Paulie who this guy was. As much as Nick didn't want to believe it, Hamilton had been right. Joey did want him, did want to rough him up, and Hamilton got caught in the crossfire.

"He's just a guy I met playing cards. We were just going to have dinner. I came up here to get my phone when all this happened."

"Let's get out of here, right now," Paulie said.

"What about him?" Ralphie said, pointing at Hamilton with the end of his pistol.

"We don't need him. We need Nick. That's it. Let's go."

Ralphie grabbed Nick by the elbow and pulled him up out of the chair.

"What do you need from me?" Nick said, looking for a response.

"We need you to do a little work for us," Paulie said. "We're putting you to work, so you can work off the money you owe us."

As they were leaving the room, Nick stopped.

"Hey, I need my bag there. I've got medicine in there I have to have, and my clothes and stuff. Take the bag with us, please.

Paulie wasn't going to argue. What was the point? He grabbed the bag and headed out the door. He saw Nick's cell phone on the bed.

"That yours?"

"Yes," Nick said.

Paulie threw it in the bag and they headed out of the room and down the stairwell. Six flights of steps, each one adding to the pain in Nick's leg, came and went quickly. When they stepped outside, there was Joey Risone, standing next to the van with a shocked look on his face.

There was his boy.

"We need to get out of here right now!" Paulie said. "Ralphie probably killed some guy upstairs in Nick's room. We need to move now."

"Jesus," Joey said. "I knew this wasn't going to be easy."

Ralphie pushed Nick into the back seat of the van and once again for effect slammed the point of his pistol toward his forehead.

"You keep being good and I won't hurt you anymore." Ralphie said.

Nick nodded, and slid up against the other door, his hands still knotted behind his back. Ralphie cut the rope, then re-tied Nick's hands in front of him. When he was done, he gave Nick a gentle nudge into the corner of the seat.

"Hey, Ralphie," Joey said from the front seat as they squeeled out of the parking lot and started heading north. "Did you hurt him already?"

"I had to, boss. He came at me. Gave him a couple of swift kicks. He's hurting a little. But he's alive, boss, just how you wanted him. The other guy, I don't know. Sorry, boss, but I whacked him pretty good. I had no choice."

Joey let out a hearty laugh. "Big, tough football player, huh?" he said to Nick. "How tough you feeling now, big boy? You got something you want to say to me now?"

Nick chose to remain silent. That was probably a good thing.

"Nice job, boys," Joey said, thrilled that his plan was on its way now. "Let's head north, to the house up on the lake. We'll stay there for the night, then get to work tomorrow. Jeez, it's almost 2 o'clock in the morning. We'll get some sleep and get ready for our big day."

North? Big day?

Nick couldn't believe all this as he sat uncomfortably in the back seat. He looked down at his brand new watch. It said 1:49 a.m.

What had he done?

He had no idea.

TOM BREW

30

A half-hour after Joey's van had pulled out of the garage there was still no word from FBI agent Marion Hamilton. As each minute had passed, his partner was more and more surprised that Hamilton hadn't checked in. Something was clearly wrong. He had called his cell phone at least a dozen times now, and always there was no answer. Just ring, ring, ring.

So he left the car and went into the hotel. He dashed through the casino to the poker room, but saw nothing. Hamilton was nowhere to be found. The agent dashed out to the hotel lobby and found a security guard. He flashed his badge and told him quickly and discreetly that his partner wasn't answering and that he was somewhere in the building. The security guard was clueless.

"He was with a kid named Nick Vincent. I think he's a guest in your hotel. You need to tell me which room he's in," the agent said.

The guard grabbed the hotel manager and filled him in. They went to the desk, punched open their guest list, and scanned for Nick's name. 'Here. Here it is. Nick Vincent is in Room 644," he said.

A few feet away, Cassie the front desk girl couldn't help but overhearing. "Yeah, his friends have been up there for about a half-hour."

The agent stared harshly at Cassie and then sprinted for the elevators, getting upstairs as quickly as he could, the portly security guard and hotel manager chasing behind, trying to keep up. He was stunned when they opened the door and saw Hamilton lying in a pool of his own blood. He was still out, but his heart was still pumping. He had a pulse, but it was very faint.

"Jesus, call 911 now. Right now," the agent said. "He's in bad shape."

Within five minutes, the paramedics arrived and quickly assessed Hamilton. Based on the wallops to his head, they were sure he had a concussion.. He also probably had some broken bones in his face. His blood pressure was low, but not terrible. They strapped a collar around his neck, carefully placed him on a gurney and prepared to wheel him out.

"This is an FBI agent. We can't be wheeling him through the damn lobby," Hamilton's partner said. "Where's the service elevator? Can we get downstairs that way?"

The hotel manager pointed the way, but the paramedics resisted.

"Hey, time is of the essence here. We can't be wasting any," he said.

The manager jumped in. "The service elevator is right around the corner. It'll be just as fast. Hey, quite frankly, I don't want anyone being wheeled through my lobby, either. It's not good for business. We can get you out of here just as fast."

So they all dashed off, and went down the service elevator. Within minutes, Hamilton was off, attached to a monitor but still out like a light. They made it to the hospital in about 10 minutes and Hamilton got the best of care.

Still, it would be hours before he would regain consciousness.

* * * *   * * * *   * * * *

Nick Vincent woke up in a tiny bedroom with sore ribs, a very sore knee, and a splitting headache. He had no idea where he was. He couldn't see much from the back seat of the van the night before, and all he knew was that they drove for about an hour, maybe more. When they got out of the van, he was quickly escorted into a pitch-black house and locked into a small room that had only a mattress on the floor and a roll of toilet paper in the attached bathroom. There was a small window, but it had bars on the outside and locks on the inside. He wasn't going anywhere; not that he knew where to go right now anyway.

He slept for about six hours, using his bag as a pillow. All that was in it was a pair of jeans and a couple of shirts, along with some socks and underwear. His Vicodin was there too, thankfully, as was his cell phone, but Joey had taken the battery out. Joey knew they might need Nick to use that phone later, when it was going to be time to start executing the plan, so he thought it best to keep it around, but with the battery in his own pocket. The sun was shining through Nick's window, and he heard voices from outside his door.

He was wishing he knew what was going on.

He knew this much: That thug Ralphie got him good last night. He could barely take a deep breath, and felt pretty sure that Frankie's second kick probably broke a rib or two. They sure hurt like hell. His first kick was a direct shot too, right to Nick's bad knee. It was swollen and unstable, and it too was throbbing in pain. He was glad the Vicodin was nearby. It would help, but not that much.

Nick was awake for about 15 minutes when he heard some rustling at the door. He heard the key go into the lock, then saw Joey and Paulie enter the room. Nick sat up at the end of the mattress and leaned against the wall.

"Here, asshole," Joey said as he flipped a bag at Nick, giving him a couple of egg muffins and some juice. "Welcome to the Hotel Risone."

"Where are we?" Nick said.

"None of your business," Joey said.

"What do you want from me?" Nick asked.

"In due time, asshole. In due time," Joey said. "For now, you just stay in here and keep your mouth shut. Don't cause any problems. We'll come and get you when we're ready."

"Ready for what? What the hell do you want from me?"

"You know what I want from you. I want my money. But for now, I want you to shut up and eat your breakfast. We'll see you a little bit later."

Joey and Paulie left the room and locked the door behind them. Nick wolfed down the eggs and muffins and figured he might as well take a Vicodin. He gulped one down with the juice, then just stared at the walls.

There was nothing else to do.

Nothing but sit and wonder.

He looked down at his new watch. It was just after 10 a.m.

* * * * *　　* * * * *　　* * * * *

Just a few minutes before FBI director Mike DiPolitto arrived at the Joliet hospital, agent Hamilton's eyes finally opened. He looked up at his partner, and the nurse who was tending to him. His eyes were still glazed over.

"Where am I? What happened?" Hamilton said.

"I was hoping you'd tell me," his partner said.

The nurse stepped in and told Hamilton to relax. "You need to keep still, Mr. Hamilton. You've got lots of tubes connected here. Just relax and I'll get the doctor, OK?"

Hamilton nodded, and closed his eyes again for a few seconds. As he was becoming more alert, he was also realizing how much pain he was in. He was still in a fog.

As the doctor entered the room, so did DiPolitto, and he was shocked at what he saw. Hamilton had huge bandages on both sides of his face, and the left side of his face was clearly swollen. When Hamilton opened his eyes as DiPolitto came in, he could see his left eye was full of blood. He clearly had been roughed up pretty bad.

"Jeez, Marion, are you OK?" DiPolitto asked. The doctor quickly raised his hand. "Please," he said. "Let him rest while I check him out, OK? He's just now becoming alert. He's been out for eight hours or more."

The doctor checked some vitals, and then asked Hamilton how he was feeling.

"My head hurts. Really bad. And I can't see out of my left eye very well. It's all blurry," he said.

"There's good reason for that," the doctor said as DiPolitto and the other agent listened in intently. "You have a pretty severe concussion and you have a broken orbital bone. You got hit with a blunt object just off your eye, which is why you can't see very well. You have a lot of blood in there, and your eye has had some trauma as well. You also have a slight crack in your jawbone, but there's not much we can do for that. It's small enough, and it will heal on its own. It's just going to hurt for a while.

"But you need to relax now. Your body has gone through a lot. It's going to take a few days to get better and we need to keep you monitored. This concussion was pretty severe."

As the doctor stepped away, he looked at DiPolitto and began to lecture him. "I'm sure you want to talk with him, but please understand he's been through a lot here. Don't overdo it with him, and make sure he gets some rest. I'll be back in about an hour to check on him again, and just have the nurse page me if there's a problem."

As he walked out, he looked back at Hamilton. "How's your pain? Do we need to up your medication?"

"Wouldn't be a bad idea," Hamilton said. "My head really hurts."

"OK, I'll have the nurse take care of it for you."

DiPolitto leaned over the bed and looked at Hamilton.

"What can you tell us, Marion? How did all this happen?"

"I don't really remember," Hamilton said, blinking his eyes to try to clear his vision. "I just walked into Nick Vincent's hotel room and bam. I got hit and went right out. Never saw it coming."

DiPolitto was startled. "Nick Vincent did this?"

"No, no," Hamilton said. "I had found him in the poker room and had talked to him for quite a while. Told him about Risone looking for him and that we had to keep an eye on him. He was pretty resistant. He's kind of an asshole, to be honest. He was giving me a lot of grief about following him around. He wanted to eat something and wanted to go to his room to get his cell phone. I walked up there with him, and as soon as I walked into the room I got hit. I never saw anything."

"So you don't know who did this?"

"I never saw the guy. He got me from behind the door, I think. But I'm sure it had to be Risone, or one of his guys."

DiPolitto was upset now and spun around to stare at the other agent.

"How the hell did this happen? I thought you were watching the van. Where'd you screw up?"

The agent got defensive, but really didn't know what to say.

"Hey, I watched that van for hours and had a good view of it. Those two guys were in the front seat the whole time, never left, and I never saw a single person come and go from that van. Even the guys back at the office checked in with me, and all they said was Risone had one long conversation with some woman, but that was it. No mention of Vincent or anything. I did my job. Watched them every minute."

"Well, clearly, you guys missed something. Now we've got an agent practically beaten to death and we have no idea where Risone is or Nick Vincent. Right?"

"No sir, we don't. I checked with the office about an hour ago and Risone hasn't been at his bar and he hasn't used his cell phone. I don't know where he is. And I never saw Nick Vincent. Marion's last call to me was that he had him and when the van pulled away to leave, to let them go. I thought Vincent was with him and we figured Risone had gotten tired of waiting for Vincent to show up at his truck. But I watched that van for hours and no one ever came or went from that van. I saw Risone and his guy the entire time."

DiPolitto was visibly upset now, both because of Hamilton's condition but also because of the mess they were suddenly in.

"Well, we need to find this kid and we need to find him fast. We certainly have to assume it was Risone who grabbed him up and we know he's up to something. We have to find them right away."

"Got any suggestions?"

DiPolitto strolled around the room. He was clearly disgusted.

"We need to come up with something, and we need to do it now."

Hamilton squirmed in his bed, moving to get more comfortable.

"You haven't heard anything from Nick?" he asked.

"Marion, I know you took quite a shot to the head, but what makes you think the kid is just going to up and call us?"

Hamilton looked at DiPolitto with his one good eye and stared down his boss.

"He's wearing one of our watches," he said, trying to force a smile.

"What!?!" DiPolitto shouted.

"I put it on him in the poker room, and I know the microphone is working. I checked it before I gave it to him."

Suddenly some life re-emerged in DiPolitto's face. This terrible mess might be fixable after all, he thought.

"So we can listen, and reach him if we need to?" DiPolitto asked.

"Sure," Hamilton said. "We can listen, but I never showed him how the buttons work or anything. We never got to that. But he put it on in front of me, and he should still have it on."

DiPolitto jumped into action. He called his office and had the surveillance guys activate the listening device in the watch. It only took a few minutes of banging on some computer codes to get it going and they did just that. DiPolitto asked about Joey Risone again, too, but his guys had nothing new for him.

"He hasn't been around the bar and we've still got nothing on his cell phone. No calls at all."

"Where the hell is he?" DiPolitto asked. "Keep an eye on things and you call me the second you know something. We need to find him, and then act fast. I need to know where he is and then make some calls. Anything that's going to happen is going to happen fast, and it's going to happen today. We have to be ready."

* * * * *   * * * * *   * * * * *

Tony Vincent finally got home late Saturday morning. He'd gone out for a few drinks after work on Friday night, ran into an old girlfriend and wound up spending the night at her apartment. When he walked into his kitchen, he saw his answering machine blinking. He had three messages, which was surprising since he didn't get many calls on his home phone. Two were solicitors, but the last one was from Ben Richardson. He hadn't seen Ben in months, and they were casual acquaintances at best. Still, he listened to the message, more and more intently as it went along.

"Tony, hey this is Ben Richardson. When you get home I need you to call me about your brother, Nick. I've got something I need to talk to you about and it's pretty important. Here's my cell phone number. Call me as soon as you get in, no matter how late. It's pretty important."

Tony didn't get it. He'd just seen Nick a few nights earlier and everything seemed fine. Maybe Ben knew something about a friend of Nick's and just wanted to pass along some information. He wasn't sure.

Still, he wasn't going to wait around to call. He needed a shower and all, but he called Ben anyway. Ben answered on the first ring.

"Jeez, Tony, thanks for calling. I've been waiting for you to call," Ben said. "Have you seen or heard from Nick lately?"

"Yeah, I just saw him Thursday night. He was in town for a day or so, but he went back to school. Why? What's up?"

"Well, a friend of mine in law enforcement heard that Nick might be in some money trouble and he wanted to talk to you to see what you knew. We stopped by your house but you weren't home and I didn't have a cell phone number for you. I'm sure he still wants to talk to you. Will you be home all day?"

"Yeah, I'll be here but I don't know what I can tell you. Nick's not having problems as far as I know. He's got some money in the bank and his scholarship covers almost everything at school. If he was having money problems, he certainly would have told me."

"You sure about that? My friend sounded like Nick had some serious issues going on, that he owed some people a lot of money and they weren't happy about not getting paid. My friend can fill you in. Let me call him and I'll get back to you. And give me your cell phone number too, just in case."

Tony gave him the number and they hung up. Ben immediately called DiPolitto, who was still at the hospital in Joliet. He stepped out of Hamilton's room and into the hallway to take the call.

"Mark, I just heard from Tony Vincent. He's home now, but he said he doesn't know anything about Nick having any problems. Doesn't know what you're talking about. I didn't say much to him, but he seemed surprised that I was even bringing up something like this."

"Call him back and tell him we need to come see him. I'm in Joliet right now and I have about 15 minutes of work I need to finish up and I'll head over there. Tell him we'll meet him about 1 o'clock. That OK with you? Are you free to come with me? He might feel more comfortable if you were there."

"Yes, Mark, anything you need. Just swing by here and get me and we'll go over to his house. I'll call him right now and wait for you."

DiPolitto popped back into Hamilton's hospital room and filled them in on what was going on. The watch was about to be activated and they had a lead on Nick's brother, so he was hoping for some good background information. He was also hoping Nick would be able to fill them in on where he was. He told Hamilton's partner to stay at the hospital, but to keep his phone handy.

DiPolitto hurried out to his car and flipped on his laptop. He checked in with the office and was told that the watch was activated. It had only been up a few minutes, but they hadn't heard a thing. With a few codes, DiPolitto could listen in himself right on his laptop and he did the same for a few minutes. Nothing. He could also track the watch by satellite, provided the reception was right, but he wasn't getting a reading to his location. The best thing about the gadget, though, was that he could send short text messages to the watch, with the only problem being he wasn't sure Nick could figure out how to read the message, or how to respond to it.

It was worth a try, but DiPolitto had to be careful. He wanted to get to Nick without his captors knowing it. Sending a message could be a problem. Still, it was a worth a try.

So he typed "ARE YOU OK?" with a preprogrammed YES and NO choice and hit send. And then he waited.

* * * * *   * * * * *   * * * * *

Nick was still locked up alone in his room, and was startled when the watch vibrated for a split second. He looked down at the display and saw DiPolitto's message, clear as a bell. ARE YOU OK? In the top corner, it said YES with a little arrow pointing to a button on the top right side of the watch. In the bottom corner was the NO, with another arrow pointing to the bottom button.

Nick's first thought was an obvious one: How the hell do I answer that one? No, he thought, he wasn't OK. He'd been beaten, slightly, and had been kidnapped. He had no idea where he was. But he also knew it could have been worse. He had seen Hamilton out cold in his room and thought he was dead. Nick knew he could have been dead by now too. If Hamilton was well enough to send him a message now, then he was lucky too. Nick hit the top button, next to the YES. A minute passed, then another message.

ARE YOU SAFE?

Again, Nick almost had to chuckle. No obvious answer there, either. Still, he quickly hit the NO button. For the moment, he didn't feel threatened, but he knew that could change any minute. He definitely wasn't safe.

The watch vibrated again.

ALONE RIGHT NOW?

Nick quickly hit YES, though that certainly didn't tell the whole story either. He was certainly alone in the room, but Risone and several others weren't far away. Then, another message.

RISONE HAVE YOU?

Finally, a question with an obvious answer. Nick quickly hit YES.

KNOW WHERE U ARE?

Nick hit the NO button.

DiPolitto called his office, his heart pounding. "I'm not seeing anything here about where he is. Are you getting any kind of reading on his location?"

"No, we're seeing the same thing you are, but keep talking to him. The interaction might get caught on the satellite the next pass."

But in a matter of seconds the computer zeroed in on the watch.

"He's in Evanston, Illinois," the agent shouted. "Evanston, Illinois!"

DiPolitto quickly banged another message to Nick.

YOU ARE IN EVANSTON. ON OUR WAY.

Evanston? Nick thought about that. Why? It had no real relevance to him, not at the time anyway. He hit the top right button again, to make sure the message went away. Several minutes passed, with no other message. Help was on the way,

he thought, but he was still very confused by all of this and how it was all supposed to play out. Then, another message showed up.

BE SAFE. DO WHAT THEY TELL YOU.

Nick clicked that message off as well. Be safe? That's a nice thought, he
said, but he wasn't sure how much control he had over that. And he was pretty sure
he was going to have to do what he was told just to stay alive, so that was a given
as well. Then, one more.

WE CAN LISTEN IN. WHISPER YOUR NAME.

Nick got up off the mattress and went into the bathroom. He turned on the
water to make sure Joey and the boys didn't hear him and then whispered into the
watch. "Nick Vincent," he said quietly into the watch. He felt the vibration on the
watch almost instantly.

NICK VINCENT. CLEAR AS A BELL.

Nick wasn't sure how to feel about all that. He had someone on his side,
clearly, but he also had a bunch of thugs just outside his door. One last message
came, but he had seen this one already. It was being re-sent for effect.

Nick took it to heart. It would be his rule for the day.

BE SAFE. DO WHAT THEY TELL YOU.

TOM BREW

31

Mark DiPolitto squealed out of the hospital parking lot and headed east to Schererville in a hurry. He wanted to interrogate Tony Vincent in person, just to be sure he didn't know anything. He had a hard time believing he didn't know something was going on with his brother, but years of experience had told him that this was a conversation best to be had in person, so he could look into his eyes and watch the expression on his face.

Schererville wasn't far anyway, and he knew he could get from there to downtown Chicago in a hurry as well to meet with his team before they converged on Evanston. He called Ben Richardson to let him know he was on his way. "Stay at your house, Ben. I will pick you up," DiPolitto said. We'll go over to the Vincent house as soon as I get there."

A few minutes later, he got a call from the agent at the hospital. There were problems with agent Marion Hamilton. Alarms had been going off and doctors and nurses were scurrying about. Hamilton had faded off again and was not responding to anything the doctors were doing. He had suffered a severe brain aneurysm and only a few minutes later, his heart was suddenly shutting down. They shocked him, over and over, but nothing was working. After 30 minutes, they gave up, frustrated by losing a patient.

FBI agent Marion Hamilton was dead.

"He's gone," the agent told DiPollito. "They tried everything, but he never responded. They said the blow to the head probably triggered something, and there was nothing they could do about it. They really tried, but they could never get him back."

DiPolitto and Hamilton had known each other for years, so this was a tough phone call for him to take. He tried to keep his wits about him as he sped east across the interstate, but he was clearly shaken.

"This assault just turned into a murder," he thought to himself.

* * * * *   * * * * *   * * * * *

The murderers were sitting around a table in the dining room of the house in Evanston, certainly unaware of Hamilton's expiring. It was time to spring their plan into action. Joey had spent the past several hours figuring out exactly what he was going to say to Nick and how this was all going to play out. It had been on his mind for days, really, and now it was time. Days were turning into hours now.

He got up from the table, and slid a chair into the corner.

"We'll put him right here and he will listen to what I have to say. We need to make sure he's scared, but we don't need to be hurting him any worse, so lay off of him, OK? I'll sit right here across from him and lay it all out. And then he'll do it."

"And if he doesn't?" Ralphie said. "If he doesn't, do we rough him up then? I'm certainly volunteering."

"Relax there, big boy," Joey said. "We need him today. He's already hurting pretty bad from you pounding on him last night. Hopefully, that'll be enough."

Joey and Paulie unlocked the door to Nick's room, and Nick quickly sat up on the mattress.

"Get up. Now," Joey said.

Nick slowly got to his feet, and Paulie grabbed him by the arm, escorting him out to the dining room and firmly placing him into the chair in the corner. Joey sat down in the chair across from him and slid to within a few feet of Nick. Paulie, Ralphie and Johnny stood right behind Joey, four pair of eyes staring a hole through young Nick Vincent.

Joey slid his chair even closer and Nick sat as far back in his chair as he could. He wasn't comfortable at all, but two thoughts were continuing to race through his mind: BE SAFE and DO WHAT THEY TELL YOU. He knew help was on its way, or at least he hoped it was, but it sure wasn't helping at this moment.

"Today's your lucky day, punk," Joey said as he stared into Nick's eyes. "You owe me twenty-thousand and change and today you're going to pay your bill in full, if you do what you're told. By the end of the night, we will be even and you will head down the road a free man, never to hear from me again. You will never call me again, see me again, think of me again or ever mention my name to anyone again. We'll be done, but you'll also be out of your debt to me. By the end of the night, it'll be over."

Nick didn't really know what to say. He was keeping the "be safe and do what they say" mantra in mind, so he treaded lightly.

"Joey, you know I don't have any money and I can't get it from anywhere else. I've told you that, over and over."

Joey looked at Nick and smiled.

"Your friend Danny Bridges is going to pay your debt for you tonight. He just doesn't know it yet and you're going to be the one to tell him."

It bothered Nick that Danny's name had come up. As embarrassed as he was by his gambling problems and all the trouble they had caused, it's mostly been about him through it all. And now here he sat, surrounded by a bunch of nasty criminals, and they were wanting to talk to him about Danny Bridges, his best friend for years. Danny, of course, had absolutely no idea what Nick had been going through.

"Danny doesn't have any money. He's never had any money."

"We don't need his money," Joey said. "We just need him to do us a favor tonight. When he does, your debt will be paid."

"And if he doesn't?"

Ralphie stepped around Joey and put his index finger to Nick's temple. "If he doesn't, you prick, I figure the bullet will go right through here. It will be my pleasure to blow your head off, right in front of your best friend."

Ralphie grabbed Nick by the neck and carefully shoved him back against his chair.

"Unless, of course, you'd rather I put a bullet through *HIS* head. He's your friend, and it's your choice."

Joey told Ralphie to back off, and he did.

Joey leaned in again. "There's really only two ways this plays out today. Either you and your friend help us, or you are a dead man. Simple as that. Win some, lose some, but this is your chance to win today. And your friend is going to help us. He does it, or your dead. Got it?

"What do you want him to do?" Nick asked, constantly reminding himself to be safe and do what he is told.

"In about an hour, we're going to leave here and head to the Pavilion Motel in Evanston. It's right across the street from the Hyatt, where your friend Danny is staying with his basketball team. You're going to call him and tell him you want to see him – you need to see him – and he's going to come over to your room at the hotel. When he gets there, we'll be there too and we're going to tell him everything that's going on with you. We're going to tell him how you've borrowed all this money from me, that you're gambling like crazy, that you've refused to pay me back after all this time and that you tore up my bar.

"We're going to tell him that Indiana is favored tonight by 10 points and that he is going to make sure that Indiana doesn't win by that many. We're going to be putting a lot of money on Northwestern and the points and your friend is going to make sure that we win."

"He won't do that. He would never …"

Joey immediately shoved Nick right in the chest, and he slammed back into the chair

"Yes, he will, and that's how you're earning your twenty-grand. It's going to be up to you to convince him, or you're dead. You'll need to tell him that, and we'll certainly confirm that to him. He'll do it, because he's your best friend and he doesn't want to see you dead. And he won't want to get hurt himself."

Nick leaned forward in his chair, angry. He forgot, for the moment, about the whole "be safe and do what they say" message.

"Danny's had nothing to do with this. You better not hurt him."

"I have no intention of hurting him, unless he doesn't do this for us. But he will. He doesn't even have to lose the game. All he has to do is make sure they don't win by too much. He can do that. He's their star."

Nick crumbled back into his chair. It didn't do any good to be angry. He knew he was out of options.

"OK, whatever you say, Joey. I'll do it, and I'll talk Danny into doing it. But if he does it, then I walk and he walks and you leave both of us alone, forever."

"Yeah, do it and we're done, and you both go on with your lives," Joey said. "You won't see me again, except in your nightmares, of course."

Do what they tell you, Nick again thought to himself.

"OK, let's go do it then." Nick said. "Let's go."

"Yep, let's go," Joey said. "Go get your bag, and make sure you've got your phone. I've got your battery here in my pocket. You'll need your phone to call Danny when we get to the hotel. It's not far away."

Ralphie walked Nick into the room and they grabbed his bag. His knee was killing him, and he was wishing this would be over. A few more hours, he thought. He grabbed his bag, and the phone was still in there, along with the clothes and his Vicodin.

"I need to take a pill before we go, OK?" Nick asked.

"Whatever. I don't care," Ralphie said.

Nick went into the bathroom and opened his Vicodin bottle. He stuck a pill in his mouth, cupped his hands to get some water and gulped it down. He put his coat on and stuck the pill bottle and phone into his bag. The five of them headed outside to the van. The sun was shining on a crisp February day, but it was cold. They got in and drove off.

Nick sat in the back seat, quiet as could be. Be safe, he thought, but mostly he wanted to be sure Danny would be safe. Off they drove.

He looked at his watch. It was a little after 2 p.m.

Nick thought some more. His first thought? He was sure hoping his watch was doing more than just telling time. He was hoping – and praying – that some-one was listening. But he hadn't seen a message in several hours now, and hadn't felt any good vibrations.

If he had rescuers, where are they? Or did he just not have rescuers? At this point, he wasn't sure. And that was a concern.

* * * * *   * * * * *   * * * * *

As Nick and the thugs drove off, DiPolitto was pulling into Ben's driveway. He honked the horn a few times, and Ben came out the front door. Within a minute or two, they were around the corner at Tony Vincent's house. Tony was opening the front door before they even got there, and invited them in.

"Tony, this is Mark DiPilitto with the FBI. We've been friends for a long time," Ben said. "And he needs your help."

"I'll do whatever you need, but I'm totally clueless here. Ben tells me something's going on with Nick, but I just saw him Thursday night. We had dinner and he seemed fine. He's still pretty bummed out about his knee, but he didn't say anything – not a damn thing – about being in any kind of money trouble."

DiPolitto was listening intently and watching Tony even closer. He had his questions ready.

"Why was Nick here in the first place? You saw him Thursday night, you said. How long was he here?"

"Not long. We had dinner and then came back here. He stayed about an hour, but I had some things to do, so I left. When I came home, he was gone. Figured he was seeing some friends and then heading back to school. I never heard from him. But it's not like we talk every day."

"So you have no idea where he's been since Thursday night?"

"No. not all."

DiPolitto continued on. He was believing Tony so far.

"So would it surprise you that he's been hiding out in a casino hotel in Joliet since then?" DiPolitto asked. "And that he's been closely watched?"

"By who?" Tony wanted to know.

It was time for DiPolitto to get serious.

"Do you know someone named Joey Risone?"

The name alone caused Tony Vincent's heart to beat a little quicker.

"Yeah, I know him," Tony said. "Owns a bar in Chicago Heights that I used to drink at now and then if I was ever working over that way. He's a bookie too. I used to place some bets with him a year or two ago, but I haven't seen or heard from him in at least a year. Why?"

DiPolitto stayed mum. He was going to be asking the questions, not answering them.

"Does Nick know Joey Risone?" he asked.

"Yeah, he's met him once or twice, but only when he was with me. I broke my ankle about a year ago and couldn't drive. So there were a few times Nick drove me over there when I had to see Joey, and he would have met him then."

"Had to see him?" DiPolitto asked quickly.

Tony stopped for a minute. Great, he thought, there was no getting around this now. Something serious was going on here, and he wasn't about to not be above board. He had to tell Mark the truth.

" I placed bets with him for a few years, but then for about six months or so, I was taking bets from about two dozen guys over here and placing them with Joey. Kind of book-making myself, and I ran everything through him. So I usually had to go see him every week or two, to settle up and swap money back and forth. But it got too hard after I broke my ankle, so I stopped. I was tired of it anyway. Too much work and too many hassles. I was busy enough with my own job."

"Are you on bad terms yourself with Joey Risone?"

"No. Hell, no," Tony said. "He was cool with it when I quit. His son Joey picked up the business, which meant he made even more money with me out of the picture. He is who he is, but we've got no problems. Just didn't care to be gambling anymore myself and didn't really have a need to be hanging out over there with him once I stopped. We're cool. But like I said, I haven't talked to him in probably at least a year."

It was a believable tale, DiPolitto thought. But, he wondered, where did Nick fit in to all of this? He had to find out.

"Do you know that Nick gambles a lot and places bets with Joey Risone?"

"No, he doesn't. He wouldn't. He knows he can't do that," Tony said.

"What makes you think so? Why are you being so naïve?"

"Nick used to place a few bets with me in high school, twenty dollars, forty maybe but nothing serious. He likes to play cards and all, but he and I talked about when he left for college, that he had to make sure he kept his priorities right, that it was all football and classes, and he had to do it right. He's going to be a professional football player someday. And he knows he can't mess that up."

DiPolitto just shook his head. If only Tony knew, he thought.

It was time to tell him.

"He's already messed it up, believe me. Here's what you need to know. If our timeline is right, after you had dinner with him Thursday, he went to Joey's bar and they got in a big argument about money that Nick owes Joey. We've had Joey Risone under surveillance for a different matter – something I cannot talk to you about – but during that time we have Nick and Joey on tape together, both on the phone – including a call from your home phone that very night – and on tape. We saw and heard them arguing, and we saw Joey point a gun at Nick. We also saw your dumb-ass brother throw a brick through Joey's front window.

"So don't be so naïve, Tony. Your brother has a serious issue with Joey and, according to our tapes, Joey talked about Nick owing him over $20,000."

"That's bad." Tony said. "He's not a guy you owe money to, especially that kind of money."

"It gets worse," DiPolitto said. "Late last night Joey and some of his guys kipnapped Nick at a casino in Joliet. In Nick's hotel room, one of his guys smacked one of my FBI agents with a pistol to the head, and earlier today that agent – my close friend – died. So we're talking murder. They have Nick and we don't exactly know where they are, but we have an idea. We think they're in Evanston, Illinois, and I'm going there now, with about a dozen of my men."

"I'm going with you," Tony said.

"You're both going with me. Right now. I might need both of you to vouch for me with Nick. But you do what you're told and you stay out of our way, OK? We have to go to my office in Chicago on the way and when we get there, we can get you updated. But we have to go now."

"Let's go then," Tony said.

They hurried out to the car and dashed off. In about five miles they were on the interstate, so DiPolitto flipped on his flashing lights and drove about 90 miles per hour into the city. Within 30 minutes, he was downtown, walking into his office.

He told Ben and Tony to stay in his office while he got his updates. They waited and waited, not knowing what was going on.

* * * * *   * * * * *   * * * * *

The flea-bag Pavilion Motel was a dump, but it served Joey's purposes for the day. It was right across the street from the Hyatt, and they weren't going to be there long anyway. He had Johnny go in and rent two adjoining first-floor room way down at the end, and he did.

They checked into the rooms, and Joey flipped Nick the battery to his cell phone.

"Call your buddy, and tell him you need to see him. Tell him to walk across the street to see you, and that you need to see him right away. If he says anything about you going over there, tell him you hurt your knee again and walk-ing is tough. Get him here, and get him here quick."

Nick dialed Danny's number, but it went straight to voicemail. He tried again about five minutes later, but still nothing. Joey stared at Nick, then made a quick phone call to one of his guys he had stationed in the Hyatt lobby, keeping an eye on things.

"They left about an hour ago, the whole team on a bus. Picked them up right out front of the hotel."

Joey hung up the phone quickly and looked at Nick.

"They probably went over to the arena for the shoot-around," Nick said. 'If they've been gone an hour, they should be back soon. They don't spend too much time over there."

The front of the Hyatt was visible from Joey's room, so he was happy a few minutes later when the bus actually pulled up in front of the hotel and the Indiana players filed out.

"Good," Joey said. "Now call him again. And leave a message if he doesn't answer. I'm sure he'll pick it up at some point.

Nick called, but it did go to voicemail again. Danny's phone was still off. It was in the bag he had over his shoulder, but Coach Garrison's rules were always no cell phones on bus rides or anytime at a gym. Nick left a message.

"Hey, Danny. It's Nick. Hey, I'm here in Evanston and I really need to see you before the game. Call me as soon as you can. I'm staying at the Pavilion Motel, right across the street from the Hyatt. Call me right way, OK?"

When Danny flipped on his cell phone, he was surprised when the only call was from Nick. He listened to the message, and didn't think twice about it. It wasn't out of character for Nick to do something spur of the moment, and he was glad to hear his voice. Nick hadn't seen him play all year, since there was no road game at Michigan. Danny's first thought was actually a good one.

The lobby was full of several Indiana fans looking for autographs and pictures, so Danny signed a few things before heading off to a corner of the lobby. He dialed Nick right away. Nick answered on the first ring. Of course.

"What's up, pal?" Danny said, excited to talk to his friend. "What are you doing here? I was surprised to hear your message."

"Well, my knee hurts like hell and I wanted to see my brother, so I drove over a couple nights ago. Thought I'd stick around for your game and go back tomorrow," Nick said. "But I've got something I really need to talk to you about. You got a few minutes to come see me?"

"Why don't you come over here, Nick? We're not supposed to leave the hotel, and my mom will be here in a little bit anyway. She'd love to see you."

"I can't, Danny. My knee's really hurting. It went out on me again a couple nights ago and it's a pain to walk. Plus, I really don't want to see anybody else. Kind of in a rotten mood, you know. I just want to see you."

Danny had seen enough of Nick's somber moods to know he could probably use some cheering up. He knew it was at least two hours before they would leave for the game, so he figured he could probably do it.

"OK, I'll pop over. What room are you in?" Danny asked.

"Room 104, all the way at the end. It's right across the street."

"Give me about 15 minutes, OK? I need to get out of my practice gear and put my bag up in the room. Let me change and I'll be right over."

* * * * *   * * * * *   * * * * *

Danny hung up the phone and walked back through the lobby. He quickly headed up the elevator to his room. His roommate on the road, Michael Trickett, was still in the lobby, visiting some friends.

As Danny opened the door to his room, he was startled to see four people standing inside by the window.

"What are you guys doing here?" he asked.

TOM BREW

32

Danny listened intently to his visitors for 10 minutes, then quickly threw on some jeans and a sweatshirt, grabbed his cell phone and coat, snapped on his new watch and headed out from his hotel room.

"I told him I'd be there in 15 minutes. Don't want to be late," he said to his four visitors as he hurried out the door. He didn't want anyone to see him leaving the hotel – coaches, teammates and fans included – so instead of taking the elevator, Danny hurried down three flights of stairs and crossed the road to the flea-bag across the street. He walked through the parking lot, spotted the door with 104 on it, and knocked.

Nick answered the door and they clasped hands and gave each other a quick hug. Danny closed the door and as he did, Nick sat back down on the edge of the bed. He was just in shorts and a sweatshirt, with a big bag of ice wrapped around his knee. He took off the bag and tossed it into the sink a few feet away, and when he did, Danny saw how swollen his knee was.

"Jesus, Nick, what happened?" he said as he took off his coat and flipped it on the edge of the bed. "It looks worse than it did a year ago."

As Danny said that, the door from the adjoining room opened and in walked four big, nasty men, Joey Risone leading the way. Ralphie stepped beside him, and went to the outside door to lock it. As they surrounded Danny, Ralphie spoke up.

"I did that. Kicked him as hard as I could. And I can't wait to do it again," he said with a toothy grin.

"What's going on here? Who are you guys?" Danny said, clearly petrified.

Joey stepped forward as the other three backed away a step. "Have a seat, kid. On the bed there, next to your buddy."

Danny sat down quickly and stared up at Joey. Risone dove right in to what he wanted to say, having practiced it in his head for several days. And now it was showtime.

"Look, the first thing I want to tell you is that I don't know you and I don't have any problem with you, so I'm not going to hurt you, OK? It's your friend here I have a problem with, and I don't have any problem hurting him again, got that?

Danny nodded.

"I understand you guys have been best friends since you were little boys, right?"

Danny nodded again.

"Well, your friend here is in some very big trouble. He gambled a lot of money with me and lost, then he didn't pay me. He gambled even more money and lost again, and still didn't pay me. Then he told me some bullshit story and borrowed some money from me and didn't pay that money back either. Your piece-of-shit friend here owes me more than $20,000 and he won't pay me. I don't like that. Since he won't pay me, we've decided to hurt him real bad, or maybe just kill him. We haven't decided yet."

"What does this have to do with me?" Danny said. "If you think I can pay you this money, you're wrong. Man, I'm just a college kid. I don't have any money."

Danny looked over at Nick, with an angry look on his face. "Is this really true, Nick?

Nick couldn't even look up at his friend. He just nodded.

"How the hell could you do this?" Danny wanted to know. Nick didn't have an answer.

Danny looked back at Joey.

"This sounds like this is his problem, not mine. We're friends and all, but there's nothing I can do about this. I can't help him pay you. I have like fifty dollars to my name."

Joey raised his hand, and put one finger over his mouth.

"Sssshh," he said. "I'm not asking you for any money. Like I told you before, I've got nothing against you. But here's the deal. I want to be paid today and your friend here can't do that. So by the end of the night, I want my money, or he's a dead man. That little fact is not up for debate.

"And that's where you come in. You are going to help your friend pay off his debt in full tonight, and when you do, he can walk away and live the rest of his life and I will erase him and his debt from my memory. I will erase you from my memory too. But for the next several hours, we're partners you and me, and your friend's life will depend on it."

Danny was confused now. Twenty thousand dollars paid off in a few hours?

"How do you expect me to do that?" Danny said. "I don't have any money and I don't know people who do. I'm just a broke college kid."

Joey stood up over Danny and put his thick hand on Danny's shoulder. He leaned from the waist and his nose was about a foot from Danny's.

"You're playing a game at Northwestern tonight. They suck, and you guys are good. You guys are favored to win the game by 10 points tonight, but we want you to make sure you don't win by that much. You don't have to lose the game on purpose, just make sure you don't win by 10."

"I can't do that," Danny said. "You're talking about my career here."

"No," Joey said, "I'm talking about your friend's life here. And you *can* do it. You are your team's leading scorer and you're the one out there who can control the pace of the game. Look, I watch 10 college basketball games a night and I know what goes on. You can turn it into a low scoring game where Northwestern can keep it close. Sure, you might have to miss some shots and maybe throw a few stupid passes by mistake, and maybe you let your guy score a few baskets the easy way. I'm not asking you to lose the game, got it? You don't have to do that. Just play slow and don't win by too much. And if you'll do that for me, your friend can walk away debt-free and alive."

Danny breathed a heavy sigh and paused for a moment.

"And what about me? Look, we get these talks about gambling on sports before every season and I've heard all the stories about guys who got caught up in this. Their careers were ruined. They've gone to jail, been ostracized, certainly never played basketball again. I can't imagine that happening to me."

"It won't happen to you, and here's why," Joey said. "Look, this is a one-shot deal. I just want my money. I don't give a shit about your friend. I want my money and I want to be done with him. And I really don't want to hurt you in any way. I hope you play basketball for another 15 years. You just do this one time, one night, and it's all over for you and your friend. But you also have to understand, if you don't do this, then we're going to leave with your friend right now and someone will be calling you tonight or tomorrow to let you know he's dead."

Nick, at long last, finally interjected.

"Look, Danny, he's serious. They already beat the crap out of someone last night and beat me around pretty good. My life is in your hands, man. I really need you to do this."

"Well, if I do this, how will I know he'll be safe?" Danny asked.

"You have my word," Joey said.

Danny gave a wry little smile, trying not to show any sarcasm. "With all due respect, I don't even know you and I'd have a hard time believing I can trust you. I'm taking on a huge risk here and I would definitely need some assurances that he would be OK if I did this and that it could never come back on me that I did it."

Joey stepped back for a second and looked at his guys, then looked back at Danny.

"Hey, to be honest, it's in my best interest if no one ever knows about this too. I just want to make my money tonight and go on living my life. Let me tell you one more thing: This is important to me because I borrowed money to give to your friend. I just want to pay that off and be done myself. This is a one-time thing and you have to believe me on that. You guys are both out of my life after tonight, one way or another."

"What do you mean by that? Are you threatening me too?"

"Well, let me correct myself then. Nick here, he's out of my life tonight, one way or another. Got it? You, you'll just have to live with your decision. But quite frankly, your decision is easy. Just keep it under 10. That's all I ask. You do it, and his debt is paid off and his life is spared. Hell, I'll even throw in five grand for you.

"I don't want any money. None." Danny said. "The only reason why I would do it is for Nick to be safe. If you can guarantee me his safety, then I'll do it."

Joey looked at his boys and smiled.

They had their man.

"But here's my concern," Danny said. "What if I can't? I mean, I'm just one guy out there. Anything can happen in a basketball game."

Joey had this line rehearsed for days as well.

"Yeah, but you are *the* guy. You're the best player on the best team. And Northwestern is a good bet anyway, even without you helping it. They really need a win to make the NCAA Tournament and it's the last home game for their seniors. They'll be playing with a lot of emotion and they can keep it close on their own. You guys are only favored by so much out of name recognition; your number is always too high. With your help, you can just guarantee it. And you can still win the game. Remember that. Who wins the game is totally irrelevant to me. Just keep it close."

Danny got up off the bed and walked around the room for a second, trying to gather his thoughts. Could he do this? Would he? Would they really kill Nick?

Yes, yes and yes.

Danny walked back over to Joey, and he felt much better standing up, since he had about six inches on him.

"OK, I'll do it, but on this condition …"

Joey snapped quickly. "You're not in a position to be making conditions."

"I don't think you're going to mind it. All I want is this: Next door here is a big sports bar, a chicken wing place with a bunch of big-screen TVs. They'll have the game on. I will leave my cell phone with one of our managers and about 10 minutes before the game I want you to text me a picture of Nick sitting in that restaurant with you – in a public place – so I know he's safe. And when the game's over, you guys leave and he stays there. I will have another friend pick him up as soon as the game is over. And you never see him again. You have to promise that. It's the only way I'll do this. And you never mention my name to anybody. That's the trade-off for you to make your money."

Joey reached out his hand to Danny, and they shook. "Deal," Joey said. "We'll go to that place and eat and drink and watch the game. And we'll leave him there when it's over. Fine with me. Be good to be rid of him, believe me."

Danny looked over at Nick, who muttered a quick thank you. Danny grabbed his coat.

"Look I have a meeting and I can't be late. No one knows I'm gone and the last thing any of us need is any suspicion."

"Go." Joey said. "And we'll send your picture. This guy here, Johnny, will be at the game too. He'll be under your basket when you're warming up and he'll hold up a piece of paper with the number on it, just in case it gets lower than 10. Got it?"

"Sure, I'll look for him when we're warming up. But I want that picture too. I want to know he's in a public place and he's going to be safe. If not, no deal."

"That's not a problem," Joey said. "We're partners tonight. You hold up your end of the bargain and I'll hold up mine. And then we're done. Do you need another player to help you?"

"Definitely not. No," Danny said. "I can do it. No one else can ever know about this. Ever."

Danny zipped up his coat, stared a hole through Nick and looked at his watch for several seconds, making sure Nick saw what he was doing.

"I have to go now," Danny said, tapping his watch and still staring at Nick. Then he looked at Joey, one last time. "My meeting is in 10 minutes. I'm going to do this, but you better be true to your word and totally forget about both of us when this is over."

"Done," Joey said. "Off we go."

Danny walked toward the door and Ralphie unlocked it. As Danny opened the door, he turned back to Nick and looked him right in the eyes.

"Nick, be safe," he said, firmly. "And do what they tell you."

He tapped his watch one more time, for effect. "I'll see you in a few hours and this will all be over."

Nick nodded. So did Danny.

"Be safe," Danny said, tapping his watch and again staring hard at Nick. "And do what they tell you."

* * * * *   * * * * *   * * * * *

As **Danny dashed back** across the street unnoticed, Joey sprung into action. "That's a hell of a friend you have there," he said to Nick, laughing. "He's going to get you off the hook."

Joey left for the adjoining room and closed the door behind him. Now that Danny was in on the plan, he had a ton of work to do. His first call was to his uncle, Albert Calabria, to let them know everything was good to go. His uncle was very happy.

"OK, this is great but don't get greedy here. You need to stay under the radar. Spread it out in Vegas over every sports book and no more than $5,000 at a time and no more than two or three bets at each place. Make some bigger, some smaller. Make the second one late, right before the game is going to start. That should get you about $200,000 in Vegas, then lay off some more with our guys in Philly, Cleveland and New York, but not too much. The last thing we need is to get them pissed off at us. Put through all the offshore bets online and we can get to about $300,000. That's enough. We need to be totally discreet here."

Joey was in total agreement. He had thought through every detail over the past several days and everything was going perfectly. He called Arturo Mustano in Las Vegas and went over every detail with him. Arturo had all the cash ready, and he had a dozen of his best runners ready to hit the strip. They would make the smaller bets first at each sports book, around $2,500, a barely negligible amount on a busy Saturday night. Then, within 10 minutes of tip-off, they'd lay down the bigger bets. Four thousand at some places, five or six thousand at others and maybe eight thousand at a few more, just to be inconspicuous. In 30 minutes, they were going to litter the town with $200,000 in bets, totally legal, and be ready to cash in big a few hours later. Arturo's guys were very experienced at laying off bets and even the guys at the sports books knew them well enough to know that whenever they placed bets that size, they were usually just trying to balance out the books for their less-than-legal book-making customers.

The sports books weren't going to notice anything one at a time and they'd be unable to react to all the big bets late anyway. Plus, Indiana was often a natural draw for bettors anyway, so things might even come close to balancing out. Plus, there were several premiere NBA games on the schedule that night and a huge heavyweight boxing match in Las Vegas, so the sports book were going to be hopping. The Indiana-Northwestern game could easily get lost in the schedule.

Every time Joey played out the scenario in his head, it always kept working out perfectly. And as it was playing out now, no stone was being left unturned. He was thrilled with the conversation with his uncle and Arturo was diligent in preparing the plan in Vegas. His guys were ready to go. And laying off bets with the families in other big cities wasn't an issue anyway. They'd all been doing it for years, just to keep their books all balanced every night. Thousands of dollars exchanged hands every week. That's just the business; that's how it works. About a half-hour before tip-off, Joey would start making the calls. It's what he did most every night. This time, he'd just be doing it from the restaurant instead of his own bar.

With everything in place, Joey and his buddies headed out the door and took the van and the other car over to the restaurant. Joey stayed in the car to make the rest of his phone calls, but he sent the others inside to grab a big table near the biggest big-screen TV. They went inside, with Nick walking right next to them.

"Get a table at the back of the restaurant and don't let him out of your sight for even one second. Got it." Joey said. They all nodded in unison. "Order up some food, but just take it easy on the drinks, OK? It's going to be a long night."

Nick listened intently to Joey. A long night, to be sure. In a few hours, this nightmare was going to be over, he thought. That was the good thought. He still couldn't stomach the bad thought, that if something went wrong he'd be in serious trouble. Danny too.

He looked at his watch. It was 7 p.m. right on the button, an hour before tip-off. The watch said 7:00 … and nothing else.

* * * * *　　* * * * *　　* * * * *

As Joey was wrapping up all his loose ends, Danny was getting ready himself. He had hurried back up the quiet staircase to his room, and when he got there his visitors were still there. They talked for only five minutes, then Danny hurriedly got dressed, grabbed his bag and headed to the bus. Right on schedule, he left with his teammates for the arena.

He had only a minute on the way out to say hello to his family, who had been waiting at the hotel all this time to see him.

"Sorry, Mom. Just trying to get ready," he said. "I'll see you guys after the game."

They got on the bus and made the short trek to the arena. Danny listened to some music on the way, making a point to not be talking to any of his teammates. This wasn't uncommon. Danny's focus was a trait all his teammates had come to respect anyway.

As they exited the bus and walked into their locker room at the arena, Danny looked at his new watch.

It said 7:00 … and nothing else.

259

TOM BREW

One hour to go, he thought.
One hour to go.
And then what?

33

With the exception of a very private five-minute closed-door meeting in his coach's office, Danny's pregame routine was the same as it always was. The only difference was that he asked one of the student managers to keep his cell phone in his pocket and to let him know when his girlfriend texted him. He made up some lie about her cell phone not working and that she'd probably text him from someone else's phone.

"Just give me a thumbs-up when I get a text, OK?" Danny told him. "And don't delete it. That way I can read it when we go back in the locker room."

Danny warmed up with his teammates and drained one shot after another. Funny, he thought, here he was feeling great about his shot and in a few minutes he was going to go out on the court and miss a few intentionally. He didn't feel good about that at all.

With about 15 minutes before tip-off, Danny, as one of the team captains, met at center court with the game's three referees and the two Northwestern captains, including Tyrone Wells, his former AAU teammate and high school nemesis from Gary who had been Northwestern's leading scorer all season, averaging nearly 24 points per game, a few more than Danny. Tyrone was by far their best player. They shook hands, listened to the officials, then wrapped things up. When they were done, Danny hugged Tyrone for a few quick seconds, right there at center court, and whispered to him.

Tyrone whispered back and then they shook hands one last time with the game officials. Then, speaking loud enough for the three referees to hear, Tyrone said: "Let's light it up and put on another show."

Both teams headed back to their locker rooms for some last-minute instructions. The student manager gave Danny a thumbs-up on the way in and handed Danny his phone in the hallway. He looked real quick, and sure enough there was the picture he was waiting for, Joey and Nick still in their jackets, sitting at the table, food and drinks strewn about. He saved the photo, tossed the phone into his bag at his locker and got ready to play a game.

* * * *   * * * *   * * * *

The four of them settled in at the table, Ralph Cerretta and Paulie sitting on either side of Nick with Joey across the table. They were all smiling, all but Nick, of course. As stressful as the past couple of days had been on Joey and his boys, they could just relax now. The drinks tasted good; so did the food. Even Nick had to admit it was nice to dive into a pile of teriyaki chicken tenders.

Joey wasn't about to divulge all the information to anyone, but everything was set. All the bets were in throughout Las Vegas; $226,000 in all, with the point spreads ranging from 9.5 to 12 points, most of the bets at 10.5 or 11. They had laid off another $50,000 around the country and placed more than $60,000 in bets off-shore through dozens of separate accounts. In all, the total dollar amount at stake was just over $330,000.

It was going to be quite the payday. A mobster's dream come true.

Joey called Johnny at the arena and Johnny took out his big marker and wrote a huge number 9 on the back of a sheet of paper. As Danny was concluding his warm-ups, he spotted Johnny behind the basket and they made eye contact. Johnny showed him the paper and Danny nodded.

They were on the same page.

Keep it under 9 points.

The television broadcast came on the big screens and there were plenty of cheers throughout the crowded restaurant. Ralphie leaned over the table and let out a big laugh. "I'm just not sure what I want more, for this to all work out or the fun I'll have beating this prick to a pulp," he said, playfully punching Nick in the chest. "It's a win-win situation for me."

"There's our boy," Joey said, looking at the TV as Danny was introduced as part of Indiana's starting lineup. A few minutes later, the ball was tossed up and the game was on.

Nick was a nervous wreck.

He kept looking at his watch, over and over.

7:58, 7:59, 8:00, and that was all. He was surrounded by people in the restaurant, good ones and bad ones, but never in his life had he felt so all alone.

And that was saying something.

* * * *   * * * *   * * * *

Northwestern got the opening tip and after several passes scored on a nice back-door cut. Joey and the boys were high-fiving each other and Danny couldn't help but think that he had nothing to do with that basket. It was actually a good thought.

The same thing happened on the other end. Indiana was just running its of-fense. Danny had the ball a couple of times, but just patiently passed off. A teammate missed a jumper and Northwestern went down and scored again. It was 4-0 Northwestern and Danny hadn't done a thing wrong yet.

The teams traded baskets for several trips and Indiana was down 9-4. Joey and the boys were loving it. Danny, content to go slow and lay back in the flow of the offense, finally took his first shot about three minutes into the game, a leaner in the lane from about 12 feet away. The shot was short, hanging for a second on the front of the rim … and then fell in. The next trip down, Danny had passed off twice when he got the ball, but then found the ball in his hands again as the shot clock was winding down. He took a three-pointer from the wing, at a perfect angle for the TV cameras to catch his shot. It was off-line too, and the TV viewers – including Joey and the boys and Nick – could see it veering to the right. It caught the inside front of the rim, swirled toward the backboard and kissed the glass … and fell in again.

"Jesus, that shot had no business going in," Nick said, shaking his head at the table. The game was now tied.

"I hope your boy hasn't changed his mind," Joey said. "That would not be good for you."

Nick said nothing, knowing full well while watching the replay that Danny's shot was clearly a miss and should not have gone in. Neither one of them, really.

Danny missed a shot on the next trip down, then had a pass tipped and stolen on the trip after that. A minute or so later, the ball got tipped out of bounds on a rebound at the Northwestern end and the horn blew. With 15:51 left, the first of the mandatory TV timeouts was called. Northwestern was ahead 15-11. Danny was 2-for-3 shooting, with the five lucky points and the one turnover. Tyrone Wells had 11 of Northwestern's 15 points. The raucous Evanston crowd was loving Northwestern's fast start.

So was Joey Risone.

* * * * *   * * * * *   * * * * *

As the broadcast went to commercial, Joey Risone was all smiles. The game was off to a good beginning. Northwestern was winning the game by a little and covering the number by a lot. Danny was out there on the floor guiding things beautifully.

So far, so good.

Nick looked at his watch for a quick second.

"Hey, there's a timeout. I need to go to the bathroom," he said as he got up from the table.

"No," Joey said, "Sit your butt back down."

"I really need to go, you know what I mean? Want me to go right here?"

Joey shook his head. He was in too good of a mood right now to argue about a bathroom break. With a wave of the hand, he shooed them away. "Ralphie, go with him. Don't let him out of your sight."

Nick straightened out his aching leg, put his hands in his jacket pockets and walked toward the bathroom, with Ralphie following right behind. Nick walked toward the stall at the end of the row and with a smirky smile asked Ralphie if he was coming in with him.

Ralphie just flipped him the bird as Nick closed the door. Ralphie stood and waited near the sinks, just a few feet away.

* * * * *　　* * * * *　　* * * * *

About a minute or so later, the first thing Ralphie saw hitting the floor was the empty Vicodin bottle. The second thing was big Nick Vincent crashing to the floor right in front of him. When Nick hit the bathroom floor, he was shaking, his eyes closed and his body thrashing. Ralphie looked down in a panic and saw the empty pill bottle. He picked up the empty bottle and saw what it was. The Vicodin prescription had been filled with 20 pills. Now, it was empty. As he bent down to check out Nick, a customer walked into the bathroom and screamed.

The customer opened the bathroom door again and yelled out to the front desk.

"Hey, call 9-1-1 fast. Someone's passed out in here."

Ralphie didn't know what to do. This wasn't like the situation in Nick's hotel room, where he could just use blunt force to solve the problem. He smashed Marion Hamilton's head with a pistol and thumped on Nick a couple of times, but this was different. There was Nick, right in the middle of the bathroom floor, in the midst of what looked like a major drug overdose. Even Ralphie could figure that out. Nick wasn't moving now.

Ralphie stepped over Nick and left the bathroom, hurrying to the back of the restaurant where Joey and Paulie were, going as fast as he could back to their table without making a scene. He told Joey what had happened and the three of them hurried toward the bathroom.

But by the time they got there, the paramedics were already there. One paramedic, a bald man who looked like he was around 50, had rolled Nick on his back and was checking his vitals. The other paramedic, a pretty young woman who looked to be in her early 20s, was on the radio, discussing the terrible situation with the hospital. In a matter of seconds, they hoisted Nick onto a gurney and hurried him out to the ambulance. Off they went, flying down the road with lights flashing and sirens blaring.

"Follow him," Joey yelled to Ralphie, tossing him the keys to the car. "Follow him now, and find out what's going on." Joey was startled. He was shocked that Nick would have just swallowed 15 or 20 Vicodin.

"Why?" he wondered "Why would he do this now?"

As Joey and Paulie were standing outside the bathroom area, staring at each other, they heard a groan come from the many patrons who were watching the game on TV. They looked up just in time to see the replay.

With Northwestern still leading 15-11, After the TV timeout, Danny Bridges had caught a pass on the left wing and drove hard to the basket for a dunk. As he went up, Northwestern's Tyrone Wells slid underneath him, trying to take a charge.

The collision looked vicious, more like something you'd see on a football field instead of a basketball court. Wells had slid forward a step further than he should have and Danny was making a strong move straight for the basket.

They fell to the floor together after the contact, Wells hitting the court first. r. Danny appeared to come down awkwardly and immediately reached for his ankle. He rolled on the floor in pain.

Trainers from both benches hurried out to the floor. The Indiana guys got to Danny first and quickly looked at his ankle. They felt around quickly and Danny told them it felt like a sprain, but a bad one.

"Happened a bunch before, but this one really hurts," he said, banging his fist on the floor. The trainers helped him up and he hobbled to the bench.

"No," the chief trainer said. "Let's go right to the locker room. He needs ice right away."

Danny and two trainers made the short walk to the locker room, Danny hopping along on one foot as two teammates helped him along. They looked over at Tyrone Wells, who was still being attended to on the floor, but kept going. The thousands of fans were still standing silently, showing concern for Wells. A few Indiana fans near the locker room entrance clapped as Danny walked by, but did so quietly out of respect for the injured Wells.

Tyrone Wells stayed on the floor for about five minutes and looked dazed when he finally got to his feet. They took him to the locker room, and he never returned.

After a few minutes, the game started back up, without Indiana's Danny Bridges and Northwestern's Tyrone Wells.

"Shit, shit, shit," Joey said. "This is not good."

* * * * *   * * * * *   * * * * *

Ralphie was doing all he could to keep up with the ambulance, but it wasn't easy. He even had to run a red light at one point, but made it through the intersection without incident. He saw the ambulance pull into the emergency room bay from about 200 yards away, and quickly found a place to park and rushed into the hospital.

When he got inside, he didn't see Nick. He went straight to the front desk.

"My friend was just brought in here. Nick Vincent. I need to be with him."

The nurse, who had seen just about everything in 20 years of emergency room care, barely looked up.

"Are you family?" she asked.

"No, he's my friend," Ralphie said.

"Sorry, but I can't give you any information unless you're family."

"But I was just with him. He's with me. I need to know if he's OK."

The nurse wasn't busy and had help at the front desk, so she shuffled through some admission forms and didn't see any with Nick's name on them.

"I don't see anything here, so let me go back and check. I probably can't tell you anything, but let me find out where he is and who's working on him."

Ralphie thanked her and sat down. He called Joey real quick, to let him know he was at the hospital.

"What's going on with him?" Joey asked.

"I don't know. They aren't telling me nothing yet, but some nurse is checking on him for me. I'll call you as soon as I know something."

Not long after Ralphie hung up, the nurse returned. She had Nick's driver's license in her hand.

"Is this your friend, Nick Vincent?" she asked. "That's who you said, right?"

"Yeah, yeah, yeah. That's him. Is he OK?"

"The doctors are working on him now. He's not doing well. But if you'll just sit here, I'll check on him again in just a little bit, OK?"

The thirty minutes she was gone seemed like an eternity to Ralphie. When she finally got back, she came out to the waiting room, with a doctor in tow.

"Hello, my name is Dr. Ryan. Do you know how we can reach his family?"

Ralphie seemed perplexed.

"I don't know. I don't have a number for his brother, but I could probably find it from someone else. Why?"

"Well," the doctor said. "We really need to talk to his family."

"You can tell me. What's going on?"

"No, sir, I'm sorry. This is something we have to discuss with his family. This is information I can't share with you."

Ralphie knew only one way to deal with difficult situations, and that was with force. He laid both hands on the doctor's shoulders and gently shoved him up against the wall.

"You tell me now," he said. "What's going on with him?"

"We did everything we could. His heart stopped and we couldn't get him back. He's gone."

Ralphie stepped back.

"You mean to tell me he's dead? You've got to be kidding me."

"No sir, I'm not. I'm very sorry but yes, he passed away. We did everything we could."

Ralphie didn't have much of a vocabulary anyway, but now he was clearly at a loss for words.

"Dead?"

* * * * *   * * * * *   * * * * *

Joey was completely at a loss for words too. With Wells out, Northwestern's offense was suddenly inept. And Michael Trickett, Danny's roommate and mentor, was having the game of his life. Northwestern could not stop him inside and before halftime Indiana went on a 28-8 run. At the break, Indiana was ahead 39-23. Jocy slammed his drink on the table.

As he did, a tall man in a staid navy blue suit walked up to his table. Several other men, nearly a dozen, were nearby and dressed similarly.

"Joseph Risone? Are you Joseph Risone?" the man asked, already knowing the answer.

"Yeah. Why?" Risone said.

"I am Mark DiPolitto from the FBI. You are under arrest for the murder of Aaron Maxwell. Put your hands behind your back and don't make a scene."

Joey's jaw dropped. He looked around, looking for a place to run, but all the suits were moving in now. "What a night this has become," he thought to himself. He had no other options, so he turned around and put his hands behind his back while DiPolitto put the cuffs on him. Paulie did the same, and off they went.

Simultaneously, FBI agents walked into the hospital and arrested Ralphie for the murder of Marion Hamilton. Two more agents quietly grabbed Johnny at the game and arrested him as well. More agents raided Joey's bar and hauled off several other people, confiscating evidence galore. Albert Calabria was pulled out of his driveway in a $3,000 suit, handcuffed and sent away to jail as well. Joey Risone, Jr., who had gone to Arizona a few weeks earlier to see his ailing mother, was the only one not corralled. He hadn't really done anything wrong anyway, other than book a few bets. That was nothing major, all things considered.

Months of surveillance finally was paying off for the FBI guys. In all, they arrested more than two dozen people in a matter of hours.

Most importantly, they had scumbag drug dealer, murderer, bookmaker, loan-shark Joey Risone. Their work was done. Almost.

* * * * *   * * * * *   * * * * *

Danny **Bridges sat** on a trainer's table in the locker room with a huge bag of ice on his right ankle. He watched the second half of the game from there on a TV and saw his roommate Michael Trickett finish with a career-high 34 points in Indiana's easy 89-61 victory, a 28-point margin well beyond the point spread. They ended the regular season with a 24-4 record and 13-3 in the Big Ten. They had second place for sure and could still tie for the conference title with an unlikely Michigan State loss the next day.

Danny's teammates filed into the locker room with big smiles, and the first one back into the trainers' room was Michael Trickett. He hugged Danny and they gave each other a smile.

"You OK?" Trickett asked.

"Yeah, I'm fine. We're calling it a bad sprain," Danny whispered to him. "Might need to take it easy for a week or so, but I'll be OK. Nice job out there."

The post-game press conferences went quickly. Coach Henry Garrison, not a big fan of the media anyway, kept it short and sweet. He told them quickly that Danny had a sprained ankle and would be day-to-day, that they would make a determination of his availability for the Big Ten Tournament later in the week. He praised Michael Trickett for an outstanding performance, sent his best wishes for Tyrone Wells and then told the media that no players would be made available because of the late hour. It was one of his favorite screw-the-media tricks after night games.

Within 30 minutes, the Indiana contingent was on a bus heading to the airport, Danny Bridges included.

* * * * *   * * * * *   * * * * *

As **Danny and his** teammates boarded the plane, Tony Vincent and Mark DiPolitto were let into the back door of the hospital by Dr. Ryan. In less than an hour, DiPolitto and Tony were out of the hospital and on their way to a funeral home in Schererville with Nick. Midnight came and went as the contingent headed south to Indiana. It was late.

The morning papers in Indiana had quickly-written stories about the game and Danny's ankle injury, and what it all might mean for the Big Ten Tournament and beyond. The Chicago papers focused more on Wells and his concussion, with some mention of Danny's injury and how the game played out. To the chroniclers of college basketball, it was just another game, an easy victory by Indiana over Northwestern. It happened all the time, year after year. They were favored by 10 and won by 28 and no one batted an eye.

There was no mention in any newspapers of the death of 20-year-old Nick Vincent from a drug overdose at an Evanston, Illinois hospital. It happened too late at night.

It would be a story for another day.

The next day.

TOM BREW

34

They knocked on the door precisely at 8 a.m. on a Sunday morning in Bloomington, Indiana, just as planned. Danny Bridges was prepared for it. He was already up, showered, dressed and ready to go. He opened the door, and in they walked, FBI agent Mark DiPolitto and Ben Richardson. Danny already had a garment bag packed, plus another smaller bag, and they were on the edge of the couch, right next to the ankle boot the team doctors had given him the night before. He was ready.

Danny shook hands with both men, but none of them shared smiles. It had been a rough, emotional night, and a carryover persisted in the early-morning hours.

"Here's what I can tell you – and what you need to know – for the moment. Your pal Nick Vincent is dead," DiPolitto said. "He died in an Evanston, Illinois hospital last night from a drug overdose and he's been successfully transported to a funeral home in Schererville, Indiana. Everyone will know about this starting this morning. There will be a two-hour viewing on Monday afternoon, from 4 p.m. to 6 p.m., and it will be closed casket, of course. The funeral will be Tuesday morning and it will be all over. You can be in back here in Bloomington by Tuesday night and back to practice by Wednesday."

Ben grabbed Danny's bags and pointed to the ankle boot. "You might as well put that on now since we're going to be walking out to the car, just in case someone sees us," he said. "It snowed a little last night anyway and it's a little slick out there. Let's continue to be careful and dot all our I's and cross all our T's."

They jumped into DiPolitto's car and there was very little conversation during the three-hour drive. Danny called the basketball office and talked to Coach Garrison, who had already been filled in on Nick's death by Ben Richardson. Garrison was fine with Danny being gone a few days. The players weren't doing much anyway. Danny had a quick conversation with Candice and filled her in on the game plan. He figured he'd be in Schererville by noon and wanted her to meet him there. She agreed. Then he and Ben talked to Tony Vincent. They agreed to all meet at Tony's house first, before Danny then went home.

A few minutes before noon, they arrived in Schererville. The three of them went into Tony's house and they all talked for about 15 minutes. DiPolitto then dropped off Danny at his house and he and Ben went to get some lunch. Candice was out front of Danny's house, waiting for him. They hugged out in the driveway, the place were Danny had shot baskets for thousands of hours, and walked into the house.

Mary Bridges was surprised to see them when they strolled into the kitchen.

"Hi, Mom," Danny said, hugging her as hard as he could. Danny, with Candice at his side, tried to choke back the tears, but he couldn't do it.

"Mom, last night … last night … Nick died. He killed himself. Took a bunch of pills and he died. He's been having a real hard time lately, and I guess it just got to be too much. I just didn't know he was hurting this bad."

Mary sat down in a chair at the kitchen table, in total shock. For the better part of 15 years, Nick had sat at this same table with them and she often thought of him as another of her children. This was hard for her, and just as hard on Danny.

"Where did it happen?" Mary asked, tears streaming down both cheeks. "Was he at school?"

"No, Mom. It actually happened in Evanston last night. He wanted to see me, and I spent about five minutes talking to him yesterday afternoon before the game. I had no idea, but I guess in some way he wanted to say goodbye. He took a bunch of pills late last night and by the time the doctors got to him at the hospital, there was nothing they could do. There's a service tomorrow and the funeral is Tuesday. I'm going to stay here until then, and I'll go back to school Tuesday night."

Mary got up to grab a tissue, then sat right back down at the table. The three of them just sat there, quiet. Mary reached over and put her hand on Danny's head.

"How are you? Are you OK?" She hurt, as much for her son as she did for Nick and his family.

"I'm still in shock, I guess. I've been through enough of Nick's mood swings to know when he's up and down, and he was definitely down yesterday, but I never expected this. He was having more problems with his knee and I think the thought of him not being able to play football again must have really bothered him. He wasn't happy; I could tell that. But this? I would have never expected it. I always thought he was too strong for that. Guess I was wrong."

Danny peeled the straps off his ankle boot and laid it aside.

"Mom, people are probably going to start calling here but I really don't want to talk to anyone. I'm not going to answer my cell phone either, unless it's Nick's brother, Coach Jackson, Ben Richardson or someone from IU. If they call on the home phone, I'll talk to them, but no one else, OK? I just want to rest."

Mary nodded and went to the cabinets.

"That's fine, son. That's fine. I'll make some lunch."

* * * * *   * * * * *   * * * * *

The **funeral home faxed** the standard one-page form to the local newspapers on Sunday, but with all the staff cuts there was no one around at the Star-Press to see it for several hours. The one news-side reporter on duty was out covering some events and no one from the sports department would be in for several hours. About mid-day, a clerk grabbed all the faxes and started doing her thing in compiling the daily obituaries. When she got to the Nick Vincent fax, she didn't think anything about it, until she saw his age.

It said 20. When she typed in the obituaries, the numbers were normally much higher. She followed protocol and called the on-duty reporter. He was a newcomer to the paper and didn't recognize the name. Neither did the clerk, a college kid herself just working a part-time job. But when she did a computerized library search on Nick, she was startled to see 200-something entries pop up from the Star-Press library.

"Oh, my gosh," she said.

She called the reporter back, and he immediately told her to call the sports editor. She did, and the editor called Mike Carey immediately. Neither had known anything about this. Carey hadn't written any stories about Nick since the month after his first surgery, so he was totally taken aback by the news. So much for a day off, he thought, and he quickly dashed to the office.

Mike Carey's first call was to Mitch Elliott, Nick's former football coach at Central Lakes. He too was shocked by the news and hadn't heard anything about it. Elliott didn't want to say anything for print, but eventually gave Carey a quote.

"He was a finest football player I've ever coached," Elliott said. "I haven't talked to him in at least a year and didn't know he was having any problems. I'm very sorry for his family. That's just way too young to die."

Carey called the Michigan sports information office, and they had been informed of Nick's death by Tony Vincent earlier in the day. They released a one-page statement, with just one quote from the head coach about how sorry they were to hear the news and that they had thought Nick was recovering well from his most recent injury.

All pretty boring stuff.

The reporter called the hospital in Evanston, but no one there had any comment. He asked for the medical records, but was denied. They gave him the time of death and the reason – heart failure due to drug overdose – and left it at that. It was standard protocol.

He called Will Jackson, the Crossroads High School basketball coach, next. Coach Jackson had just received a call from Danny, so he knew that Nick had died. He, too, was careful on the phone with Carey, and said all the right things about Nick being a great athlete and a huge competitor. He also told Carey that he hadn't talked to Nick in quite some time, being as busy as he was all winter with a basketball team of his own and the demands on a coach who'd won a state championship two seasons earlier.

"Can I ask you a favor?" Carey asked of Jackson. "I'd really like to talk to Danny Bridges for this story. Can you arrange that for me?'

"Oh, I don't know," Coach Jackson said. "I just talked to him a little while ago and he's pretty devastated. I think he'd prefer to be left alone. He's in Scher-erville already at his Mom's, but I'd please beg of you to leave him alone. You know how close those two were. This is very hard on him."

"I understand, Will, but please understand that I have a job to do here too," Carey said. "You know I'm going to treat them right. I just need some sort of comment from him to go with the story. It would sure help."

"Well, let me talk to him and I'll call you back in about an hour. Is that fair? I'll do that as long as you leave him alone."

"I will. I definitely will," Carey said. "Just call me back in an hour and I'll get started writing."

Coach Jackson was planning on going by to see Danny anyway. They had agreed to that during their phone call anyway, so when the coach got the Bridges house, he brought up the topic of talking to a reporter to Danny.

"Absolutely not," Danny said. "No interviews. I'm not going to talk to anyone about this."

"They'll probably hound you until you do, so it might be best to just make a statement today. We'll work on it together and I'll give the statement to the papers and request that they respect your privacy during this difficult time. That should keep them at bay, and you'll be left alone."

Danny nodded. "I suppose we can do that."

And so they did. They crafted a three-paragraph statement that Coach Jackson hand-wrote right at the kitchen table. It took about a half-hour and Danny read it over. Once he was fine with it, he said to goodbye to his high school coach.

Coach Jackson called Mike Carey after he got home. He had Danny's statement, and he read it to him. Jackson also called the Indiana sports information office and gave it to them, just in case any media requested some kind of statement from them.

Carey would print it word for word and, as he promised, did not bother Danny.

The statement was short and sweet, clearly from the heart.

"I was extremely saddened this morning to hear of the death of my dear friend, Nick Vincent. We have been best friends since we were little kids and we've been through a lot together, good and bad. He was always there for me when I needed him, both as a teammate but most importantly as a friend.

"We hadn't talked much lately because I've been so busy with the basketball season, but I had no idea how much pain he must have been in to do this. I know he's really struggled with his knee injury and incredibly slow rehabilitation. It's been hard on him.

"He called me on Saturday and I talked to him for about five minutes on the phone and he sounded a little down. I had no idea he was in Evanston and I certainly had no idea he was considering committing suicide. I will always remember the great times he and I had together and I will miss him terribly. He was a great friend."

Danny spent the rest of Sunday at home, half-heartedly watching Michigan State pound Iowa on TV to win the Big Ten. His phone rang often, but he just let everything go to voicemail. Kenny Dockery got a call back, but that was it. He wanted to come over, but Danny said no. He'd see him Monday at the service, Danny told him.

Mary made a nice dinner and Candice stayed around for it. Danny went to bed early after Candice left, and got a good night's sleep.

* * * * *   * * * * *   * * * * *

Danny was up early on Monday and immediately threw on a coat and went outside to get the morning paper. Before he even got back to the side door, he saw the tease to the story on the top of A-1, the front page of the paper.

Former Crossroads star dies at 20, the headline said.

The subhead told a little more: *Nick Vincent dies of drug overdose; authorities presuming suicide. Story, C-1.*

Once Danny got inside, he sat down at the kitchen table and peeled away the first two sections to get to the sports section, much as he had done his entire life. He was shocked to see a huge picture of himself and Nick, staring right back at him.

The picture was one taken the night Danny and Nick had won the state basketball championship. The newspaper had run about a half-page version of the same picture the morning after the title game, the two best friends with huge grins,

275

Nick with the net around his neck and Danny clutching the state championship trophy. It was the perfect picture, capturing all the joy of a goal accomplished, two great friends with beaming smiles. And now, they were running it again, as part of the big story of Nick's death.

The story was very long but didn't really say much. It started on the front page of the sports section and jumped to another page inside, with three more photos of Nick; one from his football days at Crossroads, one shot of him scoring in a basketball game and a third being carried off the field the day his knee got destroyed at Ohio State his freshman year.

All the news was there. The story told of how Nick died of a Vicodin overdose on Saturday night at an Evanston hospital. The reporter had backtracked the hospital's story enough to learn that Nick had been found passed out in a restaurant bathroom and immediately treated by paramedics and then hospital staff, who couldn't save him. Carey ran Danny's statement, plus the statement from the Michigan coach. He hounded the Michigan people enough to determine that the Vicodin had been properly prescribed as part of his rehab and the most recent prescription had just been filled – 20 pills – four days earlier. Carey touched on all of Nick's accomplishments, the All-State and All-American football honors at Crossroads, the state title in basketball and the Freshman of the Year award in the Big Ten from his first year at Michigan.

It ended with the details about the service on Monday and funeral Tuesday. When Danny finished reading, he flipped back to the front page and continued to stare at the picture of himself and his best friend.

He stared and stared, over and over.

That same picture already was in a frame in his bedroom, from right after the title game. It was a cherished possession then, and still was. And now, there it was again in the morning paper, and it hurt.

He wasn't going to ever see his friend again.

35

Danny saw the picture of him and Nick again Monday night at the funeral home. It was one of three pictures on display near the side of the casket, along with literally dozens of floral arrangements. Tony had picked his favorite pictures of Nick, and they were all there. There was also a picture of Nick as a very little boy, in a family photo, and one of him from picture day at Michigan, decked out in his stunning maize and blue uniform.

Tears were shed, lots of them, by everyone.

It was determined that Danny shouldn't stay long, because being upright with his ankle boot on for two hours probably wasn't a good idea. So he showed up at 4:30 with his mother and Candice. They came in and said several hellos on the way into the jam-packed funeral home. Funeral directors couldn't remember the last time they had seen so many people for a service.

They signed the book, Mary Bridges first on one line. When Danny took the pen, he wrote *Danny Bridges & Candice Wren* on the next line, and Candice gave him a soft smile.

They walked into the viewing room together, and Danny took Candice's hand. As he walked by the picture of the two of them, he touched Nick's face and continued on. They each shook hands with Nick's brother and then Danny and Candice knelt down together in front of the closed casket. They prayed together for a few minutes, with every eye in the room on Danny, the other half of this great friendship. Dozens of people began crying again, just watching Danny spend his last few minutes with his best friend. It was an emotional, heart-wrenching scene.

Danny and Candice got up and walked out of the room. They stood outside in the cold for just a minute, when Kenny Dockery came out to say hello. They hugged for a second, but that was all.

"We have to leave now, Kenny," Danny said. "I just can't stay. Please tell anyone who asks that I hope they understand."

Mary came out a second later and the three of them left. They missed out on more tears for the next hour or so, but that was probably a good thing. There was plenty of sadness, and the occasional wailing. Poor Abby Parsons, who never stopped loving Nick even after he had broken up with her a year earlier, actually passed out from crying so hard and needed help leaving. Danny heard about that a few days later, and was glad he hadn't been there to see it.

* * * * *   * * * * *   * * * * *

The funeral home had been overcrowded Monday night, but the spacious church at St. Mark's was full of even more people Tuesday morning as well. The pastor had been at the church for 20 years now and he had never seen so many people at a funeral. Nothing even close. Danny walked into the service with Candice, hobbling in with his ankle boot still on, and sat in the second row, right behind Nick's brother and a few of Nick's cousins he had never met.

The service was beautiful. The priest had several nice things to say. He touched on the point of reminding everyone that Nick was in a better place now, that any demons who had been making his life so difficult were now gone and God would watch over him forever. He talked about the importance of learning from this and how important it was to trust your faith and ask for help when you needed it. Tears flowed throughout the talk. There was some laughter, too. The priest told the story of how much of a Notre Dame fan he was and would laugh with Nick about his decision to go to Michigan. Everyone laughed when the priest re-told the story of Nick telling the priest that the reason he didn't go to Notre Dame was because of all those Friday morning marches the priest led into church for the young students to pray for a Notre Dame victory.

Tony Vincent was next and kept it short and sweet. He talked about all the joy his baby brother provided through the years and about how much Nick always missed his parents, who had died when he was so young. More tears flowed when he talked about them finally being reunited again. People cried some more when Tony mentioned how much Nick's friends meant to him, especially Danny Bridges. "That picture of the two of you, Danny. I put one in the casket too. He would have wanted that."

Tony Vincent choked his way through every word. Danny cried softly right along with him. So did everyone else.

* * * * *   * * * * *   * * * * *

The lengthy procession from church to cemetery took about 10 minutes and required the help of dozens of police officers to get the hundreds of cars through a few intersections. It was a cold February day, in the 20s but very sunny. As the hundreds of people gathered around the casket one last time, the priest said a few more prayers. Mourners dropped flowers on top of the casket as they filed out, the sun glistening off the auburn-colored casket.

When it was over, Danny and Candice walked toward the car together, hand in hand, two of the last to leave. He looked back over his shoulder one last time, squeezing Candice's hand a little tighter as he watched cemetery workers lower the casket into the ground.

Down the casket went, reflecting one last bit of shimmering sunlight as it was lowered.

And then it was gone.

Into the ground it went, the casket and the memorable picture.

The casket, the picture … and six 40-pound concrete blocks.

That was all.

TOM BREW

36

Danny **followed the script** to the letter one last time at the kitchen table, though he wasn't very happy about it. Before he left to go back to school, he had to have a little talk with his mother.

"Mom, here's what I know about what was going on with Nick. Apparently he was gambling a lot and had lost a lot of money. He had borrowed a ton of money to try to pay people back, but was really feeling a lot of pressure. It sounds like all that, combined with his knee getting messed up again, put him over the edge. It was starting to look like he might miss another football season and maybe his career would be over. I guess it just got to be too much for him."

"I would have never guessed," Mary said. "I didn't know he had a problem."

"From what they're telling me, he really started gambling a lot last year after he got hurt. He didn't have anything else to do and over a pretty short period of time it got way out of hand. He became very addicted to gambling and he did some really stupid things. Really stupid. But you have to remember this, Mom: Nick wasn't a bad person. He was a good kid who just did some bad things. And there's a big difference there. I'll never be able to forgive him for what he did, but I'm going to just choose to remember all the good times we had together and leave it at that. I want you to do the same thing. I'm not going to shed any more tears about this after today. You too, OK?"

"Do you really think you can do that?"

"Yes, Mom, I can. Look, I have so many good things in my life right now. You, Candice, basketball, my brother and sister. Just because Nick made some bad mistakes, I'm not going to let that affect me. I won't let him do that to me, to all of us. We just go on from here."

Mary understood, though inside she was certain her son was putting on a brave front for her. She would be agreeable, but she also knew she'd have to keep an eye on him.

"I'm going to go now and I'll talk to you later in the week. I'm probably not going to play in the Big Ten Tournament next week, so don't bother coming to Indianapolis. Just stay here and we'll make plans for you coming to the NCAA Tournament the next week. If I had to guess right now, I'd think we'd be coming to Chicago anyway for our first two games. So let's just wait until then. Sound fair?"

Sure, Mary said. "No sense in going if you're not going to play."

Danny kissed his mother goodbye, and Mary gave Candice a long hug as well. Ben was waiting outside to drive him back to Bloomington, so Danny made it quick with Candice. He said his goodbyes, gave her a nice long kiss and promised to call her once he got back to school.

"I'll have my phone charged," Candice said. "We'll talk all night."

"We might need to," Danny said as he walked off to the car.

He had never in his life been so happy to leave Schererville.

* * * * *   * * * * *   * * * * *

Ben drove the half-mile back to his house, and Mark DiPolitto and another agent were waiting. Danny was motioned into the back seat, and DiPolitto joined him.

DiPolitto's first question was an obvious one: "Are you doing OK?" DiPolitto asked.

Danny's answer was just as obvious. "No, I'm not OK. I hated having to lie to my mother and put her through all of this," he said. " It wasn't fair for me to have to sit there at my mom's kitchen table and tell her all that crap. It's not worth it to see her in so much pain, not worth it at all."

DiPolitto put his hand on Danny's knee and stared directly into his eyes. "Danny, I know it was hard, but it was absolutely necessary. Nick would have never been safe otherwise. They would have killed him and you saved his life. And what you did means that everyone can go on with their lives now. Everyone gets what they wanted in the long run."

"I don't feel like I've won anything at all. This is going to hang over my head forever. What if someone ever finds out about this?"

"No one ever will. Ever. I can promise you that," DiPolitto said. "The only people who know about this are the four of us in this car, Candice and Tony Vincent. Your coach, Coach Garrison, knows some things about them trying to fix the game and, to some extent, Coach Langdon and Tyrone Wells at Northwestern know something. But all they know is that gamblers were trying to throw the game and they were willing to work something out with us and Coach Garrison to get this done and stop these gamblers from affecting the outcome of a game. So no one did anything wrong ethically, and lots of very bad people are behind bars. No one else knows. No one, except Nick, of course."

"Where is he?" Danny asked. "Is he OK?"

"All I can tell you, Danny, is that he is OK and he will get all the help he needs for his gambling addiction. I can never tell you where he is and you will never have contact with him again. He's dead to you, OK? He's gone. He's safe in our witness protection program far away from here, but he's gone to you. You have to go on like he is really, truly dead."

Danny stared out the window, saying nothing. It really didn't make him feel any better that Nick was alive somewhere. He was gone to him now, and that was indeed sad. This was his best friend, after all. Flaws and all.

"It still bothers me that it all had to turn out this way. Why did it have to go so far?"

"We really didn't have any other choice, Danny. Look, first off, you have to remember that Nick got himself into this trouble in the first place. He's the one who got Joey Risone really pissed off at him. We were focusing on something completely different when Nick walked into that bar that night, and almost got killed right on the spot.

"You could have thrown the game but then if someone found out, your career would have been over. That was never going to be an option for us. You could have told them no, but then something bad might have happened to Nick, or you, or Candice or Tony. There could have been neverending mayhem. We certainly couldn't have that either. And you couldn't just not play in the game. They would have thought you might have known something.

"Once Nick was involved in this, our only goal was to get him and everyone around him out of this unscathed. That all changed when our agent – one of my best friends, mind you – was killed by one of these guys when they kidnapped Nick and Nick was the only witness. They would have never let Nick live after he witnessed what turned out to be a murder. They would have done anything in their power to make sure he could never testify. And you have to remember, these are ruthless people. They don't care about anyone but themselves, and they were all of a sudden staring at the death penalty. They would have killed Nick in a heartbeat. We had to come up with a plan that got everyone out safe, and that's what we did. It wasn't easy, and it was very risky, but it worked. And it worked without a whole lot of pain and suffering for anyone. We had to have an exit plan, for you and everyone else, and it worked perfectly. You're safe now, and so is Nick. And everyone who needs to be in jail is in jail."

Danny listened intently, and really couldn't disagree. It was a lot to go through, and he wasn't happy, but he truly did understand. Life could go on now. It was just going to be different.

"So what happens next? Where does this all go from here?"

DiPolitto had all this worked out from the beginning, so spelling it out to Danny one last time wasn't a problem.

"First, you and Candice. Because we pulled this off the way we did, I have

100 percent confidence that there is no reason to be concerned about your safety or any repercussions. Still, Jake here will stick around and blend in on campus, keeping an eye on you. We'll do the same with Candice, with one of our female agents. Candice did a great job pretending to be a paramedic with Ben here when they wheeled Nick out of that restaurant and no one ever noticed that it was her."

"I really hate that you involved her," Danny said.

"We had no choice. We didn't know what Nick had told them. If they were talking about you, maybe they would have grabbed her when you were with her. We had to be proactive, and she was a big help at the end because we didn't want to involve anyone else in getting Nick out of the restaurant. We had to keep this a secret. Candice was perfect."

Danny just stared ahead, going quiet for a moment.

"Look, I'm not worried about anything, but we'll be extra safe anyway," DiPolitto said. "Everyone we arrested will start talking and destroy each other. Your name will never come up.

"Second, you and basketball. We planned all of this the way we did so you could continue to play the rest of your life with no guilt. Technically, you did nothing wrong, Danny. All you did was tell them you'd help throw a game, but you didn't do anything. You played those first four minutes like any other game and the only thing you faked was getting hurt when you charged into the Wells kid. That was perfect. You guys both acted that out to perfection. It looked like a hell of a crash. In a few more days, your basketball life can continue without ever having to think about this again. Both coaches agreed to fake the injuries and make sure Indiana won big to screw the gamblers and assist us in all of those arrests. In exchange for that, Coach Garrison isn't going to let you play this week. He's going to tell the media your ankle needs rest and that it's much more important that you be ready for the NCAA Tournament instead of the conference tournament. Coach Garrison is on record for hating this conference tournament anyway. He can't in good conscious tank a game, but you guys will play Northwestern again on Friday if they beat Penn State and Coach Garrison won't shed a tear if you guys lose. He wants to rest everyone for the NCAAs. He's also going to hold out Michael Trickett and tell the media that he's worried about his knee and the potential of playing three games in three days. If Northwestern wins Friday and probably secures their own NCAA bid, then so be it. The two teams will play it out fair and square, but you and Trickett aren't playing."

"And that won't raise any red flags?" Danny asked.

"Not at all. It seems so legitimate. Your practices are closed anyway. Just wear the boot another day or two around campus and wear it in your street clothes on the bench that first night. Then go get 'em in the NCAAs. Believe me, we'll all be rooting for you."

"So I really have nothing at all to worry about?"

"No, Danny. It's all wrapped up now with a nice tidy bow. To everyone involved, even the bad guys, Nick is dead. And all they can ever think is that you got hurt and it was out of your control. They know that was a risk they were willing to take. And, trust me, those guys have a lot more to worry about right now than you. We have a lot of them on murder charges and they're in line for the death penalty. The others will all be in jail for a very long time on plenty of other charges. We're not even bringing up the basketball game with any of them, for obvious reasons. We just want all that to go away now and this is the easiest way. They certainly aren't going to be caring about any of these basketball issues, and we certainly aren't going to be bringing it up. They've got far bigger things to worry about."

"And Nick? What happens to him?" Danny asked one more time.

"He's dead to you, Danny," DiPolitto said. "He's gone. Don't worry about him, and don't ever ask me about him again. But he'll be fine. We'll take good care of him, and we'll help him get his head straightened out."

* * * *   * * * *   * * * *

As **DiPolitto wrapped** things up with Danny, his other FBI agents were hard at work in jail cells in and around Chicago. Everyone they wanted was behind bars, all in separate locations so they couldn't communicate with each other. So far, they had been unable to talk to lawyers. The agents acted quickly.

Ralphie Cerretta was their first target. They dragged him into a small interrogation room, turned up the heat then literally turned up the heat. Surrounded by three agents, a tape recorder and a TV monitor, fat Ralphie was sweating profusely in the steamy 89-degree room.

The agent started talking, and Ralphie started squirming in his chair.

"First thing we're going to do, Ralphie, is play a tape for you. You might recognize the voice."

The audio recording, clear as a bell, came from the device inside Nick Vincent's watch. The first thing Ralphie heard was the tussle, bodies flying everywhere and the thud of a pistol cracking into the head of FBI agent Marion Hamilton. What followed was his scrap with Nick, then his conversation with Nick once he pushed him to the ground in the hotel room. The recorder caught it all.and it was clearly Ralphie's voice on the recordings.

"Isn't hotel surveillance great?" they said, laughing at him. Ralphie wasn't smart enough to think it would have come from Nick anyway. Hotel surveillance certainly sounded real to him.

Then they turned on the TV monitor. The first tape was of Ralphie and Joey Risone in the bar, the night Nick was there and Joey pointed a gun at him. Ralphie was standing right next to him. They had him, and they knew it.

So did Ralphie.

The last video they showed him was the taped testimony of the caught drug dealer who was there the night Joey and Ralphie shot Aaron Maxwell.

"We have you, dead to rights, Cerretta," the agent told Ralphie. "You are guilty of the murder of Aaron Maxwell and we all know that. You do too, and we have witnesses and plenty of proof. What you don't know is that now we have you for the murder of Marion Hamilton. That guy you hit in that casino hotel room was an FBI agent who was looking for you and your buddies after we saw that video-tape from the bar, and a day later he died. You killed a law enforcement officer and it's all right there on tape. You have no defense for that.

"You're getting the death penalty, unless you cooperate with us right now. You cannot ask for a lawyer, not yet. You need to hear us out first, and then decide. But keep this in mind. We totally don't care about you, so you get one chance and one chance only."

Ralphie nodded, knowing he was sunk. "What do you want from me?"

"We want you to testify that you were with Joey Risone the night you both fired a dozen bullets into Aaron Maxwell, admit that two of you murdered him and that you saw Joey Risone pull the trigger over and over. And you admit that you killed that guy in the hotel room. You testify against Risone and all the others about the gambling and prostitution stuff and you testify as to Albert Calabria's involvement with all of this. You do and we'll take the death penalty off the table. You get life, no parole, but you serve it all far away from here in a minimum secu-rity prison with a new identity so you'll be safe from these guys on the inside."

It took Ralphie less than 10 seconds to agree.

He'd done enough time in prison to know that he could do more. And this sure beat the death penalty. Within five minutes, the cameras and recorders were rolling and Ralph Cerretta spent more than three hours throwing everyone under the bus. He was pure gold. When they finished, they transferred his testimony to a flash drive and prepared to go see Joey Risone.

"Don't you want to know about this basketball game we were throwing?" Ralphie asked.

"Basketball game? We don't know anything about that, nor do we care." the agent said. "We were following you guys because of these murders and this other stuff just added to it. We only care about the murders."

They led Ralphie Cerretta back to his cell. "You want a lawyer now, Ral-phie?"

"What for?" he said, trying to laugh. "It's all over for me. Your deal is the best I could ever get. I'll take it and be done."

* * * * *   * * * * *   * * * * *

The agents got to Joey Risone next. He flipped them the bird when they walked into the interrogation room.

"I want my lawyer. Now. I'm not saying a word to you pricks," Risone said. "You've got nothing on me. I want my lawyer now."

"You don't have to say anything, Joey. We just want to show you some things and then we're leaving. And then you can talk to your lawyer all you want."

They showed Joey all the videotape surveillance from the bars, which clearly busted him for his huge gambling operation. They showed him the tapes of the two witnesses describing the murder he committed and tons of wiretaps and videotape from his cocaine deals. Joey cursed at Ralphie as the tape rolled on with his confession. When they finished, they simply packed up and walked out, without saying a single word. They didn't have to. Through all the evidence, there was not one mention of Nick Vincent or the thrown basketball game. They didn't replay any of the recordings that came from Nick's watch during the kidnapping or the planning of the thrown basketball game. They didn't bother with the video of him pointing a gun at Nick that night in the bar. It wasn't necessary. They didn't need it.

Joey was a dead man.

He knew it.

Still, with little conviction in his voice, he shouted at the agents. "All lies. Those are all lies they're telling there. I've never killed anyone in my life, but I'd sure like to start with you guys right now. I want my lawyer, and I want him now."

In a matter of days, all the indictments were out. Commendations went out quickly for DiPolitto and his crew. Their superiors were thrilled and impressed with all the arrests and the major hit organized crime was taking.

Everything was working out perfectly.

* * * * *   * * * * *   * * * * *

Outside the barracks at an Army base just north of Tampa, the palm trees swayed in the warm southern breeze. From his window, Nick Vincent just stared and stared. He couldn't help but think how even though things had changed, they still remained the same. He could stare out of the window in that small room at Joey Risone's house in Evanston, too, but he couldn't leave that room either. He was in the same boat now.

"This is your home until all the trials are over," Jake the FBI agent told Nick. "First thing, we're going to cut your hair and dye it blonde; change your look a little. We'll get you checked out with the doctors here on the base and we'll do whatever we need to with your knee. Right now, everyone thinks you're dead and we'd like to think that all those mobsters don't know you had any involvement with this. But we don't know that for sure, and until then we're going to continue to hide you here. We don't want them coming after you, ever."

Nick had nothing to say.

"Once we're sure they're all going away for a long time, and we're sure we don't need you to testify about anything, we'll get you a new identity and put you in the witness protection program. But that's a long way off, pal, so get used to being here. You'll see no one, you can talk to no one. You're dead, remember."

Nick just nodded. He felt like a dead man, too.

Still, he was glad to be alive.

His life as he knew it was over. And his life as he would know it was just beginning.

That was even scarier than everything he had just been through.

* * * * *   * * * * *   * * * * *

The FBI had a private jet waiting for Mark DiPolitto at the Bloomington airport, so he took a quick nap after he boarded and the three-hour flight to Florida whizzed right by. He reviewed his notes for a while before landing at a private airport in Clearwater, then went to see Nick Vincent one last time, or so he hoped. The only stop on the way was to pick up a pizza from his favorite joint in Florida, one owned by an old college buddy.

When he walked in, Nick was thrilled to see a friendly face – or at least a face he recognized from the ambulance ride back to Schererville before he was handed off to another agent who flew with him to Florida. The pizza smelled good, too.

DiPolitto tossed the pizza on the dining room table and had Nick sit down with him.

"Dig in," he said. 'We've got a lot to talk about."

DiPolitto took off his suit coat and loosened his tie. He had a few bites of pizza, then stared across the table at Nick.

"Went to your funeral this morning. It was very nice. Lots of people, lots of tears. You would have been impressed."

"If you're trying to be funny, it's not working."

"Just enjoy the pizza, Nick. And then we'll go over some things."

Nick kept eating, his first good meal in a while.

"It is good pizza," he said. "Very good. Thank you."

TOM BREW

37

DiPolitto **settled onto** the couch and Nick joined him on the nearby recliner in his new living room inside the barracks. Nick was eager to hear what he had to say, because it had been a long couple of days in confinement, with no real knowledge of what was going on. On the ride from the hospital to the funeral home in the back of the hearse, DiPolitto had given Nick a quick rundown on what was going on, and all a petrified Nick could do then was listen. Now he'd had a couple days to think, and all of this was still very confusing to him.

"What I still don't get is why we had to go so far down the road with this hoax. Wasn't there an easier way for you to get those guys?"

DiPolitto never liked being questioned on his decisions, especially by some 20-year-old kid.

"Look, we were doing just fine gathering information on these guys when you came into our lives. We never asked you to walk into that bar, to screw him out of thousands of dollars, to nearly get your ass shot. You were the one who pissed him off even more by throwing that brick through his window. You got yourself into a lot of this trouble on your own. We had to act fast to get you out of it. It was more about helping you – you and your friend Danny – than dealing with them. Be grateful."

"It's not that I'm ungrateful, it just seems excessive," Nick said. "You're telling me now my life is over and I'll just be starting a new one. No family, no friends, no money, no nothing. That's really not so appealing to me."

Consider the alternative, Nick. You were the only witness to the murder of an FBI agent. They would have never let you live to tell anyone what you saw. You think your life is over now? Your life really would have been over then. You would have been dead. All we wanted to do with you at the time was keep an eye on you and make sure you'd be safe. That all changed when Agent Hamilton died. Yes, we had to get you back, but their plan was already in place when they killed Hamilton and grabbed you. Once that happened, many more people were at risk. We had to eliminate all that risk. But first we had to find you. Thank God you kept that watch on. I was very happy that you responded to my text."

"That was you? I thought it was the other guy. Hamilton."

"No, he had died by then. Right before."

"Why didn't you just grab them, once you knew where I was?"

"Because it was much more involved than that by then. We knew we could listen in, so we had to figure out what their plan was. We had already heard them on tape talking about wanting to throw a game and using you to pull it off. They already had someone at Danny's hotel, so they were ready to involve him, one way or another. You know, you got involved in all this through your own doing, but your friend Danny was a totally innocent bystander. We could have never let anything happen to him. So once we knew what Risone was planning and we had heard you at the hotel across the street, we just waited. We were recording your cell phone calls, so as soon as you called Danny, we pounced. But we couldn't grab you then, because they would have known you were involved in some way. We knew what was going to happen next, so we had to get to Danny first to make sure he knew what to do."

"How'd you do that? He was here 20 minutes after I called him."

"And we were in his room one minute after you called him. He walked into his hotel room to change and I was already there, plus your brother, Ben Richardson and Danny's girlfriend, Candice. Very quickly we told him what was going on with you – and we told him everything about your gambling and your debts – and we told him that your life was in danger. We told him exactly what to say and how to handle the meeting with Joey and you in the hotel room. And then we put a watch on him to make sure we could listen in, just in case something had happened to yours. We heard every word, and he handled it perfectly. He had convinced them he would throw the game. He came back to us and we sent him off to the gym with his team, and then we listened to Joey on his cell phone putting his big plan together. We tapped every call. They were in up to their noses in trouble with this and they involved lots of other people."

"Why couldn't you have sent me a message, so I knew what was up?"

"Once Danny was involved, we didn't want to run the risk of them seeing you getting a message. That would have put both of you in danger. And when Danny was there, we were right there too. We had 15 agents within 40 feet of that door. Danny was so good, we never had to present ourselves. And then he gave you that little hint when he left. You did get that, didn't you?"

"You know what? No, I didn't. Not right away. After a few minutes, it hit me what he had said and that it was the same as the message you had sent me hours earlier. But I still didn't know what to expect."

DiPolitto continued on, proud of his ploy that worked so well.

"We waited to text you again until we had everything in place at the game. When Danny got there, we snuck him and his coach into a secluded office and talked to them and the Northwestern coach and their player Wells about these mafia guys who were trying to throw a game. All we told them was that they had been deceived into thinking that a fix was in play and that we had to make sure – in reverse – that it didn't happen. We had to tell them all that Danny had been ap- proached by these thugs, but that we had been there to help Danny. Both coaches, quite frankly, were livid over the prospect of this whole thing and of gamblers try- ing to mess with their game. They're old-school guys. They hated that their games were being gambled on at all, so they were more than willing to cooperate when I told them what I wanted to do, to fake the injuries at a set time after that timeout and to let the game turn into a rout. When I suggested that Indiana might be able to sit some people the next week if they played Northwestern again, Coach Gar- rison didn't mind doing that at all. It was extremely unusual, of course, but they understood the threat involved and that we were well-positioned to make multiple arrests. The fact that this kind of gambling activity could be shut down and possi- bly be deterred for years really appealed to them. So that's what they did, and they played it out to perfection. Danny and the Wells kid played hard for four minutes, then faked their injuries. They did nothing wrong, other than act a little bit. That way they don't feel guilty and their careers go on as normal."

"I was surprised when I finally got a text back at the house where they were holding me – PUT VICODIN IN COAT POCKET. I didn't understand it at first about why you wanted me to bring my Vicodin bottle, but I put it in my pocket right away. They didn't notice at all."

"That was our hope," DiPolitto said. "We were listening in anyway, so when we did it, we figured you were alone in the room. And when we sent that first text at the restaurant – GO TO BATHROOM RIGHT AFTER FIRST TIMEOUT – I did it from about 30 feet away from you. I was watching them and I knew they weren't paying attention to you. They were busy eating and drinking and watching the game. I sent the last one at the right time, because I had my eye on the game and knew we were probably only a minute away from a timeout. The last one was key – PRETEND TO PASS OUT IN BATHROOM … OVERDOSE – and I hoped you would understand. If you didn't, we were ready to grab them up anyway, but I didn't really have a good back-up plan for you. I'm glad you did it right, and we had that ambulance sitting right there in the restaurant parking lot, with Ben and Candice in it. No one expected anything. They still don't, and hopefully they never will. Because they think you're dead, they aren't even thinking of you. If they thought you were alive, there would have been some repercussions. We could have never allowed that."

Nick squirmed in his chair.

"So are you done with me? Is this the last I see of you? Or anyone?"

"Well, we've got some things to do. Tomorrow morning, we're going to take you over to the hospital here on the base and put you back in the clothes you were wearing that night. We're going to have you tape a statement that implicates Ralphie Cerretta in the murder of FBI agent Marion Hamilton. It'll be short and sweet, but enough just in case we ever need it. We'll set the timer on the camera and make it look like it was made that night in the Evanston hospital, right when you came in but before you, you know, died. If we don't need it, no one will ever see it. We'll have some doctors here check out your knee too, some very good orthopedic guys, and if you need any surgery, we'll take care of it all for you here. We're also going to give you a new identity and we'll be giving them your X-rays and MRIs from Michigan with a different name – your new name – on them. No one will ever know it's really you.

"From now on, your name is Mitch Jackson."

Nick seemed puzzled. "How'd you come up with that?"

"I was reading your obituary and your high school coaches were mentioned. So I threw the first and last names together. It'll keep you grounded a little bit, a reminder of your past and the life you let slip away with your gambling and the crap you pulled. After the hospital tomorrow, I'll be leaving. Then you'll have one more visitor, and he'll come see you every day for a while. He's a guy Ben Richardson knows down here in Florida, and he's a treatment professional who deals with people with gambling addictions. He thinks you are Mitch Jackson and you don't tell him any of this. Just talk about your gambling with him. You need help, pal, and he's going to help you get better."

"How am I supposed to pay for that?" Nick asked.

"You just died, remember? You've got a little life insurance settlement coming since we can't let anyone know otherwise, so some of the money will go for that. Some of it will pay for your funeral, too. Your brother gets the rest and we'll use most of it to set up a trust account. Do what you're supposed to and we'll get you settled with a new identity down the road."

"How far down the road?"

"Could be six months, maybe more. Joey Risone is already being a prick, but the others are talking. Once everything is all wrapped up, we'll get you started on your new life. But it might even be a year, maybe longer."

"And I can never go home? No contact with my brother, or Danny?"

"Nope, it's over. They know that too. Goodbye, Nick Vincent. Now go get a good night's sleep and tomorrow you'll start to be Mitch Jackson."

"Do one thing. Thank Danny for me and tell my brother that I'm sorry."

"I already have," DiPolitto said as he grabbed his jacket. "They know. But they also know you really screwed up your life. They're both glad you didn't get your ass killed, but they're both also pretty upset that you messed up so much and put so many people at risk. You've got to live with that, kid. But that's what the help is for. Get yourself better. You get a second chance at life now, and we'll keep you safe, so don't screw it up."

DiPolitto headed out the door and Nick went into his bedroom. He laid on the bed and buried his head in the pillow. He hadn't cried in a while, a long while. But he couldn't help it now.

Silently, he sobbed, hearing DiPolitto's words over and over in his head.

Goodbye, Nick Vincent.

Goodbye.

38

Danny **tried to get back** into his regular routine in Bloomington. He resumed his early-morning shoot-arounds, got back to class and practiced with his teammates every afternoon, though the workouts weren't very hard. Coach Henry Garrison had learned a lot through his 40-something years of coaching to know that rest at the end of the season was much more productive to a group of tired players. He'd had enough success to know.

They left by bus late Wednesday for the hour-long ride to Indianapolis, but Garrison was scolded again by the Big Ten offices for not bringing any players to the obligatory pre-tournament media gatherings. He hated this event, always had, and didn't really care who knew about it. While he did his fifteen minutes with the media, the rest of his team was resting comfortably at their Indianapolis hotel.

Early on Thursday afternoon, Danny watched intently as Northwestern took on Penn State in the first game of the tournament, the first of four first-round games. His old friend Tyrone Wells was back on the court, playing well and scoring with ease for the seventh-seeded Wildcats. The TV broadcast had replayed Danny's crash with Wells a few times and there was some talk about it, but not much. Because Northwestern had announced all of Wells' tests were negative the day after the game and Wells had no recurring concussion symptoms, it was a story that ended quickly. Danny was happy about that. Northwestern won easily over Penn State, by 20, and advanced to the second round, where Indiana awaited the next afternoon.

Danny and Michael Trickett, as planned because of their "injuries," didn't play in the game and Coach Garrison substituted freely. Tyrone Wells, wanting to make a statement anyway, was hard for Indiana's defense to contain. Playing without a lot of energy and not shooting well, Indiana fell behind by 12 points in the first half and a late rally came up short. Northwestern won 81-74 and Indiana's regular season was over, which was just fine with everyone, Coach Garrison and Danny Bridges included. Bring on the NCAA Tournament. That's the tournament that matters.

Top-seeded Michigan State won the conference tournament on Sunday and secured a No. 1 seed in the big dance. On Sunday night, Danny and his teammates gathered at Coach Garrison's home to have dinner and watch the tournament selection show on TV. Danny smiled when the second pairing was announced –

No. 8 seed Dayton vs. No. 9 seed Northwestern in the East Regional – and he was thrilled. The fallout from their plan had worked. Northwestern got its NCAA Tournament bid – its first in decades – and he was happy for his friend Tyrone Wells.

About two-thirds of the way through the announcement of the field, the talking heads finally got to Indiana and a cheer went out. They were the No. 2 seed in the South Regional and were to play Alcorn State, a small school from Louisiana. The 2 seed was good; the uncaring loss in the conference tournament didn't change anything either.

It was all good, Danny thought. For all the covert activity that went on, nothing really was impacted. Life truly did go on.

The first weekend of the tournament was a breeze. Well-rested and clicking on all cylinders, Indiana played the first weekend in Chicago like a No. 2 seed. They routed Alcorn State 97-55 in a game that was never in doubt. Alcorn didn't play much defense, and Danny couldn't believe how open he was all the time. He also couldn't believe how open his teammates were. He made 6-of-8 shots and finished with 16 points and 8 assists in just 22 minutes of playing time. He had to laugh – to himself, of course – when Coach Garrison mentioned in his post-game press conference that he was glad Bridges and Trickett didn't have to play many minutes, considering they were coming off injuries and all.

Indiana played a very good and athletic Auburn team in the second round, but won easily again. Auburn had a bad shooting day and after about 10 minutes, Indiana was in control. They won 62-52, but it wasn't really that close. Danny scored 16 again and played well. He was feeling good about things.

After the game, Coach Garrison kept Indiana's locker room closed to the media for the second straight game. He took Michael Trickett to the press conference with him, but that was it. Some writers complained, but Garrison didn't really care. He was doing everything he could to keep his team focused, and this was one way to do it. Danny was happy about it anyway. He still didn't feel like talking. All requests for interviews during the week were rejected as well.

The regional the following week was in Memphis and it captivated the attention of the entire country. The No. 1 seed Kentucky also had advanced easily, and they were paired up with No. 4 seed North Carolina, the defending national champion who had lost several players but, as always, reloaded quickly and had a good year despite several early-season losses. Indiana was to play in the early semifinal game against the tournament's Cinderella team, Yale. The Ivy League team, as the No. 14 seed, had shocked No. 3 seed Oklahoma in the first round and then beat No. 6 seed Florida in their second game for their first-ever Sweet Sixteen appearance and the first time an Ivy League team had gone that far in 35 years.

There were plenty of good stories to be written. The Kentucky vs. North

Carolina battle of basketball legends was big, as was the Yale story, made even better by the fact that their two best players were both Indiana kids, pre-med majors with 3.9 grade point averages who grew up watching Indiana basketball. Danny still wanted to avoid the media himself because of everything, and Coach Garrison did his best to oblige. Bringing two players to the media sessions the day before the regional started was mandatory, but Garrison took two others. They did their 15 minutes, said nothing of relevance, and left.

Indiana was still on a roll. The Yale story was cute and all, but they really didn't have an answer for Michael Trickett, who was just too big and too strong and scored at will for Indiana. They also weren't quick enough, and Danny got a lot of open looks. Indiana built a big lead early thanks to a couple of 3-pointers from Danny and cruised to an easy 78-55 win. Danny had 26 points and only missed one shot all night.

NCAA officials requested Danny and Trickett to join Coach Garrison for post-game interviews and Garrison originally said no. But then he quickly pulled Danny into his office.

"Just so it looks normal, why don't you come in there with me now. I'm going to keep it very short anyway because I want to see this next game. We'll just zip in an out and if anyone asks a question about anything besides this game, I'll cut them off. Sound good?"

"Sure," Danny said. "I have to do my thing with them anyway at some point. Might as well get the first one over with."

They went up to the podium and Coach Garrison gave a quick statement. "Just a few questions," he said. "We've got another game out there."

Coach Garrison had answered two questions when an Indianapolis reporter got to the microphone.

"Danny, can you tell us about what these past few weeks have been like for you, between losing your friend and getting hurt …"

"Let's keep the questions to the Yale game," Garrison interjected. "That's why we're here."

"Well, I was getting to that, Coach," the reporter said.

"It didn't sound like it to me," he said. Garrison then went into one of his patented long-winded lectures to the media. He was very good at that. When he had a platform, he often made the most of it. He went on and on for several minutes about how sportswriters had forgotten about how to write about games and all the other stuff didn't matter. He finished, looked at his watch and barked out one more order.

"One more question. Anyone have a question for Michael Trickett about the Yale game?"

The room stayed silent for about five seconds.

"OK, thank you for your continued support of college athletics," Garrison said with a smirk as he and his two players walked off the podium. Ten minutes on the stage and Danny didn't have to say a word.

The coaches stayed to scout the North Carolina-Kentucky game, but they sent the players back to the hotel to watch the game on TV. Danny and a few of the guys watched a classic, which Kentucky finally won by a point in triple-overtime, well past midnight. It set up another Indiana-Kentucky showdown, and a chance for redemption for Danny and his teammates. Kentucky had handed them their only non-conference loss in December in Lexington, an afternoon where Danny struggled, as did the rest of his team. Danny was 0-for-2 so far against Kentucky, their bitter rivals. He was thrilled to be getting another chance at a very good Kentucky team that had lost only twice all year.

The game went as expected, two excellent teams tangled in an epic battle. Every possession was a war and neither team led by more than four points during the first 30 minutes of the game. Kentucky's front line was tall and they were taking away most of Indiana's inside game. It was up to Danny to loosen them up, and he was playing well. He had 14 points by halftime and was the coolest guy on the floor. Down the stretch, the effects of the triple-overtime game on Friday were kicking in for Kentucky. In a four-minute stretch, Indiana went on a 14-0 run to blow the game open, led by three 3-pointers from Danny, who finished with 33 points. With about 40 seconds left and the outcome no longer in doubt, Coach Garrison took Danny out of the game and they embraced on the sideline.

They were going to the Final Four.

Danny high-fived his way down the bench and took a chair. One of the student managers gave him a water bottle and a towel and as Danny plopped into the chair, all the events of the past four weeks suddenly hit him out of the blue. The joy of making his first Final Four was being far outweighed by the loss of his friend Nick. His emotions got the best of him. He leaned forward in the chair and covered his head with the towel. The tears started to flow and he couldn't stop.

It made for a great camera shot on national TV. They showed Danny, head in towel, for several seconds. And when the horn sounded, Danny got up off his chair and joined his teammates for the celebration on the court, but his eyes were red and the tears were still flowing down his cheeks.

He was happy now, and the cameras still followed him. His eyes were still red, his cheeks damp. The commentators continued on with his story, telling the national audience about Danny's background and Nick's recent death. When they finished, they also told their national television audience that Danny had just been named Most Valuable Player of the regional.

Danny and his teammates cut down the nets. They interviewed Coach Garrison on the broadcast, and Danny was next. He did his best to stay in control, and was fine when the questions were about the game and going to the Final Four.

And then …

"Danny, you've had a tough couple of weeks, burying a close friend, your best friend," the announcer asked. "Can you describe the highs and lows of your emotions?"

Danny felt a huge lump in his throat, but he worked his way through it.

"It's been hard, but I've got lots of great friends on this team who've been a big help and I've really just tried to keep my focus on basketball," Danny said. "Tonight was so important. We're such huge rivals with Kentucky and we had to have this game. If Nick had been here, he would have told me the same thing. We got it done."

"I'm sure you miss your friend," the announcer said.

"Yeah, I do. But I'm sure he's up there watching." Danny didn't say anything more, just staring straight into the camera for a few seconds, and then nodding while pounding his chest twice with his fist and pointing directly to the camera. The announcers signed off and the celebration continued. Off Danny went, to whoop it up with his teammates.

Back in Tampa, Nick caught the fist gesture on TV, and knew exactly what Danny was doing. He hadn't forgotten him.

For the first time in weeks, Nick was actually happy.

Happy for his friend.

* * * * *   * * * * *   * * * * *

Ben Richardson's treatment counselor friend in Florida was a guy named Tim Dixon. He'd had plenty of gambling issues himself as a younger man, plus a huge alcohol problem, but had straightened himself out and had been living a nice, normal gambling-free life for more than 20 years. He worked for a hospital in St. Petersburg, Florida, and dealt with drug addicts, alcoholics and sick compulsive gamblers all the time. Ben Richardson had filled him in on Nick, who was Mitch now, in witness protection and loaded with problems. Tim Dixon didn't need to know the details of how Nick would up in witness protection, and he wasn't told. DiPolittio had told Nick the same thing, and they agreed that the end of things, the kidnapping and the basketball issue, would always remain off limits.

Dixon came to visit Nick for an hour every day and Nick found his visits productive. He was reticent at first, but just the idea of having a visitor break up the monotony of his day was a good thing all by itself. The first day was nothing more than a get-to-know-you session, and Tim did almost all of the talking. He told Nick his story of his own gambling, and of his years of service working with addicts. He wouldn't judge, he said, and he was there to help. No worries, he said. We'll just visit every day and go from there.

On Tim's third visit, it was time to turn the table. It was time to start working on Nick.

"I've got some questions for you," Tim said. "Just answer them honestly. There's no right or wrong, no scores being kept. It's just a way to find out where we are with you, OK? Just answer yes or no and we can go into more detail later."

"Sure," Nick said. "It's your show, man."

Tim pulled out a well-worn little yellow book and flipped through the pages. Nick saw the words GAMBLERS ANONYMOUS on the front cover.

"Number 1. Did you ever lose time from work or school due to gambling?"

"Yes, from school, and school work, all the time," Nick said.

"Number 2. Has gambling ever made your home life unhappy?"

"Yes."

"Number 3. Did gambling affect your reputation?

"Obviously. I'm here, aren't I?"

"Four, Have you ever felt remorse after gambling?"

"Yes, all the time."

"Number 5. Did you ever gamble to get money with which to pay debts or otherwise solve financial difficulties?"

"Yes."

"Six. Did gambling cause a decrease in your ambition or efficiency?"

"Yes, totally."

" Number 7. After losing did you feel you must return as soon as possible and win back your losses?"

"Yes. I never wanted to leave."

"Number 8. After a win did you have a strong urge to return and win more?"

"Yep, win or lose, I always wanted to come back for more."

"Nine. Did you often gamble until your last dollar was gone?"

"No!," Nick said with glee, finally able to answer a question without a yes. "I gambled WAY AFTER my last dollar was gone."

Tim at least appreciated his sense of humor. "Sounds like that's a yes to me," he said.

"Probably is," Nick said. "It probably is."

"Ten. Did you ever borrow to finance your gambling?"

"Yes, thousands and thousands."

"The dollar amounts aren't really relevant," Tim said. "Don't worry about that right now. Number 11. Have you ever sold anything to finance gambling?"

"Yeah, lots of things. "Jewelry, souveniers. My soul. Tons of stuff."

"Number 12. Were you reluctant to use 'gambling money' for normal expenditures?"

"You know what?" Nick said. "I honestly think I can answer no to that one. I used my gambling money for normal expenditures all the time. If I needed a couple hundred dollars for a power bill or a car payment, I'd try to win that much and then stop – at least for a little while – so I could pay that bill. So I'd say no to that one."

"OK. Number 13. Did gambling make you careless of the welfare of yourself or your family?"

"Of course."

"Fourteen. Did you ever gamble longer than you had planned?"

"All the time. Yes."

"Number 15. Have you ever gambled to escape worry, trouble, boredom or loneliness?"

"Yep, no question."

"Number 16. Have you ever committed, or considered committing, an illegal act to finance gambling?"

Nick thought for a moment. "Yeah, I guess that's a yes too. I didn't really think some of those things were illegal at the time, but others might look at it differently."

"Continuing on. Number 17. Did gambling cause you to have difficulty in sleeping?"

"Yes. Still not sleeping."

"Eighteen. Do arguments, disappointments or frustrations create within you an urge to gamble?"

Nick hesitated again. Tim repeated the question.

"You know, I think I'd answer that one no as well," Nick said. "My urge to gamble was always there, 24/7, no matter how I felt. Happy or sad, good times or bad, I always wanted to gamble. So that answer is no."

"I understand. Interesting," Tim said. "Number 19. Did you ever have an urge to celebrate any good fortune by a few hours of gambling?"

"Constantly."

"OK, last one. Number 20. Have you ever considered self-destruction or suicide as a result of your gambling?"

Nick leaned back in his chair and ran his hands through his hair. "That's not really a question with an easy yes-or-no answer," he said.

"Actually," Dixon said, "to be honest, it's probably the easiest one to answer with one word, because I don't really care about the details right now. Maybe later, but not right now."

Nick leaned forward in his chair again and stared into Tim's eyes. Their eyes locked for a few seconds when Nick started nodding his head.

"Yes," Nick said. "My answer to that question is yes."

"You answered yes to 18 of those 20 questions. Most compulsive gamblers will answer yes to at least seven of those questions. Do you think you're a compulsive gambler?"

Nick slumped back into his chair and frowned. "Yes, dammit, I guess I am. And that sucks."

"Don't look at it that way," Tim said as he closed his book and got up from the table. "Look at it this way. It's a good thing that you know that now. Now you know what you are and you can start doing something about it."

Tim slid his little yellow book across the table to Nick. "You keep that," he said as he headed for the door. "It's good reading. See you tomorrow."

After dinner, Nick grabbed the book and started reading the first page. He read every word in the little 20-page booklet, never leaving the table for at least an hour. He couldn't help but think, over and over, about how much that book was written precisely about him.

He wasn't the first gambler to think that way.

* * * *   * * * * *   * * * * *

The Indiana team flew to New Orleans on Friday for the Final Four, all of them feeling good about their chances of winning the school's eighth title and the fifth championship for Coach Garrison. But their legendary coach surprised them all during a meeting on the flight.

"Guys, I've decided this is going to be it," the 70-year-old coach said. "It's got to end sometime and I can't imagine a better ending than to finish my career with this group of players. You've been a pleasure to coach and win or lose this weekend, you're the group I'd like to go out with."

The players, Danny included, were stunned.

But they were a focused group anyway, focused on winning a championship, and this only added to their resolve. New Orleans was abuzz over the news of this legendary coach hanging it up. It also took the spotlight - and the pressure - off the players a little, which was a good thing, and probably one of the reasons Garrison chose to quit at this time anyway.

Their opponent in the national semifinal was Missouri, a surprise Final Four entrant. They had some early dissention with player transfers and injuries, but got hot at the end of the year and as a fifth-seed in the West Regional upset UCLA and Utah to get to the Final Four.

But they played like they were just happy to be there. Indiana kept running their disciplined offense and Missouri couldn't stop them. Danny's post-season run of great play continued. Indiana jumped ahead 22-10 in the first eight minutes and their lead never dipped below double-digits. It ended at 88-65. Coach Henry Garrison had his win and Danny punched his ticket to another title game. He finished with 27 points on 11-of-14 shooting and was clearly the best player on the floor.

In the second game, Michigan State had its hands full with Georgetown. Danny was hoping for a Big Ten rematch, but it didn't happen. The title game was all set, Indiana vs. Georgetown at nine o'clock on Monday night for all the marbles.

Most of the nation would be watching.

Most of it.

* * * * *   * * * * *   * * * * *

Tim Dixon came out to visit Nick on Sunday. He brought a pizza from that place DiPolitto liked so much and he and Nick just sat around the table talking about things while they ate. He didn't stay long, but when he left he had some stunning news for Nick.

"Tomorrow, you get to take a little trip out of here," Dixon said. "I've talked to the agents and they're going to let you come with me on Monday nights to a Gamblers Anonymous meeting. They'll come with us, of course, but it'll be good for you to listen to what some other people in recovery have to say. They're Monday nights, at 7 o'clock, and it's just a few miles away. A very good meeting room, about 30 or so people. It'll be helpful."

"Monday nights?" Nick asked, knowing full well of the conflict that created. The agents had let him watch Danny's game on Saturday and they knew Indiana was playing in the finals. "Do I have to start this Monday night?"

"Yes, it's all arranged. I'll see you tomorrow."

TOM BREW

39

Nick sat in the back seat with Tim Dixon while the two FBI agents sat up front on their way to his first-ever Gamblers Anonymous meeting.

"You do know we're missing the national championship game tonight, don't you?" Nick asked Dixon sarcastically.

"Sure I do, but you don't have a bet on it anyway, do you?"

"Of course not. But I'd still like to watch it," he said.

"I know you do. We'll have you back before halftime, so just chill out and absorb the experience, OK? You've got new priorities in your life right now."

"I know, but it doesn't mean I have to like it."

"You will," Dixon said. "It's a very good meeting room, probably my favorite around here. Lots of old-timers. Keep your mouth closed and your ears open and you might learn a thing or two."

It took Nick all of about 30 minutes to realize he was in the right place. One after another, sick compulsive gamblers working hard at recovery told their stories and shared what they were dealing with. All the emotions and bad behavior that Nick had gone through were being repeated again by others. They were sick too, just like him. But they were doing something about it. Maybe he could too. Things really hit home when one gentleman told his story. He was a 40-year-old, a successful businessman now, but with a vicious past. When he talked about his past, it hit Nick hard. This was him, he thought, just a much older version.

"My name is Patrick B. and I'm a compulsive gambler," the man said. "Thanks to the grace of the God, this program and the people in it, I haven't made a bet in 3,710 days."

Nick quickly did the math in his head. A few months past ten years. Wow!

"When I came into this program ten years ago, I was a beaten man," he said. "Suicide was definitely a thought. I really wasn't sure I wanted to die, but I knew for sure I didn't want to live anymore. Not the way I was living. Gambling had completely taken control of my life. I was a sports bettor, and for years it was always just for fun. But in a short period of time, less than a year, it just took over my life. It was all-consuming. I had a successful insurance career going, I was happily married with four kids and life was great. But when the gambling got out of control, I just shut down everything else. Gambling was all that mattered. I went from making 10-grand a month selling insurance to making about three or four thousand and I never thought twice about it. Here's how sick my mind worked. I methodically tracked all my bets and that year I finished ahead by about $8,000. So I was not a gambling loser. But I never factored in how I was destroying my business and how I was ignoring my family. I still thought of myself as a winner. In just a few short months, it all blew up. I went from betting thirty or forty dollars a game to betting $20,000 in a weekend. I'd rob Peter to pay Paul all the time and I turned into a real piece of crap. I treated everybody horrible all the time. I lied like crazy to everybody. Gambling was everything to me."

Nick just shook his head. This man was telling his story, too, and Nick knew it.

The man continued. "When the losing started to pile up at the end and paying my bills was getting really tough, I just couldn't take it anymore. I was only sleeping two or three hours a night, yelling at people all the time, hating to even be in my own home. I was a mess. One night, I bought a gun and thought about it. For hours. I hated what my life had become. But I couldn't end it. Thankfully, I got some help. I came here and listened, and I stopped gambling. For a long time, I thought that was enough, but I also had to change the way I lived. Just not gambling wasn't enough. I knew I had to work on being a better person to make sure I never relapsed and that became my focus. Every day I tell myself I'm not going to bet today and I'm going to work on being a better person, because those two things go hand in hand. If I gamble, I simply cannot be a better person. And if I don't work on being a better person, then I won't be strong enough to fight off the urges to gamble.

"I still get those urges, 10 years later. But I know I can never act on them. When people have come here to these rooms and talked about their relapses, I've always thanked them and some people think that's weird. But I mean it, because when they talk about relapses, all that pain reminds me that I don't want to be there. I know I am very lucky to have never relapsed in 10 years, but that doesn't mean I won't if I don't keep working on it. My first gambling disaster, I lost my house, my car, and all my money. Those were the material things. Worst of all, I lost my marriage and lost the chance to wake up with my kids every day. That hurt. Ten years later, I've got a good relationship with my children now, but it's still not the same and I still find it hard to forgive myself for that, and what gambling did to my family dynamic. It's as good as it could be now. But if I relapsed, I know it would be even worse than the first time. I would be off-the-charts insane and destructive as a gambler and I know it. I'd be dead, for sure. So I can't do it. I'll keep coming back, going to meetings, working my program and reminding myself every day that I'm not going to make a bet today and I'm going to work on being a better person. I'll ask for God's help and I'll ask for help from the people in this program and when I do that, I like my chances. I'm optimistic that today will be a good day, and hopeful that tomorrow will be a good day, too. Thanks for letting me share."

Nick sat in stunned silence. Reading that little yellow book had given him a hint of what he'd turned into – a compulsive gambler with some very serious issues. But hearing it from the mouth of others really hit home. This guy experienced all the same things Nick did. The rapid growth of his gambling activity and subsequent addiction, the mood swings, the negative attitude and treating others badly. The lying, all of it, was all the same. This guy lost his family, and Nick could certainly relate, even as a 20-year-old. He'd lost everything – friends, family, even his own identity.

Yes, he thought, I'm in the right place. I really need to be here.

Near the end of the meeting, the moderator asked Nick – or Mitch J. as he was known there – if he wanted to say anything. He hesitated, but continued on.

"My counselor here told me to keep my mouth shut and my ears open and that was good advice, I guess," he said. "All I want to say is that I'm really glad I was here. Listening to you guys, it really hit home. I'm glad I heard it. I know I'm sick and need help, and it really makes me feel good that now I know where I can go to get the help."

"Are you a compulsive gambler?" he asked Nick.

"Yes," he said, without hesitation. "Absolutely, yes."

Nick didn't say a word on the ride back to the base. It was all a little overwhelming to him emotionally. It was a lot to absorb.

They drove through the security checkpoints and got back to the private barracks. Nick walked into the living room and quickly flipped on the TV.

"Let's watch some basketball," he said.

* * * * *   * * * * *   * * * * *

What Nick had missed was another impressive first-half performance by Danny and his Indiana teammates. Coach Henry Garrison, as always, had them well prepared. Garrison and his assistants had dissected enough film to know how best to attack Georgetown and their big 7-foot center, Antoine Day. He knew they needed to run when they could but also be patient with their offensive sets. They needed plenty of motion and deliberation, plenty of screens and ball movement to force Georgetown into making bad decision. When they got good shots, they had to hit them.

And that's what they did.

They went to the locker room at halftime leading 38-33. Danny had 10 points on 4-of-6 shooting with a couple of 3-pointers, but he had to work for everything. Georgetown did a great job of switching on the screens and tried to have a hand in his face on every shot. They covered Michael Trickett with the much-taller Day and the other four were constantly aware of Danny. Georgetown's game plan was obvious and, for the most part, it was working. Indiana was playing very well, but Georgetown was right in it.

They battled and battled through the second half. The lead hovered between two and six points much of the way, but when Day scored for Georgetown and picked up a foul on Michael Trickett – his fourth – Georgetown took a one-point lead after the free throw to go ahead by one with just two minutes to go.

Danny hit a jumper on the other end for his 26th point but Georgetown answered with a bucket of their own to go back ahead with only 14 seconds left. Coach Garrison called timeout to gather the troops for one last shot. He diagrammed a play to set up Danny for a jump shot through a maze of picks. But Danny stopped him.

"Coach, if I get a shot, I know I'll make it, but if we run that pick-and-roll from the wing, I just know they're going to overplay it. Day's going to want to step out on me, and Michael's going to be wide open. We've got enough time to run that."

The 70-year-old looked at his young star, and shook his head.

"OK, but don't force the pass if it's not there and hit the jumper off the pick. If not, attack the basket and try to get to the free throw line."

They broke the huddle and set things up. They inbounded the ball cleanly and got the ball to Danny on the right wing. Trickett came out to set the pick and, just as Danny expected, Day jumped out to stop him and his man trailed behind. Trickett immediately rolled to the basket and between the two defenders Danny made a perfect bounce pass. Trickett caught the ball cleanly and dunked over the weak-side defender who was a second late in coming over to help. He scored, and was fouled with just three seconds left and the crowd erupted.

Danny grabbed Trickett and gave him a huge bear hug.

"I knew it would work," he said. "Now make the free throw and let's go home."

Of course, he knew. That pick-and-roll had won him a state championship with Nick and hundreds of other times the same exact play had worked, going all the way back to their days as little kids at the park, beating all comers in 2-on-2, him and Nick, with the same set of plays.

Trickett made the free throw to make it 77-75 and Georgetown's long inbounds pass was tipped away. The ball wound up in Danny's hands and he held it tight until the horn sounded. As his teammates dashed onto the floor, Danny immediately ran to his coach, and handed him the ball.

"That's for you, coach. Thank you!" Danny shouted. "We did it."

The celebration went on and on in the Superdome. One by one, the players snipped off a piece of the net. Michael Trickett got his piece, then handed the scissors to the last player, Danny Bridges. Danny went snip-snip and took two pieces, then removed the net and the MVP pulled it down over Coach Garrison's head. They all cheered and roared and surrounded their coach, who was going out on top.

The network TV interview with Garrison, Trickett and Danny was a lovefest. The first question for Garrison about retiring in style never really got answered, because all he wanted to talk about was the unselfishness of his team. He told a national audience how the Hall of Fame coach was vetoed in the huddle by a sophomore and how they won this game the way they've won all year, by playing as a team and looking out for each other.

Michael Trickett had a hard time controlling his emotions. His five-year career had included two devastating injuries and two long and laborious rehabilitations. His NBA stock had dropped drastically after the injuries but had risen sharply again during this impressive senior season. Winning a title, and making the winning basket, left him virtually speechless, he was so emotional.

Then they asked Danny, who was still bouncing with excitement, about that last play.

"Well, coach had us so well prepared for this game," he said. "In all our film sessions, we could see that they kind of struggled with covering that pick-and-roll. I just felt like it would work, that they would overplay me, because I've seen it work so many times before. We won our high school state championship two years ago on the same exact play and that play has worked for me since the fourth grade. I knew Michael would make it. I was 100 percent confident."

Back in Tampa, Nick watched every minute, fighting back the tears. What he'd give to be there, he kept thinking. He hated that he couldn't, but he also knew that this was probably Danny's reward for being such a good friend. After all he'd done for Nick, it was just and right that Danny would win a national championship.

The interview ended with Danny mugging for the camera, trophy in hand. "The pick-and-roll, baby!" he yelled into the microphone, smiling from ear to ear. And then he yelled five more words before running across the court to hug Candice and his mother. He stared into the camera, tapped his heart twice with his fist, and pointed.

"That was for you, man!"

Nick felt the lump in his throat.

He knew what Danny meant.

* * * * *   * * * * *   * * * * *

The **party lasted well** into the night in New Orleans and continued the next day when they made it back to Bloomington for a parade on an unusually warm early-April day. Danny could have never imagined how much fun this would all be, and he soaked in every minute.

When all the hoopla was over and it was just the coach and his team back at Assembly Hall, they all said their goodbyes to Coach Garrison.

"Danny," he said. "Come on up to my office when you get done packing up here. I've got a few things to talk to you about."

"Be right there, coach," he said. "I've got something I want to talk to you about too."

When coach and star player gathered, it was an emotional time for both of them, along with a huge sense of relief. All that work had paid off, and now it was over.

Over for both of them.

"Danny, I wanted to talk to you about the whole Evanston thing before we part. I'm probably correct in assuming that us working with the FBI against those gambling pricks and your friend dying the same night probably aren't mutually exclusive events. I don't want to know any more than I already know, even if you know more than me. But I just wanted to tell you that I will go to my grave with what went on that night and I'll never say a word to anyone. It all worked out fine anyway, but I just wanted you to be sure you knew that I'd always have your back there. Forever. One of the bonuses of retiring now is that I'll never have to talk to a sportswriter again and I'll just figure there's no reason for this to ever come up again."

"Thanks, coach. I certainly knew I could always trust you anyway. That was never in doubt."

"So what did you want to talk to me about?" Coach Garrison asked.

"Well, I came to Indiana to play for you and win a national championship. Considering how this year went and everything, I'm thinking it's time for me to leave now too. I might as well strike while it's hot and I was wondering if you'd make some calls to your NBA people and see where they think I'd slot in the draft. All the first-round picks get guaranteed money and if I had to guess I'd probably be a 10-15 type pick at worst. That's a lot of money and especially after everything that's gone on, maybe I would be better off in a new environment and going on to the next phase too."

"Well, I certainly think you're ready. You're one of the best shooters I've ever had and you know how to play the game. The NBA, it's all about the right fit and any team would be glad to have you. Let me make some calls and I'll get back to you."

Just a day later, Coach Garrison was back on the phone. With some help from his secretary, he had set up a conference call with Steve Hamm, the general manager of the Chicago Bulls who had been a starting guard on Coach Garrison's first national championship team at Indiana 25 years earlier.

"Danny, I had a chance to talk to our scouts and if your thoughts were that you'd want to come out early if you were a top 10 or 15 pick, then you should do it," Hamm said. "The way it looks, we're probably going to be picking seventh or eighth unless we win the lottery, and we'd love to have you. We have our post-up center of the future and our point guard of the future already and we need shooters desperately. I can tell you with certainty that we'd love to have you at that pick. If that helps you make a decision, I wanted you to know that."

Danny went to Chicago the next week to talk to an agent who came highly recommended from some other former Indiana guys who were in the pros. His information echoed Hamm's, that Danny was certainly a mid-to-high first-round pick. Danny talked to his mother the next night, and although she would have preferred he finish college, she certainly understood and was happy for her eldest son. He signed with the agent the next day and had a big press conference in Bloomington. Within a few weeks, his agent had him a nice shoe deal and a contract to promote a Chevrolet dealer in northwest Indiana.

For the first time in his life, Danny had a new Tahoe, money in the bank and a couple credit cards with some very high limits. He made only one large purchase early, something for Candice.

It was a crazy couple of months for Danny, and it had wiped him out. He was looking forward to it all ending by the end of April. He had three weeks of school to go, which would be hard, and a Bruce Springsteen concert in Bloomington during Little 500 weekend, which he – and Candice – were very much looking forward to.

Every day was more of the same. He was a champion, and had the world by the tail. The smile never left his face … except for the times he'd think about his friend Nick.

He wasn't easy to forget, try as he might.

TOM BREW

40

Danny **knew his last** weekend in Bloomington was going to be a long one, so he slept in before heading off to the Indiana practice facility for a quick workout. Assembly Hall was being prepped for the Bruce Springsteen concert later that night, so it was easier to just stay at the practice facility next door. He lifted for a while, did his two miles on the treadmill and shot for an hour, ending as he always did with his 100 free throws, making 96, including the last 52 in a row.

After he showered, he walked over to the ticket office, where the school's ticket manager – who had grown close to Danny in the past two years and had been big help with tickets for Danny when necessary – had his block of tickets for the concert. There were eight in all, right in the front row up against the stage. He had tickets for Candice and himself, a couple of the IU guys and their dates, plus Kenny Dockery and his girlfriend, who were coming down from Schererville. As they were chatting and reminiscing a bit, they heard the rumble of guitars from down the hall inside the arena. After some short starts and stops, the band cranked it up, ripping off the first song of their sound check.

"*Glory Days*. How appropriate," Danny said.

The ticket manager smiled. "Well, why don't you come with me, Danny, and I'll show you where your seats are."

Danny stuck the tickets in his pocket, threw his bag over his shoulder and walked into the arena. It seemed strange seeing Assembly Hall without the basketball floor down, but Danny was overwhelmed with the size of the stage. It ran end to end on the south edge of the court, stretching out forward more than 70 feet. About 800 seats were set up on the floor, and the place would be packed later that night with more than 15,000 fans.

Danny was introduced to Springsteen's manager and the three of them sat and listened while the band ran through a few more songs. Danny thought this was so cool, hearing Springsteen live with the arena practically to himself. When they finished, the manager went onstage for a few minutes, then started walking back to Danny, the rock superstar in tow.

"Hey, I'm Bruce Springsteen. Nice to meet you," he said, shaking Danny's hand, all the while Danny thinking "No, kidding."

Danny introduced himself. "Thanks so much for doing this tonight," he said. "You can never know how much I appreciate it, and how much Candice will appreciate it. It'll mean a lot. She's a great girl and I really love doing special things for her."

"No problem. Always like a good love story," Springsteen said. "It's nice making a show special and unique. Here, this is for you. We'll do it right here."

Springsteen handed Danny a copy of his song list for the concert. It had 25 songs on it and near the end of the second set, just before the encores, Springsteen had drawn a big red arrow. And the bottom of the page, he had autographed it, with the date written in big numbers underneath it.

Danny looked at the list and smiled. "I can keep this?"

Springsteen nodded.

Danny looked at the bottom of the paper. On the last line, Springsteen's hand-written note said. "SECRET ENDING."

Danny pointed to the line and said: "I don't think I know that one."

"It's a little treat we have planned. It's a secret to you too. You'll have to wait until tonight. It's a special treat for all of our great fans here in Indiana."

* * * * *   * * * * *   * * * * *

Candice had a morning class she couldn't miss, so she didn't get to Bloomington until about 4 o'clock. Kenny Dockery showed up about an hour later and they all went out to dinner, doing nothing but talk about the concert. They were all that excited. They went straight to Assembly Hall after dinner, dropping off their donated canned goods on the way in for the local food banks, a charity thing that was important to Springsteen and his band. They worked their way down to their seats and were all smiles when they got there, especially Candice, who'd been to several Springsteen concerts before, but never had she been close enough to reach out and touch the stage. They were great seats, though it was something of a misnomer because they'd stand all night through every song.

Hour after hour the concert raged on, the crowd loving every minute of it. It was a typical Springsteen show, long, fun and loaded with energy. No one in the history of rock and roll was better live than Springsteen, and the crowd soaked in every moment.

As the second set wound down, Danny nudged Kenny Dockery and told him to get the video camera ready. Springsteen and the band caught their breath as the cheers roared down from every corner of the arena. Then he grabbed the microphone and started telling a quick story.

"These guys here, the greatest band in the world," Springsteen said, pointing to the gang behind him.

"I don't like playing music alone."

"I don't like singing alone."

"I don't like rocking alone."

"But mostly," he said, walking to the edge of the stage right in front Danny and his group, "I don't like *DANCING* alone!"

From the edge of the stage, he reached out his hand … right at Candice! "Let's dance, girl!" he said, and with the help of a security guard, Candice jumped onto the stage, a wide nervous smile on her face as the band broke into their 80s classic, "*Dancing in the Dark.*"

Kenny caught every minute of it on the videocamera and Danny loved watching it all. Candice, of course, was having the time of her life, dancing with The Boss in her cute little skirt and Asbury Park T-shirt as he sang away. Her smile lit up the room, and this was quite a room. She got a big hug from Bruce as the song ended and the crowd roared some more.

"You can dance, girl," Bruce said. "Nice T-shirt. You from Jersey?"

"Yep, born and raised, just like you, in Freehold," Candice said.

"You go to school here?" Springsteen asked, knowing the answer.

"No, but my boyfriend does," Candice said, pointing down to Danny.

"Come on up here," Bruce said, and Danny hopped up onto the stage. Danny waved and the crowd cheered as loud as they had all night.

"They must like you too," Bruce said, with a laugh.

"They do, and I love them too. This is your house for a night, but it's been my house for two years!"

Bruce laughed and the crowd cheered some more.

"So this is your Jersey girl right here?" Bruce asked.

"Yeah, she is, and we both love that "Jersey Girl" song too. It's one of our favorites."

"Well how 'bout this," Bruce said. "How 'bout we play that now and you two stay up here and dance?"

Danny looked at him and smiled. "That's fine with me, but I'll have to ask Candice if it's OK with her."

But he had a different question in mind. Instantly, Danny reached into his pocket and pulled out a beautiful diamond engagement ring. He dropped to one knee, grabbed Candice's hand, and muttered four lovely words:

"Will you marry me?"

"Yes, yes, yes, yes!" she said, pulling Danny up off the stage and into her arms. They hugged and kissed for a long time while the band broke into the song "Jersey Girl." They danced and danced, and Candice cried and cried, shedding the happiest tears of her life.

The song ended and Danny and Candice rejoined their friends as the band left the stage, taking a break before the encores. They all had hugs for the couple, Kenny letting it slip that they all knew it was going to happen. Candice was impressed with their secret-keeping skills. She cried some more, however, when her parents worked their way through the crowd to them. They had kept their appearance secret as well as they watched the concert from the main level of the arena. Candice was shocked to see them.

"We weren't going to miss this for the world," Holly Wren said and she hugged her and Danny. Mr. Wren shook Danny's hand.. What a night.

The band came back out and ripped through *"Born to Run"* and *"Tenth Avenue Freezeout,"* much to the liking of their fans. Then the lights got real low and the band disappeared into the background. On the left corner of the stage were two lone bar stools and two acoustic guitars on stands. Springsteen took a seat and grabbed a microphone.

"You guys sure know how to have a party in this town," he said to the crowd's approval. "I want to thank you for partying with me tonight. And I want to thank you for bringing all those canned goods and donations for these local food banks. They really need you right now. And they're going to need you tomorrow, too, and the day after that and you can never forget that. We're happy to support them ourselves and it felt good to donate checks to those four food banks today. Thank you for helping.

"You kids are the future of America and you need to remember that there's someone less fortunate than you out there, and they could use your help. Some of you are from big cities, and there are people there who need your help. Some of you are from small towns, some so small that you might even know everybody. But some of those people could use your help too. So be generous of your time, and be generous of your heart, and be generous of your soul.

"Who here was born in a small town?" he asked and the crowd roared, truthful for not. "I was born in a small town. She was born in a small town," he said, pointing at Candice. "And so was he," pointing at Danny.

"Big cities are great, but small towns are the best," he said.

As he finished, John Mellencamp, the rocker from down the road in southern Indiana, stepped onstage and the crowd roared. He grabbed the stool next to Springsteen, slapped hands with him and picked up a guitar.

"I like small towns too," Mellencamp said, as they both broke into Mellencamp's classic, "Small Town." It was a heck of a duet, two raspy singers and their acoustic guitars.

The lights stayed low in the arena, except for the spotlights that hit the championship banners above the stage. They were illuminated one by one, and the IU fans cheered. Just after the seventh one was lit up an eighth light appeared and slowly the newest banner was unfurled, showing off the title Danny and the boys had just won. Danny couldn't see it from his seat, but saw it all unfolding on the big video boards in the corner. This was Springsteen's nice surprise. The fans roared and roared as the band played its one last song.

Danny and Candice loved every minute of it. They all left the concert together and went downtown for a while before Danny and Candice retired to his apartment. She immediately fell asleep on his shoulder, dozing off with her sparkling new ring still on her finger. Danny dozed off a few minutes later himself, a smile on his face.

It doesn't get any better than this.

TOM BREW

41

Candice and her sparkling diamond engagement ring left early in the morning to get back to Evanston, so Danny was happy to get finals week started and finished. He had two finals on Wednesday and another Friday morning, but he also had a final paper to write for his creative writing class and he figured it would be best to get that out of the way early.

He knew that for a good reason. He couldn't just take the incomplete this time.

As busy as his life was at the moment, this little writing project was clearly hanging over his head. By design, his professor had left the topic very open-ended so his students could be creative and show off their writing ability without getting bogged down by a bunch of research. He wanted all of his students to write a 1,200-word final paper entitled "What Friendship Means to Me." As soon as he had seen the assignment a few weeks earlier, it spun him back a few years to high school, when he opted out of writing his "My Philosophy of Life," paper for Mrs. Wesson, simply because he was too busy. He always felt guilty about that, and certainly couldn't do that again.

So on an unseasonably warm, sun-drenched Sunday, he flopped into a chair on the porch behind his apartment and, with laptop in hand, was ready to start banging away. He certainly had an advantage in writing this paper, considering he'd just gotten engaged the night before in a fairly dramatic fashion, and he certainly had a new best friend for life in Candice. Their relationship was extremely special to Danny, and he was incredibly grateful that she had come into his life. He had an easy topic to write about.

But he couldn't get his mind off Nick. He tried and tried, but he couldn't get him out of his head. How could he possibly write this kind of paper without it being about a friend he had been so close to practically his entire life?

He sat and thought for a while, thinking of Nick, thinking of Candice, thinking of the concert the night before.

And then, it all came together. The words flowed freely.

For most of my nineteen-something years on this earth, I've been very lucky to have great friends and family, people I've cared about and people who have cared about me. There hasn't been a day go by where if I needed something, anything, I always have had someone to turn to.

I have a new best friend right now. My girlfriend Candice became my fian-cée last night and we're going to get married later this year. I'm thrilled; couldn't be happier. I am so looking forward to spending the rest of my life with her. She's everything I would ever want in a spouse and all of that starts with first and fore-most being great friends. In our two years together, she always has been there for me and I've tried, fairly successfully I think, to do the same for her. Our love for each other is unconditional. Even when we've had our trying moments, we always get through them before too long because that foundation of love and admiration is there. We're many things, but we're great friends first.

I had a best friend before Candice, and he was my best friend since I was a little kid. When I think of all those things I just mentioned about Candice, I can't help but think about how all of those same things related to me and my friend Nick. He died a few months ago, and his death has been very difficult for me to deal with. We were inseparable. Whenever I needed anything, like a ride to school or someone to have my back if I had a problem with something, he was always there for me. He was a very moody guy and when he was down, he relied on me all the time to help lift him back up. I did that without hesitation, because he was my best friend and he needed me. I loved him like a brother. He had a rough childhood, much rougher than mine, so when he needed some cheering up, some lifting up, I always tried to be there for him.

He took his own life recently, which is a horrible thing, and he took my best friend away from me at the same time. I have really struggled with that. Could I have done more? Did I ignore him? Should I have seen some warning signs?

Mostly, I ask this question: Was his dying my fault? I hate that I ask that question of myself, but I do and I just can't stop.

We went our separate ways after high school. I was busy with basketball and school, and he had a lot going on too, with football and then recovering from a severe knee injury. We used to talk literally every day, but as we got busy it then be-came more like once a week, then just a couple of times of month. His life got out of control with gambling over a very short period of time and I didn't know anything about it. His life was a mess and at the very end, he reached out to me, but it was too late. And now he's gone. I figure I've got 70 or 80 years to live myself and there is going to be a lot of great times in my life, and now he's going to miss all that.

And I'll miss not having him there to enjoy it with me.

That makes me angry.

Why did he have to be so consumed with gambling? He became an addict, and turned his back on his friends and family. That makes me angry.

I can't call him today, or see him, or just hang out. That makes me angry.

I can't plan a trip with him, or just go play ball, or sit around my mom's kitchen table eating fresh homemade cookies or homemade bread. It makes me angry.

Sometimes I try to justify it by thinking this gambling addiction took him away from me, but I know better. He was my best friend, and I need to blame HIM for being gone, not me or anyone else. He just should have never gotten into it, and when it got bad he should have stopped, or gotten help. This is all his fault.

I've dealt with addiction before. My father, who I was never really close with, was an alcoholic and left our family before I was a teenager. He never tried to get better, never tried to change, and I was old enough and smart enough to notice that. I didn't let it bother me. I just made sure he never hurt my mom, and I blocked him out of my own life. I was fine with that; it just let me love my mom twice as much. It really doesn't bother me one bit that I don't have a father figure in my life. It's his loss that he's missed out on all the good things that have happened in my life so far.

And it's Nick's loss now. He's going to miss out on a lot of great things from now on too. And for what? For gambling? He blew his life away over gambling. I just never thought that was possible.

My girlfriend and her parents are huge Bruce Springsteen fans and they've turned me into a big fan. He has a song I love that's had me thinking lately. There's a line in the song "Land of Hope and Dreams" that says "This train carries saints and sinners." When I think about that train, it seems to me that it would be fairly obvious who the saints are and who the sinners are. There's a clear definition there between good and bad. The next line says "This train carries losers and winners." Again, that's a pretty clear line between good and bad.

But then there's the third line. "This train carries whores and gamblers." That's the line that has had me thinking since my friend's death. Who's the good one there, and who's the bad one? I certainly can't think of whores as good people. And if sick gamblers can be so bad that they'll actually kill themselves, they certainly can't be good either. I always thought of my friend as one of the good guys, but not anymore. I hate that gambling stole my best friend away from me.

So what does friendship really mean to me? Well, I know this much now. I know that no matter how much you give to a friendship, you have to know that sometimes you can still get hurt anyway. But I won't let that emotion guide me through the future. I am not a negative person and I live my life always trying to think positive thoughts. It's the giving part of a friendship that always will be my priority, not the receiving. I have lots of friends right now. I have a great mother, a great brother and sister, some great teammates and, most importantly, a great woman in my life that I cherish every minute with. That friendship, that love, means the world to me. Just like my friendship did before with Nick. I hate that he's gone, and I hate that we can't enjoy the rest of our lives together. But life goes on, I guess, and I'm learning that at a young age. That's OK. I am fine with that. It hurts, but that pain will go away a little bit each day. I have new things to focus on now, and I'm excited about that.

Friendships have a beginning, a middle and an end. My philosophy on my friendships isn't going to change, despite all this hurt. I'm glad I have so many good people in my life and I will cherish their love and friendship every day. That's what it means to me.

Despite the pain, I still consider myself a very fortunate person. I have great friends, and I love that. Friendships mean everything to me.

Danny hooked up his laptop to his printer. He printed three copies, put one in a folder for his professor, then put another one in an envelope and addressed it to Mrs. Wesson at Crossroads High School. He put a nice little note in the envelope. "My philosophy of life is that I love having great friends in my life. I thought you might like this paper that I just wrote. Can it make my incomplete go away? I hope all is well with you. You were my favorite teacher and I miss you."

He put the third copy in an envelope and added the second strand of net he had cut down after winning the NCAA championship game. He sealed it, with no note. He wrote "DiPolitto" on the outside of the envelope. On a sticky note, he wrote "Ben, give this to your friend so he can give it to my friend if he wants to." He stuck it all in a bigger envelope and mailed it off to Ben Richardson in Schererville. He doubted that DiPolitto would ever give it to Nick, because he had been very clear about no contact ever taking place, but he mailed it anyway. It was his chance to say goodbye to Nick, one way or another.

When he got back from the post office, Candice called. She had made it back to Evanston safe and sound. They talked for hours, laughing and smiling the whole time.

Danny and his new best friend.

So in love.

* * * * *　　* * * * *　　* * * * *

About a week after Danny's letter arrived, Ben Richardson got a call from FBI agent Mark DiPolitto. They made plans to meet in downtown Schererville for a perch dinner.

"Well, I came to say goodbye," DiPolitto said. "We wrapped up the last of the cases today. That fat idiot Risone finally caved and accepted a plea. We took the death penalty off the table and gave him 35 years with no eligibility for parole.

If he hits the streets at 91, I think we'll be OK. That was the last of it, so there won't be any trials. It worked out exactly as I had hoped, though quite frankly I never thought it would be so easy. Everyone's accepted a plea, and everyone's going to jail for a very long time."

"That's great news," Ben said. "So all of this can just fade away now? That's wonderful. Danny won't ever be bothered. And what about Nick? What becomes of him?"

"I'm going to go see Nick now, and then I'm going to Washington. It looks like I'm about to get offered a big promotion there with the FBI. Danny will be fine. We've still been monitoring the phones and spying as need be, and Danny's name has never come up. They've talked about Nick a few times, but it's always just talking about him being so stupid that he killed himself. There isn't a soul in that entire crime family who's not in jail that thinks anything differently. We'll put Nick in witness protection, give him a new name, get him an apartment and a job, and he'll have a chance to start a new life. We'll keep an eye on him, but no one will ever hear from him again. Life goes on for all of us."

* * * *   * * * *   * * * *

And so it did. Life went on.

There was no need to worry about Joey Risone getting out of prison at age 91. His uncle, Albert Calabria, got 25 years on RICO charges and was convinced he would die in jail. He did, just 18 months after he went in. He got colon cancer and refused treatment. He cursed his lot in life, hated how his glamorous gangster life was ending. He cursed his nephew, Joey Risone, but did nothing about it when he was alive, out of respect for his sister. Two days after he died at a prison in South Dakota, Joey Risone was knifed in a shower and was killed. They waited on the hit until after Albert had died. All the others either died or prison or were released as very old men.

Mary Bridges enjoyed the big party at her house the week after Danny came home from school. That night he gave her a present, a copy of a satisfaction of mortgage on the house. Danny also gave her a bank statement, which was set up as a college fund for his two siblings. Mary cried and cried.

The Bulls didn't make the playoffs but also didn't win the lottery. With the eighth pick in the draft in June, they selected Danny Bridges, a sophomore guard from Indiana. Danny passed up the trip to New York for the draft, choosing to watch it at home with just family and friends. He made a point of inviting Tony Vincent, who walked over to the house right before it started and was honored to be invited to the party. The Bulls also had two picks in the second round and

Danny was thrilled when they took his Indiana teammate, Michael Trickett, with their last pick. Coach Henry Garrison, who had retired to a nice gulf-front condo with his wife on the Florida panhandle, watched the draft and smiled, happy to see his two players drafted by the same team. He lived a long and peaceful retirement in Florida, with plenty of sunshine and golf, and not a single reporter.

Danny and Candice got married in August, right before school started at Northwestern for Candice. Her mother planned a great wedding and pulled it off flawlessly despite only having four months to do everything. They got married in Key West while the sun set over their shoulders on Mallory Square in front of 70 of their closest friends. Danny paid all the airfare and Candice's father picked up the hotel bill for everyone. It was three days of fun for everyone, then Danny and Candice flew off to Ireland for a two-week honeymoon.

Ben Richardson finally got the state to fund some programs related to gambling addiction and was able to open two more treatment facilities in Indiana. He also became a speaker in high demand at high schools and colleges across the country. He told Nick Vincent's story often, chilling audiences when he told the story of how Abby Parsons' screams in the funeral home still aren't out of his head. He was a powerful speaker, and he got the message across. If he saved just one kid from addiction, it was worth it. He helped many more than that. Will Jackson coached another 20 years at Crossroads and won a lot of games, but no other state championship, before retiring. DiPolitto got his promotion and moved to Washington, but not until he got Nick Vincent settled first.

They had a long talk in Florida in June, after three months in the barracks, and this was all good news for Nick. DiPolitto made a point of calling him Mitch Jackson all the time, and laid down all the ground rules.

"We have a furnished apartment for you about twenty miles from here, in Clearwater, Florida. It's a nice little one-bedroom right across the street from the pizza place where I got you a job. You're a pizza cook for now; they'll teach you everything you need to know. You have a bank account and a credit card, all with your new name and new credit report. You're 22 now, not 20, and you have a new birthday too. You have a whole new medical history under your new name and if people ask, you grew up in Michigan and played a little football in high school before getting hurt and then you just quit. You can't be a big talker. Be shy, be quiet, assume a new life. If you want to go back to school, you can and we'll pay for it. You're in witness protection forever, which means you can never go within 100 miles of Chicago and you can never make contact with anyone from your past. You need to check in with us by phone twice a week and see us in person at the FBI office in Tampa once a month. If you see anything suspicious, you call us, but I think we're in good shape here. Everyone thinks you're dead, but we can't ever take this lightly. If you screwed up and people found out about this, Danny and Candice and lots of other people would be at risk. We can't ever let that happen."

Nick, or Mitch now, understood completely. DiPolitto drove him to his apartment and showed him around. They walked across the street to the restaurant and DiPolitto introduced Mitch to his friend, who knew nothing about Nick's background. When they walked back over to the apartment, DiPolittio pointed out a 4-year-old Chevy Malibu to Mitch, and flipped him the keys.

"It's yours, but if you ever go more than 20 miles from here, you need to let us know first," DiPolittio said. "We always have to know where you are."

Nick nodded. That was fine with him. DiPolitto didn't bother to tell him that he had a tracking device in the car and on Nick's key chain. The apartment was wired too, as was his new cell phone and laptop. The FBI wasn't taking any chances with him. They seemed certain that Nick had bought into this new life, but they wanted to be sure.

DiPolitto left and after Nick checked out his apartment he drove a half-mile down the road in his new car, a free man at last, sort of. He bought some groceries with his new credit card, made a little dinner, then crawled into his new bed to go to sleep.

This was his life now. He still wasn't sure what to make of it. About 11 o'clock, DiPolittio called. "Hey, I forgot one thing. In the drawer by your phone in the kitchen is a letter for you. Read it, then tear it up into a hundred pieces and then flush it down the toilet. Good luck, kid."

Nick walked out to his kitchen and opened the envelope. He saw Danny's name in the corner, and saw the title of the paper, "What Friendship Means to Me." And he saw the strand of net.

Nick read the paper slowly, starting and stopping. It was not an easy read. At times he wanted to be angry, but three months of treatment had at least taught him to take responsibility for his actions. At times he wanted to reach out, to tell Danny how sorry he truly was.

Mostly, he just cried.

When he was finished, he shredded the letter into little pieces and flushed it, as ordered. Then he tied the strand of net onto his key chain and went back to bed. He cried some more.

What does friendship mean to me right now, he thought. Hell, he didn't have friends right now and that was a horrible thought. It was nice to be relatively free for the first time in months, but he also realized he didn't know a soul.

Some life, he thought to himself.

But it sure beat the alternative.

TOM BREW

42

Candice and Danny moved into their new townhouse in Winnetka, Illinois, about half-way between the Northwestern campus and the Bulls' training facility in Deerfield. They lived life as newlyweds as Candice proceeded on with school at Northwestern and Danny began his career as a professional basketball player. Danny still couldn't believe his life. His first shock was being handed a check for his signing bonus after inking a three-year deal worth $3.5-million. He had never seen a check for $285,000 before and still was startled every day when he looked at his various bank accounts.

Life was good.

Direct deposits, especially big direct deposits, were a wonderful thing.

Training camp and the preseason games went great and when the Bulls opened the NBA's regular season at home against Milwaukee, Danny was in the starting lineup. He bought 30 tickets for the opener and all his family and friends were there. He invited Coach Garrison as well, but his coach was enjoying retirement – and complete privacy away from the media – too much to make the trip. Danny understood completely. His first game was a big success. He scored 13 points and the Bulls won. Not once did he think about Nick or all that he went through during his last year at Indiana, the good and the bad.

He was moving on now, and it was all good.

The Bulls' second game was on the road in Orlando. He was introduced as a starter and then the lights went out for the Magic's glitzy pre-game introductions. When the lights popped on, Danny peeled off his warm-ups and got ready to play.

Four rows directly behind the Bulls' bench, a tall young man stood up from his seat and stepped into the aisle. He was dressed in shorts, a Hawaiian shirt and flip-flops. He was tan, thin and physically fit. He took off his sunglasses and hat, showing off closely cropped, newly-died blonde hair.

He stared at Danny.

A few seconds later, they made eye contact. Beyond the thinner face and the blonde hair, beyond the tan and the flowery Florida clothes, Danny recognized the eyes.

Several seconds passed as the two stared at each other. The young man made a fist, tapped his chest twice and pointed directly at Danny. Then, almost instantly, he put on his hat and sunglasses, and turned and walked away.

At the top of the steps, he turned back to the bench and Danny was still staring at him. Danny tapped his chest twice, too. He pointed, one last time, at the young man in the hat then turned away to join his teammates on the Bulls' bench.

Nick pulled his cap down low over his eyes and left the arena.

He got in his car, flipped on the radio, and headed west.

Headed west on a lonely two-hour ride, to his one-bedroom apartment in Clearwater and his new life.

-- 30 --